He drew her close to his side.

"You are a wonderful person, Addison Hall. You have a kind heart and just enough sass to make you interesting," Jesse told her. "You are beautiful, even when it rains and your hair gets crazy, and any man on the face of this earth should be glad to have you as a friend. Grady will never, ever find as true of a friend as you are, and I'm speaking from experience. Want me to go toilet paper his house or write ugly things on his car with shoe polish?"

"No, I just want to sit here with you until suppertime and know that there's one man in the universe I can trust to make me feel better when I'm pissed," she whispered.

"I'll always be here for you, Addy. Don't ever forget it," he said.

"I know, Jesse, and I'm sorry we drifted so far apart, but I'm glad we're back in each other's worlds now."

He kissed her on top of her head. "Me, too, darlin'."

High Praise for Carolyn Brown

"Carolyn Brown makes the sun shine brighter and the tea taste sweeter. Southern comfort in a book."
—Shelia Roberts, *USA Today* bestselling author

"Carolyn Brown is one of my go-to authors when I want a feel-good story that will make me smile."
—Fresh Fiction

"Carolyn Brown writes about everyday things that happen to all of us and she does it with panache, class, empathy and humor."
—Night Owl Reviews

"Carolyn Brown always manages to write feel-good stories."
—Harlequin Junkie

"Fans of romance series filled with small-town charm and a cast of supportive family and friends will appreciate this."
—*Publishers Weekly* on *Cowboy Rebel*

"Lighthearted banter [and] heart-tugging emotion...make this a delightful romance."
—*Library Journal* on *Cowboy Bold*

"There's no one who creates a rancher with a heart of gold like Carolyn Brown."
—*RT Book Reviews*

Second Chance at
Sunflower
Ranch

Second Chance at
Sunflower
Ranch

CAROLYN
BROWN

FOREVER

NEW YORK BOSTON

Copyright © 2021 by Carolyn Brown
Small Town Charm copyright © 2021 by Carolyn Brown
Cover design by Sarah Congdon. Cover images © Shutterstock.
Cover copyright © 2021 by Hachette Book Group, Inc.

Forever
Hachette Book Group
1290 Avenue of the Americas, New York, NY 10104
read-forever.com
twitter.com/readforeverpub

First mass market edition: July 2021

Forever is an imprint of Grand Central Publishing. The Forever name and logo are trademarks of Hachette Book Group, Inc.

The publisher is not responsible for websites (or their content) that are not owned by the publisher.

The Hachette Speakers Bureau provides a wide range of authors for speaking events. To find out more, go to www.hachettespeakersbureau.com or call (866) 376-6591.

ISBNs: 978-1-5387-3561-9 (mass market); 978-1-5387-3562-6 (ebook)

Printed in the United States of America

CW

10 9 8 7 6 5 4 3 2 1

To Tammie Edwards,
with much love!

Dear Readers,

As I finish this book, winter is slowly pushing fall into the history books. The yards are full of leaves, and the poor trees are naked. Even with all the unusual, difficult situations that 2020 has thrown into our laps, the time seems to have flown by this year. For Jesse Ryan, going home to Honey Grove, Texas, is like going back in time twenty years—is he ready for that? For Addy, who hasn't seen Jesse in twenty years, it's a little scary—can she continue to keep a two-decade-old secret?

There are several people who have helped me take this book from a rough idea to the finished product you hold in your hands. The process is a lot like taking a chunk of coal and turning it into a diamond. All those people deserve more than just a simple thank-you for their hard work, but my sincere gratitude and a few virtual hugs are what I've got to offer them today.

Thank you to my publisher, Grand Central and the For-ever imprint, for continuing to support my cowboy series. Thank you to my friend and editor, Leah Hultenschmidt, for working with me to make this a stronger book. To all those folks behind the scenes who created the amazing cover, who copyedited, who worked in promotion, and those who helped in any way to take this from a figment of my imagination to the book it is today, thank you!

Thank you to my agency, Folio Management, and to my agent, Erin Niumata, for all you do! We've been together for twenty years—longer than most Hollywood marriages!

Thank you, once again, to Mr. B, my husband who endures long days of living with an author who walks around arguing with the voices in her head. And to my son, Lemar Brown, who went with me and Mr. B to research the town of Honey Grove and who took pictures of the area for me.

And a big thank-you to all my readers who continue to support me by reading my books, by telling your neighbors about them, for writing reviews, for sharing them with your friends and everything else that you do. Without readers, there would be no need for authors so y'all really are the wind beneath my wings.

Until next time, here's hoping that 2021 is a wonderful year!

Happy Reading,
Carolyn Brown

Second Chance at

Sunflower
Ranch

Chapter One

*H*oney Grove billed itself as "The Sweetest Town in Texas." Jesse Ryan certainly hadn't agreed with that when growing up there, but as he drove back into town, he hoped things had changed in the past twenty years. The morning he had left— a lifetime ago—the sun had been low in the eastern sky. He'd hoped his best friend, Addy, would have at least shown up to wave goodbye, but she hadn't. Jesse remembered all too well the lump in his throat that morning and the same feeling returned as he drove past the familiar sights in the small town.

He remembered how his mother, Pearl, had managed to hold back her tears until she had hugged him in front of the Air Force recruiter's office in Paris, Texas. She had clung to him and wept on his shoulder.

"Mama, this is no different than if I was going to college," he had said.

"It seems different to me." She'd stepped back and looked at him like it was the last time she'd ever see him. "I love you, son."

His father, Sonny, had kept a stiff upper lip, but had shaken his hand firmly. "This has always been your dream. Go make us proud."

"Call and write when you can," Pearl had whispered.

"I promise I will," he had managed to get past the baseball-sized lump still in his throat. "I'll be back before you know it."

"We'll look forward to that." Sonny had grabbed him in a fierce hug.

Jesse had kept his promise and come home when he could, sometimes twice a year, but most of the time just around Thanksgiving so his team members with wives and kids could be with them at Christmas.

The sun peeked up over the horizon beyond the rolling hills of North Texas. That he had left at sunrise and was now coming home twenty years later at dawn seemed fitting. With the sun rising ahead of him, he was beginning a new chapter in his life—right back on Sunflower Ranch, where he'd grown up.

Not much had changed. The OPEN sign in the window of the same old doughnut shop that had been there forever flashed on just as he passed, and he was tempted to stop and buy a dozen to take home. But he forgot all about that when he saw a banner strung up across Main Street, announcing the Honey Grove Rodeo in a few weeks.

The banner wasn't the same one that he'd seen in the rearview mirror when he left all those years ago, but it reminded him that not much ever changed in a small town. He made a left-hand turn at the first of two traffic lights, drove down the familiar road about three miles, and braked before he entered the ranch property. He rolled down the window of his pickup truck and inhaled the fresh country air. A south wind kicked up and caused the Sunflower Ranch sign above the cattle guard to squeak as it swung slowly back and forth on rusty hinges.

"First order of business after breakfast is to grease that sign," Jesse said as he drove under the sign and down the long lane to the house. When he'd left, his two foster brothers, Lucas and Cody, had waved goodbye from the porch, but they weren't there to greet him that morning. Cody was working for a program similar to Doctors Without Borders, and Lucas traveled all over the world training cutting horses.

A light from the kitchen window sent a long, yellow shaft out across the yard. He glanced down at the clock on the dashboard. "Mama will be making breakfast, and Dad will be sitting in his recliner reading the newspaper," he muttered as he parked the truck beside two others just outside the yard gate. "I hope I can get used to rural life again."

Truth be told, he was a little leery about getting out of his vehicle. Every time he called home—which was at least twice a week when he could get service—his mom and dad talked about what a good job Addison Hall was doing since she had moved to the ranch several years ago to help take care of Jesse's father.

Addy would be in the house, and Jesse hadn't spoken to her in nearly twenty years. Up until he went to the Air Force, she had been his best friend. His first memory of her was the two of them mutton bustin' at the Honey Grove Rodeo and tying with her for first prize. They had been inseparable from then on, but that old saying about "out of sight out of mind" was sure enough true when it came to him and Addy. About six weeks after he left for basic training, her letters and calls had stopped, and he hadn't seen her since the night before he left home— the only time they'd crossed over the friendship line.

He opened the door of his black pickup truck, slid out of the seat, and rolled his neck to stretch the kinks out before he made his way up on the porch, which wrapped around three sides of the long, low ranch house. His father would have already come out and gotten his paper off the porch, or maybe from out in the yard if the person throwing it didn't have good aim, so the door would be open.

A blue heeler dog turning gray around the muzzle got up from where he'd been resting under the porch swing and came to greet him. Tail wagging, the animal sat down right at Jesse's feet.

Jesse knelt on one knee and scratched the old dog's ears. "Good mornin', Tex. You still keeping the cows herded?" He was procrastinating, but he just wasn't ready to face Addy after all these years, or to meet her daughter, either, for that matter.

"Pearl, darlin', are we expectin' company?" Sonny's voice rang out from the living room. "I hear someone talkin' out on the porch."

"That's my cue." Jesse straightened up. "See you later, Tex."

He yelled as he opened the front door, "Is breakfast ready?"

"Jesse, is that really you?" His father tossed the newspaper to the side and grabbed a cane. Leaning on it, he opened up his other arm for a hug. "Hurry up, son, before your mother gets in here. I won't get a bit of attention when she finds out one of her boys has come home."

"Oh. My. Goodness!" Pearl joined them for a three-way hug. "We weren't expecting you until the first of next week."

Jesse swallowed the huge lump in his throat. When he'd been home eighteen months ago, his dad only had to use the cane sporadically, but the way he leaned on it now meant that things were definitely on a downhill slide. "I wanted to surprise you," he said.

"Well, you surely did that." His mother took a step back but kept a grip on Jesse's arms. "Let me look at you. You've got a few gray hairs in your temples, and your eyes look tired. You need some good old home cooking and hard ranch work to put the sparkle back in your life, my son."

"I'm thirty-eight years old, Mama," Jesse chuckled. "I've earned those few gray hairs. It's been a long week of getting things done so I could retire from the Air Force, but a few days on the ranch and I'll be right as rain. I hope that's breakfast I smell cookin'?"

"I know exactly how old you are, son," Pearl said, smiling, "and that is sausage gravy and biscuits that you smell. I hope you haven't eaten already."

He bent and kissed his mother on the forehead. "When it comes to your cookin', Mama, I'd never settle for second best."

Her eyes looked weary, too, he thought. Somehow every time he came home, she seemed smaller. When he was a little boy, she had looked to be ten feet tall and damn near bullet-proof, but these days she barely came up to his shoulders. She had always had chin-length hair, but it had more salt in it these days than pepper. Seeing Sonny on the decline had to be tough on her, but Jesse was home now, and he could and would take a load off her shoulders.

"And I'm glad you're home. This old man right here"—she glanced over at Sonny—"needs your help running this place. Addy and Mia do what they can, and Henry is still a fine foreman, but he's past seventy." She talked as she pulled him into the kitchen.

"Don't you be callin' me old, darlin'," Sonny called after her and started that way.

"The MS is getting worse," his mother whispered. "It won't be long until you will have to make all the decisions."

Jesse draped an arm around his mother's shoulders. "I'm here. What can I do to help with breakfast?"

"Good morning." A voice from Jesse's past floated through the air. "I've got the waterin' troughs cleaned out and..."

Addy stopped in the middle of the floor. Her face lost

all the color and she stammered, "Jesse, what...when...we weren't..."

"Surprise!" he said, but his voice sounded hollow in his own ears.

Addy certainly didn't have any gray in her kinky, dark brown hair, which she had swept up in a ponytail. Ringlets escaped and framed her delicate face. She met his stare, and their gazes locked over the top of Pearl's head. Her crystal-clear blue eyes still mesmerized Jesse as much as they had in the past. She had put on a few pounds, but every one of them looked fine on her. Her jeans dipped in at a tiny waist, and her T-shirt dipped low in the front to show a little cleavage. She probably still got carded when she tried to buy a six-pack of beer.

"I thought you were a nurse. Why would you be cleaning troughs?" He wanted to kick himself the moment the words were out. Not a hello, how are you doing, good to see you, like he should have said.

"I am, and when Sonny or Pearl needs my nursing skills, I'm right here, but I'm also a farmhand. If you'll remember, I was raised on the ranch right next door to this one, so I know how to clean troughs, herd cattle from one pasture to another, and—"

"Mornin'." Another woman came into the kitchen by the back door. "Hello, Jesse. I'd know you anywhere from the pictures Nana and Poppa have on the mantle. You're early."

She stuck out her hand to shake with him. Her grip was firm, and her green eyes sparkled. "I'm Addy's daughter, Mia. Does this mean the big welcome home party next week is off, Nana?" She let go of his hand and went over to the kitchen chair where Sonny was sitting to kiss him on the forehead. "Did he almost give you a heart attack, Poppa?"

"Yes, he did," Sonny admitted. "We've talked so much about Addy and Mia the last few years that you probably feel like you already know all about them."

"Yes, I do, but it's really good to put a face to a name." When his mother had told him that Addy had a baby and was raising the child on her own, Jesse figured that Addy had gotten involved with someone right after he had left for the military. At least knowing that made him understand why she had cut him off so suddenly and wouldn't even take his phone calls all those years ago.

"Well, now that we're all here, let's get breakfast on the table. We're burnin' sunshine," Mia said. "I've got hay ready to bale, and then this afternoon, I need to spend some time in the office with the books."

Jesse shot a look over toward his father. Sonny flashed a smile and said, "Mia just got home from college last week, and she's missed the ranch."

Mia opened a cabinet door and took down six plates. "I wouldn't even be in college if I hadn't promised Nana and Poppa that I'd go. I can learn more right here on the ranch than I can sitting in a classroom."

"If I'm going to turn all the bookwork over to you, then you need to understand agriculture business and learn all that computer crap that you can. It confuses the hell out of me, and Pearl refuses to have anything to do with it," Sonny said.

"Some of us old dogs don't want to learn new tricks." Pearl took a pan of perfectly browned biscuits from the oven.

Jesse watched as Mia set the table. There were only five of them, but she was getting ready for six people.

"Is someone else coming for breakfast?" he asked.

"Dr. Grady Adams comes on Saturday morning," Mia answered. "He comes early so he can check Poppa before he does his rounds at the hospital over in Bonham."

"You'll remember Grady Adams." Pearl dished up a bowl full of scrambled eggs. "He graduated with you and Addy. He's your dad's doctor."

Of course Jesse remembered Grady. As a kid, he had always had his nose in a book, so it wasn't any wonder that he had become a doctor. But Grady Adams wasn't the person causing his heart to pound out of his chest, and his breath to come in short gasps.

At that very moment, Grady poked his head in the back door. "Anybody home?"

"Come on in." Sonny motioned him inside with a flick of his wrist. "We was just about to say grace, so you're right on time. Have a seat, and we'll have some breakfast before we go talk medicine and cures for this disease."

Grady set his black leather briefcase on a side chair and stopped to kiss Addy on the cheek. "How's my patient today?"

"I'm fine. This new trial drug seems to be helping a lot," Sonny said.

Grady hadn't changed all that much. His light brown hair was a little thinner, and he'd either traded his thick glasses for contact lenses or else he'd had Lasik surgery. He still had a round, baby face and he'd put on a few pounds that had collected mostly around his middle.

"Hello, Grady." Jesse took a step forward and stuck out his hand. "Been a long time."

"Well, hello to you, too. You weren't supposed to arrive for a few more days. So you're out of the service now?" Grady's handshake was firmer than Jesse thought it would be. "It's good to have you back home, and yes, it has been a long time. I don't think I've seen you since the night we all graduated from high school."

"That sounds about right, but it's great to be back home." Jesse pasted a smile on his face. "So you're a doctor, and you make house calls?"

"Just for Sonny," Grady answered. "I'm the head of the ER

over in Paris, but I come out here once a week to check on this new trial drug that Sonny is taking, and to get a free breakfast." He winked across the table at Jesse.

"Married? Kids?" Jesse asked.

"Was married. No kids. My wife died a while back, but I'm moving on a baby step at a time. I'm dating a really nice woman who works in pediatrics at the hospital. She can't make biscuits and gravy like Pearl does, though." Another wink.

Jesse almost sighed with relief. *At least Grady wasn't dating Addy.*

"I'm so sorry to hear about your wife," Jesse said.

"Thank you," Grady replied. "You and Addy were best friends if I remember right. Bet y'all have got a lot of catching up to do."

"Yep, we sure do." Jesse shifted his focus over to Addy. Their eyes caught for a moment, and then she blinked and turned toward Mia.

"Before you start on the books, you should take care of your sheep and the alpacas. They're your responsibility when you are home," Addy said.

"I'll start that tomorrow," Mia said.

Her expression and tone reminded Jesse of a few recruits he'd gone through basic with—full of defiance and attitude.

"No, darlin'." Addy smiled. "You'll start right after breakfast."

"Yes, ma'am," Mia said with a head wiggle. Jesse was glad that he had never married and had kids if that was the way they acted.

Chapter Two

Addy thought she'd have another week to prepare herself before Jesse came home to Honey Grove. Seeing him there in the kitchen, with a chest that seemed to be an acre wide and his green eyes with those gold flecks, had left her speechless. She'd thought that twenty years would erase all those old feelings. But she still felt a thrill at seeing him.

Like "Delilah," the song that Blake Shelton sang a few years ago, she thought. The lyrics said that she couldn't blame anyone but herself because she never bothered to look at the best friend sitting right beside her. She'd been afraid to tell Jesse how she truly felt, and she'd paid the price.

Like always, Sonny said grace before they ate. As soon as he said "Amen," Addy began to pass the food around the table.

"Jesse, I understand you were a medic in the Air Force," Grady said as he helped himself to the scrambled eggs. "See much action?"

"Little bit," Jesse answered.

Addy almost smiled. Jesse had never been a guy who talked

a lot. He had probably exchanged more words with her than anyone else in the world. She wondered if he'd overcome the "man of few words syndrome" as she had tagged it when they were in high school.

"Any overseas? Did you ever run into Cody?" Grady asked.

"My brother and I were in different places. Haven't seen him in almost two years now. We all made it home for Thanksgiving a couple of years ago. He couldn't get away last fall," Jesse answered.

Addy was surprised that he had answered with more than a simple yes or no. She could feel Jesse's eyes on her, but she couldn't look right at him again.

Stop it! she scolded herself. *You've got to live on the same ranch with him, so you can't avoid him forever.*

Her hands trembled as she took a biscuit from the platter and sent them on to Sonny. "Mia and I will be glad to move out into the bunk house, and let you have your old room back."

"Oh, no!" Pearl shook her head. "The whole reason we hired you full time was so you'd be right here close by if I need you to help with Sonny."

"I'm glad to unload my stuff in the bunk house," Jesse said. "As kids, us boys couldn't wait to grow up and get to live out there. Last time all three of us were home, we stayed out there. I got to admit, it wasn't as glamourous as we thought it would be, but it will suit me just fine."

The only time he said more than a couple of words was when he was nervous. Despite her resolve not to look at him, she stole a quick glance across the table and caught his eye again. Just like old times when they didn't even need words, she could actually feel his angst. Was it because seeing her affected him as much as seeing him did her?

"Well, you got the bunkhouse all to yourself unless Cody makes up his mind to come home," Sonny said.

"Has he mentioned that kind of thing?" Grady asked.

"I can hear it in his voice when he calls us," Pearl answered. "He's weary with that way of life."

"With Addy and Mia's help and the locals that we hire from town during busy times, we don't use the bunkhouse anymore," Sonny said. "You might have to chase out some spiders and mice and talk your mother out of some linens. No one has stayed out there since you boys were all home the last time."

Addy felt her cheeks burning at the thought of what had gone on in that bunkhouse twenty years ago. She and Jesse had been emotional about him leaving Honey Grove, and she had cried, and...

The blush deepened, and she shook the memory from her mind.

"Great!" Mia said. "I didn't want to move out there anyway, and I doubt that Jesse would feel comfortable in a bedroom that's painted lavender. Mama loves that shade of purple."

"I remember," Jesse said softly.

Addy wondered if he remembered anything else about that night. She had spent endless nights staring out the bedroom window at the bunkhouse in the distance and reliving that night she and Jesse had spent in the bunkhouse.

"Earth to Addy," Grady chuckled.

"I'm sorry." She turned slightly to focus on him. "Did someone say something? I was off in another world."

"Evidently." Grady grinned. "I asked if you would pass the muffins. I've got time to eat one for breakfast dessert before Sonny and I have our weekly visit."

Addy passed the basket of blueberry muffins to Grady and then lowered her gaze to her half-full plate of food. Even after twenty years and so many life events had passed, she still got flutters in her stomach when Jesse Ryan was anywhere near her. They had discussed everything from the time neither of them could even talk plainly. He knew when Addy had gotten her first kiss. She knew that he had had a crush on Jenny Lynn Baker in the seventh grade. Then that last night before he left, things had gone from a goodbye kiss to a helluva lot more right out there in the bunkhouse. The next morning, she had awakened earlier than Jesse and she had slipped away before daylight. That was the last time she had laid eyes on him until right now.

She had thought that not being at the ranch when Jesse and his brothers came home would help, but maybe running from him had been a mistake.

"I don't want to ruin our friendship," she had said that night just before they started making out. "If we dated or even had a fling, things would be awkward between us. I don't want to chance that."

"What if we're meant to be together?" Jesse had toyed with a strand of her hair.

"We're eighteen, Jesse. We've got so much to do before we even think like that." But he'd kissed her, and the rest was history. She had used the Jesse Ryan yardstick to measure every man she had dated since then, and they'd all come up short. Now Jesse was back. Time could not be turned back, and life had gone on for both of them.

"You're doing it again," Mia told her mother.

"I'm sorry—again." Addy blushed and passed the muffins to Grady.

Grady chuckled. "My best friend's mind is off in la-la land this morning. I already finished a muffin, and even though I could eat another one, the elastic in my scrub pants is already stretched pretty far. Sonny and I are going to the office for a checkup now."

"I'll help Pearl do the cleanup while Mia goes to take care of her sheep." Addy pasted on a smile.

"See you tomorrow in church?"

"Of course. I'll save you a seat in case you get pulled into an emergency," she said.

"And dinner right here afterwards," Pearl said. "Maybe we'll have a game of dominoes in the afternoon."

"Sounds good." Grady laid his napkin on the table and stood up.

Sonny did the same and used his cane to lead the way to the office.

"So you and Grady are best friends?" Jesse asked.

"He's a good man." Addy sounded defensive even to her own ears. "And we have a lot in common, him being a doctor and me a nurse, so we kind of speak the same language."

"Hey, everyone needs a best friend." Jesse smiled.

"I wish he was more than her friend." Mia got up and started toward the door. "I like him, and he makes her laugh. Maybe things won't work out with him and his new girlfriend. We can always hope."

"Grady is a good friend, nothing more, not even in the future." Addy didn't leave room for argument.

"Speaking of the future, remember that I told you about this new trial drug for MS? It seems to be slowing down the symptoms, and we're grateful for that."

"Does he get out to check fences or—" Jesse started.

"Every day," Addy butted in. "We help get him in the truck and drive him around the fence lines. We let him check the cattle and make decisions about moving them from one pasture to the other."

"But Mama and I have been helping with the bookwork." Mia turned around from the back door. "He hated doing it anyway, and it gives me work experience for my degree."

Pearl reached over and laid a hand on Jesse's. "You can't know how glad we are that you are home, son. If you could drive him around after breakfast, it would be a big help."

"Whatever you need, Mama," Jesse replied. "I've also had medical training."

"That's great," Mia said. "Now we've got a nurse *and* a medic on the ranch. Can you do vet work? We could save a lot of money if we didn't need a vet a couple of times a month."

"Sorry, but that's not in my field," Jesse answered. "But if you break a leg or get on the wrong end of an IED, I can fix you up enough to get you to a hospital."

"I don't think there's any bombs on Sunflower Ranch," Addy said.

Other than the one about to go off in your heart right now? Her grandmother's voice popped into her head.

She ignored the question and stood up. "I'll help with cleanup, and then when Mia gets back from the sheep pens, we can get out there to get a pasture full of hay baled and ready for the barn. Think Sonny will ever go for the big round bales?" Keeping her hands busy would keep her crazy emotions in check—hopefully anyway.

Pearl shook her head. "He says there's too much waste in those things. Besides he likes to give jobs to the high school boys in the summertime. Says it teaches them hard work."

Mia laughed out loud. "What it does is teach them to go to college and do something where they won't have to sweat."

Jesse turned to look at her, and Addy's heart skipped a beat. He'd have to know before long, and it would turn everyone's life upside down.

"Is that why you're going to college?" he asked.

"No, sir," she answered without hesitation. "I'm sitting through all those classes because Poppa says I have to if I'm ever going to be the foreman of this place. That's been my goal since I moved onto this ranch, but..."

"But what?" Addy asked.

Mia shrugged and looked guilty as hell. "But I might..." Another shrug. "It's nothing."

"Thinking about changing your major?" Jesse asked.

"What I'm thinking about isn't a whole lot of your business," Mia smarted off. "I'm going to feed the sheep. I'll meet y'all at the hay field." She slammed the wooden screen door on her way out.

"What's that all about?" Pearl asked.

"Who knows?" Addy answered. "She's been different since she came home from college this semester, but she's said that ranching is in her blood, and she would never want to do anything else."

"Teenagers." Jesse headed into the living room.

Addy's pulse raced. "I'm on duty to drive a hay wagon today. When you get back from driving Sonny around, we can use you in the field."

"Go on," Pearl said with a wave of her hand. "If Jesse is going to take Sonny out for his morning drive, I'll have plenty of time by myself in the house. And I'll appreciate every minute of it."

Mia pushed back into the house. "I forgot my hat. Where's Jesse?"

"Right here." He poked his head around the kitchen door.

"You should know that I'm a rancher." She glared at him. "I was born on my great-grandmother's place out near Cactus, Texas, in the middle of a tornado. Granny couldn't get Mama to the hospital, so she delivered me in a storm cellar. When everything cleared out, she put me and Mama in her old pickup truck and took us to the hospital. The next day, she took us home, and I've lived on a ranch my whole life. So don't look at me like I don't know what I'm doing."

Addy wondered who Mia was trying to convince—Jesse or herself—and why she was being so belligerent. She had been the kind, sweet daughter that Addy had raised when she had come home for the Christmas break, but the girl who arrived

at the ranch for the summer had changed into a sassy, sometimes even hateful person. Could it be that knowing Jesse
was coming home had made her question her own place on
Sunflower Ranch?

"Well, I, for one, am glad that you've been here to keep the
ranch going while I've been out running missions for the Air
Force," Jesse told her.

"Thank you," Mia said as she took her cowboy hat off a
rack by the door and settled it on her head. "When you get
done with Poppa, I'll expect you out in the hay field."

"Mia Pearl Hall," Addy fussed at her.

"Pearl?" Jesse raised an eyebrow.

"It's my grandmother's middle name as well as mine,"
Addy answered.

"And my first name, so I claim her, too," Pearl said.

"Enough about names," Mia said. "Can I expect you in the
hay field? Those young boys don't want to listen to me, and
Henry has a crew fixing fence this morning."

"I'll be there as soon as I get back with Dad," Jesse promised.

"Good." She nodded and left by the back door.

Jesse raised an eyebrow at Addy. "Looks like she's well on
her way to making a pretty fine foreman. She's certainly bossy
enough, but then she comes by that honest. I remember you
being pretty sassy."

Addy crammed her straw hat down on her head. "If you
don't have a hat anymore, you'd better rustle one up. This hot
sun will fry your brains."

"It can't be any hotter than it was in Iraq or Kuwait," he
said, grinning.

"And you had a hat there, I'm sure," Addy said as she
pushed the back door open.

She went straight to the old ranch work truck. The thing had
been new the year that Jesse left for the Air Force. Now the

paint had rusted off in places, and the bench seat inside was cracked so badly that she kept a quilt thrown over it. But the engine still hummed like it was new. She started the engine, clutched and put it in reverse, then just sat there for a few minutes. Hoping to quiet her racing thoughts and all the memories, she leaned her head on the steering wheel. When that didn't work, she rose up and backed the truck out of the yard.

"I should have stayed in Cactus," she said. "I should never have come back here. When Granny went to the nursing home five years ago, and Mama and Daddy moved out there, I should have stayed."

Driving to the hay barn, she remembered coming out to Sunflower Ranch five years ago and all the old memories that flooded her that day. Mia was fourteen that spring, and Addy had just started managing a home health care facility. That's when Sonny was first diagnosed with MS, and Pearl had made arrangements for Addy to come see him every two weeks. Pearl had whispered that he was too damn stubborn to see a doctor as often as he should. The disease progressed quickly at first, and before long, Addy was out at the ranch almost every day.

"Mia loved it here, and Pearl said that she was the grandchild they had never had," Addy muttered as she got out of the truck and hooked up the hay hauling trailer to it. "So here we are, and Jesse is here. And what am I going to do?"

"Who are you talking to, Mama?" Mia came out of the tack room with two new pairs of gloves.

"Myself," Addy answered. "Don't you ever have a conversation with yourself?"

Mia nudged her with a shoulder. "Of course. I have to talk to someone who's as intelligent as I am every now and then."

"If you were all that smart, you'd figure out a way to keep your hired hands working," Addy told her.

"I'm only a year older than some of those guys," Mia reminded her.

"Dated any of them?" Addy asked.

"Hell, no!" Mia got behind the wheel.

"What does that mean?" Addy slipped into the passenger seat.

"I love you, Mama. I'm glad you kept me and didn't give me away, but I damn sure don't want a baby at my age. I've got plans, and babies aren't a part of that until I'm at least thirty." Mia backed the trailer out of the barn and drove toward the hay field.

"Good for you," Addy said.

"Besides, who knows what kind of man my father was. You don't want to talk about him, and I respect that, but he could be a serial killer for all I know." Mia didn't even grind the gears as she shifted from low into second.

"That's not showing a lot of faith in my judgment," Addy told her.

"No shade on you, Mommy dearest. He might have been a good man at the time, but I would like to know what kind of genes he threw into me before I have kids of my own." She slapped the steering wheel. "Not a boy in sight. If they show up to work at all today, I'm firing the lot of them, and calling a bunch of girls to come help me next week."

"Temper! Temper!" Addy scolded. "Look over there under that big scrub oak tree. I do believe that's four guys all hugging what shade they can before you start cracking the whip over their heads."

"It's a good thing they're here." Mia braked and brought the truck and trailer to a stop. "They don't know how close they came to losing their jobs."

"I'll drive. You get out there and make 'em sweat. Nothing sexier than a guy with big muscles and a sweaty body," Addy teased.

"God, Mama!" Mia shook her head.

"No, I'm not a god, but thanks for thinking I am," Addy giggled.

"If that's the truth, then why aren't you flirting with Jesse? He's pretty darn sexy, and he kept stealing looks at you all during breakfast." Mia jumped out of the truck and whistled for her crew to get to work.

Oh, my sweet spitfire of a daughter, you may come to regret saying that in the next few weeks.

Chapter Three

"You all settled in, Dad?" Jesse asked.

"Ready to go." Sonny laid his cane to the side of the passenger seat. "I'm so glad you're home, son. I was wondering if any of you boys would ever come back to the ranch." He patted Jesse on the shoulder. "I keep saying that, but I want you to know that I really mean it. Henry wants to retire as soon as summer ends, and you'll need to take over, but that's not the only reason I want you here. Your mama is going to need you if... when..." he stammered.

Jesse leaned across the console and gave his dad a quick hug. "That gives me six months to get a handle on things, Dad. And the new trial meds are helping so I expect to celebrate your hundredth birthday with you here in about twenty years. Don't you disappoint me!"

"You know I've always loved you as much as if you belonged to me and your mama by blood, don't you? I regret that I didn't tell you boys that as often as I should have." Sonny wiped away a tear hanging on his eyelashes.

"You did just fine, Dad. We all three knew we were loved," Jesse assured him and then started the slow drive around the property line fences.

Sonny cleared his throat, took out a hanky from the bibbed pocket of his overalls and blew his nose, then put it back. "Thank you for that, Jesse. These damned drugs make me as emotional as a teenage girl, but while we're on the subject, do you ever wonder about your biological parents? The other boys asked questions years ago, and we answered as best we could."

Jesse sure hadn't thought about having this conversation the very morning he got back home. "I looked into it myself a few years ago. I found out my birth parents' names and that they had died. Maybe that should have bothered me, but it didn't. Some guys I knew in the service that had been adopted had issues, but I never did. You and Mama loved me so much that it didn't matter. The only thing I wondered about was why you and Mama didn't adopt me right away, rather than waiting until you did the paperwork for Lucas and Cody."

Sonny sighed, inhaled deeply, and let it out slowly. "All your mama ever wanted was a family, and it was my fault we couldn't have kids, not hers. She loved me enough to stay with me even after we found out why after almost twenty years of marriage, we didn't have children. If we couldn't have our own flesh and blood, I didn't want to have any kids at all, but I love your mother more than life, and she wanted children, no matter how we had to get them."

Jesse felt his heart fall down into his cowboy boots. His own parents hadn't wanted him, and that didn't bother him, but the thought of Sonny not wanting him was another matter. Jesse felt tears welling up in his eyes, but he blinked them back.

Sonny went on, "Your mother talked me into trying out foster care, just to see how it would go."

"Dad, you don't have to tell me all this." Jesse got out of the truck and opened a gate, jogged back to the truck and drove through it, then hopped out again to close the gate.

"Sorry that I couldn't do that for you," Sonny said when Jesse was behind the steering wheel again.

Jesse patted him on the shoulder. "No problem."

"Now, where were we?" Sonny asked, then went on before Jesse could answer. "Oh, yeah. Back to when the foster lady brought you to our house. You were a big baby at nine pounds, but you scared the bejesus out of me. I was terrified that I'd drop you or do something wrong. There I was the same age as you are right now with a baby in my arms. I'd always managed to steer clear of even my buddies' newborn babies, but Pearl was so in love with you from the first moment she took you from that social worker's arms, that she wanted me to feel the same thing."

Jesse had held his friends' babies, and he'd felt the exact same way. Flying into war zones on a rescue mission, tornadoes, and red-haired women didn't scare him as much as a tiny baby did.

"Merrylee, the social worker, who was a childhood friend of your mother's, said she could pull some strings and we could adopt you right away," Sonny said. "I was the one who wanted to wait. Your mother wanted a family, not an only child, and I wanted to see how we'd do with one before I consented to having more babies in the house. When you were two years old, Merrylee called and said she had a three-year-old and his year-old brother who were available to foster like we did you, and in six months we could probably adopt them. I was in a turmoil. I always figured that if we did take in another child or two, you'd be the oldest and inherit the farm when I was gone, and by then you were mine...my son...my child. I didn't think I could love any others the way I did you."

Jesse's tears that time were of joy, not disappointment, but he still kept them at bay. "That would have been a big decision. Three boys who were stairsteps. A lot of work would be involved in raising us boys, but why are you telling me this now?" Jesse stopped beside a fence that was almost on the ground.

Sonny whipped his cell phone from his shirt pocket. "Henry, we're about a quarter of a mile west of that old fallen oak tree. Fence needs fixin' today if you can see your way to get it done. We'll need to move cattle into this pasture tomorrow, and there's no way this fence will hold them."

"Tell him I'll take care of it this afternoon. He shouldn't have to work on Saturday afternoon," Jesse said.

He listened for a few seconds and then said, "Thanks a lot. Jesse made it home a few days early. He'll take care of the fence. Why don't you come on over for supper tonight?" He listened for another minute, and then put the phone back in his pocket. "He says to tell you welcome home, and he's looking forward to seeing you tonight."

"It'll be good to get a visit with him, too. Now, tell me, Dad, where is this Merrylee lady now?" Jesse asked.

"She married and moved to California right after we got Lucas and Cody. Died last year with pancreatic cancer. She and your mother kept in touch, but they hadn't seen each other in years." Sonny sighed. "I wanted Pearl to fly out for the funeral, but she wouldn't leave me, said she wanted to remember Merrylee like she was when she brought you boys to her. I'm telling you this history because you need to hear it and understand that..." He paused.

"Understand what?" Jesse asked.

"That it doesn't matter whether a child comes to you as a baby or already up and running around, that kid becomes yours as much as if it was flesh and blood. I worried about bringing

Lucas and Cody into our lives because I was afraid that I couldn't love them as much as I did you," Sonny said. "I'm a rough and tough old cowboy, son. I don't cry very often, and I'm not as romantic as I should be with your mama and saying all this ain't easy for me. I love all three of you boys, and you need to know that. I haven't even given you a choice about steppin' up and runnin' this place when Henry retires, so I'm givin' it to you now. I took over this place from my dad, and he took it over from my grandpa. It's Ryan land, and it needs a Ryan to run it. Each of you boys have taken a different path up to now, and I don't want you to feel—"

Jesse laid a hand on Sonny's shoulder again and gave it a gentle squeeze. "I'm here, Dad, because I want to be, and I'm not going anywhere. You raised me to be a rancher. I've given enough of my time back to helping others. I'm glad to be home, and I'm glad to take over the reins for Henry."

"And someday for me?" Sonny glanced down at the cane.

"Like you said, a Ryan needs to run this land, and I'm a Ryan, maybe not the oldest son, but I can do the job—but not until after we celebrate your hundredth birthday," Jesse teased. "And thanks, Dad, for telling me all that. It's not easy to open up like you just did."

"No, son, it's not," Sonny said, and nodded, "but sometimes it's very necessary."

The last time Jesse had been this emotional was when he came home in the back of a plane with two flag-draped caskets carrying a couple of his friends. That was a sad, heartbreaking day. Today was a happy one. He was home. His father had just told him how much Jesse meant to him. But the emotional roller coaster left him as drained as the time he had escorted his friends back home for their funerals. He had to man up just like he did all those years ago, compartmentalize, and think about something else.

"Hey, how on earth did you get Addy to give up her job and come to work for you on a ranch?" Jesse asked. "Mama said she is an RN. She must have been making really good money."

He drove slowly around the last half of the fence line. When he had been younger, he and his brothers checked the fences on trail bikes. They had wanted horses, but Sonny thought bikes and four-wheelers were more efficient. Pearl had told Jesse that it had nothing to do with what worked better. But the truth was that when Sonny lost his beloved horse, he swore that he would never get attached to another one.

"It's not all about the money," Sonny chuckled. "Mia couldn't raise sheep to show at the fairs while she lived in town, and your mama was so worried about me that she wanted a full-time nurse in the house. We offered Addy room and board and a good salary. Mia could have the whole ranch to grow up on, plus said we would pay for her college expenses. We didn't intend for Addy to do farm work when she moved in, but pretty soon she was out there on a tractor and doing what she could to help out. They're both good ranch hands, and until the last few months, Addy made sure all my medical stuff was in order. She helps Grady do all that now. If they hadn't gotten to be friends before she moved in with us, I doubt that he'd make the trip to the ranch every week. I'd hate to think I'd have to go to the clinic and sit for hours waiting to see my doctor. Grady reports back to him, and I only have to go in to see him every other month this way."

"Is he Mia's father?" Jesse's brow wrinkled when he frowned.

"Have no idea, but I can't imagine it," Sonny answered. "She moved out to the Panhandle right after you left for the Air Force. I expect Mia belongs to someone she met out there. I always thought maybe you would ask her out, thick as y'all were back in high school."

"We didn't want to ruin a friendship." Jesse wondered what life might have been like if they had dated, and maybe she had settled down in one of his home bases. They would probably have a family by now. Sonny and Pearl would have the grandchildren they'd always wanted.

"Friendship, huh? That's crazy thinkin' there, Jesse," Sonny said. "Your mama and I were good friends before we married. That just made everything better afterwards. We already knew how to talk to each other..." he chuckled again, "and how to argue. You and Addy always reminded me of me and Pearl when we was young. Like I told you, your mama wanted a family and grandkids. You three boys are all starin' forty in the eyeball right now, and ain't a one of you brought us home grandbabies, so Mia stepped in to fill that place for us."

"You really don't know who her father is?" Jesse asked.

"I didn't ask, and from what I hear, Addy has never told a soul," Sonny answered. "Not even her parents. Did your mama tell you that they moved out to the Texas Panhandle about five years ago when Addy's grandmother died? Little town called Cactus. Strange name for a town if you ask me, but nobody did. They put their acreage up for sale, and since it bordered Sunflower Ranch, I bought the place."

"Are you renting the house that was on the property?" Jesse wouldn't mind living over there. He would have space of his own and yet still be on Ryan property.

"I offered it to Addy and Mia since it was her old home place, but she said she feels more comfortable living in the house with me and Pearl. That way if we need a nurse, she's right there," Sonny answered.

"Do you think she's embarrassed about who the father is?" Jesse asked as he drove the last leg back to the ranch house.

"Don't know. Don't care," Sonny answered. "Mia is a great kid, and we love her no matter who she belongs to. I wish we had a dozen grandkids who loved the land as much as she does."

Jesse parked as close to the yard gate as possible so that Sonny wouldn't have to walk very far. "Need me to help you or should I go on out to the hay field?"

"I can still get up the stairs fairly well, so get on out there and help Mia with those rowdy boys." Sonny grinned. "She's still working on making them believe she's boss. And thanks for listening to me, son. My door is open if and when you ever need to unload on someone."

"I'll remember that." Jesse gave a brief nod and sat still until Sonny was on the porch before he put the truck in reverse and headed toward the hay field. He hummed an old tune by Travis Tritt, "Where Corn Don't Grow," and remembered the day that he'd told his dad he wanted to go to the Air Force and be a medic.

"I've taught you to mend fences, to run a ranch, how to bait a hook, and clean fish for supper," Sonny had said. "I wanted you to be a rancher, but I won't hold you back. If that's your dream, then go chase it. But always remember where home is, and that there's a ranch waiting on you if your dreams don't work out the way you planned."

Jesse wondered if he'd stayed on the ranch, maybe gone to college and gotten a business agriculture degree, if he would have a son by now. Maybe one that had a dream that didn't involve ranching but would come home someday—one that could step into his shoes and run the Sunflower Ranch.

The lyrics of the song talked about a young man and his father sitting on the porch. The son asked his father if he ever wished he had a life where corn didn't grow. The father told him that there would be dusty fields no matter where he went in life. Jesse had never believed anything more than he did as he sang the last words of the song on his way out to the hay field.

"I've been so many places where corn don't grow that I can't even remember them all," Jesse muttered as he thought of all the places in what his team had called "the sand box."

When he parked at the edge of the hay field and stepped out of his truck, he left his career as combat medic behind, settled his old sweat-stained Stetson on his head, and changed into a cowboy. He had come home to Sunflower Ranch and was staying no matter what the circumstances.

"You ready to work?" Mia wiped sweat from her face with the tail of her T-shirt.

"You ready to try to keep up with me?" He unsnapped his chambray shirt, took it off and tied it around his waist, pulled a pair of gloves from his hip pocket, and picked up the first bale of hay. "This is what you want me to do, isn't it, boss?"

Mia nodded, grabbing the hay from him, and stacked it on the trailer.

The four boys who were working eyed him cautiously. "Who are you?" one of them finally asked.

"I'm Jesse Ryan," he said. "You guys going to ask questions or earn your paychecks?"

"You called her boss." A scrawny red-haired kid tossed a bale up onto the trailer.

"Yep, because that's who she is on this mission, and we'd all do well to listen to her. She's a tough one, I hear," he said.

Chapter Four

$\mathscr{A}$ddy drove with one elbow stuck out the window of the truck that pulled the trailer the boys were stacking hay on. She saw Jesse coming out across the field from his truck, and her breath caught in her throat when he removed his shirt. His chest had always been broad, but sweet lord, looking at his bare skin glistening with sweat gave her a case of hot flashes that had nothing to do with the sun beating down on her arm.

She turned the radio on and upped the volume so the kids could hear. Garth Brooks was singing, "If Tomorrow Never Comes." Right then she wished that tomorrow would never come, that she would never have to tell her daughter the truth about her father.

She glanced in the side mirror to catch Jesse staring at her reflection. When he caught her eye, he tipped his hat and went back to work. Could he be thinking the same thing that she was? The words to the song asked if the love they had known from the past was enough to last if there was no tomorrow. She and Jesse had agreed when they were only thirteen that they couldn't ever be more than good friends, because if they were, it might ruin their best friend status—and then that last night before he went to the military, they had crossed the line. Who could know if that one crazy night would have developed into something else if she had been willing to keep in touch with him? The only thing she knew for sure was that, for her, the love they had shared that night had lasted twenty years—but it was past time to let all that go. She and Jesse were adults now, and the choices they had made had changed them.

"Mama!" Mia yelled over the top of the music on the radio.

Addy realized the truck was veering right toward a hay bale and quickly got it under control. She did her best to keep her eyes on the field in front of her, but every few minutes she stole a fast glance at Jesse. Why did he have to be so damned sexy?

When no more bales could be loaded onto the trailer, the kids hopped into the bed of the truck. Just as she started driving toward the barn, Jesse opened the passenger door and slid into the wide bench seat beside her. He twisted the cap off a bottle of water, handed it to her, and then did the same with a second one and turned it up for several long gulps.

"Thank you, but the hay haulers are supposed to be back there together." She took a sip and set the bottle between her knees.

"I'm too old to sit back there," Jesse said. "I don't want those kids to hear me groaning after only two hours of hard work."

"You *are* getting pretty damn old," she said.

"Hey, now!" Jesse raised an eyebrow. "If I'm remembering right, you are four days older than I am."

A strand of kinky brown hair had escaped her ponytail and was hanging in front of her oversized sunglasses. She tucked it behind her ear and kept her eyes on the rutted lane back to the barn. "You've been out on a twenty-year adventure filled with danger, and that makes you look"—she lowered her sunglasses and glanced at him—"about five years older than me."

You are flirting. Her grandmother's voice was loud and clear in her head.

Am not, she argued. *I'm just being a friend to Jesse like I used to be.*

"I missed you, Addy. Why didn't we keep in touch?" he asked.

"You had your dreams to follow that involved getting away from this ranch," she answered. "I had mine, and they went in separate directions. Our paths just separated, Jesse."

"And yet, here we are right back where we started," he said.

"Yep, hauling hay like we did when we were kids," she agreed as she backed the trailer into the barn. "Guess it's tougher than we thought to get away from our roots."

"Ever wonder where we'd be if we had stayed in Honey Grove?" he asked.

Just every single day, she thought. "There's no use in thinking about what happened in the past. Those days are gone."

"What about the future?" he asked as he opened the truck door.

"No use in worrying about that either. We just have today, and right now the important thing is that we get this hay stacked so these boys can collect their paychecks and knock off work by noon," she told him.

"I'd forgotten it was Saturday," he said with a grin. "You going to the Wild Horse tonight?"

"Those days are in the past, too," she told him.

"Still got your fake ID?" he asked.

"Of course I do." She didn't tell him that she had an old

cigar box with everything they had ever shared through their eighteen years as best friends and neighbors.

"Me, too," he said.

* * *

Mia had already formed a hay-tossing brigade and had several bales stacked when Jesse got out of the truck and back to the trailer. "We've got this if you want to go on to the house and visit with Poppa."

"Reckon I'd best stick around and earn my keep." Jesse stepped in front of the line and caught the next bale that she threw over the side of the trailer.

Mia shrugged and shot him a dirty look. "Suit yourself."

"You got a problem with me, boss?" he asked.

She cut her eyes over to the other side of the barn where her mother was gathering up bottles of water for everyone. "Not if you stay away from my mama. I teased her about flirting with you, but she doesn't need a boyfriend at her age." She bent down and whispered for his ears only.

"I'll be living right here on the ranch. How do you propose I stay away from your mother?" he asked.

"Find a way," Mia whispered. Then she yelled: "You guys need to hustle. I'm not paying overtime, and you don't get a check until these bales are stacked."

"Tough boss, aren't you?" Jesse asked.

"Tougher daughter," she shot back at him.

Addy brought over the water and a stack of envelopes. "Looks like you guys are going to be done by noon for sure."

"Yes, ma'am," said the tall, lanky blond kid named Pete.

"What are you boys going to do tonight?" Jesse asked.

"We're going to score some beer, take it to the creek, and build a bonfire," he answered. "Hey, Mia, you want to go with us? I'll pick you up at seven. You can bring a six-pack of your favorite beer."

"Not tonight," Mia said.

"Well, you know where we'll be," he said. "And Ricky will be there, if that changes your mind."

"Ricky?" Jesse asked. "Boyfriend?"

"That would be none of your business," Mia answered.

It didn't take a brain surgeon to know that Mia wasn't happy about Jesse being back on Sunflower Ranch. Maybe she was jealous of his relationship with Sonny and thought he was there to usurp whatever authority she thought she had. Or maybe she had felt the vibes between him and her mother, and she didn't want to share Addy.

Jesse had just thrown the last bale onto the stack when he caught a movement in his peripheral vision. He whipped around to see Grady coming into the barn. The doctor was wearing light blue scrubs and white shoes and didn't have a drop of sweat on him.

"Hey, I thought y'all shut down this business at noon on Saturday," he yelled.

"We're almost done." Mia jumped down off the wagon and ran over to him. "I'd hug you, but I'm a mess, and I still have to sweep the trailer and truck."

"I'll take care of that," Jesse offered.

Mia turned slightly and said, "It's my job, so I'll take care of it. You're finished for the day, Jesse. Go on to the house."

Jesse downed half a bottle of water. "Not me, boss. I'm going to help Henry fix a fence that's down." He brushed against Addy's shoulder when he passed by her. "See you around. Is your best friend Grady coming for supper as well as Henry?"

"Nope. He has to be at the hospital on Saturday night, but he has Sunday dinner with us," she answered as she handed the boys their checks.

"Afternoon, Grady." Jesse nodded as he untied his shirt and slipped his arms into it on his way out of the barn.

"Jesse." Grady nodded back. *I'm her best friend, not Grady*, Jesse thought.

But that was yesterday, the voice in his head reminded him. Jesse could feel Mia's cold stare on his back all the way out to his truck. He'd love to know what he'd done to get under her skin so badly. She hadn't been particularly warm that morning at breakfast, but at least she hadn't sent him go-to-hell looks or practically told him to drop graveyard dead.

Tex came out of nowhere and jumped into the vehicle as soon as Jesse opened the door. The dog sat down in the passenger's seat, barked once, and then stared out the front window as if telling Jesse to get on with the program.

"Well, at least you're glad I'm home," Jesse said as he got behind the wheel, rolled up the windows, and turned the A/C on high. "Grady is treating me like he's afraid I'll take Addy away from him. Mia is acting like I'm Lucifer come up from the pits of hell. And Addy...I don't know if she's got room for another guy friend in her life or not. And why is he here again on the same day anyway?"

Tex stuck his nose right against the vent and wagged his tail.

"Or maybe you just want some cool air and don't give a damn who you ride with," Jesse said. "You got any idea why Mia is acting so harsh?"

Tex licked him on the hand and whipped around to the side window to watch a rabbit bounding across the pasture.

"Maybe tomorrow I won't let her be boss if she's going to treat me like something she stepped in out in the pasture," Jesse chuckled. "Whatever her problem is, she can get over it, old boy"—he reached over and scratched the dog's ears—"because I'm here to stay. I probably should never have left. Dad needs me now, and I'm not going anywhere."

Tex barked once in agreement.

"I've had enough traveling in dry desert places and wondering if I would ever get home to see green grass again. I'm ready to settle down and maybe even give the folks some of those grandbabies they seem to want." Jesse braked and parked in front of the tool shed.

Tex sat still when he opened the truck door.

"Are you planning on going with me to fix that fence or not?" Jesse asked.

He could have sworn that the dog nodded his head. "Well, then sit tight. I'll be right back with what we need."

He tossed the tools and supplies in the back of the truck, along with an extra set of gloves. The one thing he forgot was water, so he was almighty glad that the little chore only took an hour. The way the sun was beating down on him, he could feel dehydration setting in by the time he'd finished the job and got back to the barn.

Tex bounded out over the top of Jesse's legs the second that the truck stopped, and the dog set up a howl as he chased a rabbit into a mesquite thicket not far from the barn. Jesse didn't stop to watch the race but rather headed straight on into the tack room and went to the refrigerator for a bottle of water.

Mia came out of the tiny bathroom and propped her hands on her hips. "I'll take care of this. You can call it a day."

"I don't need any help, Mia. I want to work the rest of the day in here. I need to reacquaint myself with where everything is. Tomorrow, I'm going to make sure my old four-wheeler and my dirt bike are completely in running order. I want to know if I've got all the tools I need or if I need to make a trip over to Bonham," Jesse said.

"Don't tell me what to do." Her green eyes flashed anger.

"All right then, I'll make a suggestion. You said that you

needed to do some computer work in the office when we were eating breakfast. Maybe you could do that, and let me have some time out here," Jesse said.

"I'm nineteen years old, and I've worked on this place more in the past few years than you have. Hell, I've worked on a ranch more than you have since you left this one." Mia glared at him.

"Yes, you have, but I've got about twenty years of life experience that you don't have, and I had eighteen years of ranch work under my belt before I left here, so you can shed your pissy attitude. It would break Mama and Daddy's heart to know that the two of us couldn't work together, so let's start all over and try to get along." Jesse pulled a wooden box out from under the worktable.

"Hmphh," Mia all but snorted. "Don't test me."

"Same back at you." Jesse started to reach out and brush a spider from her hair but kept his hands to himself.

She inhaled so deeply that she almost busted the buttons off her shirt, and then let it out in a whoosh. "I don't like you."

"That's plain as a snout on a hog's nose. I don't have any idea why, but you can get over it," he chuckled.

"What's so funny?" she demanded.

"Your mother could get on a soap box pretty quick when she was your age. She had that same fire in her eyes, and the same attitude," Jesse said.

"Don't you bring Mama into this," Mia said. "This is between us."

"I think maybe you've got a burr under your saddle because of something else going on in your life. You blushed when Pete mentioned Ricky. Who are those boys anyway?" Jesse asked.

"That's my business and not a bit of yours. I saw the way Mama was lookin' at you. I know you were friends, but you left her behind, so leave her alone now. She and Grady are good friends. She doesn't need another guy friend." Mia glared at him.

"You don't even know me. I'd hoped we could get along with each other. The folks have sung your praises every time I've talked to them. Why have you taken such a dislike to me when we've just met?" Jesse asked.

"Integrity," Mia answered, then stomped across the room and slammed the door behind her.

* * *

Addy's hair was still damp from her shower when she checked Sonny's vital signs and wrote down her findings on his chart. With the new trial medicine, Grady insisted that Sonny's blood pressure, heart rate, and temperature be recorded twice a day. Bless his heart, he'd stopped by that morning for a second time just to see if she was all right. He'd said he could feel the tension at the breakfast table, and he wanted to know if she needed to talk. She had assured him that she was fine, and he'd given her a friendly hug and gone on his way.

"I'm glad Jesse is home," Sonny said. "I'd like for all three of my boys to come back to Honey Grove, but to have Jesse is special. He'll always be our first."

"Seems like just yesterday that we adopted him," Pearl sighed.

"Hopefully, he'll take some of the worry about this place off you," Addy said as she put her stethoscope back into her little tote bag, "and I agree about time slipping by. Seems like only yesterday that Jesse and I graduated from high school, and he left to go to the Air Force. It's like time stood still, and he's only been gone a few hours."

"That's the way of it when really good friends get together

again," Sonny said. "Doesn't matter if it's two years or two months. True friendship don't know time or distance."

"I guess that's right about me and Jesse. The heart doesn't know about time and years, does it?" Addy agreed.

"No, it doesn't," Pearl said.

Mia came into the kitchen in a whirlwind. Her long, brown hair was twisted up on top of her head in a messy bun that was still a little damp from her shower. "What can I do to help?"

"Set the table and then get the butter and strawberry jam out of the fridge," Pearl said. "Jesse is going to be starving. He took a biscuit with him this morning, and that's all he's had all day. He's always loved hot rolls with my jam on them."

"I suppose he's going to want to go over the books, too?" Mia asked.

Addy could tell from her daughter's tone that the idea wasn't setting too well with her. "And why wouldn't he? He needs to see what's going on here on Sunflower."

"Forget I said anything." Mia took down five plates. "But don't expect me to show him the ropes."

"Six plates," Sonny said. "Henry will be eating with us, too."

"What's got you all in a tizzy today?" Pearl asked.

"I'm fine," Mia said.

"Missin' your friends at school?" Sonny asked.

"Not one bit," Mia answered. "We only need five plates. I'm going to go into town and grab a burger with some of the kids I haven't seen yet this summer."

Addy got her by the arm and marched her out of the kitchen, across the formal dining room and into the living room. "I don't know what you're angry about, but I won't tolerate your attitude. Pearl and Sonny have been too damn good to you for you to blow off supper tonight."

"I don't like Jesse," Mia said.

"That's too bad, because as of this morning, he's *your* boss.

Sonny is turning over the whole operation to him in a few months. Henry is retiring, and Jesse will be the new overseer and foreman of this place. So suck it up, get your butt back in there, and put a smile on your face," Addy said.

"You're treating me like a child."

"Act like an adult, and I will treat you like one." Addy pointed toward the door.

Mia pasted a fake smile on her face. Addy followed her into the kitchen and took down another plate. "You can get the silverware and Jesse's strawberry jam out of the fridge."

"Did I hear my name?" Jesse's silhouette blocked the light coming through the door into the kitchen. His dark hair had been combed back. He filled out a fresh pair of creased jeans just right, and he had polished his boots. His plaid, pearl snap shirt stretched across his broad chest like the thing had been tailored to fit him. Addy's pulse jacked up a few notches, and her breath caught in her chest.

"Yes, son. Come on in here and get washed up. "I made that freezer strawberry jam just for you." Pearl took a step to the side and hugged him. "I know how you like it on your hot rolls."

"You're going to spoil me, Mama, and I'll love it." Jesse kissed her on the top of her gray hair and then sniffed the air. "Is that one of your famous pot roasts I smell?"

Pearl grabbed two pot holders and took the roast from the oven. "Got to feed you good so you won't get a wandering notion again."

"Never happen, Mama." Jesse grinned. "I'm right back where I should've been all along."

Chapter Five

Jesse turned away from his mother to find three sets of eyes staring at him. His father looked downright happy. Addy had questions in hers, and Mia was shooting daggers at him.

Henry rapped on the back door and came into the kitchen without waiting for someone to invite him inside. "Smells good in here, and can you believe what the cats have drug in?" He crossed the room and wrapped Jesse up in his arms in a fierce bear hug. "Boy, I'm glad you finally came home. These old bones of mine are getting tired of long days of fencing and hay and pulling baby calves. They're ready to go to the cool mountains of Colorado and fish all day."

Jesse patted him on the back and took a step to the side. "It's sure good to see you again, Henry! Dad told me that you're retiring at the end of the year, but you sure you don't want to stick around 'til spring? In the wintertime up in that part of the country, you'll be more likely to catch forty winks than a fish anyway."

Henry hung his cowboy hat on the rack beside the door.

"It's right good to see you, too, son. We're all gettin' older by the day on this place. I'll miss all y'all, too, but my sister left me a cabin in the mountains, and it seems like an omen. Sonny tells me that you'll be taking over before long. Soon as you're ready, I'll be willin' to step down. Don't want to rush you. You need to get comfortable with everything." He headed for the table, where Sonny was sitting. "You just tell me when the time seems right to you, and I don't care if I catch a fish or them forty winks, it'll be good to rest my weary bones and not have to deal with teenage boys anymore."

"Tell me more about this cabin." Jesse followed him over to the table. It would be so easy to drag his feet and keep putting off the day when Henry could really retire, but that wouldn't be fair. Maybe if Jesse really buckled down, Henry could at least drop a fishing line in the water before it got too cold. Jesse had gone on missions when he had only a couple of hours to get ready, so hopefully, he could step up to this job by the beginning of fall.

"Oh, yeah." Sonny answered from his place at the head of the table. "Like he said, his sister bought a cabin at the base of a mountain right near a river. When she passed away last year, she left it to him. He's invited me and Pearl to come up there and visit him."

Henry sat down at the other end of the table. "And Sonny promised that next summer he and Pearl would fly up and stay a couple of weeks with me."

Pearl set a bowl of potatoes and one of carrots on the table. "You just want me to come up there and cook for you two old codgers."

"Well, if you're offering." Henry flashed her a grin.

Mia brought the platter of roast to the table. "I went skiing with my Sunday school class in Colorado, and I loved the place. I met this really nice boy, and we texted for a few weeks when I got home. Maybe Mama can go up there sometime and find a husband."

"Mia Pearl Hall!" Addy gasped. "Whatever makes you think I'm looking for a husband?"

Mia shrugged and shot a sly smile in Jesse's direction. "I'm grown now, and you're getting a little long in the tooth, as Grandpa says."

Addy's expression was one of total bewilderment. "I am not that old. Haven't you heard? Forty is the new thirty!"

"Yeah, right," Mia said. "I'd hoped you and Grady might get together and be more than friends, but I guess that's not going to happen."

"No, it's not!" Addy said. "I value his friendship more than a relationship with him."

"I was sorry to hear about his wife." Jesse waited for his mother to take her normal place at his dad's right hand, and Mia and Addy to take their places on the other side of the table before he pulled out his chair. "I didn't want to drag up old hurts so I didn't ask him, but what happened to her?"

Pearl bowed her head. "Henry, will you say grace for us?"

Henry said a quick prayer. The moment he said, "Amen," Jesse picked up his napkin and laid it on his knee. He wasn't prepared for the shock that went through his body when Addy's knee made contact with his. He jerked his head up and their eyes locked for just a brief second. From the width of her eyes, he had no doubt that she had felt the same sparks.

Jesse had forgotten all about asking about Grady's wife, and was trying to deal with his feelings.

"Amelia was in a bad car wreck," Pearl said. "Drunk driver T-boned her. You might remember her, Jesse. She was smart and very shy, a lot like Grady."

"Wasn't she in chemistry class with you, Addy?" Jesse asked.

"Mama!" Mia nudged her after a long pause.

"I'm sorry, what did you say?" Addy asked.

"Jesse asked if you had chemistry class with Amelia," Mia said.

Addy took the bowl of beans from her daughter and put a spoonful onto her plate before passing them on to Henry. "Yes, I did. She was a junior and we were seniors." She glanced over at Jesse. "She always had her nose in books, like Grady."

"And she wore wire-rimmed glasses, and her team always won the academic bowl contests," he said. "I remember her very well. I'm not a bit surprised that she and Grady wound up together, and I'm sorry to hear that he lost her. To have something like that happen so sudden would be devastating."

"He's coping pretty well," Mia said. "Mama has helped him get over his grief. They talk several times a week. A guy friend is a good thing to have."

"Your mama was always a good listener," Jesse told her. "Would you pass the hot rolls, please, ma'am? And do you have a guy friend, Mia?"

Mia picked up the basket of rolls and passed them over to him. "Of course I do. A woman needs a guy friend who'll help her see things like men do."

"What's his name?" Jesse asked.

Mia blushed. "That's my business."

"I'd be interested in knowing who this guy friend is, too," Addy said. "You never mentioned him before."

"He's a secret," Mia whispered. "We'll talk about this later."

"All right." Addy shrugged. "Used to be that you told me everything."

"I'm a grown woman now," Mia said.

Henry chuckled and steered the conversation back to the ranch business. "I drove past the fence that was down and saw you got it fixed, Jesse. Fine job. The whole section needs some work done next week, but at least now if one of the Hereford bulls from the pasture across the road gets loose, it won't be flirting with our Angus cows."

The tension was still so thick that Jesse couldn't have cut through it with a machete when he looked across the table at Mia. "I took care of that before I organized the tack room this afternoon. Thought I might fix my old dirt bike and four-wheeler on Monday if that's all right."

"What are you looking at me for?" Mia asked. "You're going to be the boss soon enough. I guess you can do whatever you want."

"Just wondering if you can handle that bunch of wild boys all on your own," Jesse teased.

"I'm good at what I do," Mia shot back.

Jesse shifted his gaze to his father. "But before I do get all greasy and dirty working on a bike, I'd like for you to walk me through the computer program, Dad."

"I'll be glad to," Sonny said, "and more than glad to turn the whole thing over to you. I've hated all this technology stuff."

"I'll do it," Addy said. "Computers stress you out, Sonny."

Sonny looked down the table at Addy. "That's a great idea, and takes a load off my mind. I didn't like doing the paperwork when it was in ledger books, but I just hate it now that everything has gone technical."

"Thank you both for helping Dad with the computer work," Jesse said, "and Addy, I'm a pretty quick study on computers, so maybe I'll catch on pretty quick."

"Don't pass plumb out when you see how much feed and fuel costs these days," Henry chuckled. "It's probably doubled in the past twenty years."

"Just like everything else," Jesse agreed, "but if you hear me groaning and trying to catch my breath, come rescue me."

"Addy can give you some mouth-to-mouth if that happens," Henry teased.

"No, she will not!" Mia said.

Addy cut her eyes around at her daughter. "Honey, I'm sure that Jesse was teasing."

"I just want you to meet a nice man that makes you happy before..."

"Before what?" Addy asked.

"Nothing," Mia answered. "Great pot roast Nana, and I'm sorry to eat and run, but some of my friends are waiting for me uptown."

"Go have fun," Pearl said.

"Remember that you've got a full day ahead of you tomorrow," Sonny cautioned her. "Better not stay out too late."

"I won't, Poppa." She kissed him on the top of his head on her way out of the room.

Jesse wished he knew how to fix Mia's problem with him. His folks and her mother sure didn't need this kind of tension every time they sat down at the table. If it didn't get better, he would beg off having supper with them as often as possible and take a plate out to the bunkhouse.

* * *

After supper and cleanup, Addy checked Sonny's vital signs, wrote them in the notebook for Grady, and went to her room. She tried to read a book, but finally tossed it over on the bed when she realized she hadn't gotten past page one. The television didn't have anything she wanted to watch, and she was still in turmoil over Mia's behavior all day.

Mia had been a happy baby, a great little girl, and had become Addy's best friend when they moved to Sunflower Ranch—right up until last Christmas. She was supposed to come home for spring break in March but had said she needed to stay at the college and study for midterms. Addy wasn't used to her acting so surly and didn't like the snarky little witch that had taken over Mia's body. She finally marched across the hall and knocked on her daughter's bedroom door.

"Come in," Mia yelled.

Addy found her lying on her bed, both thumbs doing double time as she sent texts to someone. "I thought you were going into town."

"Changed my mind. I might go later this evening for a while. Are you here to yell at me some more about supper?" Mia laid the phone on the bed beside her.

"Who are you texting, and do you feel like I should yell at you?" Addy sat down on the edge of the bed. "You might tell me why you're being so rude and hateful. This isn't *my* Mia. This is some woman that I don't know, and she's not been the same since she came home from college this semester."

"I've got my reasons, and I don't want to talk about it," Mia answered.

"We've known for weeks that Jesse was coming home and taking over the ownership of the ranch. Sonny's problems are stabilizing with the new drug, but if it stops working, he could go downhill pretty fast," Addy reminded her.

"I don't like Jesse," Mia sighed, "and I'm *not* having this conversation right now." Her phone pinged and she picked it up again. "Ricky can get away quicker than he thought he could, so he is going to be at the bonfire down on the creek tonight. He's picking me up and bringing me back home."

"You do know how I feel about Ricky, and you know how he treats girls, don't you?" Addy asked. "His reputation for using them and then throwing them away has been with him since y'all were in middle school. Why on earth would you even want to be around him?"

"I'm an adult now, Mama, and folks have accused him of mean things when they don't even know him. Don't worry about me." Mia hopped up off her bed, grabbed her phone and purse, and headed out of the room. "You don't like Ricky. I don't like Jesse. At least I'm honest about stuff. You and Jesse have been flirting with your eyes all day. What is it with y'all? Were you more than best friends?"

"Like you just said, I'm not having this conversation tonight, and I don't appreciate the way you're talking to me," Addy said through clenched teeth.

"I'm an adult, and I *will* speak my mind," Mia smarted off.

Addy stood up, crossed the room, and closed the bedroom door behind her. Then she opened it and said, "You might tell Ricky if he honks for you to come outside, I'll be the one who goes out the door first. If he can't respect you enough to come inside for you, then he can stay away from this place."

Mia rolled her eyes toward the ceiling and started texting again. "You are so old-fashioned, Mama. Guys don't do that anymore, and I won't ask Ricky to, so forget it, and if you go out there, I'll just leave the ranch and get a job in town for the summer."

Addy pointed a finger at her daughter. "Respect doesn't change with age, my child. If you want to get a job elsewhere, just get after it, but remember, you'll have to pay rent, utilities, and if you move away from here, you can damn well expect to pay your own phone bills and car insurance."

"Whatever..." Mia did a world-class head wiggle.

Addy closed the door again and headed across the hallway to her bedroom with a full head of steam and anger. She was almost to her bedroom when Jesse called out to her, "Hey, got a minute?"

"Sure, but I promise I don't know what's gotten into Mia. She's not at all the snippy little witch she's been all day. She's had a dose of smart aleck since she came home from college this semester, but not as bad as today. I think it has to do with Ricky O'Malley, the boy that she keeps saying is just her friend," Addy said.

He stopped so close to her that she got a whiff of his shaving lotion—something woodsy with a hint of musk—the same scent he had used in high school. She inhaled deeply and forced a smile. Whatever was going on with Mia wasn't his fault.

"Must be having a rough day. Maybe she's more serious about Ricky than she's letting you believe, or maybe it's the heat," Jesse said. "I was wondering if you'd seen a red tooth-brush in the bathroom. I looked and it's not there. If you threw it out, that's fine, but I forgot to pack that and my hairbrush, both. I never worried about it before because I knew I had those things here."

Mia swung her door open in time to catch what he'd said about his toiletry items. "How are you ever going to run a ranch if you can't even keep up with your hairbrush and tooth-brush?" She stomped down the hallway toward the kitchen.

"I'm sorry," Addy said. "I may send her to summer classes just to get rid of her if she doesn't straighten up. I assure you she wasn't like this before she went to college."

"She'll grow up," Jesse reassured her. "Remember when we thought we were old enough and smart enough to set the world on fire?"

"Oh, yeah. We were full of spit and vinegar back then, but it didn't take us long to figure out that we had to have matches to set the world on fire, and to get those we had to find jobs that paid money." Addy smiled back at him. "But I haven't seen your toothbrush. I do keep a couple of extra ones. Be glad to share one with you, but you're on your own when it comes to your hair."

"Thank you," Jesse said.

"Be right back out." The door to Addy's room was open so

she went in, opened a drawer, and picked up a blue toothbrush. "It's not red, but it'll work until you can get a red one."

Her fingertips brushed against his as she handed it to him. She could have sworn that sparks flew at his touch, but she quickly forgot all about it when she heard the blast of a car horn and the front door slam. She took off in a dead run and made it to the porch in time to see the taillights of an older model pickup truck driving away. Mia was waving out the passenger window as the vehicle disappeared into the night.

"You okay?" Jesse asked right behind her.

"I guess she's decided to go through the rebellious stage later than most kids," Addy said. "That Ricky kid was supposed to come to the door, not honk for her."

"I'm not very smart when it comes to teenage girls, but if you ever need to talk, I'm out in the bunkhouse," Jesse offered.

"Thanks," she said.

"See you in the morning." He held up the toothbrush. "And thanks for this."

"Sure thing." She tried to keep calm, but what she wanted to do was stomp a hole in the wooden porch.

She waited a few minutes and then went back into the house. She could hear Sonny, Henry, and Pearl all visiting in the living room and overheard something about a cabin in Colorado. She couldn't blame them if they wanted to get away before next summer. Who knew what condition Sonny might be in by that time if this new treatment plan took a wrong turn and he got worse? Now that Jesse was home, they should go as often as they possibly could.

She went back into her room—Jesse's old bedroom. Packing up all his trophies, ribbons, and even some of his clothing and toting them out to the bunkhouse to store them had not been easy for her. Learning back in the spring that he was coming home to stay had almost sent her right back out to the Texas

Panhandle to her parents' ranch. She knew she could live with them until she got a job in a nearby hospital or nursing home, but she sucked it up and decided to stay in Honey Grove. Mia had gone to high school here, and some of her classmates, including Ricky, had even attended college with her. Mia loved Sunflower Ranch, and Pearl and Sonny loved her like she was their own granddaughter.

Addy went to the window overlooking the backyard and pulled open the lace curtains. Out there in the distance, a light came on in the bunkhouse. She saw a movement and wondered if Jesse had a girlfriend, someone just waiting for him to ask her to be with him here in Texas. The thought caused jealousy to shoot through her body.

"You have no rights to him," she said, but she couldn't keep her mind from going back to that night they had spent in the bunkhouse. They hadn't turned on the lights, but had only a small candle, and they had promised to be honest with each other from that time on, and never keep secrets about how they felt.

"Yeah, right," she muttered as she dropped the curtain, got her things together, and headed for the bathroom at the end of the hall. "Like that last part could ever happen, given the results of that night."

Chapter Six

$\mathcal{T}$he congregation was singing the first song on Sunday morning when Grady slipped in beside Addy on the third pew from the front. The lyrics of the hymn "Leaning on the Everlasting Arms" talked about being safe and secure from all alarms. Addy was a strong, independent woman who had proven that she didn't need a man to complete her, but it would be nice to cuddle up next to a guy at night. Sure, she could talk to Grady about anything, and he had turned out to be a good friend, but a boyfriend would be nice. For some reason Mia seemed to be pushing her in that direction now that she was grown. All through her childhood she didn't want Addy to date anyone. Addy glanced over her shoulder at her belligerent daughter, who was sitting on the back pew with Ricky O'Malley—just another of her many acts of defiance.

"Sorry I'm late," Grady said. "My relief doctor had a flat tire on the way to work."

"We just started the first hymn." She handed him her song book, and Jesse immediately moved his hymnal over to share with her.

His shoulder had pressed into hers when they all had to scrunch down a little to make room for Grady. Now she had all kinds of chemistry happening on her right side, and she didn't talk about her feelings where Jesse was concerned to anyone— not even Grady.

She and Grady worked well together, spoke the same medical lingo, and they had shared lots of feelings when Amelia had died, but Jesse Ryan was off–limits for her and always would be.

The preacher stepped up behind the lectern, cleared his throat, and said, "Good mornin', everyone. I'd like to welcome Jesse Ryan home and back to our congregation, and to say that we all appreciate your service. Now, if you will open your Bibles to the thirteenth chapter of First Corinthians, we'll have congregational reading of the verses four through seven."

Addy flipped her Bible open to the familiar chapter and read with the rest of the folks in the church: " 'Love is patient, love is kind. It does not envy, it does not boast, it is not proud. It does not dishonor others, it is not self-seeking, it is not easily angered, it keeps no record of wrongs. Love does not delight in evil but rejoices with the truth. It always protects, always trusts, always hopes, always perseveres.' "

"We have four weddings this week in Honey Grove," the preacher said when the reading was done. "That's why I chose this passage to talk about this morning, but the more I thought about it, the more I realized that this is a message to all of us."

"Amen," Sonny said loudly.

"Glad you can agree, Sonny," the preacher said.

He went on to talk about each aspect of the verses, but Addy only heard the droning of his deep voice somewhere off in the distance.

Love doesn't have to be all fire and heat, the voice in

her head whispered. *It can be a quiet companionship, a re-lationship between two people who have similar interests and respect for each other.*

I want both, she argued. *I want it all.*

You've kept your secrets, but if you ever want to have a marriage, you're going to have to open Pandora's box and let them out.

"No," she muttered.

Jesse nudged her on the shoulder. "Don't argue with the preacher."

"Shhh..." She put her finger on his lips and wouldn't have been surprised if lightning had shot through the ceiling and zapped her into a pile of ashes right there on pew three. No one with a boyfriend as special as Grady should be letting an old flame make her feel like that.

She would simply have to get over her silly infatuation.

When the services were over, folks gathered around Jesse to welcome him home with hugs and pats on the back. She and Grady headed for the door, shook the preacher's hand, and went straight to his car.

"I don't have time for Sunday dinner today," Grady said, "but I can take you home. Has the tension eased up between Mia and Jesse? It can't be easy on you for her to act like she is. I'd hate it if she treated me like she does Jesse."

"I believe she feels threatened so she's lashing out." Addy got into Grady's SUV and closed the door. "You don't pose a threat. You're just my good friend. Jesse is going to be her boss before long."

"It'll all work itself out, Amelia," he said as he got in behind the wheel. "Oh! I'm so sorry. I was thinking about her when the preacher talked about love. I didn't mean to call you by her name."

Addy patted him on the shoulder. "It's all right. She was a

big part of your life for a very long time. It's only natural that you'd think of her when the subject of love came up."

"Thanks for that. I don't know what I'd do without you to talk to."

"That's what friends are for." Addy wondered if she was always going to be *just a friend*. Not that she wanted more with Grady, but Jesse could be a very different matter.

"Yes, and I love having you for my best friend." He started the engine, backed out of the parking lot, and started driving toward the ranch. "You want me to talk to Mia? Maybe I could help her see that Jesse is a good person."

"Not right now," she said, "but I might take a rain check and ask for help if she doesn't straighten up."

"Just let me know," he said.

Addy's phone rang, and she fished it out of her purse. When she saw that it was Mia, she sighed.

"Mama, I won't be having Sunday dinner with the family. Ricky and I are going to Bonham to eat at that little café over there, the one that serves those wonderful chicken fried steaks. See you later. Don't wait up for me. I might be late coming home tonight."

"Whoa, girl! You've got evening feeding chores," Addy said.

"Tell Jesse to do them." Mia ended the call before Addy could say another word.

"Want to cash in that rain check now?"

"Not just yet, but there are times when I wish I could ground her like I did when she was in high school," Addy admitted.

"Amelia wanted to start a family when we first got married, but I wanted to wait until I was established. Look what it got me. You ever going to tell Mia who her father is?" Grady asked.

Addy shivered in spite of the heat. "Maybe someday, but not today. She's not in the right frame of mind to tell her anything. I can't understand how she turned into a person I hardly know."

"Jesse came home," Grady said as he drove toward the ranch.

"What's that supposed to mean?" Addy asked.

"He has always been the wonder boy, and she could live with that. But now that he's back, she feels like her place on the ranch is threatened, like you said before, and one other thing. Ricky is bad news, and he's probably encouraging her behavior," Grady answered.

"Jesse's not like that. He's doing his best to get along with her, but she just won't cut him any slack at all," Addy defended him.

"It wouldn't matter if he had wings and a halo. The point is that she has always had first place in your life, in Pearl and Sonny's and now she's having to take a step down to second place," Grady said. "I know how she feels."

"What are you talking about?" Addy shivered again.

"I had a crush on you for a while in high school," he admitted, "but the only boy you could see was Jesse Ryan, and he didn't ever even ask you out. I would have been so honored to take you to either of our high school proms. And there you were with Jesse in your eyes, and he didn't even ask you."

"Was it really that obvious?" Addy asked.

"Yep, it was, but then Amelia woke me up and made me feel like I was somebody even better than one of the almighty Ryan boys who were always best at everything. I knew I'd fallen in love with her the night we won the academic bowl. I wouldn't have even joined the team, but she talked me into believing that together we could beat the socks off Jesse Ryan's team, and we did." Grady's whole face lit up at the memory.

"I never knew that," Addy said.

"Doesn't matter now. We're all adults. I'm just trying to make you understand how Mia feels." He patted her on the shoulder.

"Jesse was always just my best friend, like you are now," she said. "We decided in junior high that we couldn't ever get involved because it would ruin what we had."

"Honey, everyone knew how you felt about him back then except you. I'm just glad that he's not Mia's father. I'd rather it was anyone but him. Was it a guy who worked on your grandmother's farm?" Grady asked.

"Her biological father isn't important. She belongs to me." Addy air-slapped him on the shoulder.

"You'll have to tell her someday. That could be part of her attitude right now. Everyone she knows has a dad, whether he's worthless or a wonderful person, and she's needing to know where she comes from." Grady parked in the front yard and said, "I'll see you at the end of the week. Call me if you need a listening ear."

Addy undid her seat belt with one hand and opened her door with the other. "Thanks for the ride and for the therapy session."

"Honey, you know you are welcome. God only knows how many times you've gotten me through the tough spots." He nodded.

Her high-heeled shoe got stuck between two boards on the top step and she stumbled, threw out her hands, and tried to grab something, but all she got was an armload of hot Texas air. Then Jesse's strong arms scooped her up like a bride. She wrapped her arms around his neck and took a deep breath.

"Where did you come from?" she asked.

"I heard a vehicle drive up and thought maybe Mama might need help with Dad," he said. "I slipped out the side door after church and came straight home. I don't remember you being clumsy," he chuckled as he carried her into the house and set her on firm ground. "But back then, you wore cowboy boots everywhere, even to church."

"Thanks for..." she huffed, "saving me from a fall."

"Anytime. I'm a knight in shining cowboy boots, just look-ing for fair damsels to rescue. I thought Grady was coming to Sunday dinner." Jesse sat down on a ladder-back chair in the foyer and pulled off his boots. "Been a while since I wore these except when me and the guys went out. I'll have to get used to them again."

Addy sat in the chair beside him. "Grady can't come after all, and Mia is off with who I assume is now her boyfriend." She kicked off her shoes and wiggled her toes. "Give me cowboy boots over these things any day of the week. I'm not so sure I like this boyfriend of hers. He's one of those wild, bad-boy types who would cause any mother to worry."

"She seems to have her head on straight, except when it comes to me. She does a pretty fine job out there of running a hay crew, so I reckon she can take care of herself," Jesse said.

"Grady says that she's jealous of you. Maybe we should have stayed here at Thanksgiving when you guys came home instead of going out to Granny's place, so she could have gotten to know you back when she was just a kid," she said.

"Don't know why she'd be jealous of an ugly old cowboy like me. She's the princess around here," Jesse laughed. "Why *did* you leave when we came home, Addy?"

"Seemed like the thing to do at the time. Y'all could help with the ranch work, and spend some time with Sonny and Pearl without us interfering. You were a medic and Cody is a doctor, so I wasn't needed. We had always gone to Granny's for Thanksgiving ever since I was a little girl, so she expected us to be there." She shrugged.

But the real reason was that I didn't want to... She couldn't even complete the thought.

"I figured that was it," he said.

Pearl came in the front door with Sonny right behind her.

"Y'all going to chew the fat all afternoon or wash up for dinner?"

"I'll do that soon as I get out of these Sunday clothes and into my overalls." Sonny headed down the hallway.

"I'd rather chew on some of those chicken and dumplings," Jesse said. "Do I have time to run out to the bunkhouse and get into some more comfortable clothes?"

"Of course." Pearl stopped long enough to kiss him on the cheek. "Just don't take too long. Where's Mia?"

"Off having dinner with her boyfriend." Addy stood and started down the hall toward her room.

Jesse was halfway to the kitchen when Sonny stopped for a moment and set his jaw. "I don't like that Ricky kid. He's been trouble since the day he was born. Why'd she have to go and take up with the likes of him anyway? If he hurts her, I'll—"

Pearl locked her arm through his and said, "Mia is smart and independent. We might have to haul him to the hospital if he does anything she doesn't like, but we don't have to worry about our girl. Now, go on and get changed while I finish getting the food ready, sweetheart."

"Yes, darlin'." Sonny leaned over just enough to give her a kiss. "Have I told you how much I love you today?"

"Three times, but I never get tired of hearing it," Pearl answered.

Addy was stripping out of her off-white sundress when she remembered what Mia had said about her finding a guy to make her happy. "I have to get beyond this"—she frowned—"blast from the past before I can give anyone my heart. That saying really dates me."

She pulled on a pair of faded jeans, a T-shirt with a horse-shoe on the front, and her comfortable boots. She gave the high heels that had caused her to fall a dirty look as she left the room. Mia was going to be so mad when she found out Pearl had made chicken and dumplings. That was her daughter's favorite Sunday dinner.

"Serves you right for being so bitchy the past couple of days," Addy said as she entered the kitchen.

"Who was bitchy?" Pearl looked up from the stove, where she was dropping bits of dough into a pot of boiling broth.

"My daughter," Addy answered. "She's been horrible. Didn't you see it?"

"Of course we did," Sonny chuckled. "But, honey, she doesn't do well with change. She'll be fine in a few days. I just wish she wasn't going out with that O'Malley boy."

"Hopefully, she'll get tired of him and show him the road real soon," Pearl said.

"Get rid of who and what road?" Jesse asked as he hung his hat on a nail in the utility room and came on into the kitchen.

"We were talking about Mia's boyfriend," Pearl answered.

Jesse leaned over and sniffed the steam coming off the pot of broth. "That smells so good. I bet if she brought him home to Sunday dinner, that would tame him right down."

"Well, now!" Sonny thumped the table with his fist. "That's a great idea. Next Sunday I'm going to invite him myself, and then after we eat, me and him are going out on the porch for a come-to-Jesus talk."

Addy had no doubt that one of those talks wouldn't do a bit of good. It might even push Mia farther away from the family and right into Ricky's arms. After seeing her sitting so close to him in church, and the way they were holding hands as they crossed the parking lot to his truck, Addy had no doubt that they were more than friends.

Chapter Seven

*J*esse would have waited another few days before coming home if he had realized that Monday was Honey Grove Family History Day. He wouldn't disappoint his mother for anything, but he sure didn't look forward to hitching a couple of borrowed mules to the old wagon and driving it into town.

Pearl Ryan's grandmother had been the president of the Town Planning Committee to celebrate the Family History Day, then Pearl's mother took over, and when she passed away, Pearl herself had held the position for the past thirty years. The celebration was always held on June fourteenth. It didn't matter what day of the week it fell on. If it happened to be on Wednesday or Sunday, then there were no church services that evening. Pearl declared that God understood the importance of family.

Everyone around the community gathered in town that day, most of the locals on horseback or in wagons to commemorate those days when Honey Grove was a booming town. In 1890, the town was a central hub for area farmers, who used the railroad to ship their products all over the South. Pictures of early days were displayed in each building, so folks got a sense of how things had been down through the ages, and guides expounded on some of the more historic places that still remained. Then there was the tour of homes since Honey Grove had the most historic old houses of any small town in Texas. Each tour ended at the oldest church in Honey Grove, where Pearl and the refreshment committee served cake, cookies, and punch.

Jesse felt like he'd been shot through a time machine when he drove the wagon around to the front yard that evening. His mother and Addy were dressed in vintage long dresses and bonnets and were putting cakes and cookies into the backseat of Sonny's pickup.

His father wore bibbed overalls and a straw hat and waited on the front porch swing. "Hey, son." Sonny waved. "I sure wish I could go with you, but Addy and your mother vetoed that. Last year, the horses got away from me and we had quite a ride into town. It would be tough on me to climb up in the wagon, so I'll just let you have that job."

"I'm in agreement with them," Jesse said. "Anyone going with me? Where's Mia?"

As if on cue, the girl stepped out onto the porch. She wore a pair of cut-off jean shorts, a halter top that showed half her back, and cowboy boots. "I'm right here, and the answer is no, I'm not going with you or anyone else. I've got better things to do," she said. "Ricky and I have plans."

"You be careful, darlin'," Sonny said. "That boy has been in a lot of trouble."

"Ricky and I don't have secrets, Poppa. I know everything about him, and people have spread rumors about him that simply are not true." She took time to kiss Sonny on the top of the head and then jogged out to her pickup truck.

"Don't stay out too late. You've got sheep shearing to do tomorrow morning," Addy yelled across the yard.

"I've decided to sell my sheep soon as they're sheared. I've already got a buyer who'll be picking them up tomorrow evening." Mia waved as she got into the vehicle and drove away.

"What brought all that on?" Sonny picked up his cane and got to his feet. "She's named each one of those sheep and sat up at night with them when they were lambing."

"I'm wondering if I'm the cause of all this," Jesse said from the wagon seat. "Y'all tell me that she was a sweetheart until this past weekend."

"She'd only been home from college three days when you arrived," Sonny said. "She hasn't been the same girl since she got here, but you're right, it did get worse after you got here. I'll have a talk with her tomorrow."

"I've tried," Addy said, "but she shuts me out."

Pearl stepped up on the porch to help Sonny out to the truck. "I imagine she and Ricky have been keeping company at college, and he's leading our girl astray. I'll see what I can do, too."

When Sonny was in the passenger seat, Pearl took a look at what all was in the backseat and said, "Looks like you're going to have to take your own car, Addy, or else ride with Jesse. We'll have plenty of room to bring you home."

"I'll just ride with Jesse," Addy said.

Jesse hopped down from the wagon and circled around the back side of it. "Let me help you," he said. His big hands circled Addy's small waist and lifted her up into the wagon. "There you go, Miss Hall. I'll try to keep from hitting too many potholes, but you might want to hang on to your bonnet."

Addy's clear laughter rang out across the yard. Jesse had missed hearing her laugh like that right along with their long

visits when he went to basic training. She had written to him
and sent cards while he was in basic training, but by the time he
got to his next phase of training, all communication from her
had stopped. In her last letter she had told him it would be best
if they just moved on and forgot about each other. He had to
follow his dreams, and she had her own life to think about.

"Don't blame yourself for Mia," Addy said.

"Can't help it." Jesse flicked the reins, and the mules started
a slow walk down the lane. "Maybe part of it is Ricky, but
me coming home was the straw that broke the camel's back.
I don't know what to do about it, but I plan to have a talk
with her, too. Adult to adult. She can vent and get it out of
her system."

"You are all welcome to give it a shot, but I don't think it
will do a bit of good," Addy said. "I'm in shock that she said
that about selling her sheep. She's worked so hard at building
up her flock, and she makes a lot of money selling show
animals to the local kids. She keeps her flock over on the part
that was my folks' place. When she's at school, Henry takes
care of them, but the shearing is always saved for when she's
home. It's a big job," Addy answered. "And she's always loved
to do that part. You should have been around when she got her
best ones ready to show at the county fair. She won the grand
champion trophy almost every year."

"Maybe she's just yanking your chain," Jesse said.

"She sounded pretty serious to me," Addy sighed.

"How many sheep are we talking about?" Jesse asked.

"Thirty ewes, a ram, and maybe twenty lambs. I can't
believe she's even thinking about selling. She's been working
on that project for five years," Addy sighed.

"Why would she do that without talking to you or to Dad
about it?" Jesse asked.

"I can't even begin to understand why or what she's

thinking these days." Addy put her head in her hands. "It's got me totally baffled, but like you said, maybe she's just messing with me."

"Remember when we were that age?" he asked.

"Oh, yeah." Addy removed her hands and held them in her lap. "We were ready to set the world on fire with our dreams."

"I was going to save veterans in the war zones, and you were going to be a nurse. Maybe Mia is having trouble deciding where her place is in this world."

"What happened to those two kids?" she whispered.

"You tell me," Jesse answered. "I missed you so bad. I felt like I'd gotten a Dear John letter when you told me we shouldn't even call or write anymore."

"Why didn't you try to change my mind?" she asked. "Like I told you in my last letter, you were off chasing your dream, and I…"

"You had a baby," Jesse finished her sentence, "and didn't even tell me. I was your best friend, and thought we were a little more than that after that last night. I didn't even know about Mia until I came home after the second phase of my training. I figured you'd found someone else and didn't want me in your life." He still remembered feeling like he'd been gut-punched when he'd gotten the news.

"Mia was born on the last day of February. I was pretty busy with a newborn and trying to finish up my second semester of nurses' training by the time you got done with your training," she whispered.

Jesse nodded and kept driving, and then it hit him right between the eyes. His mouth went dry, and his hands trembled so badly that he had to focus on keeping the reins tight. His heart missed a beat, and his chest tightened. "Mia is my daughter, isn't she? Why didn't you tell me?" He couldn't believe that it had taken him so damn long to figure it out.

Addy shrugged. "You never talked about anything but joining the Air Force and getting away from the ranch. I loved
you too much to ruin that dream for you. If you had known
I was pregnant, you would have done something stupid, like
gone AWOL, and insisted on marrying me. I didn't want to be
married at eighteen, so I refused to tell anyone about you."

"Is that why Mia's been so hateful. Does she know?"
Jesse asked.

"No, and I don't want her to know until she gets through
this rebellion." Addy turned to look at him. "Promise me you
won't say a word. I'll tell her when the time is right."

"Does Grady know?" Jesse felt like he'd been kicked in the
gut by a two-ton bull. He felt panicked—coming home to an
ailing father, and now finding out he had a nineteen-year-old
daughter who hated him. It was too much to take in. He slipped
over into that fight-or-flight mode, with lots of emphasis on
the flight right then.

Addy shook her head. "Promise me, please, that you won't
say or do anything to make her suspect. I have to be the one to
tell her, and the time has to be right."

"I promise, but Addy, I'm a father"—he winced at the
word—"of a young woman I've never supported or acknowl-
edged. How do I ever make that up to her or to you?"

Addy laid a hand on his knee. "Not one bit of this is your
fault. I made the decision not to tell you or anyone else, so I'll
take the responsibility."

"How did you..." he stammered, "hide it from..." He
cleared his throat and tried to think, but everything was a blur.

"When I found out I was pregnant, I called Granny. She
said she needed me to help her on her ranch and offered to
pay for my college in exchange for some help. I simply moved
from here to Cactus. My folks didn't even know until they
came home for Thanksgiving, and we let them think the baby

belonged to one of the summer hired hands. It wasn't all that difficult," Addy answered.

"I wish you would have told me." The first burst of anger replaced the shock, and he slapped the edge of the buckboard. "Even if we didn't get married, I would have done right by her."

"Water under the bridge," she said. "We've both moved on."

Jesse was glad that they were nearing the church, and that Addy had business to attend to there. He needed time to think, to get everything in perspective. God Almighty! He had a daughter who hated him and was dating a boy that Sonny said was worthless. A father would take care of that, but under the circumstances, he had no right to say a word.

He brought the wagon to a halt in front of the church, and like a gentleman, he hopped off the wagon and helped Addy down. When her feet were on the ground, their eyes met and locked for a moment. He knew her well enough to realize that she was begging him to keep quiet about things.

"Please," she whispered.

"I promise," he said.

"Hey, mister!" a little dark-haired boy yelled from across the parking lot, and the moment was gone.

A dozen kids came running up right behind him, all talking at once.

"Can we ride down to the square in the back of your wagon?" the first kid yelled above all the rest.

"Miz Pearl told our mamas that it would be all right," a blond-haired girl about ten years old said. "My name is Kelsey. Can I ride on the seat with you?"

"Why should you get to ride up there?" the dark-haired boy asked.

"Because I'm the only girl, and because I'm the one who asked Miz Pearl if we could ride in the wagon, and because

I'm the one who heard her talking to Miz Joyce about the wagon, and because I asked first," Kelsey blurted out before stopping for a breath.

"I guess that's reasons enough." Jesse started to lift her up into the seat, but before he could turn around, she had scaled the side of the wagon like a monkey and plopped down.

"Who is going to take care of you once we get to the square?" Jesse asked.

"Our mamas done already called our daddies and they're meeting us at the store with the white elephant on top," Kelsey said.

With very little difficulty, Jesse could see Mia acting just like Kelsey at that age. She would have had dark hair and green eyes like Kelsey and been just as sassy.

"You are Miz Pearl's son?" Kelsey asked.

"Yes, ma'am, I am," he said.

She cocked her head to one side. "Where's your kids? Why ain't they ridin' with you?"

"Well, I've got a wagon load and there wouldn't be any room for more," he answered without telling the big secret.

"Bet they're too old to ride in a wagon," she said.

"Little bit." He nodded.

Kelsey folded her arms over her chest and sighed. "They're missin' a lot of fun. Do you think I could ride on one of them mules the rest of the way?"

"I don't reckon we'd better chance that." Jesse managed a smile. "The boys would be jealous."

"Yep, they would." Kelsey grinned.

Several grown men, some Jesse had even gone to school with, waited in the middle of the crowded town square for their kids. He had shaken hands with them and gotten several pats on the back and lots of welcomes back to Honey Grove before an elderly lady grabbed him by the arm.

"You are right on time. Pearl said you would be leading the first group of folks on the tour," Darla Jo Whitney said. "I'll be sending out ten at a time every fifteen minutes. I know it's been a while since you've done this, so here's your paper with the pointers. Make it interesting. They're paying five bucks a person, and the money goes to the Town Planning Committee for scholarships."

Jesse took the paper from her and nodded. "Yes, ma'am. How many tours am I responsible for tonight?"

"Just the one," Darla Jo answered. "You'll end up at the church with your group. Follow me, and I'll get this kicked off."

Of all things, one of the ladies in his group had a baby strapped to her front in one of those carrier things. A little dark-haired girl that gave him a big toothless smile when he stooped to have a look at her. His chest got that tight feeling again. So much had happened during the last twenty years, and he had missed every bit of it, from Mia's birth to her first smile, her first steps, all the way up to now with her first rotten boyfriend.

He had to compartmentalize everything if he was going to make it through the evening, so he put the shocking news in a box and closed the lid. Then he smiled at his group and said, "David Crockett discovered the area of Honey Grove when he camped there on his way to join the Texas Army at San Antonio in 1836." The history of the area came back to him as he slowly led the group around the square, but then, he had done this tour from the time he was fourteen until he left home. "Davy sent letters back home to Tennessee telling about this area and its abundance of honey-filled trees. That's where the town got its name. In 1873, Honey Grove was officially established. If you will turn to page three of your booklet, you'll see pictures of the town square as it looked back in the early days when cotton became king in this area and farmers got rich, back when businesses on this very square prospered. In 1888, Honey Grove had seventy-two houses, twelve dry goods establishments, two banks, seven churches, four huge hotels, two lumber yards, many restaurants, and several boardinghouses. The railroad business was booming, taking the farmers' goods all over the place."

Family History Day, he thought as the folks found the right page and talked about the pictures. *Seems fitting that, today of all days, I'd find out that I have a daughter.*

Chapter Eight

Jesse awoke the next morning with a sense of dread. How could he shear sheep with Mia, knowing that she was his own blood kin daughter? He dressed in faded jeans and one of his dark blue Air Force T-shirts and headed up to the house without a single answer to his question.

"Good mornin'." He tried to be cheerful when he entered the house, but it came out more than a little flat.

"It's a wonderful morning," Mia said. "We're shearing the sheep today. My buyer will be here at noon, and if he likes what he sees, he'll write me a check and take them all away."

"I bought the alpacas, and they aren't up for sale," Sonny said. "And why have you got this bug in your britches to sell your prize stock anyway?"

"I want the money, and I don't want to worry with them anymore. Plus, Henry will be retiring, and who will take care of them when I go back to school? It's a smart move, and the timing is right. The buyer wants them all and the alpacas, too," Mia answered.

"I believe you've got something else in mind that you're not telling me," Sonny said. "Has this got something to do with that O'Malley boy?"

"I make my own decisions. Ricky doesn't tell me what to do," Mia protested, "and Poppa, my buyer really wants the alpacas. They'll bring a good price, and you won't have to take care of them," Mia argued. "What are you going to do with alpacas and no sheep for them to guard?"

"I'm just going to bring them up close to the barn and look at them. I like the babies," Sonny answered.

"That's not good business sense. On a ranch, everything has a reason to be here. Even Tex is a working dog." Mia wrapped a pancake around a piece of sausage. "At least talk to my buyer."

"My alpacas are not for sale," Sonny said. "I got to say that I'm disappointed that you're selling the sheep, but they're yours. Just remember, every decision has consequences. If you sell out and spend the money, it will take years to build up a flock as good as this again," Sonny said. "You've got good stock, and the kids around here appreciate buying a lamb from you for show for their FFA and 4H projects. We made enough money the last two years to feed the whole flock for the winter and still have a profit."

"*My* sheep," Mia reminded him with an edge to her voice. "I don't have time to take care of them anymore, and I need the money."

"For what?" Jesse sat down and forked a stack of pancakes over onto his plate.

"That would be none of your business," Mia answered. "You any good with clippers?"

"I can manage," he said.

"Well, then you can meet me at the shearing barn over on my grandparents' old place in thirty minutes. I'll get the flock mustered up and ready," Mia said.

Addy yawned as she came through the door. "What's going on?"

"I'm going to muster up my sheep. The buyer will be here pretty soon." Mia crammed a hat down on her head.

"Mia Pearl!" Addy propped both hands on her hips. "This has gone on long enough. What's gotten into you?"

"I've made my decision, and no one, not even you, can talk me out if it," she said.

"Why? Just tell me why?" Addy was almost in tears. "Mia, you've never lied to me, so tell me the truth. At Christmas you went out to see the sheep in pouring-down rain just minutes after you got home. How can you sell them when they've meant so much to you?"

"I'm not having this conversation with you, Mama. My mind is made up, and no one influenced me," Mia declared.

"And you are lying to me because you won't look me in the eye," Addy said.

Mia just shrugged and slammed the back door.

"Good Lord!" Addy sat down and put her head in her hands. "Did you talk to her, Sonny?"

"Tried to," he said. "It was like pouring water on a duck's back," he sighed.

"I got the same response," Pearl said. "She says she wants the money. I sure don't understand why she needs money. She's got a pretty good savings account from her years of working here, and she's always got a nice-sized checking account. She doesn't have a vehicle payment or any bills."

"Then what does she need the money for? Those sheep will bring in thousands from the right buyer. They're prime stock," Addy said.

"Told me it wasn't any of my business," Jesse answered.

She was right, he thought. He hadn't been there for her all these years, so it wasn't a bit of his business what she did with her sheep or her money. That didn't keep her attitude toward him from stinging. He had no right to say anything to her when she got short with Sonny, but he intended to bring it up when they were shearing sheep. As good as his folks had been to her, she should show them some respect.

"How many sets of shears do you have?" he asked.

"Three," Addy said. "I learned to shear sheep when we still lived out near Cactus. Mia is good at it, and Henry usually helps."

"I can take Henry's place," he offered.

"You ever done that kind of work?" Pearl asked.

"Few times," Jesse answered. "My team got..." Most of what he was about to say was classified so he tiptoed around the story. "...tied up in the middle of Afghanistan for a couple of days. We were staying with an old shepherd who needed help with shearing, so we learned the art. I may not be fast, but I can get the job done."

He couldn't tell them that the helicopter that was coming to rescue them and the pilot of a plane that had crashed had gotten shot down. Or that the old shepherd was really an undercover agent, working behind the scenes.

"Then you're elected," Addy said. "Give me time to get some coffee and a pancake in me, and I'll go with you over to the shed."

He and Addy should be dealing with Mia together, like parents, but that would probably never happen, and even if they could work things out, Mia would never accept him—not with the attitude she had. Like Addy had said, they had moved on. Jesse needed to get comfortable in the backseat, or the bunkhouse as was the case.

* * *

Addy had expected things to be totally awkward between her and Jesse that morning when she got into the truck with him, but they weren't at all. He had every right to scream at her or give her the old silent treatment, but he drove down the lane, took a left-hand turn, drove a mile, and made another left onto the property where she had grown up.

"I wish I had done things different," she admitted. "I thought I was doing the right thing, but now I need help in the worst kind of way, and she doesn't even know you are her father."

"Want to tell her this morning?" he asked.

Addy shook her head. "No. Not until she gets over this phase. She's always been such a good girl. So grounded and stable that I've patted myself on the back for raising her without a man in the picture. Guess I let my ego build up too soon."

"I imagine you did a fine job. Some kids just have to go through that painful rebellious age and hit bottom before they realize what they've always had right in front of them. But Addy, I'd like to be there when you tell her," Jesse said.

"Sure," Addy said. "Looks like she and Tex have them herded up. That's the last one going into the shed."

Addy still had high hopes that she could talk Mia out of selling off the flock, right up until they got the first three animals out of the shed and into the shearing area. "What kind of price are you getting for Nellie?" she asked.

"That would be my business," Mia said as she switched on the first set of shears and started to work.

"How about Buster Boy, here?" Addy began the job on the prize ram that had cost Mia all her wages one summer.

Mia gave her a drop-dead look and kept working. "You can't guilt me into keeping them by reminding me that I named them. And for your information, Mama, Ricky and I are leaving this afternoon for a little vacation."

"You can't leave today. Father's Day is Sunday," Addy said.

Mia cut her eyes around at her mother. "I don't have a father, remember?"

"You have a poppa, who has given you a lot of leeway on his ranch and has paid for your college. You know how much Father's Day means to him. Give this idea of a vacation a week at least. Stay until after Sunday," Addy begged, hoping to have time to talk her out of leaving with the local bad boy.

"I have some questions." Jesse started on a second ewe. "Is Ricky selling off something of his to help pay for this trip, too? Where are y'all going, so we'll kind of know where you are in case you need help? Are you taking your vehicle or his?" Jesse started on a second ewe.

"We're going on a road trip and we're taking my truck, because it's in better shape than his, and the rest is none of your business. I keep telling both of you that I'm an adult and that Ricky and I can make our own decisions," she answered. "We've been dating for months."

Addy's world was falling apart at the seams. Mia had always talked to her about everything. Why had she kept this a secret? The sudden changes in Mia made sense now.

"Are you eloping?" Addy whispered the question and held her breath, hoping that Mia would talk to her.

"Hell, no!" Mia shouted over the top of the noise of the shears. "We don't need a piece of paper or a fancy ceremony to know that we're in love. We're just going on a trip to find a place where we would like to settle down and live together. I want to see more of the world than Texas. I deserve to do what I want. I've worked hard here."

"What do you intend to do when you run out of money?" Jesse asked.

"We'll both get jobs on a ranch," she answered. "We've worked on them our whole life, and it shouldn't be hard to find work. There are ranches everywhere."

Addy finished shearing Buster Boy and turned him out into the corral. She gathered up the wool and put it into the packer at the end of the room, wiped the tears from her eyes, and tried to flush the anger from her heart. Addy couldn't bear seeing her daughter leave town with that boy; hence the tears. But the anger came from her sensible daughter not being able to see that she was giving up her own dreams for a guy who would break her heart.

"Aren't you going to help us finish the shearing?" Mia yelled.

"No, I am not," Addy said. "I will put the wool in the packer and sweep, but that's as much as I'm doing to help with this foolhardy idea of yours. If you're going to be an adult and take your life and money into your own hands, then have the guts to go tell Sonny you won't be here for Father's Day."

"I'll tell them when I go back to the house to get my things. I'm not talking about this anymore. My mind is made up." Mia stomped her foot on the wooden floor for emphasis.

Addy hoped that when Mia saw the effect her leaving had on Pearl and Sonny, she would take a step back and think about things. Her sheep would be gone, but she could use the money to build another flock, or maybe even invest it in cattle. Addy's thoughts chased around in her head so fast that she was a little dizzy when the shearing was finished. She gathered up the last of the wool from the floor and put it in the packer.

"What do you want to do with this bundle of wool?" Addy asked.

"Sell it and put the money in my checking account." Mia brought out three bottles of cold water and tossed one each to Addy and Jesse. She twisted the top off hers, took a long drink, and then wiped the sweat from her face with the tail of her tank top, showing off a belly ring that Addy had no idea her daughter had gotten. When Mia sat down on the floor across the room from her mother, her shirt rolled up in the back and there was a tattoo of a rose across the small of her back.

"When did you get a tat?" Addy whispered.

"Ricky gave me this one for my birthday." She shrugged. "I've been thinking about getting another one, maybe two hearts entwined with mine and his initials in them, right here." She pulled down the neck of her shirt and pointed to her chest.

Addy downed half the bottle of water to keep from saying anything.

"Did you want a tat?" Jesse asked.

Mia jacked up her chin in defiance. "Ricky wanted me to have one, and I thought it was sweet of him to pick out a rose. He says I'm his beautiful red rose, and this will always remind me of how much he loves me. If I get another one, it will show him that I will love him forever."

"So you've been dating him since February?" Jesse asked.

Mia shook her head. "We've been seeing each other since right after Thanksgiving last year."

"Why didn't you tell me?" Addy asked.

"I knew how you would react," Mia told her.

Jesse's body glistened with sweat and his hair was soaked when he sat down on the floor of the shed not far from Addy. Just having him close gave her strength, but she still thought maybe this thing with Mia was just a dream—no, not a dream, a full-fledged nightmare.

Jesse turned up his bottle, took a long drink, and said, "That's pretty amazing shearing for a nineteen-year-old girl."

"Are you one of those men who think women can't do something good?" Mia's tone was cold enough to scare away the sweltering heat.

"Not at all. I served with women, even knew a couple of snipers who were female," he said. "If that's all you got out of my statement, then you missed the point altogether."

Addy tried a different approach. "I can't stop you from

going, but I can freeze your bank accounts since I'm the primary on both of them."

"I don't need any of that money. I'll just cash the check I'm getting today. That should be enough to keep us in hotels and food until we find where we want to live. Ricky thinks we'll start driving toward California and maybe find a place in Nevada. I want to check out the mountains in Colorado or maybe Wyoming before we make a decision," Mia said.

"Will you call your mother every day?" Jesse asked. "She'll worry about you."

"Nope, but I will call her once a week on Sunday afternoon if we aren't somewhere that has no service." Mia pointed at him. "But this isn't any of your concern. It's between family, not outsiders." She turned back to focus on her mother. "Ricky and I've been living together this last semester of school. He got kicked out of the dorm for smoking pot, but it was his roommate who had the stuff, not Ricky. We rented an apartment together. We passed most of our classes, so we have a full year of business courses under our belts, and I have ranching experience so finding jobs won't be a problem."

"Sweet Jesus!" Addy muttered. "What do you mean, most of your classes? Last semester you had all A's."

"Well, this semester I failed three classes." Mia shrugged. "I'll retake them later if I go back. Ricky and I haven't decided what we're going to do at the end of summer. If we don't want to work on ranches, we may both join the Army, if they'll promise to station us at the same places. I hear the truck coming to get the sheep. I can get them herded in without y'all's help. I just have to go by the house and get my stuff, then pick up Ricky . . ." She smiled at her mother. "I'll call you on Sunday." She dashed out the back door without so much as giving Addy a hug.

Jesse moved over to sit closer to Addy. "Are you going to survive all this?"

Addy pulled her knees up, propped her elbows on them, and buried her face in her hands. "Wake me up, Jesse, and tell me this was all a nightmare. What did I do wrong? How could I have been so blind as to not know she had moved out of the dorm. Pearl and Sonny paid so much for her to live there."

He slung an arm around her shoulder. "I'm so sorry, but today is very real. Want me to call Grady? Does he know that I'm Mia's father?"

"Hell, no!" Tears flowed down her cheeks. "He wouldn't understand any of this, and he'd have a million questions about why I didn't see it happening. I failed by not giving her a father figure...and now she's about to ruin her life. I can't even imagine her...in the Army," Addy said between sobs.

"Right now, that might be the best place for her and Ricky both." Jesse pulled her closer to his side. "There's no way they'll promise them the same duty stations, so she'd be separated from him and have some time to think for herself without him telling her what to do. From what y'all have told me about him, he probably wouldn't last past basic training. But before that happens, it's a sure shot that he's about to spend every bit of that money she's getting today. You would be wise to freeze her accounts, or he'll use that up, too."

"I hate to do that." Addy laid her head over on his shoulder. "What if she gets off somewhere and needs the money to get home?"

"I have no rights here, but you would be protecting her interest. She knows that you love her and that she can call you," Jesse answered.

Mia blasted through the door like a whirlwind. "I forgot—" She stopped dead in her tracks. "So I was right. You have been flirting with Jesse, haven't you?"

"Jesse has always been my good friend," Addy said. "You just broke my heart, and he's here for me."

"Grady would be here for you if you'd call him, and he's supposed to be your best friend," Mia huffed, "but if you want to sleep around and get pregnant again in your old age, that's your business. I forgot the papers that show what good stock my buyer is getting. See you later, Mama, but be careful about sleeping with dogs. You might get up with fleas."

Addy was a blur as she got on her feet and took several steps toward Mia. "You are certainly one to talk about sleeping with dogs. Go on and have your fun, and when the money is gone, call me. I'm your mother, and I'll always be here for you, but don't you dare ever talk to me like that again. I raised you better than that."

Mia glared at Addy. "Ricky loves me. You're all wrong about him, and I'll prove it."

"I hope you do." Addy wiped tears from her wet cheeks. "But right now, all I see is a girl who is about to get her heart broken. And, honey, for your information, I was not sleeping around. Someday when you grow up a little, I'll tell you all about your father."

"I'm not sure I even want to know." Mia picked up her envelope of pedigree papers and left.

Jesse stood and wrapped Addy in his arms. "Evidently, she has to learn the hard way, but I'm here for you anytime and anyplace. We can get through this together."

"Helluva homecoming for you, isn't it?" she said as she laid her head on his chest and listened to his heartbeat. If only she could go back and get a do-over, Mia would be facing both her parents that day, and Jesse would be having one of those come-to-Jesus talks with Ricky.

"The night is always the darkest just before the sun comes up" Jesse whispered.

Chapter Nine

The afternoon heat beat down relentlessly on Addy as she jogged from the truck to the house. She was glad Sonny was in the office and Pearl was in the kitchen. She couldn't face either of them right then. She went straight for the bathroom, adjusted the water in the shower, and stripped out of her dirty, sweaty clothing. She pulled the shower curtain back and stepped over the side of the tub. Tears and water mingled together as she sat down on the far end of the tub and sobbed until her sides ached.

How could she love her daughter so much and yet be so angry with her at the same time? Had her mother cried like this when she realized that Addy was six months pregnant and wouldn't even tell them who the baby's father was? Was this her payback for the choices she'd made?

She had no answers, only a heavy feeling in her chest that nothing would ever be right again between her and her daughter. It took all her strength to stand up and finish her shower, and yet, she still had to face Pearl and Sonny. She turned the water off, wrapped a towel around her body, and padded barefoot to her bedroom. Dressed in underwear, a T-shirt, and a pair of denim shorts, she finally looked at herself in the full-length mirror.

"I am strong," she told the woman looking back at her, a woman who seemed to have aged twenty years in the past few hours. "Mia will get over this boy and come home, and things will be normal."

She had to believe that, or she couldn't go out there and face the family. She rounded the corner of the hallway and ran smack into Jesse. He wrapped her up in his arms for the second time that day to keep her from knocking them both on the floor, and he held her there for several seconds. Water droplets from his quick shower still hung on his dark hair, and he had changed from his dirty shirt and jeans into clean ones.

"Have you talked to them?" he whispered.

She took a step back and shook her head. "No. I needed to get myself together first."

"Then we'll do it together." Jesse laid a hand on her shoulder. "I'm here to support you, Addy, like I should have been all these years."

"Thank you. I guess we might as well get it over with." She took a deep breath and started for the office.

Sonny looked up from the desk. "Looks like you two got cleaned up after that job. Did she really sell the sheep, or was she just testing you?"

"She really sold them. Did she come by here and talk to you?" Addy answered.

"Nope. I heard someone come in the house and leave again, but she didn't say a word to me and Pearl. What's going on?"

"Reckon you and Mom could come into the kitchen or the living room? We need to talk," Jesse said.

"Sure thing, and here's something for you." Sonny handed her an envelope. "Henry had to go into town for more barbed wire, so he brought us the mail on his way back down the lane. I reckon that's Mia's grades. I'm sure she's got a solid four point, just like last semester." He picked up his cane and started for the kitchen.

Pearl finished sliding a cake into the oven as they trooped in together. "Y'all must be starving. I went ahead and made sandwiches." She brought a plate out of the refrigerator and motioned for them to sit down at the table. "Mia didn't really sell the sheep, did she? She's just having growing pains this summer and spreading her wings."

Chips and pickles were already on the table when Pearl set the plate of sandwiches down. She poured four glasses of sweet tea, and Addy helped her carry them to the table.

"We said grace at noon, so you just go ahead and dig in." Pearl pulled out a chair and sank down into it. "So, about the sheep?"

"She sold them," Jesse said. "I'll let Addy tell you the rest."

Addy opened the envelope, which was addressed to Addison Hall, and took out the single sheet of paper. She gasped when she looked at it, and three sets of eyes stared at her.

"Are you all right?" Pearl asked.

Addy's hands shook so badly that the paper slipped right out of her hands and fluttered to the floor. Jesse reached down, picked it up, and handed it back to her.

"I've had my head stuck in the sand for six months." Addy's voice quivered.

Jesse draped his arm over the back of her chair. "This is not your fault."

"I should have seen the signs. When she called home, she only talked a few minutes. When I talked about coming to see her for a girls' shopping day, she put me off." She took a deep breath and tried to hold back tears. "Look at this, Jesse. She has failed every single class, not just half of them. They're putting her on probation next semester." As mad as she was, Addy couldn't sit still. She pushed back her chair and paced around the table. "I'm so sorry, Sonny. I can't begin to apologize for her wasting your money like this."

"There's a mistake," Sonny declared. "I'll call the school and get this straightened out. A kid doesn't go from perfect grades one semester to failing the next."

"She's let Ricky control her life the past six months," Jesse said. He took Addy's hand in his when she passed by his chair. "She's said some pretty hateful things to her mother about—"

"Jesse is Mia's father," Addy blurted out. "But she doesn't know that. She caught him with his arm around me and accused me of fooling around and getting pregnant again." She slumped down in her chair.

Pearl shot a knowing look at Sonny and then reached across the table to pat Addy's hand. "We figured that out years ago, and we know that you and Jesse have always had a special connection."

Addy was shocked speechless. How did they know when her own parents had never figured it out?

Jesse blinked several times and then said, "Why didn't you tell me if you knew all this time?"

"That was Addy's place, not ours, and we figured it would all come out when the time was right." Sonny nodded. "That's part of the reason we wanted you and Mia to move in here with us. We wanted to be a part of our granddaughter's life."

"But how?" Addy whispered.

"The timing for one thing. She was born nine months after that last night before Jesse went to the Air Force. She's got his eyes, and she's tall like Jesse, and if you look at his baby picture and hers, you can't tell them apart," Pearl answered.

"Does anyone else know?" Addy asked.

"Not even Lylah O'Malley, who as you know, is the biggest gossip in Honey Grove," Sonny chuckled. "She spread the rumor that you got pregnant by one of your married professors."

"Good Lord!" Jesse threw both palms up. "Is that Ricky's mother?"

Pearl nodded. "That's exactly who it is. She's about your age, Jesse. And for the record, we never believed a word of what she said about you, and when the next bit of gossip reached her, you were old news."

Sonny picked up the platter of sandwiches and passed them over to Addy. "This will be a hard lesson for her, but we hope it will make her stronger."

"I couldn't swallow anything right now." Addy set the plate down between her and Jesse. "Thank God, Jesse was there to support me. Bless his heart, he didn't even know that he was her father until today, and..." The next words stuck in Addy's throat.

"I would have done things different if I'd known," Jesse said. "Why didn't you tell me, Mama?"

"We figured Addy would tell us all when she was ready," Sonny answered. "This is all that bad boy's doing, and we just need to keep Mia in our prayers and hope that when he's done spending all her money, she will call us instead of letting him talk her into something horrible."

Addy pulled her phone from her hip pocket. "Speaking of money, I need to take care of that right now."

"Fannin Bank," a lady answered. "This is Betsy. What can I help you with today?"

"This is Addy Hall. I'd like to check the balance in both the checking and savings accounts I hold jointly with Mia and maybe move the money over into another account," she said. "How are Justine and the new baby?"

"The baby's doing great. Justine is doing better with him than I thought she would be. She's turning out to be a good mother, even if the father is a bastard. You should come by some evening, have a glass of tea with us and see the baby. She's named him Levi Matthew, after her father and grandfather. We've nicknamed him Matty," Betsy said. "I've got those accounts pulled up. The savings has fifty dollars in it, and the checking is down to ten dollars."

"Last January, we had five thousand dollars in savings and a thousand in checking," Addy said. "Are you sure you've got the right numbers?"

"Looks like Mia has been pulling out money right along. Still want to transfer what's left and maybe close out these accounts?" Betsy asked.

"No, leave them alone," Addy said.

"Call me when you have time to come visit. I heard that Ricky and Mia are off on a vacation together. I didn't even know they were dating," Betsy said. "But then teenagers don't tell mothers much, do they? I hope he's nicer to her than he was to Justine. You do know that he's the father of Justine's baby, don't you?"

Addy shivered. The situation with Ricky was even worse than she thought possible, and now Mia was all enamored with him. "I didn't know, but I'm so, so sorry to hear that."

"Guess we all have to pay for our decisions in some way," Betsy said. "I should've paid more attention to the signs."

"Amen to that." Addy almost groaned, and wished she'd known about Ricky and Mia before things had gone this far.

"Here I am a grandmother at forty, so what can I say? At first Justine wouldn't put Ricky's name on the birth certificate, but one of our friends who is a lawyer told her to do so, so that she could sue him for child support. Justine said that she hoped that she never saw that boy again, and wishes she'd never let him talk her into that rose tattoo on her back. Oh, and one more thing before you hang up. I know you and Grady are good friends. Have you met his new girlfriend? She's a ringer for Amelia."

"Nope, but he keeps saying he'll bring her around sometime," Addy said. "Bye, now." Addy ended the call and turned back to the Ryans, a dreadful knot in the pit of her stomach. "Mia has used all the money she had saved, and her checking account is almost dry. Between the two accounts, she's got about sixty dollars, and Ricky O'Malley is the father of Justine's new baby. Can it get any worse?"

"Whew, that's a lot to take in," Pearl said.

* * *

"Hey, anybody home?" Grady yelled from the front door.

"We're back here!" Sonny hollered. "Come on in and have a glass of tea and some pie."

Grady took a chair at the head of the table so that Addy was on his left. "That sounds good. I thought I'd stop and get copies of Sonny's medical charts today since I can't come by tonight. Got a long, boring meeting at the hospital, starting right after rounds."

Addy got to her feet and poured Grady a glass of tea. Since the pie was already on the table, she took a dessert plate down from the cabinet and grabbed a fork from the cutlery drawer. "Will we see you before Sunday morning?"

"Doesn't look like it." He cut himself a large piece of pie. "The whole week is swamped down with meetings. That's what I get for being head of the ER, but it's also what I've worked for, so I can't complain. How have things been here?"

"Same old, same old," Sonny said. "But got to say, these new pills are keeping my problems at bay."

"That's great," Grady said.

Couldn't the man see that Addy was upset? Her eyes were swollen and red from crying, and every vibe coming off her spelled sadness in big bold letters. Jesse didn't feel like he was in a position to say a word. If Addy wanted Grady to know what had happened that morning, she could tell him. But Jesse didn't have to sit there and stew in his jealous juices.

He pushed his chair back. "I'm going to take my sandwich to go and help Henry mend fences. See y'all at supper."

Grady didn't even look up from his pie, but just waved.

Addy caught Jesse's eye and mouthed, *Thank you.*

Sonny grabbed his cane and said, "I think I'll go with you, son. I can't help, but if you'll park up under a shade tree, I'd sure enjoy watching."

"Don't forget your hat," Pearl said. "And Jesse, pick up his lawn chair. It's that long, red tube thing settin' beside the washing machine. If he gets too hot, call me, and I'll drive out and rescue him."

"Will do." Jesse waited for his father to head out the back door and then followed him.

"What was that all about? You jealous of Grady?" Sonny asked when they were in the truck. "He and Addy are just good friends. You ain't got nothing to worry about with him."

Jesse started the engine and drove around to the back of the house, then went through the procedure of opening and closing the gate. That gave him time to think about what his dad had asked before he answered.

"I guess I am jealous," he admitted, "but as a friend. She deserves someone who can see she's upset and has a lot on her mind. All Grady seems to be interested in today is Mama's pecan pie. A real friend would invite her out to the porch and let her vent. I couldn't sit there another second and watch her want him to ask about *her* day."

Sonny nodded in agreement. "Ever think that maybe she's not ready to tell him that you're Mia's father? That she just wants him to eat his pie and go so she can have some time to process all this? And speaking of Mia, how are you holding up after finding out you had a daughter all these years? I figured you'd be stomping holes in the porch floor or rippin' and snortin' around on that old dirt bike to get past the anger that Addy kept such a big secret for so long."

"I'm still in shock," Jesse answered. "If I would have asked when Mia's birthday was, I could have figured it out on my own. I just figured that Addy had met someone at college or out in the Panhandle, and that's why she stopped writing and calling me. I should have known we were better friends than that."

"Should have, could have, would have," Sonny said. "Those are all in the past. What are you going to do about the future?"

"I feel like I'm navigating uncharted waters at the dark of midnight in a horrible storm," Jesse said. "I hope that someday Mia and I can have some kind of relationship, and that Addy and I can at least be friends like we used to be."

"We didn't even know you kids were dating," Sonny said. "It wasn't until she moved in with us and Pearl saw a picture of Mia when she was a little baby that we began to put things together. Those two pictures are identical. Then we did the math, and your mama remembered that Addy didn't even come tell you goodbye on the morning we took you to the recruiter's place. We figured y'all had had a falling-out, and that's why she didn't want anyone to know that you were the father."

Jesse pulled the truck up under a shade tree, not far from where Henry and the boys were working. "We only had one night together, Dad. That last night before I left, and we both cried and swore we wouldn't let that night ruin our friendship.

She slipped out before daylight without even telling me goodbye."

"Guess God had other plans," Sonny said. "I just wish we would have known before Mia was fourteen. We could have done more to help them. And I damn sure wish I could get a hold of that kid she's run off with. I would kick his ass all the way to the Gulf and then kick him off in the water."

Jesse chuckled. "I'm sorry for all this mess, Dad. You sure don't need all this stress when you are trying to keep this disease from getting worse."

"Family don't always mean there's smooth sailin', son. Sometimes the waters get rocky, but we've always got each other to lean on," Sonny told him.

"Amen." Jesse got out of the car and propped Sonny's chair up against the tree. He set a bottle of water in the holder on the arm. "Thanks for coming along and supporting me today."

"Anytime, son, anytime." Sonny slid out of the truck and made his way to the chair.

Chapter Ten

Addy could not sleep at all that night. She tossed and turned, beat her pillow into submission, threw the covers off, then pulled them back up over her body, and finally gave up even trying. She padded down the dark hallway to the kitchen, got down the Jack Daniel's, poured a double shot, and carried it out to the porch swing. The night was considerably cooler than the day had been. She had just set the swing in motion with her foot when Jesse walked up on the porch with a beer in his hands.

"You couldn't sleep either?" He stopped the swing, sat down on the other end, and then set it in motion again.

"I keep going over the past nineteen years and wondering what turning point brought all this about. I think it was moving here. If we hadn't come back to Honey Grove, she never would have met Ricky and made all these bad choices," Addy said.

Jesse shook his head. "It's plain that you've been a good mother, so stop blaming yourself."

She took a sip of her whiskey. "Thanks for saying that, but

if I hadn't wanted to come back to Honey Grove, none of this would have happened."

"Maybe. Maybe not," Jesse said. "All you have to do is kick a mesquite bush or an old scrub oak tree and a dozen bad boys will come running out. There would have been someone like Ricky out there in the Panhandle. Those guys aren't worth their salt, and they're always lookin' for an easy target. When they're together full time, and she's not doing something behind your back that seems thrilling right now, the novelty will wear off."

Addy took a small sip of her whiskey. "I figured you'd be angrier than you are."

"Shock can kill anger pretty quick," he said. "We can't undo what's done, but we can move on. I'd like for her to know that I'm her father when she comes home."

"*If* she comes home," Addy said. "And it's just been the two of us for so long, that I think it's best if I tell her all by myself."

"Oh, honey, she'll come in here with her tail tucked between her legs, begging you to forgive her," Jesse assured her. "And if you think it's best to have that conversation with her by yourself, then that's what you should do. I haven't been in the picture enough to ask for any favors."

"What makes you so sure that she'll come home?" Addy asked.

"You and this ranch are her stability. When she gets tired of Ricky, she'll want her roots again. I know because I came home," he admitted. "That last hitch in the Air Force seemed like it took forever. By the last year, all I could think of was coming home to the ranch, wearing my cowboy boots, and never having to stand at attention again. Then I got scared that something would happen to me, and I'd never eat Mama's cookin' again or see Daddy before it was too late."

Addy's eyes misted. That was exactly the way she felt the

last year Jesse was in the service. Every time she looked out her bedroom window at the bunkhouse, the ache in her heart for her best friend grew even more, and she regretted not being up front and honest with him.

"Well, we sure slapped you in the face with drama when you got here, didn't we?" she whispered.

"It's still good to be home. I'll take the good with the bad." Jesse finished his beer and crushed the can in his bare hands. "Good night, Addy. See you at breakfast."

"I'll be there." She smiled for the first time that day. "And thanks again for everything—most of all, for understanding."

"Hey, you had your reasons." He touched her cheek. "Get some sleep. I understand that we have to move some cattle from one pasture to another tomorrow. Don't want you to fall asleep and wreck one of the four-wheelers."

"I can still keep up with you, even in the face of drama," she assured him.

"There's my strong friend." He smiled.

Friend.

She couldn't ask for more, but sitting there under the stars, she wished she could.

* * *

Jesse hummed Blake Shelton's "Home" all the way back to the bunkhouse. The song had been one of his favorites the past year, but now it had even more meaning when he remembered the lyrics saying that he understood why she couldn't come with him because it wasn't her dream.

He opened the door, and Tex ran in before him and curled up on the sofa. "Like the song says"—he stopped and rubbed the dog's ears—"I just wanted to come home, and even with the problems, I'm glad to be here."

He kicked his boots off, stripped out of his jeans and shirt, and curled up on his bed. This time, he went right to sleep and couldn't believe it was morning when his alarm went off.

By the time he got dressed, poor old Tex was dancing around and barking at the door.

"Just a minute, old boy. I've got to get my hat," Jesse said.

When he finally opened the door, Tex made a dash for the nearest bush and then ran back to the porch.

"Don't rush me, feller," Jesse yawned. "We'll get to those cattle soon as we eat some breakfast."

The sun was barely peeking over the horizon when he opened the back door and stepped inside to the aroma of coffee, bacon, and something that smelled suspiciously like cinnamon rolls.

"Mornin', Mama." He headed straight for the coffeepot. "Daddy, did you sleep well?" he asked as he poured two mugs full and set one in front of his father.

"Better than I expected after the way yesterday turned out." Sonny picked up the mug and took his first sip. "You reckon Addy is going to be all right?"

"She's tough." Pearl pulled a pan of hot yeasty cinnamon rolls from the oven. "She'll be fine, but when Mia gets around to calling us, I intend to have a word or two with that child."

Jesse heard footsteps coming down the hall, poured two more mugs of coffee, and took them to the table. "How you doin' this mornin?" he asked when Addy came through the door.

She smiled wearily at Jesse. "Pearl always says that things look better after a good night's sleep and dawn comes around. I feel better than I did last night."

"Come out back with me for a minute. I've got something to show you," Jesse said.

Addy followed him out the back door in time to see a gorgeous sunrise.

"Isn't that a beautiful rainbow?" Jesse asked. "A new day. A new outlook, and new hope."

She nodded and wiped away a tear. "I hadn't realized how much I'd missed our friendship until you came home. Remember when we used to talk about everything. I believe the only secret I ever kept from you was Mia."

"I missed talking to you, too," Jesse said. "I guess we'd better get on back in there and help Mama get breakfast on the table."

"I suppose so," Addy said. "Thanks for the sunrise and the encouragement."

"Anytime." He smiled.

He escorted her back into the house with his hand on her lower back and went straight to the stove to carry a platter of bacon and eggs to the table in one hand and the pan of cinnamon rolls. "Mama, you're going to make me fat."

Sonny chuckled. "As hard as I intend to work you, there's no way you'll gain an ounce. Eat up and then get those cows moved over to the next pasture. That way we can plow that one under and replant it. If that cockamamied weatherman isn't lying to us, we've got a rain coming at the end of the week, so it would be good to get the seed in the ground tomorrow."

"Cockamamied," Jesse laughed. "The guys on my team used to tease me about our Southernisms. They nicknamed me Dr. Cowboy."

"Doctor?" Addy asked.

"I was the combat medic, remember?" he said.

"Say grace for us, Sonny," Pearl said. "These two need to eat and then go muster some cattle."

Sonny bowed his head and said a short prayer, then chuckled again. "I don't think it's mustering when all they do is herd them through a gate to another pasture. Mustering is what you do when you stay out there two or three nights like we used to do back when we were young and couldn't afford to hire extra help."

If only, Jesse thought, then shook the idea from his head. He and Addy were back on friendly ground. She had Grady now, whether Jesse liked him or not.

* * *

Addy loved being a nurse, but the first time she got on a four-wheeler and helped Henry herd a bunch of cattle across the huge ranch, she knew what she'd been missing. She had thought that she had to choose between the two things she loved, but Sonny and Pearl had offered her both worlds. She had never regretted the choice she had made to come help on the ranch that day, especially that morning when she started up the engine of the four-wheeler.

"Move 'em out," Jesse yelled over the noise of the two engines. "Round 'em up, Tex!"

The dog chased a rangy old bull from out of a mesquite thicket, while Jesse and Addy worked the stranglers into a herd. She yelled and waved her hat in the air to make the cattle move along. The distance from one side of the pasture to the other was only a half a mile, but this bunch of cows had evidently made themselves a home right where they were.

"I thought Mia had a home here, too," she muttered as she helped Jesse round up the cows. "I guess the grass was greener on the other side. But if that's the case, why don't these damned cows see that?"

Several of the cows, especially those with calves, had hidden in the corners of the pasture, and Tex had to work to get them headed in the direction they needed to go. When they were all moved and the gate was closed, Jesse and Addy sat down on the ground and leaned their backs against his four-wheeler.

He had brought two bottles of water from his saddlebag. He twisted the top off one and handed it to her.

She took a long drink and then brought out a sack with protein bars and apples in it. "Thought we might want a little pick-me-up before we get on the tractors and start plowing."

"Ranching must go on." Jesse took an apple and an energy bar from the bag. "If we get the pasture plowed by dark, we can seed it tomorrow and then pray that cockamamied weatherman is right about the rain."

"You think it's raining on Mia today? Think she's already missing the ranch?" Addy asked.

"Don't know about the rain, but I bet she's missing home. She won't admit it for a while longer, but she's wondering already if she made a mistake," Jesse answered.

"How can you be so sure?" she asked.

"Think about it, Addy," he said. "When did you start missing home when you left to go to your granny's place? Don't know about you, but the morning after..." He stared off into space for several seconds before he went on. "After we spent that night together, I wished I wasn't leaving. I had already signed on the dotted line, so I had to go, but I didn't want to. I wanted to be here with you and all that was familiar to me."

"When I found out I was pregnant, I just wanted to run away, but I cried the whole seven hours it took me to drive out there," she answered truthfully. "When I got the opportunity to come back, it seemed like a dream come true. Like I was being given another chance, but Mia wasn't happy living in town, so..." She hesitated.

"So when Sonny got sick and needed a full-time nurse and some farm help, did it seem like an answer to a prayer?" Jesse asked.

She nodded. "It really did, but enough nostalgia. We've got a pasture to plow under. I'd hate to be that weatherman if he's wrong about the rain. Sonny needs someone to be mad at right now, and he might put a curse on that guy."

They didn't take time to go in at noon, but kept plowing until it was dark, and then used the tractor lights and the light from the moon to finish up the last couple of acres. All day long, Addy's thoughts ran in circles. She would think about how wonderful it was to have her good friend back. Then she would go back to worrying about Mia, hoping that her daughter was all right and happy. Then the next moment, she would hope that Mia was so miserable that she would learn her lesson and be ready to come home. Not once did she think of Grady until she and Jesse were in the truck and on the way back to the ranch house.

"You remember Betsy Massey?" she asked.

"Wasn't she in a grade or two above us in school?" Jesse answered with another question.

"That's right. She works at the bank," Addy said.

"Is that who you talked to this morning? Julie's mother?"

"Justine," Addy corrected him. "The seventeen-year-old mother of Ricky's most recent baby. If the rumors are right, he's got one over in Bonham and maybe one or two more scattered around this area. Anyway, she says that she saw Grady having lunch with a woman in Bonham last week and said that the woman was the image of Amelia, Grady's wife who was killed. I'm worried about him, Jesse. I don't think he's recovered from her death, and he's grasping at someone to take her place."

"He's the chief over at the hospital," Jesse said. "That could have been a drug rep, or an insurance rep, or maybe a lawyer. Hospitals are always getting sued for one thing or another."

"You really think so?" Addy asked.

"Hell, no!" Jesse said. "I think he's seeing a woman he met at a strip club. Her name is Cotton Candy, and she's twenty years old, and he doesn't want to talk to you about her any more than you want to talk to him about me."

Addy air-slapped his arm. "You are crazy."

"Do you want Grady to be more than a friend?" Jesse became serious.

"No, I do not," Addy answered. "I might need a how-to book to even know what love is. I've had a couple of relationships that I thought might turn serious in the past twenty years, but for the most part, I've just concentrated on taking care of Mia. But there is no chemistry between me and Grady. We're friends, and I care about him in that respect, but that's as far as it goes."

"Well, maybe Cotton Candy loves him so much that he can't get her out of his mind. Maybe she keeps those little blue pills in her purse for all the times when—"

This time Addy slapped him for real. "The Air Force certainly didn't make you grow up. You're just as ornery as you were when you left. I'm trying to be serious."

"Let him have his secrets. He'll bring his new woman around to meet you when he's ready?" Jesse asked. "What makes you think he's not ready to move on anyway?"

"He called me by his dead wife's name when he drove me home from church."

"Sounds like he's got some sortin' out to do for sure, but that's his business." Jesse parked his truck at the back of the house.

"You sound like Mia," Addy said.

"In some ways she was right, you know. Some stuff is her business, and she'll have to learn from her mistakes, just like we did," Jesse said.

"I don't want to talk about that anymore. It makes me sad," Addy said. "I'll race you to the refrigerator. I'm starving."

She was out of the truck in a flash, jumped the fence, and

beat him to the back door. "That cold fried chicken leg is mine, buster."

"Not if I grab it first." He picked her up and set her behind him, then hurried over to the refrigerator and grabbed the container with the leftover chicken. "Would you look at this?" He grinned. "There's four legs in here. Three for me and one for you."

"I'll tell Pearl if you don't share fair and square," she threatened.

"Tattletale." He handed over the container to her.

She took out two legs, one for each hand, and gave the open container back to him. "Reckon there's any chocolate cake left?"

"If there is, I get half of it, or I'll tell Mama you don't play well with others," he teased.

I might learn how to play well with others again now that you are home, she thought as she bit into the cold fried chicken.

Chapter Eleven

Grady didn't make it to church on Sunday morning. When he called, he said that he couldn't be there for Sunday dinner, but that he would stop by around three o'clock to check on Sonny's progress. He also said that he had something to talk to Addy about, but not on the phone. Grady was always on time, so when he had not arrived by three thirty, Addy began to worry. She tried calling his phone but got the voice mail message telling his patients if they had an emergency to go to the nearest hospital.

"What do you do if the doctor himself is the emergency?" she muttered.

She finally went out to the porch and waited on the swing, and at exactly four o'clock, he parked his car beside her truck next to the yard fence.

"You *are* late," she called out when he got out of his vehicle.

"Sorry about that. We'll talk later. Right now, I need the reports on Sonny, and could you start faxing them to me at the hospital on Friday morning from now on?" he asked as he made his way across the yard.

"Sure, but you've always picked them up here." She stood and headed into the house. "I would have appreciated a call if you weren't going to be here at three. I've been worried."

He opened the screen door and talked through it. "Time got away from me. We'll talk as soon as I visit with Sonny. I'd like to do a private exam today, so if you'll wait on the porch, that would be great."

She raised an eyebrow. "Sure thing. Bring out a couple of beers when you come back."

"I'll bring one for you, but I'd better pass," he said. "I'm driving, and I need to be in Bonham at five."

He went on into the house, and Addy sat back down on the swing. Something definitely was not right. She might have blinders on when it came to Mia, but not with Grady. He was an open book for the most part. He hadn't been around in a week. Yep, something was amiss, and it didn't take a rocket scientist to figure out that it had to do with the woman Betsy had seen him with. She had her phone in her hand to call her friend and ask for directions when Jesse came round the house.

He rested his arms on the porch railing and smiled. "You look like you could chew up fence posts and spit out toothpicks. What's going on?"

"I'm not sure, but Grady says we need to talk," she answered, "so you need to get lost."

Jesse snapped to attention and saluted her. "I'll be down at the bunkhouse if you need me."

"Thanks, Jesse," she said.

He dropped his hand and whispered, "One more thing. Have you heard from Mia?"

She shook her head. "Now, go. I'll see you in a little while. You got beer down at the bunkhouse?"

"Yep, and whiskey, both." He waved and disappeared around the end of the house.

Addy sat back down on the swing for a think. She hadn't quite figured out what could be so important that Grady couldn't talk to her on the phone by the time that he came out of the house and sat down in one of the wicker chairs instead of on the swing beside her.

"We need to talk." Grady pulled out a clean white handkerchief from his pocket, removed his glasses, and cleaned them. "I don't know how to say this other than just spit it out: I've met someone, and I've fallen in love with her. I'm in love with Aurelia, like I was with Amelia."

"Really?" Addy asked. "Tell me more about her."

"She's the head nurse at the hospital, and I don't know why we have taken so long to realize that there's something between us."

"It sounds like you should be really happy. So why the need for such a serious talk?" Addy said.

"Well..." Grady fidgeted in his chair. "I told her about you, and she's not comfortable with me having a woman for a best friend." He wrung his hands the whole time he talked.

"So because she says so, you're going to give up our friendship? Just like that?" Addy could barely believe it. "Is this why you didn't tell me about her before? How long have you two been together?"

"I've been seeing her since New Year's, and I didn't tell you because I knew this is what you would say," Grady answered. "We moved in together this morning."

"Wow, that's mighty fast. And don't you think it's odd that her name is so close to Amelia's? Betsy said she looked just like her, too. Are you sure you're not confusing love with grief?"

"I would have told you sooner, but with Mia and Jesse both coming home and..." He let the sentence hang.

"Hey, don't blame this on Jesse or Mia. I think you need to

take a step back and think this over. First, are you really over Amelia? And second, do you want to move in with a woman who says you can't even talk to a good friend? Neither one sounds healthy."

"I'm sorry I kept you in the dark, but you haven't always told me everything either. Like who Mia's father is, and I had to hear it through gossip about Mia leaving with Ricky O'Malley. I was here the day that she left, and you didn't mention it," he said. "Or is it because you had Jesse here to talk to instead?" His gaze came up to meet hers. "I can see there's something between you two and that it was hindering our friendship."

"Hey, Jesse's been home a week and you've hardly even been around the whole time he's been here. In fact, I don't think you once asked how *I* was doing. Maybe then it would've been easier to tell you about Mia and Ricky." She suddenly realized just how one-sided their friendship had been, and that made her even madder than him telling her that he couldn't talk to her anymore.

Grady stood and headed toward the porch steps. "You can just fax Sonny's reports to the hospital every week from now on."

"Fine, Dr. Adams." Addy stood too and crossed her arms over her chest. "I wish you and Aurelia the best of luck. I have a feeling you might need it."

As soon as Grady had driven off, Addy marched out to the bunkhouse and slung open the door without knocking. Jesse was sitting on the sofa with his feet propped up on an old coffee table that had seen lots of scuffed-up boots in its lifetime. Everything that she had packed away and stored out there had been taken out of the boxes, and the living area of the bunkhouse looked a helluva lot like Jesse's bedroom had when she first moved into the house.

"Did he ask you if y'all could be more than friends?" Jesse asked.

"Why did you put all this stuff out?" She slumped down on the sofa beside him.

"My question first." He picked up one of the two beers from the end table and handed it to her. "Is Coors still your favorite?"

"Yup." She downed a third of the long-neck bottle before setting it down on the coffee table and burping. "That wasn't very ladylike, but then I don't feel much like a lady today. Grady didn't want to take our friendship to a new level. His new girlfriend doesn't want him to talk to me anymore. She's not comfortable with him having a woman for a best friend. Now, your turn about all this." She waved her hand around the room.

"I've lived in barracks for twenty years. I wanted to feel like I was home. Now back to you, why are you so pissed?" he asked. "You can kick any bush between here and the Gulf of Mexico and find a dozen best friends. There's one sitting here drinking beer with you if you don't want to start kicking."

"He shouldn't let a woman control him, especially one who's named Aurelia, and looks like his deceased wife, Amelia," Addy said.

"He hasn't been out here to the ranch in days. Didn't that give you a clue that something was going on?"

"You'd think it would have, but I was giving him all the benefits of doubts." She turned up the bottle again. "And that pisses me off."

"I'm not surprised that Grady let a woman railroad him into doing what she wants. He always was kind of a pushover." Jesse dropped his feet down to the floor. "I'm having another beer. You want one, or do you want a shot of Jack Daniel's?"

"Beer, please," she answered.

He went to the kitchen area and brought back two more long-neck bottles. "I missed good beer when I was out on a mission. Sometimes all we could get was nonalcoholic."

"Monkey piss tastes better than that." She reached out for the bottle he offered her.

"How much monkey piss have you tasted?" he asked.

"None, but I have an imagination." She was glad that Jesse was home, happy that their friendship was coming back, but she wanted to get serious now. She had never been one to beat around the bush, especially with Jesse, so she came right out and asked, "What's wrong with me, Jesse? I can't even keep a best friend."

"Nothing that I can see, except maybe your hair is a fright on rainy days," he chuckled.

"I'm serious," she declared. "You wouldn't ask me out in high school. We had a one-night fling because we were both sad that you were leaving. I haven't been able to hold on to a relationship since, so something has to be wrong with me. Tell me what it is. I don't want to grow old by myself."

Jesse didn't answer for so long that she thought he was avoiding her question altogether. Finally, he said, "We didn't want to ruin the friendship, remember. We had been best friends since we were maybe four years old. I couldn't imagine not having you to talk to or to lean on in times of trouble. That didn't mean I wasn't interested in you, Addy, or that I didn't dream about you. That night here in this very room was..." He paused and gazed into her eyes. "More than words can ever describe."

"And now?" she asked.

"Now we have a smart-ass daughter we have to figure out how to handle." He blinked and studied his beer bottle. "We can't go back and recapture that night. We're not eighteen anymore."

"Tell that to this room," she said with another sweep of her hand. "I'd say that you've done a pretty good job of it."

"Well, then..." He wiggled his eyebrows.

"Don't tease me," she said.

He slid down to the middle of the sofa and drew her close to his side. "You are a wonderful person, Addison Hall. You have a kind heart and just enough sass to make you interesting. You are beautiful, even when it rains and your hair gets crazy, and any man on the face of this earth should be glad to have you as a friend. Grady is a stupid ass for not seeing that and treating you like the queen you deserve to be. He will never, ever find as true of a friend as you are, and I'm speaking from experience. Want me to go toilet paper his house or write ugly things on his car with shoe polish?"

"No, I just want to sit here with you until suppertime and know that there's one man in the universe I can trust to make me feel better when I'm pissed," she whispered.

"I'll always be here for you, Addy. Don't ever forget it," he said.

"I know, Jesse, and I'm sorry we drifted so far apart, but I'm glad we're back in each other's world now."

He kissed the top of her head. "Me, too, darlin'."

Chapter Twelve

The temperature had already risen to eighty-nine degrees by ten o'clock that Tuesday morning when Addy and Jesse got on the four-wheelers and headed over to her old home place to check on the alpacas. They crossed two pastures, waved at Henry and the hired hands who were putting up new fencing, and then drove across the dirt road. Since alpacas didn't do well when the weather got hot and needed a shady place to get under, Henry had moved them into the corral next to the hay barn, which had a lean-to shed attached to its side.

Addy brought her four-wheeler to a stop, slung a leg over the side of the seat, and counted the animals before she stood up. "Looks like they're all here," she said. "I'm seeing the male or macho in the middle of his harem, six hembras, and two crias. You ever dealt with alpacas before?"

"Nope. I've seen a few but never dealt with them," he answered.

Jesse nodded as he parked, got off the four-wheeler, and went over to the corral fence. "Dad wants us to move them over closer to the ranch house on Sunflower Ranch so he can enjoy them more. Maybe that pasture right outside the yard fence?"

"Great idea," Addy agreed. "The shed at the end of the barn could provide shelter for them in hot and cold weather, and there's a water trough up there close by. We'd just have to be careful to keep the barn door closed. All that hay and feed would be like a never-ending buffet to them. We'd be calling Stevie out every week to take care of them if they ate too much."

Jesse propped a foot on the bottom rail of the corral and leaned on it. "I never thought Stevie O'Dell would turn out to be a vet. She was so prissy in high school. Is she still single?"

"Yep," Addy answered. "You interested?" A shot of jealousy stabbed her in the heart.

"Nope, never did like prissy girls," Jesse answered. "I prefer women with a little sass in them."

Addy cocked her head to one side. "I hear a cria crying from inside the barn. One of them must've found a way in, and now it can't find its mama."

"That's not a cria," Jesse said. "It sounds more like a human, not a baby, but a child. Maybe somebody's kid got lost."

Addy took off in a run around the end of the barn. She slid the door open enough to slip inside and stopped dead in her tracks when she saw Mia's truck. Had the vehicle been sitting there the whole week and no one noticed it? If so, had she left with Ricky in his truck?

"Holy smoke," Jesse gasped. "Isn't that Mia's truck?"

Addy's hands trembled, and her stomach twisted into knots. Something was dreadfully wrong. She felt like a boulder the size of an elephant was sitting on her chest. Her child was out there without a way to get back home.

"Yes, that's her truck," Addy whispered. "And I think there's someone inside it."

Jesse closed his hand around hers. Together they eased across the scorching hot barn. The windows were rolled down and the truck was covered with a layer of dust. When Addy peeked inside, the whole world around her disappeared and everything went black. Jesse caught her as she started to fall backward and held her tightly against his chest.

"It's Mia," she gasped when she got her bearings.

"Mama?" Mia sat up and slung the door open at the same time. She fell into her mother's arms, laid her head on Addy's shoulder, and sobbed until she got the hiccups.

"I should go," Jesse said.

Addy shook her head. "Don't you dare leave."

She led Mia over to the side of the barn and pulled her down to sit beside her on a bale of hay. "How long have you been here? Why didn't you come to the house?"

Mia kept her eyes glued to her boots. "I've been here since midnight last night. I didn't want to wake up the whole house. Poppa might have had a heart attack."

"You could have called me, and I would have let you in the house. You didn't need to sleep in your truck," Addy said.

Mia shook her head but still didn't look up. "No, ma'am. I don't deserve to come home, and you have every right to say that you told me so."

Jesse sat down beside Addy. "We're just glad you're safe."

Addy put her arm around Mia and drew her close to her side. "What happened, sweetie?"

Mia put her head in her hands. "I was a fool. I trusted Ricky." She hiccupped through her tears.

"Do you want to talk about what happened?" Jesse said.

Mia shook her head again. "I don't want to say his name or talk about him or anything, but Mama, Poppa and Nana deserve to know what happened. "On Sunday night we had this big argument. I went out to get food..." She closed her eyes and shivered in spite of the steaming hot barn. "When I got back, there was another woman in our room, and he was kissing her."

Addy's mother instincts kicked in and anger boiled up from depths that she didn't even know existed. Not only had Ricky taken advantage of her child, he had broken her heart. The guy had better stay out of Fannin County for a long time because it would take years for her to be able to look at him without wanting to strangle him.

"He said that she kissed him and..." Mia wiped tears away from her cheeks and sat up straight. "I was a fool to believe him, but I did. That night he lost the rest of our money at the poker table."

"How much money did he put in with yours when you left together?" Jesse asked.

"That's none of your business," Mia said through clenched teeth.

"I'd say it is our business," Addy disagreed. "You need to face the fact that you've been conned, not only for the past week, but for six months. How much did Ricky contribute to the living expenses when you two moved in together last semester? Did he get a job and help with food and rent?"

"Did you get a job?" Jesse asked. "Is that why you failed every class?"

Addy was about to ask the same question, but hearing it said out loud made her angry at her daughter as well as Ricky. Mia should have known better than to throw her entire future away on a smooth-talking bad boy.

"Did you?" Addy asked.

"When my money was gone in my savings and checking account, I worked as a waitress in a café not far from our apartment. I couldn't go to school and keep up with the bills. Ricky liked to have his friends over to play poker and drink beer. That took money." Mia shrugged. "I was happy if he was."

"Do you want me to go find that worthless guy and kick his ass?" Jesse asked.

She nodded. "I wish you would, but he's not worth driving all the way to Vegas for. Mama, I have no money and no sheep, and..." Mia started sobbing again.

"You'll make more money. Time will heal your broken heart. You can go back to school in the fall and repeat last semester. There's an old saying that what doesn't kill us makes us stronger," Addy told her. "But you will take your fall classes online and pay for them yourself. You are going to apologize to Sonny and Pearl. Then you are going to talk to Jesse, one on one, not here but after you talk to Sonny and Pearl. It's up to him whether you have a job on the ranch."

"Why not Henry?" Mia asked.

"Because he's retiring pretty soon, and Jesse will be the fore-man and boss then. If you're going to stay on the ranch, then you will be working for him, and it's only right that he makes the decision," Addy answered. "You wanted to make your own decisions and you have. Now it's time to be accountable. Sonny paid out money for your tuition and books, and your dorm and meal ticket. You wasted every bit of that, so you can study and work at the same time next year. Then we'll talk about whether you can go back to the campus to live in another year."

"But—" Mia started to argue.

Addy shook her head. "I love you. I'm glad you're home. I'm sorry that Ricky did this to you, but there are no buts, Mia. Accept the fact that you messed up."

"I already did," she whined. "I told you I was sorry, and I didn't have a right to come back home."

"That's the first step. The second one is proving it." Addy hugged her again.

"Where is Ricky?" Jesse asked.

"I don't know. I guess he's in Vegas still, but I never want to see him again." Mia brushed her kinky dark hair away from her wet cheeks.

Her eyes and height are from Jesse, but at least she got her curly hair from me, Addy thought and then wondered why on earth she would be thinking about genetics at a time like this.

"I feel ugly again," Mia whispered. "Ricky made me feel pretty. I should have known that he only saw my money. I'm like a tall, lanky old sunflower growing wild in the field. The girl he left with was a tiny blonde with blue eyes, like a delicate little rose."

"Being tall does not make you ugly," Jesse said. "How do you know that he left with a girl?"

"He wrote a note saying that he was leaving with the love of his life, that I should be out of the hotel by noon, and that he was taking the rest of the money we had. *We!*" She doubled up her fist and hit the hay bale beside her. "He didn't put a dime into the trip and spent all of my money at poker. He kept saying that he could feel a lucky streak, and when he won enough, we'd travel around the world."

"How did you get home if you didn't have any money?" Addy wasn't sure she even wanted to know the answer.

Mia looked at the ceiling. "After the kissing fight, I hid a hundred-dollar bill in the pocket of the hotel bathrobe. I didn't have enough for a hotel, so I drove the whole distance. I only stopped for gas, and I got hot dogs and chips when I filled up the truck. The trip took almost twenty hours, and..." She started weeping again. "My life is ruined. Everyone will know what he did to me."

"I expect if Justine can hold her head up, then you can, too." Addy wanted to cry with her. Mia didn't deserve what had happened, but she had made bad choices. Addy realized two things in that moment. One was how much she loved her daughter. The second was that she had never fully appreciated all the love and support she had had through the years.

Mia's brow wrinkled, reminding Addy of Jesse when he frowned. That she hadn't seen herself in Jesse's mannerisms was a mystery. Addy thought of clearing the air completely and telling her that Jesse was her father, but that could come later. One crisis today was enough for all of them to get through.

"Why would you say that about Justine? What has her being pregnant got to do with me?" Mia asked.

"Ricky is the father of her baby," Jesse answered.

Mia's green eyes popped wide open. She stared at Jesse like he had horns, a pitchfork, and a long-spiked tail. "You're lying."

"Nope, he's not," Addy said. "After the way he's treated you, why would you think Jesse was lying to you?"

"Because that would mean..." She jumped up to her feet and began to pace again. "I can do the math. That means she got pregnant at the end of last summer. Ricky and I were secretly dating back then. He was cheating on me."

"Maybe he was cheating on her," Jesse said. "Ever think of it that way?"

Addy did some math in her head, too. "So you were dating him your first semester of college? When you came home on weekends..."

"Dammit!" Mia crossed her arms over her chest. "He said we had to be careful because Poppa didn't like him. He was seeing Justine the whole time, wasn't he?"

Addy had thought she was a blessed woman when Mia was growing up. Her child never gave her any problems, but now she realized that her daughter had been saving it all up for one big boom—like an exploding bomb that rattled every emotion and hit every raw nerve in her body. "Betsy told me that Justine wouldn't tell anyone who the father was until the baby was born. Guess Ricky was telling her the same things he told you, that they should keep things secret, too. You should go talk to her. Y'all were friends before you went to college."

"What would I say to her, Mama? I didn't know it at the time, but I was the other woman back then," Mia said softly.

"Just being able to share might be good for both of you," Jesse offered.

"But first, you have to go home, talk to Sonny and Pearl, get a shower, and unpack your truck. Then after lunch, you and Jesse will have a long visit about whether you can work on the ranch or if you'll need to find a different job. Betsy might hire you to clean her house. She mentioned a couple of months ago that she wasn't happy with her cleaning lady," Addy said.

Mia groaned.

Addy stood and was surprised that her legs supported her. She took a few steps, went up on her tiptoes, and hugged her daughter. "Get in your truck and go to the house. We'll be along in a little while. Mia, I know this seems like the end of the world right now, but it will pass, and you'll be stronger on the other side of it. I love you, and I'll help you."

"Will you come with me to talk to Poppa and Nana?" Mia begged.

Saying no was one of the hardest things Addy had ever done, but she slowly shook her head. "That part you need to face on your own, hon."

Mia sucked in a lungful of air, let it out in a loud whoosh, and marched over to the barn doors. She slung them both open and headed back to her truck.

"Do you think she'll be okay?" Addy asked Jesse.

"Of course she will. She's got us."

* * *

Jesse liked the sound of that word. *Us.*

Addy was pacing the barn, clearly wrestling with her thoughts.

"You know I'm going to give her back her job, don't you?" he said.

"I never doubted that for a minute, but don't give her any authority, Jesse. Make her work like the summer help, with either Henry or you to supervise her," Addy advised.

"Tough love?"

She plopped down on the floor and leaned back against a bale of hay. "Yes, but it's tough on both of us, all three of us really. My first instinct is to shower her with love, give her back her position, and not ever mention this again."

"But?" Jesse sat down beside her.

"But that wouldn't teach her anything. She needs to be accountable." She laid her head on his shoulder. "I'm going to ask a tremendous favor of you right now. Make her work right along beside you all summer. She'll be surly at first, so it'll be a pain in your ass to work with her, but she needs to know you better before we tell her that you are her father."

"You forget that I was in the Air Force for twenty years. I've dealt with lots of folks who were a pain in my ass," he chuckled. "That's the least I can do after not helping you raise her."

"Thank you, Jesse," she sighed. "You are a good friend."

"Our first job, hers and mine, will be to bring the alpacas over, one or two at a time on foot."

"They're tough to herd," Addy said.

"Maybe I'll learn something." He grinned. "That should give us the better part of a day to spend together."

"You are the boss. Just don't let her forget it. Now, can I please fall completely apart?" she asked.

"Have at it." Jesse got ready for tears and weeping.

Addy slapped the barn wall so hard that the metal rattled, then she kicked a bale of hay, sending two field mice running across the floor. "I'm so mad at Ricky that I could chain him up to the back of a four-wheeler and drag him out to the back forty for the coyotes and bobcats." She drew in a breath. "If Mia was ten years old, I would ground her to the house for five years with no phone, no tablet, and no computers."

"That's pretty mad," Jesse said. "I expect her having to work with me is far worse than that, and honey, it would be best for Ricky if he stayed in Nevada. I imagine Justine's daddy and I would both like to take a turn at teaching him a lesson, too."

"This isn't all his fault. If Mia had been honest with me"—she waved her hand around the barn—"with all of us, we could have talked to her."

"Think she would have listened? All those secrets were exciting, and making her own decisions made her feel like a grown-up," Jesse told her. "Ricky is a con artist and she got took. We'll put that behind us and move on to the future."

"You are such a good man, Jesse Ryan," Addy said.

Jesse didn't feel like such a good man. If he had been, he would have realized that something wasn't right twenty years ago when Addy stopped writing and didn't take his calls anymore. A good man would have pursued the issue to find out why his best friend was brushing him off—especially after that incredible night they had just shared.

Chapter Thirteen

"This is the second time in the five years I've lived here that I hate to go into the house," Addy said as she crawled off the four-wheeler and sat down on the porch step.

"When was the first time?" Jesse followed her and sat down beside her.

Addy closed her eyes and sighed. "Last week when Mia left. She broke Pearl and Sonny's hearts. How could our lives get in such a mess in such a short time?"

Jesse laid a hand on her shoulder. "They love her, so they will forgive her."

She covered his hand with hers and gave it a gentle squeeze. "Forgiveness when you love someone is easy, but trust has to be rebuilt."

"Are we still talking about Mia?" Jesse asked. "If we're talking about us, then I want you to know that I trust you, and I forgive you. I understand your reasons."

"Do you wish I would have done things different?" She

kept her hand on his because simply touching him brought a measure of peace to her in all the turmoil of the day.

"Right now, I sure do. I want her to know, but then I'm afraid of her reaction when she finds out I'm her father and that everyone has kept it from her. She's as bullheaded as both of us combined." He leaned over and kissed her on the cheek. "Back when I was in basic training, I'm not so sure I would have wanted to know that I was going to be a father. I was so gung-ho on saving the world that I might have felt trapped. I like to think that I would have been wise, and I do know down deep in my heart that I would have done right by you and by our baby if I'd known."

"Everything seemed clear cut back then. Not so much right now." She removed her hand and stood up. "We'd better go see how Pearl and Sonny are doing. I hope this doesn't jack his blood pressure up too high. I probably should check it before dinner."

"Face the music." Jesse smiled.

"Sounds like the title of a country music song, doesn't it?" Addy said.

"Would be a good one," Jesse answered as he stood and extended a hand to help her up.

"We could write it for sure, couldn't we?" She put her hand in his and smiled up at him. "Thanks for understanding."

"Always." He winked like he used to when they were in high school.

"I was afraid you'd—" she started.

He laid a finger over her lips. "I could never be mad at you for looking out for me. We're best buddies, remember?"

"Always." She laid a hand on his cheek, turned, and went into the house.

"You're just in time for dinner," Pearl called out from the kitchen

Addy checked Sonny for signs of high blood pressure as she went into the kitchen. His face wasn't flushed, but his eyes were red, no doubt from crying. She hoped that he had stood firm in front of Mia and she hadn't seen that she had upset him to the point of tears.

"How are you holding up after all this drama?" Addy asked. "Should we do a midday check on your vital signs? Jacked-up blood pressure isn't good."

"About like you, I suppose, and we should check him over after we eat," Pearl answered for him as she wiped her eyes on the tail of her apron. "But we're getting it all sorted out, and we're so glad she came home. She could have been too stubborn to even come back."

"Did she apologize and talk to you about a job?" Addy asked.

"She was very sorry," Sonny said. "I believe it was harder on me to be firm with her than it was when I had to make you responsible for your mistakes, Jesse."

"She has to learn, but that don't mean it's easy on us," Pearl added.

"So what's the verdict?" Jesse asked.

"She has to work for minimum wage. She's not a boss over any of the summer help because she quit her job without notice. She has to report to you every morning and work beside you," Pearl said.

"That's for both of you, so y'all can get to know each other," Sonny explained. "She has to tell her mama where she's going and when she will be back, and if we catch her lying, she's fired. All this is only if you see fit to hire her."

Jesse cocked his head toward Addy. "Did you call them before she got here? This sounds a lot like what you told her."

She nodded. "While you were loading the alpaca feed, I called and asked them to back me up, and to add in anything else that would teach her a lesson. I didn't want them to be shocked or feel sorry for her when she walked into the house looking like something the dogs drug up."

"That was a smart move," Jesse said.

Addy heard footsteps in the hallway and busied herself getting chips from the pantry. Mia looked a little better after her shower, but she still needed a good night's sleep and maybe some ice packs for her swollen eyes. She took her normal place beside her mother at the table and bowed her head for grace.

Sonny's prayer was a little longer that day, and when he finished, there was a lump in Addy's throat the size of a lemon. At that moment, Addy would have given anything if she could have told Mia that Jesse was her father. She wanted nothing more than to hold her daughter and tell her that she would be working beside Jesse so that she could get to know him. But deep in her heart she knew that she shouldn't rush things. Mia had to really get to know Jesse first.

Mia took two sandwiches from the platter and piled chips on the side. "I'm starving," she said. "I only had a hot dog and some chips all day yesterday. I had no idea how much gas money I needed to get here, so I was afraid to use too much for food."

"Well, you are home now," Pearl said. "We're happy that you made it. Eat good. If Jesse hires you, you'll have a long afternoon of work ahead of you."

She didn't even glance his way but kept her eyes on her plate. "What's for supper?"

"Chicken pot pies and banana cake for dessert," Pearl answered. "Pretty simple food after you've been having all that fancy stuff from a Las Vegas buffet. Sonny and I thought about going to Vegas a few times to see the bright lights and some of the shows, but it just never worked out."

"Nana, I'd rather be sitting right here in this kitchen eating sandwiches than in that fancy hotel blowing all my money on food and the poker tables," Mia said.

"I can add a hearty amen to that," Jesse said. "I felt the same when I was able to get home for visits. My job with the Air Force was often dangerous and exciting, but there's nothing like home." He reached for a sandwich at the same time Addy did.

His fingertips brushed against hers, sending her on an emotional roller coaster that brought back memories of the day and the weeks after he had left.

The timing had just never been right.

Addy's grandmother's voice was clear in her head. *I told you to tell your baby's father about her. If you had, you wouldn't be facing this turmoil today.*

If I had, he would have insisted on marrying me, and then resented me for the rest of his life. He was my best friend. I knew him, Addy argued.

Forget about the past, Mia's situation, your jobs, and everything else, and listen to your heart, the voice said and then went silent.

"Mama?" Mia nudged her on the shoulder. "Are you all right?"

"I'm fine." Addy managed a weak smile. "I was just having an argument with my grandmother."

"Granny talks to you. That's kind of creepy." Mia shivered. "What did she say?"

"That I should listen to my heart." Addy glanced across the table to find Jesse staring right at her again. Back in their younger days, they could practically read each other's minds and didn't need words to communicate. That morning, it seemed like they were back to knowing what the other one was thinking.

"Sounds like good advice to me," Pearl said. "The heart can't hear or see, but it has feelings, and it will guide you right, if you'll just listen to it."

"Amen, Mama." Jesse shifted his focus over to her. "If only we had paid attention to that when we're young, things might have turned out better for us."

"Are you talking about me?" Mia asked.

"No, my child," Addy answered for him. "He's talking about all young folks. We made our mistakes when we were your age, but hopefully, we learned from them, just like you will."

"So I'm a mistake?" Mia's old surliness returned.

"No, you were made out of love." Addy avoided glancing at Jesse but kept her eyes on her daughter. "And you've been loved every day since you were born."

"Then my father wasn't a one-night stand or a bum off the streets?" Mia asked. "Maybe we are cursed to like deadbeats who love us and leave us, Mama. Like the old saying says, 'Like mother, like daughter.'"

Addy's forefinger came up so fast that it was a blur and stopped close enough to Mia's nose that she jerked back. "Your father is not that kind of man, and I'm not having this conversation today, young lady. Right now, we are taking care of what you've done, not the trouble I caused twenty years ago by not telling your father that I was pregnant with you. Understood?"

Mia shrugged. "When *are* we having this conversation?"

"When I think you can handle it without running off again," Addy answered. "Finish your dinner so you and Jesse can talk about whether you'll be doing ranch work or searching for another job. You're going to need money to pay for your online courses next fall."

"You were serious about that? I really can't go back to college?" Mia gasped. "I promise I'll make good grades again. I'm never looking at another guy again, so you don't have to worry about that."

"I was serious," Addy said. "Online courses that you will

pay for out of your earnings this summer. One grade below a B, and you can begin paying your own cell phone bill and your truck insurance."

"One mistake in my whole life. I might as well go to jail," Mia pouted.

"This time it was misjudgment. Just be sure that when you mess up next time, it's not something illegal," Addy told her.

Chapter Fourteen

Jesse sat down in a rocking chair, stretched his long legs out so that he could prop his boots on the back-porch railing, and waited for Mia. He didn't look around when the door opened until the tingle on the back of his neck told him that Addy was nearby. He brought his legs down, sat up a little straighter, and turned to face her.

"Did she back out and decide that waitressing or working in a fast-food place would be better than facing me every day?" he asked.

"No, she's putting her hair up, so she'll be ready to work," Addy answered as she sat down in the chair beside him. "I've changed my mind about sitting in on the visit if that's all right with you."

"Not at all, but why?" Jesse asked. "Do you think I'll break if she starts crying?"

"Maybe." Addy sighed. "I remember a few times when I cried. You would have tried to shoot the moon out of the sky to get me to stop."

"Did you cry when you found out"—he checked the door and lowered his voice—"that you were pregnant?"

"Nope," she answered. "I just called Granny, and we put together a plan. We took precautions that night, if you'll remember, so I couldn't blame you, and tears wouldn't undo what was done. Granny said that the two of us were alike. When we were faced with a problem, we just plowed into it with all our might."

"You sure showed that today, even if it did break your heart to do it," he said.

They sat in comfortable silence for a few minutes until Mia came out onto the porch and sat down in the swing. "I'm not sure how this is supposed to go. So, I already had the rules laid out for me twice, but I'm still not sure how this is going to go. What am I supposed to do now?"

"I'll leave you two alone to discuss the job." Addy stood up and went into the house.

"How did you apply for the job as a waitress when you quit going to classes?" Jesse asked.

"I went in and asked for the job, filled out a form on the computer, and they hired me," she said.

"Are you asking for a job as a hired hand on this ranch?" he asked.

"I guess I am," Mia said.

"There's no guessing to it. Ranch work is hard. It's demanding, and it requires long hours. Either you know you want to work here, or you don't," Jesse said.

"All right then," Mia said. "I want a job here. I already know what it takes to do ranch work. I'm experienced. I've had responsibilities right here that you already know about."

"Are you willing to do what I say without back sassing and without attitude?" he asked.

"I guess..." She clamped her mouth shut. "Yes, I am. I'll

work hard to show all of you that I'm sorry for the choice I made and walked away like I did."

"Then you have a job. Minimum wage like the summer hired help. Tomorrow, you and I will bring the alpacas over to this side of the property. This afternoon, you can get out the lawn mower and weed eater and take care of the yard work. If you're done before supper, then go ahead and weed Mama's flower gardens," Jesse told her.

"Henry usually has one of the boys do that..." She stopped and took a deep breath. "I'll get the mower out and get busy."

"Ever mowed before?" Jesse asked.

She shook her head.

"Then I think I'll sit here and supervise, just to be sure you do it right." Jesse propped his feet up on the rail again and tipped his cowboy hat down over his eyes.

Mia slammed her straw hat down on her head. Her boots sounded like shotgun blasts on the wooden porch as she stomped across it, but Jesse didn't even blink an eye.

"Good job," Addy said from just inside the screen door, "but I can't see you sitting here doing nothing."

"As mad as she is, she'll have this done in an hour or two at the most. She and I are going to go straighten up the barn the rest of the afternoon. The stalls need to be ready for the alpacas in case we have to bring them in out of the heat or weather. She's going to sleep like a baby tonight." Jesse yawned.

"Think you can keep up with her?" Addy smiled.

"I'll do my damn best," Jesse answered. "This raisin' kids ain't for wimps, is it?"

"Nope, and especially after they get to be as old as Mia," Addy answered. "I'm going to take Sonny's vitals. Just to be on the safe side, I'm going to insist on doing Pearl's, too. Neither of them needs this kind of drama. It broke my heart when Pearl mentioned how much she wanted to go to Vegas."

Jesse sat up again and hung his hat on the back of the rocker. "Mine, too. I figure when Henry gets settled in Colorado, I'll buy them tickets to fly up there, and then in the spring, I'll insist they go to Vegas. They need to make every minute count before Dad gets any worse."

"Sounds like a plan." Addy stood up.

"You think you'll ever go back to nursing full time?" Jesse asked.

She patted his shoulder. "I've got the best of worlds right now. I'm a full-time nurse to the folks, and I'm also doing what I can on the ranch. I'm happy, Jesse. Why mess with that?"

"Amen," he said. "You might as well come on out here where I can see you."

"I'll be out in a few minutes," she said.

The door opened a few minutes later, and Addy and Pearl both came out on the porch. Pearl brought out two glasses of sweet tea and Addy carried a couple of bottles of water. Pearl handed Jesse a glass of tea and sat down on the swing. Addy opened a bottle of water and hiked a hip on the porch railing.

"We could have had one of the hired hands take care of the yard," Pearl said.

Jesse took a long drink. "She needs to work off her anger before we do a job together."

"This something you learned in the Air Force?" Pearl asked.

"It is." Jesse nodded. "I learned it real quick, too. A team is only as good as its members working together, but if there's a problem between two of them, then it has to be settled before the team can go on a mission."

"You would have been a good father all these years," Pearl whispered.

"I'm not so sure of that, but I do know I had some good role models in both you and Dad. We'll get through all this, Mama, and when the time is right, Addy and I will tell her the whole story." He turned to focus on Addy. "How's Dad's blood pressure?"

Addy took another drink of her water. "Surprisingly enough, it's not up too much. He hasn't slept good all week for worrying about that child."

"And you, Mama?" Jesse turned back to her.

"I was thirty years old when we got you," Pearl answered. "I haven't slept good since that day. It's a mother's job to worry about her kids, and you boys all chose paths to travel that have been scary to me. I'm glad you are home, and I wish Cody would come on back and start a practice around here. We have sick people here just like they do in the Sudan or in one of those other places where he goes. And Lucas, running all over God's creation training horses, scares me, too. He's promised us a visit when he gets done in Argentina after the first of the year. I'm looking seventy right in the eye now, and your dad had his seventieth birthday a couple of years ago. We need you kids to be close by."

"I didn't know how much I missed home until I came back for good. When I came in for a visit, there was always a deadline as to how long I could stay. Maybe my brothers will get to the point that they miss it, too," he said.

"We can hope so," Pearl said. "She looks pretty hot. You might take her that bottle of water. It's a shame we have to treat her like this. She's always been so grounded that we could depend on her for anything."

"Sometimes the hardest lessons reap the greatest rewards," Jesse said, "and yes, Mama, I'm speaking from experience."

"Gentle but firm," Pearl said as she started into the house. "That's what she needs most."

"And a little teamwork to teach her to depend on others and be dependable. Thanks for the tea and the visit," Jesse said.

Pearl and Addy both went back into the house. Jesse stood

up, crammed his old straw hat down on his head, and headed out across the yard with the bottle of water in his hand.

"I'll take over for a few laps while you hydrate." He tossed the bottle of water her way. She caught it midair and sat down with her back against a shade tree. "Thanks."

Jesse mowed three laps, leaving the very last one for her, and then motioned for her to take over. "Get that done, and we'll get to work."

"What I've been doing isn't work?" She finished off the water and carried the empty bottle to the trash can on the back porch.

"That was just the warm-up. Now we get to go shovel out stalls that haven't been touched in years, put down fresh straw, and get the barn ready for the days we might need to keep the alpacas inside. I don't know much about them, but I'm willing to learn, and I bet they like to be in out of the heat when July gets here."

She nodded. "We probably should keep them in the barn a couple of days. Then after they get used to the move, we'll let them roam free in this pasture and use the lean-to at the end of the barn for shelter from the heat. If bad weather comes, we'll want to keep them in the stalls."

Mia took a bandanna out of her hip pocket and wiped the sweat from her forehead before she started moving again. When she'd finished the last bit of the backyard, she got out the water hose and cleaned the mower.

Jesse was impressed with her attention to doing a job right. "I bet they're missing the sheep?"

"Probably, but they'll be used to not having them by now," Mia said.

"Dad says they're going to be his pets and breeding stock. We might make some money on them when folks realize they really are good for keeping the coyotes and bobcats away from the lambs." Jesse started out for the barn.

She had to run to catch up, but then her stride matched his, step for step. "Do you think we can ever get into the sheep business again?"

"I doubt it," Jesse said. "Sheep require a lot more care than cattle and don't have nearly the return on the dollar. The only reason Sunflower Ranch ever had sheep to begin with was for you, and you sold out."

"My second mistake," she grumbled. "I was making good money selling lambs to the kids around here for show."

A blast of hot air hit them both when he opened the barn door. "I can't judge you, Mia, since I've made lots of mistakes. Maybe someday if you are still interested in sheep and willing to do the work yourself with them, you can start the business again."

Jesse slid the door open as wide as he could and then crossed the barn to the other side to do the same with the one that led out to the corral. "That might give us a breeze of some kind. You can get a shovel and the wheelbarrow and start on the stalls."

"Are you going to sit on a hay bale and supervise?" she taunted.

"Nope, I'm going out in the corral to string some wire around the fence rails so the babies won't be able to slip out." He took a pair of gloves from a shelf beside the back door and shoved his hands down in them.

She pulled a pair of work gloves from her hip pocket and put them on. The shovel made a clanking sound when she tossed it into the wheelbarrow, and with a huff, Mia stormed off down the aisle to the left, where six stalls awaited.

Tomorrow, they would work together bringing the alpacas over, but today she still needed space.

* * *

"Move, dammit!" Addy fussed at the clock that afternoon. She was busy putting data about the cows into the computer, and the hands on the clock seemed to be stuck, moving as slow as a sleepy sloth.

At four, she finally called Jesse and was about to give up when he answered on the fifth ring. "Is everything all right out there?"

"Yep, I'm getting the corral ready for alpacas, and Mia is working on the last stall. We'll have some panels to get set in place before we come in for supper, but I expect we'll be there by six," he answered. "Are Dad and Mama all right?"

"Sonny is taking a nap in his recliner. Pearl has been making cookies all afternoon. They're having a church bake sale on Saturday afternoon," Addy answered.

"And you?" Jesse asked.

"Sonny asked me to do some data entry, and I sent Grady a mid-week chart. With all the drama, I just want to be sure everything is looking good," she answered.

"Got an answer back on Dad's chart?" His voice calmed her just like it always had.

"Grady said that everything was fine, which was a relief. I would never forgive myself if the stress brought on by all this caused problems with his new medicine regimen. He's really doing good on it," Addy told him. "I should let you get back to your work."

"Probably, but it's good to hear your voice. See you in a couple of hours. Maybe you could come down to the bunk-house and have a cold beer with me tonight. I'll give you the rundown of our day, and you can tell me what's on your mind," he suggested.

"I'd love to. Be there about dark." Her world suddenly seemed brighter.

The next two hours went by a little faster, and when Mia and Jesse came through the back door, Addy was pouring sweet tea over ice in glasses. Mia picked up one, downed it, refilled it and took it to her place at the table, then headed to the bathroom to wash up.

"A little thirsty, are you?" Sonny asked.

"Don't know about her, but I'm spittin' dust." Jesse went to the kitchen sink and washed all the way to his elbows.

"How did she do?" Pearl whispered.

"Worked hard," Jesse answered. "Probably just to show me, but I believe she's worked some anger out, and that's good."

Addy tossed him a towel and then carried the rest of the glasses to the table.

"Thanks. I'd smile but it would take too many muscles. It's been a long day," he said.

"Yes, it has." Mia yawned as she sat down at her normal place at the table. "I'm almost too tired to chew."

Addy sat down beside her. "You've worked this hard before."

"Not after driving for twenty hours, sleeping for maybe four, and crying for another five or six." Mia bowed her head.

After grace, Addy nudged her. "Are you thanking God for a home and a job, or did you fall asleep?"

"If you're asking both of us, I think it was the latter," Jesse answered.

"I heard her snore," Sonny added.

"I'd argue with the lot of you, but I just want to eat, take a shower, go to bed, and sleep until noon tomorrow," Mia said.

"You can do all but that noon thing," Jesse said. "We'll be up early so we can clean out that watering trough and feed bin before we walk the alpacas over here. I want them to think they're coming to a five-star hotel."

Mia took out a big serving of chicken pot pie when Sonny passed it to her. "Don't even talk to me about fancy hotels."

"You didn't like living like a queen?" Addy asked.

"Sure, for about two nights," Mia answered. "Then I saw all my money dwindling away, and it wasn't fun anymore."

"Fun is expensive." Sonny took out a helping of cranberry salad and handed the bowl off to Mia.

"Yep, Poppa, it is, and making the money is harder than spending it, or watching someone else lose it at poker tables. I don't want to talk about that right now," Mia said. "I've been thinking about Justine all afternoon. I'm going to call her in a few days. We need to talk."

"That would be nice of you," Pearl said. "Lots of her friends have turned their backs on her. I'm sure she would appreciate you reaching out. Oh, and before I forget. I've put you down to help with the church bake sale on Saturday afternoon. I think Justine will be there. Maybe you can talk to her then."

"Nana, I can't face the people that soon," Mia whined.

"Yes, you can," Addy said. "And on Sunday morning, you'll be sitting on the pew with us, just like always."

"But Mama, everyone will know what happened," Mia argued.

"They probably knew you were on the way home before we did," Pearl told her. "Ricky O'Malley is a mama's boy who can do no wrong in her eyes. He would have called and told her some big tale about how you broke his heart, and Lylah O'Malley is the biggest gossip in Fannin County."

Addy had gone to school with Lylah back when she was Lylah Green, long before she and Patrick O'Malley married. The girl had been the biggest gossip in town even back then, and marriage had not toned her down one bit. Addy felt sorry for Mia, but her daughter couldn't hide forever.

* * *

Jesse took a shower, put on a clean white shirt and a pair of faded jeans, and sat down on the sofa to wait for Addy. The dust from all the drama of the day had settled, and now it was time for them to talk about what they should do next with their daughter.

"Our daughter," he said out loud for the first time.

"What about a daughter?" Addy startled him when she closed the door and joined him on the sofa. "Do you have other children hiding out there?"

"Nope," he said. "No other kids, boys or girls."

"Are you sure?" Addy pulled her feet up on the sofa and faced him. "You didn't know about Mia, so maybe there's more surprises out there."

"I've been in a couple of relationships, but neither lasted, and both of those women are now married. Their children didn't come along until a couple of years after they got hitched," he answered. "Now that we've got that out of the way, what are we going to do about this parenting thing?"

"Take it a day at a time," Addy said. "You promised me a beer, and I've been looking forward to it all evening."

Jesse stood and rolled his neck to get the kinks out. "Been a while since I fenced that long and hard, but I couldn't let Mia get done with the stalls before I finished the corral. A good boss works every bit as hard as his employees."

He went to the kitchen area and brought back two long-neck bottles of beer, then gave one to Addy. She twisted off the top, took a sip, and set the bottle down on the coffee table.

"Want a massage?" she asked.

"For real?"

"I studied massage therapy after I finished my nursing degree. Sometimes, Sonny needs me to work on the muscles in his calves and back to relieve the pain," she told him.

"I can't see Dad on a massage table."

"I do his massages in a chair, but I have a table. We stored it in what used to be the pantry over there." She pointed toward the door leading into a room where they used to store staples for the hired hands. "If you want a really good neck massage, you can get it out and pop it up. If not, you can just lay on the floor," she said. "Got any lotion or oils in here?"

"Lotion in the bedroom on my nightstand. Do I need a sheet?" He gave her a sly wink.

"Nope, you just need to take off your shirt," she said as she headed toward his bedroom.

"How much is this going to cost me?" He stripped out of his shirt and tossed it over on the sofa.

"How many beers have you got?" she asked.

"Two cases of the regular stuff we like, and a six-pack of Jack Daniel's Watermelon that I picked up when I came through Sherman on the way home." He crossed the room and found the folding table right where she said it would be. He popped it up in the middle of the living area and stretched out with his face in the hole on one end.

She brought a bottle of unscented lotion from the bedroom and squirted some into her hands. "That might be enough to pay for tonight's session, but if you want to book another one in a week, you better make a beer run for another six-pack of that JD Watermelon. I like it a lot, and we can't get it except at liquor stores," she teased as she began a deep massage on his neck.

"Oh, honey, I'll buy a case next time for a massage like this," Jesse groaned.

"You've had massages before, haven't you?" She filled her hands again with lotion and started on his shoulders.

"Only one, and that was two years ago. We'd come in from a tense, ten-day mission and every muscle in my body ached. The doctor on post suggested a massage rather than pain pills. He was right," Jesse said. "You could make big bucks in this area doing this kind of thing."

"I don't need the money, and I'm already committed to being a full-time nurse, part-time ranch hand for Sonny, and a helper for Pearl. Don't have the time or the inclination," she told him.

"That means I get you all to myself. Oh, darlin', right there, that feels so good," Jesse said.

"I hope this place isn't bugged. Can you imagine the rumors if Lylah O'Malley overheard what you just said?" Addy giggled.

"Don't even mention that woman to me," Jesse growled. "I might not have known about Mia until a few days ago, but she's mine, and just the thought of Lylah's son talking her into leaving with him makes me—"

"Tie up in knots," Addy finished for him. "I can feel it in your shoulder muscles."

"She caused trouble between us in high school," Jesse reminded her.

Addy moved down to his sides. "I'd forgotten about that."

"I'll never forget it," Jesse declared. "Those two days were horrible. We didn't talk, and I was so lonesome for you that I couldn't even eat. How could you ever forget?"

"I guess I just packed it away and shut the lid on it, but I remember confronting her about the whole thing. She threatened to whip my ass, and I told her to bring her lunch because it would take all day. The whole thing was something over the Student Council election, right?" Addy asked.

"She said that the reason I won over her was that you counted the ballots wrong, and that I paid you to do it. When I stepped down, you got mad and said she was getting her way, and it made me look guilty. I just wanted to protect you," he said.

Addy moved slowly back up to his neck. "I knew that, but I didn't need protecting, Jesse. I still don't. Maybe that's what's wrong with me. Guys want a pretty little rose, like Mia said, who they can watch over. They don't want a sassy, independent woman who can take care of herself."

"Not me," Jesse said. "I want a woman who loves me for me and who doesn't see a hunky, retired military guy who can field dress wounds."

She slapped him on the shoulder. "Your ego is showing."

"Downright sexy, ain't it?" he teased.

"Yep, and now, your thirty minutes are up, so roll over and put your shirt on before I start hiring you out as a male escort," she told him.

"Will you be my first customer?" he asked as he pulled the shirt over his head.

"Nope. I got a baby when I slept with you the last time. Now, put the table away while I wash my hands and then drink the rest of my beer," she told him.

"Even though she's ornery, sassy, and willful, you wouldn't take a million bucks for her." Jesse broke down the table and put it away. "Thanks for the massage. That was wonderful. I'll sleep really well tonight."

He sank down on the sofa, picked up his beer, and downed the rest of it even if it was warm. "Want another one?" he asked as he got up and headed to the kitchen.

"Yep, one of those JD things," she answered.

Jesse took two from the fridge and twisted the tops off both before he took them to the living area. He handed one to her and then sat down again. "I really like living out here rather than in the house. It gives me privacy, something I haven't ever had before. Cody had gone to college when I left for the Air Force, but Lucas and I were still home, and I've lived in barracks ever since then."

"Why didn't you get an apartment?" she asked.

"Seemed like a waste of money since I would hardly ever be there. Mostly, I was on one mission after another. There's never any rest for a combat medic. Sometimes, I would be in the field six months at a time, and sometimes, for just a few days, but I was never home more than a week at a time," he answered.

"Do you ever have nightmares about the missions?" she asked.

"Not very often. I was fortunate. We only lost one team member, and that was more than ten years ago. He got shot all to hell, and I couldn't patch him up enough to get him back to base. We were over there in the sand box, and he died on the way back. I blamed myself, drank too much, and pretty much fell apart. My captain refused to let me go back out with the guys until I had some therapy." He was telling her things that only his teammates knew, but then he'd always been able to talk to her.

"I'm sorry I wasn't there for you during the rough times," she whispered.

He held his bottle over toward her. The two of them made a clinking noise when they tapped them together. "I could say the same thing, but the two of us are back together now."

"Yes, we are," she said, "and on that note, it's time for me to leave or else sleep on this sofa tonight. I'm emotionally drained from this day, but I want you to know I couldn't have survived it without you."

"This coming from the woman who doesn't need protecting?" he teased.

"I still don't, but I do need a friend to lean on occasionally," she said.

"Give me time to get my boots on, and I'll walk you up to the house," he offered.

"Just to the door is good enough. I know the way home." She smiled.

He stood up and offered her his hand. She downed the rest of her drink, set the empty on the table, and put her hand in his. "Quite the gentleman," she said.

"I'm almost thirty-nine years old, but Mama would still take a switch to me if I was anything but a country gentleman." He kept her hand in his all the way to the door. "Thanks again for the massage and for keeping me company this evening."

"Thanks for the beers and for being here for me," she said.

He tipped her chin up with his fist, looked deeply into her eyes, and kissed her—not a quick brotherly peck on the cheek or forehead, but a scorching hot one that told him that he had deep feelings for Addison Hall.

When the kiss ended, she took a step back and said, "Do you think that's wise?"

"Oh, yeah." He grinned. "I really do. Good night, Addy. See you at breakfast."

* * *

Addy sat down in one of the rockers on the back porch and touched her lips. They felt hot, but they were surprisingly cool. She'd been there only a few minutes when Pearl came out wearing a white cotton nightgown that was six inches too long for her.

"You couldn't sleep either?" She eased down in the chair beside Addy and set a can of root beer on the table between them. "I'm not surprised after this day."

"I had a beer with Jesse," Addy admitted. "I hope that helps me sleep. Is Sonny all right? His blood pressure and everything was good, but I worry that we're causing him too much stress. You will tell me if you think we need to move out into our own place, won't you? There would be no hard feelings, and I would still come out here every day to be your nurse."

Dark clouds shifted over an almost full moon. Thunder rattled off in the distance, and a streak of lightning zigzagged through the sky. For some reason it seemed fitting that the day would end with a storm. It had, after all, started with one.

"If you and Mia left, Sonny would go crazy. Y'all being here and Jesse coming home has helped him more than any new trial things or his medicine possibly could," Pearl said. "Do you think that you and Jesse will ever get together?"

Addy wasn't sure she was ready to even think about such a thing, much less answer the question. "Would we blow an amazing friendship if we did?"

"Did I ever tell you that Sonny and I were best friends when we were growing up? That was back in the days when no one believed a girl and boy could be friends without getting involved." Pearl picked up a farmer's magazine from the table and fanned with it. "The air seems so close when there's a storm brewing, doesn't it?"

"Yes, it does," Addy agreed. "Evidently, y'all became more than friends."

"Oh, yes, we did." Pearl smiled. "We had declared that we would never even kiss each other because that could lead to a relationship, and we couldn't imagine ever losing each other for a friend. But one night, on a hayride, I almost fell off the wagon and he saved me. We had that first kiss and threw caution right out in the pasture. We were married a year later, right here on this ranch. It was called the Ryan Ranch in those days."

Addy was suddenly wide awake and intrigued. "When did it change?"

"They weren't using the bunkhouse in the winter, so we took up housekeeping out there. Sonny's mama took sick in the spring and passed away the first of summer, and his dad, God love his soul"—she stopped and took a drink of her root beer—"couldn't boil water, clean a house, or even do laundry. He offered us the ranch, free and clear, if we'd move into the house with him and help him until he died." Pearl drew her knees up and wrapped the tail of her gown around her ankles. "Sonny's

dad was killed in a tractor accident a year after we moved in, and Sonny inherited the whole place. I had a bouquet of wild sunflowers that Sonny picked for me the day we got married. I saved the seeds from those flowers, and we planted them out there by the gate posts where you turn into the lane. Those reseed the land every year and produce more, reminding us that we are still best friends as well as an old married couple these days."

"That's a beautiful story. Is that where you got Sunflower Ranch then?" Addy asked.

Pearl smiled and nodded. "Sunflowers because I love them, and the new brand became the SR ranch for Simon, or Sonny as he's been known his whole life, Ryan. It all fit together so well that it seemed like it was divine. Now, this old lady has rattled on enough about the past. We should both get some sleep. Good night, Addy, and please don't ever leave us."

"Okay, but only if you promise to tell me if all this turmoil starts to upset Sonny," she agreed.

Addy hurried inside when the first drops of rain blew in from the southwest. She went straight for Mia's bedroom to be sure her daughter was all right. Even as a child, she had hated storms. Last summer, she had still come into Addy's bedroom, dragging her favorite blanket behind her, to sleep on her mother's bed when it stormed.

Staring at her from the doorway, Addy was reminded of just how much she did look like Jesse with all that dark hair and heavy lashes laying on her high cheekbones. She tiptoed across the room just as a flash of lightning lit up Mia's face. Memories flooded Addy's mind like a video of her daughter's life.

The first picture was one of Addy holding Mia on her shoulder while she worked on her college classes. She had taken two weeks off after the baby was born but had kept up with all her assignments—then for the rest of the semester, she had worked with Mia in her arms.

Then there was one of Mia when she had cut her first teeth. Addy and her grandmother had walked the floor with the baby night after night, trying to ease her pain and get her to sleep. Other images followed one after another. Mia when she took her first wobbly steps in the living room, and when she said her first words. With her first sheep and her first blue ribbon, and then sitting on the porch of the house where they'd first lived here in Honey Grove those few months before moving to the ranch.

"Your father missed all that because I didn't tell him about you," she whispered as she tucked the sheet up around Mia's shoulders.

She tiptoed out of the room and eased the door shut, then went to her own bedroom. A flash of lightning jumped out of the sky and seemed to land right below her window when she pulled the curtains back. A glimmer of yellow showed in the bunkhouse window through the rain. Was Jesse having trouble sleeping, too?

Addy sighed as she dropped the curtain and touched her lips again. It was still there—the same sensation she'd felt before. "If I'm honest, I've always loved him for more than a friend. That's probably why I can't seem to last in a relationship with anyone else. I can't give them my heart when he's got it in his pocket."

Chapter Fifteen

Jesse sipped on a cup of coffee as he set the table for breakfast and then got the jams and jellies out of the refrigerator. "Quite a storm last night wasn't it, Dad?" he asked.

Sonny looked up. "I didn't hear a thing, but I did see that we had gotten a little rain when I got my paper off the porch."

Pearl refilled his coffee mug. "Darlin', we had lightning and thunder, and it rained cats and dogs and baby elephants."

"I slept right through it, but you should tell Henry to make a drive around the fences and count the cattle this morning," Sonny said.

"Want me to do that rather than bring the alpacas over?" Jesse asked.

"No, Henry can take care of it. Those animals will be better off over here so we can take good care of them," Sonny answered.

"Will do." Jesse nodded.

"Will do what?" Addy asked as she entered the kitchen. "I should have been up thirty minutes ago to help with breakfast."

"Don't worry about it. Jesse already had coffee made when Sonny and I got in here this morning," Pearl said. "We were talking about that storm last night and bringing the alpacas over here today."

"What storm?" Mia yawned. "I could have slept until noon."

Addy gave her a brief hug. "You *must've* been tired to sleep through that one. You've always been terrified of storms."

Jesse noticed that Mia wiggled free of Addy's embrace and then headed for the coffeepot. She poured herself a cup and carried it to the table without even asking if her mother wanted some. Jesse quickly made Addy a mug full and handed it to her.

"Sorry, Mama." Mia shrugged. "I figured you'd been up long enough to get your own."

"Thank you, Jesse." Addy smiled up at him.

"So are we still walking the alpacas over this morning, or do you want me to do some other stupid jobs?" Mia asked.

"Thin ice," Addy said in a low voice.

"All right," Mia huffed, "other *meaningless* jobs."

"Getting thinner," Addy said.

"Sorry, Jesse," Mia said. "I'll try not to offend anyone else this morning."

"That's better," Addy said.

"Yes, we are moving the alpacas," Jesse answered, "and Mia, there are no stupid or meaningless jobs on a ranch. You should know that by now. Everything that needs to be done is important and deserves our best efforts."

"Whatever." She raised one shoulder in half a shrug, as if he didn't deserve a full one. "Nana, after we get the alpacas over here, I thought I'd help you bake cookies this afternoon."

"You'll have to take that up with Jesse," Pearl said. "Say grace, Sonny, before the gravy gets cold."

Everyone bowed their heads, and Sonny gave the shortest

prayer Jesse had ever heard. When he raised his head, he smiled at Mia. "Honey, your mama can help my precious Pearl make cookies. You are needed on the ranch, but Jesse is the boss."

"Even over Henry?" Mia split a biscuit open and covered it with sausage gravy.

"That's right." Sonny took out a portion of scrambled eggs and passed the bowl on to Pearl. "Even over Henry. Jesse will even be my boss at the end of the summer. He will be running the whole ranch by then."

"What if Cody and Lucas come home?" Mia set the bowl of eggs on the table when they reached her.

"They are all equal owners of Sunflower and will share in the profits, but Jesse will be the boss and get a salary since he'll be working on the place," Sonny explained.

"Who's going to take care of the bookwork?" Mia pressured for more.

"Addy took over when you left us," Pearl answered. "She's going to show Jesse the program in the next few days."

"I messed up pretty bad, didn't I?" Mia added two spoons full of sugar to her coffee.

"Yes, you did, but maybe someday, you'll prove yourself again," Sonny told her.

Mia's gaze across the table at Jesse made him uncomfortable, and he seriously thought about giving her the whole afternoon off to bake cookies. "So what's the verdict... *boss*?" Her tone was so cold that he changed his mind.

"When we get the alpacas over here, we will be driving into town for a load of feed, and then we need to clean as many watering troughs as we can this afternoon. I noticed green algae growing on a couple of them. We also need to put a little oil in the windmill bearings. It was squeaking last time Dad and I made a drive around the fence line. I'm thinking that, tomorrow, we'll help Henry and the hired hands put up new fencing around the property across the road, and Friday, you and I will clean out the shearing shed real good," he answered. "I can't spare a good hand like you to make cookies."

"Yes, sir!" she smarted off.

"I'll try to make sure we're all done by noon on Saturday so you can go to the bake sale with Mama and Addy, though." He smiled brightly.

"We always knock off at noon on Saturday, and pay the hired hands for their week's work," she reminded him.

"You'll be paid for three and a half days of work," Jesse said. "Please pass the eggs. If no one else wants any more, I'll finish them off. We've got a long day ahead of us. Mama, would you fix up some sandwiches for us? I've already got a cooler with bottles of water and tea in the truck. We probably won't have time to come in for dinner."

Mia groaned and filled another biscuit with strawberry jam.

Jesse made a second plate of biscuits and gravy. "This can be a good day or a bad one. I choose for my part to make it a good one because you and I get to work together. It's up to you whatever kind of day you have."

Mia shot him a dirty look. Jesse wondered if she'd be so surly with him if he had been in her life the whole time. She had had a big disappointment because of bad choices. Getting over that and accepting that the blame was as much hers as Ricky's would take time, and hopefully, in the end, she would be ready to accept him as a friend if not a father.

Addy nudged her with a shoulder. "Remember that you put yourself in this position. You can bring yourself up out of it with hard work and determination, but it won't be an overnight or even end-of-summer thing. The choice is yours."

"I don't make good choices anymore," she muttered. "Jesse, you're the only one who isn't totally biased toward me at this table, so you have to choose for me from now on."

"I'm up for it," Jesse said without a moment's hesitation. "Does that include everything, like what you are wearing to church on Sunday, or just boys and job schedule?"

"I can pick out my own clothing and my own food, but if I am going to date another boy, which I'm not for a long time, then you have to check him out first," she said.

"I can do that," Jesse agreed. "But first, tell me in detail why I get the job."

"Poppa, Nana, and Mama have always trusted me to make my own decisions. You are practically a stranger, so you don't know me. I'm good at getting my way, but you are former military so I'm trusting you to see through me like you did this morning. I know my faults, and I loved Ricky for not giving in to me all the time. He did teach me a few things," she answered. "Does that make sense?"

"What on earth did that kid teach you?" Sonny asked.

"Not to trust someone until they earn that trust. That compromise is the basis of a friendship and a relationship. I gave in too quick on every issue and let him have his way because he told me I was pretty. I didn't really want this tattoo, and I've taken my belly ring out to let the holes close up. He wanted me to change to suit him, and I loved him just the way he was until he broke my heart," she said.

The first hard pains of fatherhood hit Jesse right in the heart. He wanted to hug her and protect her from any further hurts. For now, he would have to be content to have her opening up and talking to him without those go-to-hell looks.

"Do I get to stay in and make cookies now?" She almost grinned.

"No, we've got alpacas to move and a fence to build," Jesse answered. "Meet you at the barn in ten minutes."

"Oh, well," she sighed. "Can't blame a girl for trying."

"I can smell saccharine a mile away." Jesse pushed his chair back and carried his plate to the kitchen.

"What's that supposed to mean?" Mia followed him.

"Think about it. All that BS you were just putting out wasn't real sweetness, it was fake. Good try. I'll give you that much." Jesse settled his straw hat on his head.

Mia pushed her own chair back, jumped up and took her plate to the sink, then dashed off down the hall.

Jesse leaned around the corner of the utility room and winked at Addy. "See y'all later. Addy, would you please bring Dad out to the corral to see the alpacas when we get them all over here?"

"Just call either me or Sonny when you are ready," Addy agreed.

Jesse whistled all the way to the barn, where he made a final inspection of the fencing and the stalls. Mia had done a good job in getting them cleaned out and fresh straw put down. He'd checked the books, and according to Dr. Stevie, two of the hembras would be ready to give birth within the next month.

"Things will be ready for them or for any other emergency with them," he muttered. "I think they're an unnecessary expense, but if Dad likes them, then the money doesn't matter."

"Who are you talking to?" Mia asked as she came up to the stall.

"Myself," Jesse answered.

"I hope you're getting good answers." She picked up two ropes and a couple of halters. "You ever handled alpacas before?"

"Once or twice, and I work through some of my problems by talking to myself," he said. "You should try it sometime."

"No, thank you," she said. "Which vehicle are we taking?"

"We'll walk over there," Jesse answered. "I see you've got rope and bridles. I figure we can each bring a hembra and baby the first trip, then we'll have two more trips to get the rest of the ladies over here, and we can bring the macho last."

"What'd you do? Read up on the alpaca lingo?" Mia headed out of the barn.

"Something like that." He followed her outside.

Her stride was long, and she walked like she had somewhere to go. There was no lollygagging around with this girl. "Anyone can know what to call them. It takes experience to know how to handle them, and for your information, Tex could help us herd them over here all at once. He's helped me muster up the sheep before."

"I prefer to move them slower." Jesse put a hand on the fence post and hopped over the barbed wire in one easy jump, only to find out that the ditch between him and the road was filled with water from the rain.

"Be careful," he called out as she made the same jump.

She just gave him one of her famous looks and rolled her eyes. Jesse hopped over the ditch, crossed the road, and jumped over the other fence, then started out on the last quarter mile to the alpaca shed. If the old Hall Ranch had been separated from Sunflower with a dirt road, going from one place to another would have been a lot easier.

"This should have been my ranch," Mia said. "I am the oldest grandchild, so it should have been passed down to me, not sold off."

"Your grandparents probably needed the money to buy out your aunts and uncles' interest in your Granny's ranch out near Cactus," he suggested. "Are you angry because of that?"

"Yes. No. Maybe a little," she said.

"Would you have sold the place if Ricky asked you to?" Jesse asked.

"That's downright mean and harsh." She almost gritted her teeth. "Honestly, I don't know, but we'll never know, will we?"

"How many cousins do you have?" They weren't far

away from their destination now because Jesse could hear the alpacas' strange humming noises as they communicated with each other.

"Uncle Nate has twins who are about eight years old. Uncle Quinn has a daughter who is ten now," she said.

"I remember Nate and Quinn. They were about five years older than us, so they were already gone from home when we were in high school," Jesse said.

"And yet, their kids are younger than me," Mia sighed. "You were always her best friend, right?"

"That's right," Jesse answered about the time they reached the corral. He climbed over the side, looped an arm around one of the mama hembras, and talked softly to her. "We're going to a better place for you. We've got it all cleaned up and ready, and you're going to love it." Mia handed him a bridle, and he gently eased it into place then attached the lead rope.

"Not bad," she said as she did the same with the other mama.

"Thank you. I did a little research on them last night," Jesse said.

The animals were tame enough that it didn't take much to get them separated and out of the corral. Then it was a simple matter of leading them over to their new home. Right up until they reached that ditch full of water, and the hembras set their heels. The crias had been romping behind their mothers like little wind-up toys. When the grown-ups decided that they weren't wading through water and climbing up a hill to a barbed wire fence, the babies balked, too.

"Let's take them on down the road a bit to where the gate is," Jesse suggested.

"If they'd just hop over the puddle, we could lead them down the fence line and we wouldn't have to be so careful with the crias and the traffic," Mia said.

"If plan A doesn't work, we move to plan B. If we hear a

car, we may have to carry the babies until it gets past us." Jesse slipped an arm around his alpaca and whispered in her ear.

"Now you are an alpaca whisperer?" Mia asked.

"Nope, but that mama told me that she'd prefer to go down the road rather than jump the ditch. It's only a few hundred yards." Jesse tugged gently on the lead rope, and the animal followed him.

Sure enough, when they got to the place where Jesse could open the gate, the alpaca sailed over the ditch and then turned around and called its baby to it. The cria ran up and down the ditch and then made a jump, landed on the other side, and nuzzled against its mama's neck. Crazy animals, Jesse thought. but then realized the first place had water in it and that's probably what spooked the alpaca.

Mia hopped over the water, tugged on the lead rope, and her animal made the leap. When the baby started over, it misjudged the distance and landed neck deep in the water. The mother panicked and pulled against her rope, and the other female became agitated.

Jesse handed both ropes to Mia and waded right out in the water to get the baby, put it on his shoulders, and started up the slippery slope. He'd only gone a step or two when he fell backward into the water, but he managed to hold the cria up high enough to keep water from getting in its little nose.

In seconds, Mia had tied the two mother alpacas to a fence post and waded out into the water to get the cria. She managed to get it up onto dry land so it could run to its mama for comfort before she made a misstep and landed firmly on her butt in the water right beside Jesse.

"I'm sure glad this is not mud." Jesse stood in water nearly to his knees. "I'm cooled off. How about you? Getting those mamas tied up was fast thinking. You did good."

Mia got to her feet. "Aren't we going to go to the house and get into dry clothes?"

"Nope," Jesse answered. "We've got three more trips to get the animals crossed over. Why change when we might have the same problem next time?"

She kicked at the water, sending a spray all over him.

He chuckled and did the same right back at her.

Before long, they were soaked from head to toe, and Jesse was sure that the folks back at the ranch could hear their laughter.

She reached out and gave him a push, and he fell backward to sit in waist-deep water. He grabbed her by the ankle and pulled her down beside him.

She looked over at him and grinned. "Bet I can beat you to the top of the ditch," she challenged.

Before he could answer, she jumped up and scaled the slippery bank like a monkey going up a tree. Jesse had to concentrate to get up to the top without falling backward, but he made it on the first try. He poured the water out of his boots, put them back on and untied his hembra from the post. "Come on, pretty lady. The worst part is over. From here, it's clear sailing to your new five-star home. Hey, Mia, close the gate before you untie your animal."

"Yes, sir...*boss*!" Her tone was cold but not quite as bad as it had been that morning.

"Progress," he muttered under his breath.

She had to hustle to catch up to him, and when she did, the first words out of her mouth were, "So you and mama were, like, friends and nothing more?"

His worry radar shot up into the red zone. "Why are you asking?"

"She never mentioned you one time when I was growing up. I didn't even know you existed until we moved in with Poppa and Nana. They told me that you and Mama were inseparable until you went to the Air Force right out of high school. What happened that y'all didn't stay friends?" Mia asked.

"Time and distance," Jesse answered.

"Since you came home, y'all are good friends again, right? I know that she tells you stuff, and you tell her things," Mia said.

"Yes, that's right." Jesse wondered where she was going with this line, so he answered with as few words as possible.

"So," Mia sucked in a lungful of air, and then blurted out, "has she told you who my father is, or does she even know? Was she sleeping around with more than one guy, and is that the reason she's never told anyone?"

"Yes and no," Jesse answered.

"What does that mean?" Mia frowned.

"It means that I will never lie to you. Yes, I know who your father is. Yes, your mother knows who he is. No, she has never been a person who sleeps around. You were conceived out of deep love between two people," Jesse answered.

Mia stopped in her tracks and locked eyes with him. "Who is it? I have a right to know."

"Yes, you do, but it's not my place to tell you. Your mother has worked hard to make sure you have a good life, so she should be the one to tell you, and I'm sure she will when she feels like the time is right," Jesse answered.

"I don't like you so much," she said.

"Well, darlin', I'm not too fond of you either," he said. "But maybe we can remedy that in the future."

"Why should we?" she asked.

"Because working for a boss you like is a lot easier than working for one you hate," he answered.

* * *

Addy drove Sonny out to the barn after dinner so he could see the alpacas. She set up a folding chair for him and wrestled a bale of hay out of the enclosure so he could prop his feet up. The two babies ran back and forth from their mothers to inside the barn, where they checked out every corner. At the faintest sign of something strange, they took off back to their mamas for protection.

"Nosy little devils, aren't they," Sonny chuckled.

The small side door at the end of the stalls opened and Jesse waved. "Hey, y'all. I thought I might find you out here. What do you think, Dad? Do we need to do anything different?"

"Just keep the big doors that lead out into the pasture closed for a few days," Sonny said. "I'm thinking maybe we need to rope off a section on that side for them, rather than turning them out in the whole twenty acres."

"I'll get Henry and the boys on it the first of the week." He closed the door tightly and started down the aisle separating the stalls.

Addy's heart pounded with each step that he took toward them. She stared at his lips and wished they were alone so she could see if another kiss would be as hot as the one they'd shared.

"How much trouble was it to get them over here?" Sonny asked.

"Tell you in a minute." He went straight for the tack room and returned with three bottles of cold water. "It's hot in here even with that little breeze. You need to stay hydrated, Dad." He handed the first bottle to Sonny and the second one to Addy. "So do you. We can't have either of you dropping from heat stroke." He sat down beside Addy and chuckled. "Mia and I both got cooled off on the first trip, but we're pretty well dried out now, except my boots are still a little sloshy." He went on to tell them the story about the ditch.

Sonny laughed until he got the hiccups, and tears rolled down his cheeks. "I would love to have seen that. You do know you could have loaded them in a trailer and brought them over in less than an hour, don't you?"

"And miss all that fun?" Jesse chuckled with him, and then grew serious. "She tried to manipulate me into telling her who her father is, Addy."

Her breath caught in her throat and she forced herself to remember how to breathe. "And?"

"She played on the fact that we were best friends and asked me if I knew who it was. I told her I would never lie to her, that I knew but that I wouldn't tell her because it wasn't my place," he told her.

"Good answer," Addy said. "She needs a few weeks to get over this thing with Ricky before we tell her."

"I agree," Jesse said. "Got to get back to the fencing. See y'all at supper."

"I think I'm ready to go, too, Addy," Sonny said. "Heat is a little worse than I thought it would be. Just put my chair over behind the panels by the hay. I'll probably be ready to come back in the morning when it's cooler."

See you later? Jesse mouthed at Addy over the top of Sonny's head as he headed toward the tack room.

She gave him a brief nod and handed Sonny his cane. Tonight, she would get the full story of what all happened between Jesse and Mia, but that was secondary to the idea that she would get to spend time with him—alone.

* * *

Jesse picked up another wire stretcher from the shelf and walked with his dad and Addy out to her SUV. He held his dad's cane while Sonny hiked a hip into the passenger seat and grabbed a hold of the hand grip on the ceiling.

"All settled?" Jesse asked.

"Yep, but it gets harder to get in and out of a vehicle every time," Sonny admitted. "Don't wait until you are past seventy to retire, son. Do it as soon as you can and enjoy a few years when you can travel."

Jesse patted him on the shoulder and stretched the seat belt over his chest. "Been there, done that already, Dad. I'm ready to do ranchin' work until I drop now. Fasten this thing. Addy's always driven too fast."

"That's the pot calling the kettle black. I've never had to call Sonny to bring the tractor and get me out of a ditch," she smarted off to him.

"Hey, don't go draggin' up the dead bones of old mistakes." Jesse flashed a brilliant smile across the top of the SUV.

"Then don't make me," she said with a grin.

He tossed the stretcher over into the back of his truck, got in, and drove across the pasture to where Henry, Mia, and the summer help were all working on putting up a new fence and taking down the rotted old wooden posts. Mia came over to the truck and got the stretcher and jogged back.

"You and Pete tighten up this length while me and these other two boys get the next few posts in the ground," Henry said.

Pete whipped off his cowboy hat and wiped sweat from his brow with a bandanna he pulled from his hip pocket. "Put me with someone else. I'm not working with her. She's ruined our family by dragging Ricky off to Las Vegas. Mama is crying because he won't come home, and Daddy is mad all the time. He says he'd sue her if he could afford a lawyer."

Mia didn't waste a bit of time getting right up in Pete's face. "It was Ricky's idea to go to Vegas, and he went through thousands of my dollars at the poker tables, then ran off with another woman and left me stranded. How can this be my fault?"

"He told Mama that he felt sorry for you, and you begged

him to move in with you. Then you promised him anything he wanted if he'd go to Vegas with you. You're the reason he flunked out of college last semester and why he left town. You ain't no better than that slut Justine, who says her baby belongs to him." Pete jacked his chin up a notch so that he was looking down at Mia. "Daddy says I can work here, but I'm to stay away from her."

Mia's hand knotted into a fist, and she drew it back to deck Pete, but Jesse closed his big hand around it and held tight. "Pete, you collect your gear, whatever it is, and go home. Don't bother coming back. The next time you even remotely insult Mia, I won't hold her back from knocking you on your ass."

Pete turned around and stomped back toward the house, then he turned with a sneer and said, "You'll be sorry you did this to us, Mia. Ricky is a good guy, and he just felt sorry for a big old plain girl like you. You shouldn't have ruined his life."

"We've got fences to build before quittin' time," Mia said through clenched teeth, "so let's get with it. Thanks, Jesse, for standing up for me."

"Anytime," he said, then turned to the other three guys. "Any of you have something to say?"

"No, sir," Tommy said. "I'm glad you fired him. I got tired of hearing him bad-mouth Mia. We all know what kind of person Ricky is."

"Then we'll all get back to work," Henry said. "Jesse, why don't you help Mia with the wire while we put down some more posts?"

"Be glad to," Jesse agreed.

As soon as the others were out of hearing, Mia turned around and glared at Jesse. "Why didn't you let me hit him? He deserved it."

"Yes, he did, and it took all the willpower I could muster to keep from knocking him cold myself, but think about it, Mia,"

Jesse answered, "if you had hit him, Patrick O'Malley would have brought assault charges against you, and that would feed the gossip that Lylah is spreading. We want it to go away, not keep spreading like weeds in a pasture."

"You're right, but it would have felt good to put him on the ground." She shoved her hands down into her gloves.

"You'll have your chance, but when it comes around, do it with your brain, not with your fists," Jesse advised.

"What does that mean?" Mia asked.

"You'll figure it out," Jesse answered and changed the subject. "Your feet dried out yet?"

"Nope, but I've kind of gotten used to the warm slushy feeling of wet socks." She smiled. "How about you?"

"Same here. Are you thirsty?" He pulled a bottle of water out of his hip pocket and handed it to her.

"Thanks," she said as she opened it and downed a third of it before tucking it away in the back pocket of her jeans. "Now let's get this wire stretched. We can probably catch up with the other crew by suppertime if we work hard."

A little more progress, Jesse thought.

Chapter Sixteen

Addy had spent the afternoon in the office and was more than ready to get out of the house that evening after supper. She ran a brush through her shoulder-length hair and twisted it up on the top of her head with a wide hair clamp. She didn't bother with makeup, since the only place she was going was to the pharmacy to pick up the next month's supply of medicine for Sonny. She was looking forward to some time alone to think about whatever this was with Jesse, and how to tell Mia that Jesse was her father.

A blast of heat hit her in the face when she stepped outside that evening. Mia was sitting in the porch swing. Jesse had just rounded the end of the house with Tex right beside him.

"Hey, where are you going?" Mia asked.

"Got to make a run to the pharmacy in Bonham," Addy answered without slowing down.

"Hold up," Mia said. "I'll go with you if we can stop at the ice cream store afterwards. I've been wanting a hot fudge sundae for days."

"My treat and I'll even drive if I can crash the party," Jesse offered.

So much for a nice quiet evening to think before she took a walk down to the bunkhouse after dark. "Can't turn down an offer like that," she said.

Addy expected Mia to say that she'd just stay home if Jesse was going, and then Jesse would suddenly remember that he had something he needed to take care of somewhere on the ranch so the two women could have some time together. But neither happened.

The swing looked a little lonely when Mia left it going back and forth, and poor old Tex pouted when Jesse told him that he had to stay home. Mia rushed out to Jesse's truck and got into the backseat. Evidently, things weren't going well enough for her to call shotgun and ride next to him all the way to Bonham.

Jesse stuck his head in the door and yelled, "Hey, Mama. Addy, Mia, and I are going to Bonham. Y'all need anything?"

"Just Sonny's medicine." Pearl's voice floated out to the porch.

Tex dashed into the house while the door was open, and Addy felt much better about leaving the poor old boy behind. She got into the vehicle and fastened her seat belt. "After that big supper, I shouldn't have an ice cream sundae, but I'm going to," she said.

"Me, too, but it sounds so good on a hot night like this," Mia said. "Poor old Tex. I bet he misses his rides to the feed store when Poppa was able to drive."

"I'm sure he does," Jesse said as he slid behind the steering wheel. "Dad used to take Tex's daddy with him before Tex was born. Addy, do you remember Hondo?"

"Oh, yeah." Addy smiled. "He came over and bred our dog on Hall Ranch. Daddy wasn't happy about it since his dog was a registered blue heeler, and Sonny didn't know exactly what Hondo's blood lines were."

"At least Tex knows who his father was, even if Hondo didn't have a pedigree," Mia said.

Addy turned around enough that she could see Mia. "And we're not having this conversation tonight."

"Oh, all right!" Mia huffed. "If you won't talk to me about that, then can I have a consolation prize and not have to go to the bake sale?"

"Not happening," Addy said.

"All right then, can I have a banana split instead of a sundae?" Mia pressured.

"That's doable," Jesse said. "I was thinking of having one myself. I have an incurable sweet tooth, and ice cream is my favorite dessert."

"Did you know that about Jesse, Mama?" Mia asked.

"She knows everything about me." Jesse smiled.

Except how I feel about him, Addy thought.

Jesse had to slow down just slightly to go through Windom and Dodd City, two little communities that each had less than four hundred people. Addy remembered spending lots of Saturday nights in an old barn halfway between the two little towns. That's where the teenagers went to drink beer, turn up the radio on Jesse's old pickup truck, and dance to the music. That's where they had both lost their virginity—but not to each other—and where Addy had gotten drunk for the first time when her first had dropped her for another girl. It's where Jesse held her hair back for her when she threw up, and where he held her while she cried over the breakup.

"Bet I could read your mind right about now," Jesse said as he drove past the WELCOME TO BONHAM sign.

"Probably so." She smiled at him.

"What?" Mia looked up from her phone. "What are y'all talking about?"

"Where did you kids go to party on Saturday nights?" Addy asked.

"That's classified." Mia went back to whatever game she was playing.

Jesse pulled into the pharmacy parking lot and said, "I'll run in and get the medicine." He was out of the truck and halfway across to the pharmacy door before Addy could gather her thoughts together and argue with him.

"What's it like to have Jesse for a guy friend?" Mia asked.

"Pretty nice," Addy said. "They aren't as whiny as girls, and they are pretty straightforward. Wasn't Ricky your friend before you became more involved?" She winced at the visual of that boy even kissing her daughter.

"Ricky was my first love," Mia said. "I was afraid to have sex in high school like all the other girls were doing because I didn't want to wind up getting pregnant like you did. I don't want children until I finish college, do something exciting and other fun things."

"I see." Addy remembered saying something like that when she was only a little younger than Mia.

A person supposedly never forgot their first love or their first sexual experience. *Not so*, Addy thought. *I can remember Mason Jones very well and the pain I felt when he broke up with me, but I wouldn't want to be with him, or for him to be Mia's father. The one I can't forget is Jesse. It's always been Jesse, but we're right back where we were all those years ago except for a few kisses. I like having my friend back, but I'm worried that what he really feels is guilt about Mia.*

"Mama, what are you thinking about?" Mia asked. "You look like you're a million miles away."

"You mean like you do when I'm talking, and you don't even look up from your phone?" Addy asked.

"Point taken," Mia said.

Jesse jogged across the parking lot and got into the cool truck. "Man, it's hot out there. Got that job done. Now it's time for ice cream. Want to go inside the store, or get it at the drive-by and eat in the truck?"

"Truck, please," Mia answered.

"Too messy," Addy said. "Let's go inside and eat at a booth."

"Ma—ma," Mia whined.

"Got to face the outside world sometime," Addy told her.

"What if Lylah or Pete is in there?" Mia asked.

"Smile sweetly, say hello, and walk away from them," Addy advised.

"I'd rather knock Pete through the glass window," Mia said.

"Mama always told me to pray for my enemies," Jesse said.

Addy bowed her head and said, "Dear Lord, I've been reminded that I should pray for my enemies. Please open Lylah's eyes to see that her son isn't the guy she thinks he is, and while you are doing that, can you make her mute for a few weeks, so she won't spread gossip about me and mine. And one more thing, Lord, forgive me for what I will do if she gets all up in my space about my daughter. Amen."

"Amen!" Mia giggled. "Now that's a prayer I can get into. Let's go get some ice cream."

Jesse slid a sly wink at Addy. "Mama just said pray for them. I never thought about a prayer like that."

"It does put a whole new spin on talking to God," Mia giggled.

Addy hadn't heard her daughter laugh like that in ages. Hopefully, that meant her old Mia was coming back, and that hateful girl who had recently taken over her body was on her way out.

"Motherhood brings out a whole different side to a woman," Addy said as Jesse snagged a parking spot close to the front door of the ice cream shop. "God must've heard me because the ice cream shop has only one elderly couple in there tonight."

Mia hopped out of the backseat and beat both her mother and Jesse into the cool store. "Slowpokes," she teased as she waited in front of the counter to order. "Y'all are getting so old."

"Hey, now, I kept up with you all day, didn't I?" Jesse argued.

She cocked her head to one side. "That's because I took pity on such an old man and went slow so you could keep up."

Jesse made the same gesture, and Addy held her breath for a brief second for fear that Mia would see the similarity between them.

"I was going slow so you wouldn't feel bad," Jesse assured her.

"Yeah, right!" Mia turned toward the young man behind the counter and told him what she wanted on her banana split. Then she went to a booth and took out her phone again.

"You two have the same expressions," Addy whispered.

"Our eyes are alike, too," Jesse said out the side of his mouth. "She's going to figure it out, Addy. We need to tell her soon."

"Maybe next week," Addy agreed. "But for tonight, let's just enjoy the fact that she's not biting our heads off."

Jesse carried the tray with three banana splits on it to the booth and passed them out according to what each of them had ordered. Addy could tell that he wasn't quite sure where to sit since she was on one side and Mia on the other.

"You can sit beside me," Addy said as she dipped deep into her ice cream.

"Thanks." Jesse slid in beside her.

Thank God for cold ice cream, Addy thought when his hips and thighs were pressed against hers. *I bet if I dropped a spoonful on my leg, it would sizzle.*

Mia only took time away from her ice cream to text on her

phone. Addy sent up a serious prayer that she wasn't getting or sending messages to Ricky. Finally, when she could stand it no longer, she asked, "Who are you so involved with on the phone?"

"Well, it's damn sure not Ricky, Mama, so don't worry your head over that," she answered. "I've been playing a game, not talking to anyone. The truth of the matter is Ricky said he didn't like sharing me with other people, so I kind of lost my friends. They all told me he wasn't a good man, but I didn't listen, and now I'm out here in the world with no one."

"That's not true," Jesse argued. "You've got me and your mama, Poppa and Nana, and Henry. And, honey, you can make new friends or maybe even rekindle old ones if you reach out to them."

"I was rude to most of them," Mia admitted.

"It doesn't take much to apologize and tell them that they were right," Addy told her.

"Maybe later," Mia said. "Right now, I'm on level nine of this game, and if I can get to ten, then I'll be higher than Ricky ever got, and that's important to me."

"Well, then get after it," Jesse chuckled. "Beat him however you can if it makes you feel better."

Addy could have kissed Jesse right there in front of the elderly couple who were heading out of the store, her daughter, and even God right then. She just kept shoveling banana split into her mouth instead and wishing that it would cool off all the heat that Jesse was causing by sitting so close to her.

* * *

Dark had settled around the county and brought with it a nice cool breeze, taking the temperature down at least ten degrees when they finished eating their ice cream and went back out to the truck. Mia hadn't even looked up from her game when they drove through Windom.

Addy was staring out the front window without seeing a thing when suddenly she realized that a car was swerving across the yellow line and coming right toward them. "Holy crap!" she squealed.

"What?" Mia dropped her phone, covered her head, and screamed.

Jesse turned the wheel hard to the right, sending Addy and Mia into a hard lean and then whipping them back upright as the truck went nose first into a ditch full of water. The other vehicle grazed the backside of Jesse's truck and slid, back end first, into the same ditch only a few feet away.

"Is everyone all right?" Jesse's voice sounded like it was coming from the bottom of a rain barrel.

"I'm fine," Mia said, "but I can't find my phone."

"I'm good. Let's get out of here and see if those other folks are hurt." Addy unfastened her seat belt. If she hadn't braced herself with her hands, her head would have hit the dashboard. Jesse was already out of the truck and knee deep in water when she opened the door.

"Are you sure you're all right?" he asked.

"I'm good. Go see about those folks," Addy said.

A loud scream pierced the air, and Jesse disappeared in a blur.

"Mia, get out easy, and be sure nothing hurts or is broken," Addy cautioned.

Another scream came from the other vehicle and a man's voice begging Jesse to help him get his wife out of the car first. Adrenaline rushed through Addy's veins and her nursing training kicked in. She sloshed through the water to the car, found a very pregnant woman lying back in the seat with her hands on her stomach and screaming at the top of her lungs.

"Can you walk?" Addy asked.

"This baby is coming right now," she yelled.

"But are you hurt?" Addy glanced over her shoulder to be sure that Mia was walking all right and not holding a shoulder or an arm.

"No, but this baby is coming out of me." The woman reached out through the open window and grabbed Addy's hand in a death grip.

Jesse and the driver slipped and slid in the mud and water several times before they made it around to the other side of the car. Addy forced the woman to let go of her hand, and then Jesse opened the door. The seat belt was stuck, so Jesse cut it away with his pocketknife, and then he picked the woman up like a baby.

"What can I do?" her husband asked.

"Stay up on the top of the ditch and let me pass her up to you," Jesse said. "Then we're going to lay her down flat and call an ambulance. Mia, call 911."

"No time for an ambulance. I've had three kids, and I know when they're crowning," the woman said between gasps.

"I'm a nurse, and Jesse is a combat medic. We'll take care of you until the ambulance gets here," Addy tried to reassure her.

"I don't care if you're Minnie and Mickey Mouse, just help me get this baby out," the woman said.

"I'm sorry," her husband said as he took her from Jesse.

Mia reached out and slipped Addy's phone from her mother's hip pocket and made the call. "Ambulance is on the way. They said no more than ten minutes. I can help. I've pulled calves and delivered alpacas and lambs. What do I do?"

"Give me the lace from the sleeve of your shirt. Is there a dry blanket or shirt anywhere in either vehicle?" Addy asked. "And I need a match or cigarette lighter."

The husband pulled a lighter from his pocket. "What's that for?" he asked.

"Give it to me," Jesse said. "I'll sterilize my pocketknife with fire."

"I'm Walter Johnson, and this is my wife, Gloria," the guy said.

"Mia, would you please grab that blanket out of the backseat of my truck," Jesse said as he helped the woman out of the car.

She hurried to the truck, brought back the blanket, and spread it out on the grass.

"She's only been in labor an hour or so. I don't think…" the husband said.

"Walter, I know when a baby is coming," Gloria yelled and drew her knees up. "I'm going to push…"

Addy dropped to her knees. "My name is Addison Hall. This is my daughter, Mia, and Jesse is the man who took you out of the car. I'm going to check you right now to see how far you are. If you can keep from pushing for just a few minutes…"

"I can't," Gloria huffed.

Addy tried to keep the woman's dignity as she raised her wet gauze skirt. "You are right. This baby is coming, and it's time to push, ambulance or no. Take a deep breath with the next contraction and give it all you've got. Mia, have you got that string ready for me?"

Mia held it up. "And it's even dry."

Gloria sucked in all the air she could and pushed. "Is she here?"

"Not quite. She's got lots of black hair, though," Addy answered. "One more, and we'll see if we can get the shoulders out, then it'll be easy going."

Mia knelt beside her mother. "You must love me a lot to have gone through this."

"Yes, I did, and yes, I do," Addy said. "I've got an arm.

And now another one. We're almost there, Gloria, and I hear sirens."

"I wanted drugs," Gloria huffed. "I've never done this without drugs."

"You're doing great." Walter kissed her on the forehead. "Just give me one more good one."

The ambulance came to a screeching halt right beside the two vehicles. The back doors swung open, and the paramedics brought out a stretcher. They shifted Gloria over onto it, and in minutes, had moved her from the ground to inside the back of their vehicle.

The two of them seemed to be everywhere at once, and when the next push finished bringing a squalling baby into the world, they had the right equipment to cut the cord, wrap the newborn in a clean blanket, and hand her to the mother. Just like that, it was over, and Addy felt cheated that she hadn't got to finish the job.

"You the father?" One of them looked at Jesse.

"No, this man right here is." Jesse patted Walter on the back. "Go on with her."

"My car?" he moaned. "I'm so, so sorry for all this. A skunk ran across the road, and I swerved to miss it. I didn't want Gloria to have to smell that all the way to the hospital."

"I understand," Jesse said. "Where do you live? I'll call a wrecker and have them take it to your front yard."

"Thanks, man. I live in Dodd City just a block off the highway. I own Walter's Auto Shop. Just have them put it there, and send me the bill," Walter said as he crawled into the ambulance.

"We'll send another one for you folks," the paramedic said.

"Don't bother." Addy waved him away. "We're all fine."

The ambulance sped away and Mia sat flat down on her

butt. "Did that really happen or am I having a nightmare? I can't ever do that, Mama. I just can't."

"You've pulled calves and helped alpacas and sheep. Birthing is birthing," Addy told her.

"No way. You'll have to adopt your grandbabies," Mia told her.

"You'll change your mind, and don't you ever say that in front of Pearl and Sonny," Addy said.

"Why?" Mia rubbed her shoulder.

"Think about it." The adrenaline rush dissipated and left Addy feeling flat. She sat down on the side of the road and put her head between her knees.

"Oh! Because they adopted their three boys." Mia dropped down beside her mother. "Are you all right, Mama? Did you bump your head? Jesse, call the hospital, and tell them to send that other ambulance."

Jesse whipped around and dropped to his knees in front of Addy. He cupped her cheeks in his big hands and raised her head. "I don't think you have a concussion, but it would be good to get all of us checked." He started to get his phone out of his shirt pocket.

Addy reached up and touched his hand. "I'm fine. It was just the adrenaline leveling out. I've delivered babies, but never on the side of the road and without some decent supplies. I can't tell you what all went through my mind."

"But you were so calm," Mia said.

"So were you and Jesse, but I could tell y'all were on edge," Addy said. "I'm fine. Don't call an ambulance. We're probably all going to have seat belt bruises, but we don't need to go to the hospital for that. They'll heal in time."

Mia rubbed her shoulder again and stared at the two vehicles. "What if we both hadn't swerved? We could have had a head-on crash. Jesse, you were wonderful during all of it."

"It was all instinct and training," Jesse said.

At the thought of perhaps losing Mia and Jesse in a split second, Addy's hands began to tremble, and tears dammed up behind her eyes. She refused to cry. Mia needed a strong mother at times like this. "Jesse, you better call that wrecker, and then call Henry," she said. Planning always made her feel in control. "Start out by telling him that we're all fine, but to let the folks know what's happened. If they see a wrecker coming down the lane, Sonny's liable to have a heart attack."

"Good idea." Jesse whipped out his phone and made the calls.

Mia draped an arm around her mother. "What if something like that would have happened when Ricky and I were going to Las Vegas? He drove so fast that it scared me sometimes, and he even played chicken a few times with folks on the road."

Addy opened her mouth, but words wouldn't come out past the tightness in her throat and in her chest. Finally, she managed to say, "Thank God, you came to your senses and came home."

"But that's just the thing, Mama. I didn't come to my senses. I would still be with him if he hadn't left me. He had that kind of power over me. He made me believe that it was my sole duty on earth to please him. How can a person do that to someone that they keep saying they love?" Mia asked.

Jesse finished making his calls and sat down on the other side of Mia. "I heard the last of what you said, honey. That's not love. It's manipulation and control. Ricky is a con man, and he'll only get worse as he gets older."

"Until today, if he'd called me and asked me to meet him somewhere, I would have gone," Mia admitted.

"What changed your mind today?" Jesse asked.

Mia picked at the green grass around her and hesitated so long that Addy thought she was going to ignore the question. The only noise around them was a rangy old bull who had come up to the pasture fence on the other side of the ditch. Every few minutes he snorted loudly as if telling them to get away from his area.

"In that instant when I didn't know if we were going to live, I realized that Ricky had carved away so much of who I am, that the wrong person was about to die," Mia finally said. "Does that make sense?"

"More than you'll ever know," Jesse answered.

She swiped a tear away with the back of her hand. "I don't want to be remembered as that girl he created, but as the girl who had a backbone and made her own decisions. I wish I'd never gotten this tattoo, but it will always remind me to never think that I have to . . ." She wiped another tear. ". . . to do anything a guy wants me to do to be his girlfriend. I'm just lucky he ran away with that other girl. I hated her at first for taking him from me. Now I feel sorry for her."

Addy hugged her tightly. "I'd send her a thank-you card if I knew her name."

"He'd better stay out of Honey Grove for a long time," Jesse said through clenched teeth.

"I hear a truck coming around the curve." Mia pointed. "That didn't take long, and, Jesse, he's not worth going to jail over. We need to forget him and move on."

The sound of a big truck filled the air, and then the wrecker came around the slight curve and stopped. A bald man with a full gray beard opened the door and yelled, "Which one you want me to take care of first?"

"The truck, and if we could ride with you back to Honey Grove, that would be great," Jesse told him.

"No problem. That's why I've got a backseat in this thing," he said. "By the way, I'm Tommy Forestall. Y'all crawl on up in there. I'll get this thing hitched up and we'll be on our way." He hopped out of the vehicle. "After you get your wife and her sister up in the truck, you could put these up on either side of us to stop the traffic for a few minutes." He handed Jesse a stack of orange cones. "Don't want someone to come around that curve and make a mess of my new wrecker. Honey Grove, huh? Do you know Sonny Ryan?" the guy asked.

"That's my dad," Jesse answered.

"Good guy. I graduated from Honey Grove High School with him all them years ago. We had us some good times together. Maybe I'll just run in and say hello to him when we get there," Tommy said.

"I'm sure he would like that." Jesse set the cones down and helped Addy and Mia up into the backseat of the wrecker.

"Why didn't you tell him that I'm not your wife?" Addy whispered.

"Then I'd have to explain that Mia is your daughter, not your sister, and that would just complicate things." Jesse grinned.

When he'd closed the door, Mia fastened her seat belt and then asked, "Did you ever think about dating Jesse before he went to the Air Force?"

"Like I've told you before, we were best friends," Addy answered. "You don't ruin something that important with a fling."

"Too bad," Mia said. "It might have led to something pretty nice for both of you, but then what do I know? I let Ricky lead me around like a puppy on a leash."

Addy laid a hand on Mia's knee. "But now, you've broken that leash, and you will never make that mistake again."

"Other than this damned tattoo, I don't want anything to ever remind me of him again." Mia sighed.

Jesse got into the passenger seat. "I heard what you just said. Just forget him, darlin', and move on with your life. One bad choice doesn't have to define you."

"Thanks, Jesse," Mia said.

"Amen," Addy added.

Chapter Seventeen

*J*esse paced the bunkhouse floor that evening, his nerves strung like a rubber band stretched to the breaking point. All he could think about was that rotten Ricky O'Malley and what he'd done to Mia. Jesse was seething when Addy came through the door and crossed the floor, wrapped her arms around him, and held him close.

"I need to feel your arms around me," she said. "I'm still reeling from everything. I thought that the drama we'd been through was the toughest we would ever see, but I was wrong."

Jesse wrapped her in his arms and held her so close that he could feel the calming effect of her heart beating in unison with his. "I've been in really tough situations, Addy. Some to the point that I wanted to kill whoever had hurt my buddies so badly, but never have I felt such anger as I did today when Mia told us how controlling Ricky had been with her."

"Me, too, and I needed to be close to you tonight to calm this roller coaster of emotions that's making me want to cry one minute and hurt a spoiled boy the next," she whispered.

Jesse slipped one arm under her knees and the other around her shoulders, picked her up, and carried her to the sofa. He sat down, keeping her in his lap. "How on earth did Ricky play at the poker tables anyway? He's only nineteen, right?"

"I'm sure he and Mia both have fake IDs," Addy answered, "just like we did when we were their age. Only we just wanted to drink beer and dance at the honky tonks."

"How did our parents survive us?" Jesse sighed.

"We must be paying for our raising." Addy looked up into his eyes.

"If we are, then I worry about any children that Mia might have, even if they are *bought* children like me and my brothers," Jesse said.

"She speaks before she thinks." Addy blinked and focused on something across the room.

Jesse leaned forward and kissed her on the forehead. "We did too when we were young and stupid. Still do sometimes. No worries. I seldom ever think of us as being foster kids and then adopted."

"Neither do Sonny and Pearl," Addy said. "I should 'fess up to something. When I had Mia, things didn't go well. She was a big baby, ten pounds and three ounces, and I had a lot of problems. The doctors had to do an emergency hysterectomy when she was two days old. Maybe the fact that I couldn't have more made me hold her a little too close. She should have had her wild streak when she was in high school so that I could have still been here for her."

Jesse tipped her chin up again. "I'm sorry that you had to go through that alone."

"I survived with Granny's help, and even kept up with my online classes," she said and moved out of his lap to go to the kitchen. "I thought you should know. Want a beer?"

"Yes, please," he answered. "Since we're confessing, I've

always had a fear of having kids," Jesse said. "I was given away by my parents. They were both very young from what I found out when I looked into it. I investigated a little deeper and learned that they're both dead. I've wondered if they were like Ricky—reckless and dangerous, and if that gene would come through if I had kids. Then there's always the thought that if I did father a child, I wouldn't want it after it was born. My biological father didn't want me, so what if I was like that?"

Addy brought back two cans of beer and handed him one, then she settled down on the sofa right next to him. "I don't think you've got a thing to worry about. As angry as you were about Ricky, you are a good father even if you came into the picture when your daughter was grown."

"I did have a moment there"—he opened his beer and tipped it up for a swallow—"and then several more when we got home."

"So did I, but she's got her feet back under her now, and I believe she's going to be all right." Addy set her beer down and laid her palm on his cheek. "What is this between us, Jesse? We're not kids anymore, so what are we?"

"What do you want us to be?" He covered her hand with his, then moved it away from his face to kiss her palm.

"I'm not sure. We live on this ranch together. It could get awkward if..."

He put a finger over her lips. "We'll never know if we don't give it a try."

"How do we do that?" she asked. "We've both got a lot of baggage here."

"Yes, and hopefully, we are good enough friends to help each other unload all that baggage." He smiled and leaned just slightly to cover her lips with his.

She tasted like cold beer, and her damp hair smelled like the beach. That was quite a heady mixture. He tangled his fingers in her kinky hair and braced her head for more and more steamy, hot kisses.

When she finally pulled away, they were both panting. "Haven't felt like that..." He stopped and caught his breath. "In almost twenty years."

"Oh, come on, Jesse Ryan," she said. "You can't tell me you haven't kissed a girl since we spent the night together in this bunkhouse."

"I can tell you that none of them ever made me feel like you did and still do." He brushed another sweet kiss across her lips.

"Right back at you," she said.

A knock on the door brought them both to their feet. "Hey, anyone home?"

"That's Mia," Addy said as she raced across the living area and threw the door open. "Are you all right? Are you hurting somewhere?"

Mia stepped into the bunkhouse. "I'm fine, Mama. I was too wound up to sleep, so I went to your room, but you weren't there. I thought you might be down here. Y'all having trouble getting everything from today out of your minds, too? And did you see that moon out there? Nana told me it's called a Strawberry Moon." She talked as she headed across the room and sat down on the floor on the other side of the coffee table. "I keep seeing that woman in so much pain, and then Nana and Poppa were so worried that I was afraid they would have a heart attack. Nana told me while you were in the shower that she wasn't sure she could survive losing one of her boys, or me or you, Mama. I would feel just horrible if I caused her to die."

"We come equipped for the grief that comes when we lose a parent or a grandparent." Addy took a long drink of her beer. "We grieve and we hurt when that happens. But losing a child is an unnatural grief, one that we never get over."

"How do you know?" Mia asked. "Did you lose a baby? Is it all right if I get a bottle of water from the fridge?"

"Of course," Jesse answered. "There's also root beer and bottles of sweet tea."

She popped up onto her feet, crossed over to the kitchen area, and brought back a bottle of root beer.

"I didn't lose a baby," Addy said, "but your granny did. My mama had a little brother who died when he was six years old. He fell out of a tree and broke his neck, and Granny said that she still wasn't over it when she was in her seventies."

"I don't want to think about losing you or my grandparents or Nana and Poppa." Mia shivered. "I need all of you in my life—even you, Jesse."

"Well, thank you for that." He smiled so big that his face hurt.

She held up her bottle, and Jesse touched his can to it. "Mama?" She raised an eyebrow.

Addy leaned forward and made it a three-way toast. "To surviving and bringing a new baby almost all the way into the world."

"To realizing that life is important," Mia said.

"To family," Jesse added.

"And on that note, we'd better get back up to the house. One of us needs to be there in case Sonny needs us. He was so upset about the wreck that his blood pressure was up quite a bit," Addy said.

"Thanks for letting me crash your party," Mia said.

"Anytime," Jesse said. But the truth was that he would rather have had a whole night with Addy all to himself.

* * *

To Addy, Thursday and Friday seemed to pass in the blink of an eye. She wanted to go to the bunkhouse both nights, but Mia stuck to her like glue, as if she was afraid that if Addy got out of her sight, she would never see her again. Jesse stayed in the house both nights until bedtime, but Addy didn't even get a good night kiss. By Saturday morning, she was ready to grab Jesse by the hand and lead him off to that old barn up near Dodd City for a make-out session.

When she reached the kitchen that morning, Jesse was making a pot of coffee. "Where is everyone?" she asked.

"Sleeping in a little while, I guess." He finished his job and drew her close to him for a hug. "I've wanted to kiss you since Wednesday night, and there just didn't seem to be a time. "Good morning, darlin'." He ran a forefinger down her cheek and then his lips met hers.

She took a step back when she heard Sonny's cane tapping down the wooden floor in the hallway. "Good mornin' to you. How has Mia been doing the past couple of days? She's either texted me or called every hour."

"She's been quiet, but she's kept up with her work. She's not surly like she was the first couple of days. That wreck really shook her up," Jesse answered.

"Crazy how things work, isn't it?" Addy was setting the table when Pearl and Sonny entered the kitchen. "What are we having this morning?" she asked Pearl.

"I thought maybe we'd do bacon and pancakes," Pearl said. "Were y'all talking about Mia and the change that's come over her? Seems like there was Mia that we helped you raise and knew, then the ugly one that came home from Las Vegas, and now, there is this clingy one. I didn't like the Vegas one, but this one worries me. Think we need to take her to a therapist? She's been through a lot in a short while."

Addy had gone to a therapist for a couple of years after she'd had the hysterectomy. She had always thought that someday she'd fall in love, get married, and have a whole yard full of kids. Then suddenly, she was told that she couldn't have any more children when she was only nineteen years old. She kept up with her classes, and took good care of Mia, but she went into a deep depression. Her grandmother had made the first appointment with the therapist, and Addy had argued with her, but after three visits, she was feeling better.

"Maybe so," she finally said. "Let's give her a couple of weeks, and if she's not better, I'll find one and make an appointment for her."

"What do you think, Jesse?" Sonny asked.

"I've been to a therapist," Jesse said. "Mine helped me a lot, so I'm all for it if Mia needs to go. I'll even drive her there and back."

"Mornin', everyone." Mia yawned as she came into the kitchen. "What's on the agenda today, Jesse?"

"We've got to start with taking care of the alpacas. Then we'll need to finish up the morning with Henry and the boys. After that, you are supposed to help with the church bake sale, right?" Jesse answered.

"Full day," Mia said. "Mama, what are you doing today?"

"Breakfast, Sonny's vitals and meds, some data work on the computer, dinner, and then the bake sale," Addy answered. "I'll be in the house until we go to the church for the sale."

"Okay, then." Mia tucked a strand of dark hair behind her ear. "What can I do to help with breakfast, Nana?"

"Get out the jams and butter while I start frying bacon," Pearl said. "And when you get that done, get a can of orange juice from the freezer and make it up."

"Yes, ma'am." Mia headed for the refrigerator. "What are you and Poppa doing today?"

"I'll be going over the books before we take them to the CPA for our quarterly tax payments. Pearl will be making more cookies," Sonny answered. "Honey, we are all fine. You don't have to worry about us."

"Yes, I do," Mia disagreed. "These old worthless boys you've got didn't give you any grandkids to worry about you, so it's my job."

"Well, thank you for that," Jesse said.

"Just sayin'," Mia said. "The whole bunch of you need to settle down, fall in love, and live happily ever after so Nana can rock her grandbabies."

"Bossy this mornin', ain't you?" Addy arranged the five plates around the table.

Mia shrugged. "Yep, I am, but a near-death experience can sure enough wake a person up to what's important."

Sitting across the table from Jesse Ryan can do the same thing, Addy thought as she slid a sideways glance over toward him.

With the briefest of nods, he let her know that he was thinking the same thing.

* * *

The church parking lot was already filling up when Pearl, Addy, and Mia arrived that Saturday afternoon. The pale blue sky had a few puffy, white clouds, and the temperature was hanging right at a hundred degrees.

Jesse nosed his truck right in beside his mother's vehicle, got out, and helped Sonny get his feet on the ground, and then began unloading baked goods for the sale. Pearl grabbed a lace tablecloth, looped her arm in Sonny's, and the two of them talked to each other all the way into the church fellowship hall.

"Isn't that sweet?" Mia sighed. "When I fall in love for real, I want what Nana and Poppa have."

"Don't we all?" Addy picked up a box filled with plates of cookies.

"That kind of commitment takes a lot of work." Jesse toted two applesauce Bundt cakes into the sale. "If Mama hadn't made one of these to leave at home, I would buy them both."

"So you still like anything with cinnamon?" Addy smiled.

"There were times when I was on deployment that I would have given my whole paycheck for just a piece of this cake," Jesse answered, "and if I'd had a whole cake, I would have sold it off piece by piece and made a fortune."

"Too bad that I didn't know that," Addy teased. "I would have made a dozen cakes and sent them to you, and we could have split the profits."

Mia held the door open for them. "What's too bad is that you two lost touch."

Pearl waved from one end of the tables that had been set up in a U-shape around the floor of the fellowship hall. "Bring the boxes of cookies to this end. Cakes down there, and pies and miscellaneous things in the middle."

Jesse set his two cakes on the table and headed back out the door to get the rest of the things. Out of the corner of her eye, Addy watched him walk away. With his boots and hat and that bit of a swagger, he was the sexiest man in the whole room—at least in her eyes.

"I'll be over there at the checkout table taking in money and making change, but you two"—Pearl flicked her wrist to include Mia and Addy—"are going to take care of this end. Keep things pushed forward and looking pretty. Oh, there's Justine and Betsy. Doesn't look like they brought the baby. I was hoping to get to hold him."

"And there's Lylah," Addy whispered.

"I've got her at the other end with the cakes," Pearl said out the side of her mouth. "I put her with Vivien. They're cousins and just alike."

"Hey, Mia." Justine smiled. "I guess we're working together."

"Looks like it," Mia said. "I'm sorry about how things have happened. I didn't know that..."

Justine, a tall blonde with bright blue eyes, laid a hand on Mia's arm. "It's not your fault. It's not mine. We'll lay the blame where it belongs. We were both conned by the same guy."

"Thank you," Mia said, "but I was the other woman."

"So was I," Justine said. "When I finally admitted that Ricky was the father of my baby, I found out that he's got another one over in Bonham who's about a year older than my Matty. And that girl has a tat on her back, just like I do."

"Me, too." Mia blushed.

"Guess he brands all his women." Justine's tone was icy cold. "Be glad you didn't get pregnant like me and Willow. We've both got a son to raise now."

"Tattoos and baby boys," Mia whispered. "He leaves his mark wherever he goes, doesn't he?"

Betsy and Pearl set about arranging the cookies on a table.

"The people waiting in the sanctuary will be turned loose pretty soon," Pearl said. "It's always a madhouse for the first half hour, and then we'll get another rush about four o'clock. And, girls, just learn from all this trouble, and move on with your lives."

"Amen," Addy agreed. "And Justine, even though Mia's father was a good guy, we are both lucky women. Just like me, you have a lot of support and love to help you raise your baby as a single mother."

Mia raised her hand. "If you ever need to do some Ricky bashing, I'm your lady."

"I'll take you up on that." Justine grinned. "How about tonight? Can I call you after supper?"

"Give me your phone, and I'll put my number in it for you," Mia said.

Addy heaved a quiet sigh of relief. Mia had made a friend.

Now, maybe she wouldn't be quite so clingy, and together, she and Justine could help each other get past their experiences with Ricky O'Malley.

The citizens of the little town of Honey Grove turned out in masses to support the church's Strawberry Moon Bake Sale every year. The money raised went to support the Clothes Closet and Kitchen, where folks in need could come for clothing or food. The clothing was secondhand, but several volunteers made sure each piece was washed, ironed, and put onto hangers so that the place looked like a department store and not a rummage sale. The food bank always had canned food, dry beans, and cake mixes on hand, and Pearl tried to be sure eggs and milk were in the refrigerator at all times. When Pearl first organized the bake sale twenty years ago, she wanted to make enough money to buy a washer and dryer for the Closet. This year, her goal was to replace those old machines with new ones and, if there was leftover money, to buy more supplies for the food bank.

Betsy pulled her chair over close to Addy's and whispered, "I'm so glad Mia and Justine are talking. Justine has drawn away from all her friends, and today is the first time I've gotten her to get out in public like this."

"I know exactly what you mean." Addy got that antsy feeling that told her Jesse was close by, and then he appeared right behind her. He laid a hand on her shoulder, sending sweet little shivers sliding up her spine, and then leaned down to whisper in her ear.

"Thought I'd come by and tell you that Dad and I are going over to Bonham to look at a bull he's got his eye on. We'll be back in time for me to help y'all take care of putting the tables and chairs away."

The warmth of his breath on her neck added to the sensation. "Sometime around five?"

"I'll be here," he said.

"Thanks," she said.

He straightened up and smiled at Betsy. "Good to see you. Looks like Justine and Mia are having a visit over there."

"Yes, they are, and we both think it's great," Betsy answered. "The other old men in the sanctuary will miss y'all."

"I thought maybe it was best to get Dad out of there when Patrick O'Malley showed up," Jesse said in a low voice.

"That's why Danny opted to stay home with the baby," Betsy whispered. "Best to avoid trouble when we can."

"Yep." Jesse tipped his hat toward them and left by a side door so he didn't have to walk past the table where Lylah and Vivien were taking care of the cakes.

"I've always wondered why the men come to these things anyway," Addy said.

"Tradition, I guess." Betsy shrugged. "But they look forward to a couple of hours of talking politics, sports, and believe me, they gossip more than women."

"Oh, really?" Addy asked.

"I'll miss that part since Danny stayed home today," Betsy giggled. "He always brings home all the dirt on everyone. Those men know things that I don't even hear at the bank."

"Since Jesse and Sonny are leaving, Pearl and I will have to rely on the old gossip vine right along with you," Addy laughed with her.

"Honey, we are probably the topic of what's being said in the other room," Betsy said. "Our daughters have corrupted Ricky O'Malley, the poor thing."

Addy laughed even harder and then stopped abruptly when she saw Lylah coming toward them. Her eyes were fixed on Justine and Mia, and her mouth was set in a firm line. Her light brown ponytail swung back and forth like a frayed flag in a hard Texas wind, and her hands were knotted into fists. Addy and Betsy both got to their feet, rounded the end of the tables, and met the woman in the middle of the room.

"Get out of my way, Addison Hall." Lylah's freckled face was scarlet with anger. "I've got something to say to those girls, and I intend to get it off my chest."

"This is not the time or place," Addy said low enough for Lylah's ears only. "If you want to yell at them, accuse them, or anything else, do it somewhere other than the church. Matter of fact, you can come by Sunflower Ranch tomorrow afternoon and tell them off there."

"But if you want this to be the time and place, I'd be glad to take the first swing," Betsy told her.

Lylah looked down on them like they were something she had stepped on out in the pasture. "Get out of my way, or I'll put you both on the floor."

Pearl stepped between the two women and held out her hands. "We aren't doing this here, Lylah."

Lylah pointed at Mia and Justine. "Those two are spreading rumors about my boy, and your son fired Pete for refusing to work with Addison's bastard kid."

"Enough!" Pearl's voice went all high and squeaky. "Either go man your table or get out of here, Lylah."

"You would take up for her and that brat of a daughter she's raised," Lylah smarted off. "You're not running me off. I've supported this church my whole life, but I will have my say one of these days. Those two over there have lied about my boy so much that he doesn't feel like he can even come home."

"What about the girl over in Bonham raising your other grandson?" Addy asked. "Is she lying about him, too, and what about the fact that he's talked all three girls into getting the same tattoo on their backs, kind of like branding them as his property?"

"What are you talking about?" Lylah asked.

Addy motioned for her daughter to come over. "You should see something."

Mia and Justine left their posts and came over to stand in front of Lylah.

"I would like for you girls to show Lylah the tattoos that her son convinced you to get," Addy said.

They turned around backward and raised their shirts.

"And there's another one in Bonham," Justine said. "Ricky is your son, and he can't do anything wrong in your eyes, but he's a different guy around us girls, Miz O'Malley. All you would have to do is look at Matty, and you wouldn't have a single doubt who his father is, but after what you've said and the rumors you've spread about me, and Mia, too, now, that ain't likely to happen. I don't want you anywhere near my son or for your influence to ever be a part of his life."

"I'll see him when you bring him to church." Lylah's voice had lost some of its cutting edge.

"But you'd have to prove yourself to ever hold him or acknowledge him as your grandson, and I don't think you are capable of that." Justine didn't raise her voice and even smiled a couple of times. "Come on, Mia. I think the bake sale is going to start in about two minutes. We've got a job to do."

"If I believed you, and if that baby is really Ricky's, then I have grandparent's rights," Lylah said.

"Not if Ricky doesn't pay me child support, and I'm sure he's too busy getting some other girl a rose tat these days to do that." Justine turned around and marched back to her post with Mia right behind her.

Lylah went back to her chair beside Vivien and slumped down into it. They were still whispering when Pearl unlocked the door into the fellowship hall and folks began to pour inside.

"Good job," Mia said to Justine.

"I couldn't have done it without you being right there beside me," Justine said.

Betsy nudged Addy on the arm. "What Justine just said."

"What Mia said." Addy couldn't wait to go to the bunkhouse that evening and tell Jesse exactly what had happened.

Chapter Eighteen

Addy set the last glass of sweet tea on the table and made sure everything was ready before she took her seat. When she did, her bare foot touched Jesse's, and a whole new set of sparks danced around the kitchen.

Sonny said a quick grace and then grinned at Pearl. "Looked like your bake sale went well."

"We had a sell-out except for one chocolate pie that Vivien brought," Pearl said. "Bless her heart, she tries, so I bought it there at the end. That way we could say that we sold everything that was brought."

"Why are you saying *bless her heart*?" Jesse asked.

"It's a bought one from the frozen department at the grocery store. She takes it home, thaws it out, and adds a layer of whipped cream to the top," Addy said.

"According to her, the whipped cream out of a squirt can makes it homemade," Pearl explained. "It's over there on the counter if anyone wants some for dessert."

"Not when there's an applesauce cake waiting for me,"

Jesse said. "Did you make enough for the new washer and dryer?" He moved his foot over a few inches so that he could play footsies with Addy.

When she pulled her foot back, he just stretched out those long legs a bit more and massaged her foot with his toes.

"Yes, we did and more. We can restock the pantry with those canned hams that go so fast when folks need help," Pearl answered. "Did you two buy a bull?"

"Thinkin' about it." Sonny helped himself to a second slice of the pizza they had picked up in Bonham. "It's a fine bull, but Vernon wants a little too much. I'll wait a few days and make him an offer. What's this about you stepping into the middle of a big fight, Pearl?"

"Somebody"—she cut her eyes around at him—"stole my thunder."

"Gossip travels fast, Mama," Jesse chuckled, and tucked his feet back under his chair.

He was flirting big time, and Addy liked it, but she wasn't one hundred percent sure their friendship was worth losing if things went south. "Lylah was just smarting off, but Pearl put her in her place real quick."

"I'd say that Justine stepped up to the plate and did that far better than I could. When she and Mia both showed off the exact same tattoos on their backs, Lylah kind of settled down," Pearl said. "If those things had been acceptable for girls back in my day, I would have had a sunflower put on my back, or maybe my hip. That way, it would be for Sonny and no one else."

"Nana, if you want a tat, you can still get one." Mia got a second slice of the pepperoni pizza and took a bite.

"Honey, gravity got my skin a long time ago. My sunflower would have so many wrinkles in it that it would look wilted," Pearl chuckled. "I was glad to see you and Justine talking this afternoon."

"We're going for ice cream this evening. I'm picking her up at seven, and we're taking Matty with us so I can meet him," Mia said. "I guess y'all can survive without me, right?"

"We'll do our best," Addy assured her in a serious tone.

"I'll be home by eight. Justine says an hour is enough of an outing for the baby," Mia said.

"You do know that you can stay out as late as you want," Jesse said. "You are a grown-up now."

"Yes, sir!" She snapped a smart salute to him.

"And there's our sassy girl back in her skin," he teased.

"That wreck just spooked me, but I'm fine now," Mia announced.

After supper, Addy took Sonny's vitals, gave him a neck massage and his evening meds, then left him and Pearl alone to watch their favorite Saturday evening shows on television. She went right to her window and stared out at the bunkhouse in the distance. Some evenings, Jesse sat in the living room or on the front porch with his parents at the close of a day, but not that night. He said he had to return some phone calls to his old teammates and had gone to the bunkhouse.

Addy had lived in the ranch house for five years. She had been content, if not ecstatically happy there, just knowing that Mia was loved and had a stable environment. But tonight, for the first time, the place felt more than a little lonely.

Jesse walked up to the window that faced the house. His silhouette showed that he had a hand up to his ear, so evidently, he had indeed needed to make a few phone calls. For some crazy reason, that made Addy feel better. She waited until she saw him drop his hand and lay the phone down before she slipped down the hall and out the kitchen door.

He was on the porch when she arrived. He'd changed from the jeans and pearl snap western shirt he had worn to the bake sale into a pair of loose-fitting pajama pants and a faded T-shirt with a bull rider on the front. He was barefoot, and his hair was still wet from a recent shower. When she was still five feet away, she caught a whiff of the shaving lotion that always set her senses to reeling.

"I was hoping you would come tonight. I came out to look at the Strawberry Moon." He pointed up at a full moon hanging right above the treetops. "Has Mia come home yet?"

Addy hiked a hip on the porch railing. "Not yet, and she hasn't called or texted. That's a good thing after the way she's almost set my phone on fire every day since the wreck."

Jesse crossed the wide porch and hugged Addy, then kissed her on the forehead. "Seems right to be here with you and that big old lover's moon so close, it feels like we could reach up there and touch it."

"I thought it was the Strawberry Moon, not a lover's moon." She wrapped her arms loosely around his neck.

"It's both," he said. "Mama talked about the bake sale when I would call her, but I didn't know until today that they had named it the Strawberry Moon Bake Sale. She said they always have it on the last weekend in June, and that's when the Strawberry Moon is out. The Native American culture called it that because that's when the wild strawberries were ready to pick, along with other fruit. Mama said it seemed fitting to name their fundraiser after that because some of the ladies brought jams they made from the fresh fruits they had harvested. Tonight, I'd rather it would be a lover's moon."

"Why are you telling me all this, Jesse?" Addy asked. "You only go on and on about something when you are super nervous."

"You know me too well," Jesse sighed.

"Are we really going to give this a try?" she asked.

"I'd sure like to." He removed her hands from around his neck. He kissed each knuckle separately and then turned her hands over to kiss the palms. "But first, I think we'd better be up-front and honest with Mia. Her reaction to us might make you change your mind."

"Mia means a lot to me, but I can make up my own mind about what I do. What about how you'll take her reaction?" she asked.

"My mind is pretty well made up." He flashed a grin so brilliant that it would have paled the sun. "When I came home, from that first minute, I could feel something still between us even after all these years. I'm not making the same mistake I did all when I was too young and stupid to realize what I had right in front of me."

"All right then, we'll tell her tomorrow after church," Addy agreed. "But, Jesse, let's take it slow. We're not kids anymore, and we need to be sure that this is more than a physical attraction."

"Anything you want, darlin'," he said. "As long as I can hold you, and—"

The door flew open before he could even finish his sentence. Mia rushed outside and dropped to her knees in front of her mother. She laid her head on Addy's lap and burst into tears. "I'm so sorry, Mama."

Addy's mind went into high gear. Had Mia wrecked her truck, decided to run away with Ricky again, or robbed a bank? Whatever it was, she would be there for her daughter. *But please, Lord, don't let it be something illegal or that worthless Ricky coming back into her life*, she prayed as she wrapped Mia up in her arms.

"What's happened?" Jesse laid a hand on Mia's shoulder. "Are you all right? Do we need to take you to the doctor?"

Addy sucked in air and held it. "Has something happened to Sonny?"

Mia raised her head. "I'm fine. I think Poppa is good. I

didn't go through the house. I came straight here, and..." Her chin quivered, and tears continued to flow down her cheeks. "I hoped you'd be here. I'm so so sorry for..." Her voice broke, and she buried her face in her mother's lap.

"For what?" Jesse asked.

Mia raised her head again. "For being such a horrible person, and for all the mean things I've said about my father being a bum off the streets. And for lying to you and Jesse, and Poppa and Nana tonight."

"Did you go see Ricky?" Jesse asked.

"Of course not!" Her tone turned a little edgy. "I lied about going to see Justine. I went to the drugstore."

"Are you sick?" Addy's stomach turned over and nausea set in.

Mia shook her head. "I went to the drugstore to buy a pregnancy test. I'm a week late."

The room spun a couple of times and started to fade into a gray fog before Addy remembered to straighten up and take a deep breath. "Have you taken the test?"

"I went to a truck stop and did it in the bathroom. That was the longest three minutes of my life. I thought they would never pass, and then I was afraid to look at the test. I knew I would be sick if it was positive and guilty for hating Ricky so much if it was negative since it wouldn't be a little baby's fault," Mia said. "It was negative. I guess I'm just late because of all the stress."

"Then why are you so upset?" Jesse asked gently.

"Because of the way I've felt and treated Mama about my own father. I didn't want to be pregnant with Ricky's baby. Like Justine, I would be terrified to even tell all y'all, and I'd live in fear that my baby would grow up to act like Ricky." She stopped talking long enough to wipe her eyes with the back of her hand. "Then I got to thinking about how you felt, Mama, when you looked at me. Did you see my father in me? Did you worry that I'd grow up and act like him?"

"Yes, and yes, but your father is a good man. It was my decision, not his, to not tell him. If he had known about you, he would have married me, and I wasn't sure it would have been for the right reasons," Addy explained.

"Then why wouldn't you tell me who he is or was all these years?" she asked.

"Because if he had known, he would have given up on his dream and rushed back here to do the right thing, and well..." Addy glanced over at Jesse.

"After a time," Jesse said, "I imagine it just got easier to move on with her life, right, Addy?"

"Did you ever forget him? Did you love him?" Mia asked. "I don't want to remember Ricky, and I don't think I ever loved him. I just wanted someone to love me like Poppa loves Nana. We even talked about that before we moved in together, and he said he wanted the same thing. How can I ever trust another guy?"

"Question one." Addy held up one hand. "I never forgot him." She held up another finger. "And I did love him, but I wasn't sure it was the marryin' kind of love. I thought it was most likely the best friend love that got out of hand one night."

Jesse patted her on the back. "When the right guy comes along, he will respect you, and he will never want to change you."

Mia's eyes shifted from Jesse to Addy and back again several times. She finally cocked her head to one side and then blinked rapidly a dozen times. "Best friend love..." she whispered. "Jesse, are you my father?"

"Yes, he is," Addy said before he could answer.

"And everything your mother said is true. I'd always talked

about making a career out of the military. I would have given all that up in a split second if I'd known about you. Our friendship was so strong that she didn't tell me about you so that I could have my dream," Jesse added.

"I had dreams, too," Addy said. "I wanted to be a nurse, and I am one. I have a beautiful daughter that has brought joy to me… well, until she got all sassy and headstrong and ran off with a bad boy. I have no regrets about the decisions I made, except that I feel that I've cheated you two out of knowing each other. That's the one thing I'm sorry for."

Mia stared at Jesse the whole time both he and her mother were talking. Addy wondered if she was in shock or in a trance. She started to snap her fingers in front of her daughter's eyes when the girl finally spoke.

"I have your eyes, and that's why I'm so tall."

"Yep." Jesse nodded.

"You really didn't know about me?" she asked.

"Not until I came home. I knew Addy had a daughter, but I didn't know you were my child," Jesse answered.

"Did you ever wonder?" she asked.

"No, I didn't. We only had that one night together," he said.

"Didn't Poppa and Nana talk about me? Did they ever send pictures, like at Christmas, or didn't you see the ones on the mantel of me and Mama?" Mia pressured for more.

"They did, and yes, I saw the pictures when I came home, but I never made the connection until I came home a few weeks ago. If I had, I would have gotten to know you," he said.

"Part of Jesse not seeing you is my fault. When he came home, I made sure we were in Cactus for Thanksgiving," Addy said.

"I didn't figure it out for myself until I was told when your birthday was," Jesse told her.

"I've got to think about this for a while," Mia said as she

stood up. "I should have known it all along because Mama has always had a picture of you in her wallet, but..." She frowned at Jesse. "I figured my dad was someone she was ashamed of, not her best friend. I don't think I'm ready to call you daddy or dad."

"You might not ever be ready for that, but I do hope we can be friends," Jesse said.

"We'll see." Mia started for the door. "Is this a dream, Mama?"

"No, but you might lead with 'I'm not pregnant' next time," Addy said.

Mia turned around and drew her eyebrows down into a dark line. "Are you coming with me?"

"Of course I am." Addy followed her into the house.

"If you've got any more questions for me, I'm right here," Jesse said.

"Thanks." Mia turned around and smiled. "And I'm glad it's you that's my father, Jesse."

"Me, too," he said.

Mia reached over and took Addy's hand in hers. "I meant it. I'm glad Jesse is my father. That means that Poppa and Nana are my real grandparents, and..." She paused.

"And what?" Addy asked.

"And I've been a horrible granddaughter." She sat down in the grass and pulled her mother down beside her. "Do they know?"

Addy pulled her hand free and hugged Mia. "Yes, they figured it out years ago, but I didn't tell them until after Jesse came home."

"Do you think Lylah knows?" Mia asked.

"Nope. If she did, she would have already spread it all over the whole state. I heard that she spread rumors that I got pregnant by one of my professors," Addy answered.

The stars glistened in the night sky just like they had twenty years ago when Addy slipped out of the bunkhouse and jogged all the way across the pastures to her own house. There was comfort in knowing that some things never changed.

"Jesse is a good man." Mia seemed to be trying to wrap her mind around him being her father even yet.

"Yes, he is. He's always been a good person," Addy agreed.

"He's a tough boss, but I like him. Do you think I can ever think of him as a daddy?" Mia asked.

"What I think doesn't matter. That is totally up to you," Addy told her. "Give him some time. Nothing has to be decided tonight."

"I wish it could be so that I wouldn't worry. Oh, no!" Mia gasped.

"What?" Addy looked around to see if there was a snake or maybe a tarantula near them.

"I've treated him like crap. What if he never likes me?" Mia asked.

"You are his daughter, and he already likes you," Addy assured her.

"Are you sure?" Mia wiped more tears from her eyes.

"Positive," Addy answered. "Let's go on to the house. You need to get some rest. You've had nothing but one crisis after another lately."

"I'm not sure if I'll ever sleep well again, but I'll try." Mia stood up and extended a hand to help Addy. "At least Jesse was good to you, and y'all are still friends."

Addy's heart was still beating too fast when they made it to the house, and Mia had disappeared into her bedroom. There was no way that she could sleep, so she grabbed a bottle of water and headed to the front porch swing, only to find Jesse already there. She collapsed beside him and laid her head on his shoulder.

"God, I'm glad she's not pregnant. It never entered my mind that she might be. She's been on the pill for a while." She closed her eyes and leaned her head back on the porch swing.

"We're living proof that failures happen." Jesse slid down to sit closer to her and take her hand in his. "What do you think she'll say after she's slept on the news?"

"Six months ago, I would have said that she would have another million questions to ask and she would take a while, but she would accept you. Today, I don't know. I'm kind of glad she doesn't have enough money to run away, because after the stunts she's pulled, I'm not sure," she said. "Jesse, are you ready for all this responsibility? She's concerned about feeling like you are her dad, but she's also worried that you won't like her."

He removed his hand from hers and draped an arm around her shoulders. "It's all been a bit of a shock. I'll admit that, but darlin', I'm ready. She's part of the bargain if we're going to get involved, and besides, I already love that kid. I didn't realize how much until tonight. Hearing her say that she was glad I was her father—I can't begin to tell you how that made me feel."

Addy laid her head on his shoulder. "I'm glad we told her tonight, but I think we were talking about us when she barged in and scared the hell out of me with that news of a pregnancy test."

"We could have been discussing dinosaurs or ice cream for all I remember," Jesse admitted. "I feel like we just jumped over a hurdle, but we haven't landed on solid ground yet."

"Me, too," Addy agreed. "I need to talk about something unrelated to drama."

"With our background, we're not drama?" Jesse made lazy circles with his thumb on the soft spot on her neck.

"What's between us is nothing compared to everything

we've been through. Do you think we should get in to breakfast earlier than usual and tell Sonny and Pearl that she knows?" The adrenaline was leaving Addy's body. That combined with Jesse's gentle touch on her neck made her drowsy. "I can't believe that I'm sleepy."

"No, we don't need to get up that early," Jesse said. "We'll tell them at breakfast if she hasn't already, and, honey, we're both worn out emotionally."

One minute, Addy was resting her eyes, the next her face was warm from the sun pouring in from what she figured was her bedroom window. Her eyes snapped open when she realized that she'd overslept. That's when she realized that Jesse was spooned up against her back and his arm was slung around her to keep her from falling off the swing.

"Good Lord!" She moved her arm and sat up so fast, she got dizzy. "It's daylight and—"

"Good morning, beautiful," he said. "I slept better than I have in years. How about you?"

"Yes, but we've got to go inside, and I hear rattling in the kitchen, so the folks are already up," she answered.

"Don't be in such a rush. Mama and Dad already know we have a daughter together. We just slept in the swing. It isn't a big deal." He sat up and stretched.

"It's a big deal this morning. We should have been there when Mia came out of her room"—she tapped her phone, which was lying on the porch—"it's seven thirty. She will have been up for an hour."

"Betcha five bucks we have to knock on her door and wake her." Jesse headed across the porch with her right behind him.

"You look like you slept in your clothes," he teased.

"That's because I did," she responded. "At least if anyone sees me, they'll know we weren't in here getting naked."

"We can remedy that anytime you want." He winked.

"Slow down, cowboy." She went into the house when he opened the door for her. "Remember, we decided to take it slow."

"I can go slow, or I can go fast." His eyes twinkled as he took her hand in his and led her to the kitchen.

Sonny looked up from his coffee. "Good mornin'. Y'all already been out feedin' the alpacas and checkin' cattle?"

"No, we both fell asleep on the porch swing last night," Addy answered.

Pearl raised an eyebrow, but before she could respond, Mia padded barefoot into the kitchen. "Good mornin'. Blueberry muffins! My favorite breakfast." She went to the refrigerator and brought out the milk, poured a glassful, and carried it to the table. "I guess we should talk about things, right?"

"What things?" Sonny asked.

"That I'm your real granddaughter, that I was afraid I was pregnant but I'm not, that I've been a real brat, and that I still don't know how to feel about Jesse being my father." She slathered butter on a muffin as she talked. "But Poppa, you should say grace before we talk about anything at all."

Pearl looked like she'd just won the lottery. Sucking on a lemon couldn't have erased the grin on Sonny's face. Jesse laid his hand over Addy's and gave it a gentle squeeze.

Mia had sure enough put all the information in a nutshell, and, suddenly, it didn't seem as much of a crisis as it did the night before.

Sonny bowed his head and thanked God for the food, the hands that prepared it, and asked for strength for the day's battles. When he opened his eyes, he focused on Mia, who was busy taking the first bite of her muffin. "Okay, Mia, what on earth is going on?"

"All right. Last night, Mama and Jesse told me that he is my father."

Sonny looked like he was trying to hide a smile. "And how did you feel about that?"

"To be honest, I'm still in shock. I couldn't get to sleep for hours last night, and I still don't know how to feel." She looked at Jesse. "I'm sorry."

"No need to be sorry," he assured her. "It's a lot to take in, and I know it will be an adjustment."

"I am glad you didn't marry some other woman, at least." She took a bite of her muffin.

Addy was glad about that, too.

Mia took a sip of milk and looked to Pearl. "I'm also glad to know that you and Poppa are really my grandparents. You've always treated me like one of your own, but, somehow, it's different to know it's true."

Pearl wiped tears away from her cheeks with the tail of her apron. "We had our suspicions that you might have been Jesse's daughter, but we never wanted to say anything out of respect for your mother. And even if it hadn't been true, you know you're always part of our family."

Addy struggled to hold back her own tears. Would things have been different if she'd told the Ryans sooner? Had she robbed them of time with their grandchild, times when Sonny was stronger and could have taken Mia out on the four-wheelers or hiking through the pastures?

Mia pushed back her chair and stood up. She hugged Sonny first and then Pearl. "I'm glad y'all are my real grandparents, and…" She stopped short of hugging Jesse. "And I'm glad that my father is here now and someone I can get to know."

Addy glanced across the table and locked gazes with Jesse. His eyes were swimming with tears, but he blinked them away.

"Thank you for that much," Jesse said. "We'll work on that *getting to know* each other, starting this morning. After we clean the watering troughs, I thought we would unload a new trough in the pasture, fill it, and see how the alpacas do with a little more space to run and play."

"What's that got to do with getting to know someone?" Mia asked.

"Working together is the—" Jesse started.

"Best way to get to know a person for who they really are," Addy finished for him.

"Seems like Nana told me that same thing." Mia smiled. "Now, I have the right to call you that, don't I? It's really my right."

"Yes, darlin', it is," Pearl answered.

The guilt left Addy's heart and soul. She glanced across the table at Jesse, and they shared a moment of happiness without either of them saying a single word.

Chapter Nineteen

*J*esse felt his phone vibrate in his back pocket, so he pulled his four-wheeler under a big scrub oak tree and stopped. Mia pulled up beside him and raised a dark eyebrow.

"Phone call from one of my military buddies," he answered her silent question. "Take a break and get a bottle of water out. We've been running hard all morning."

"No arguments from me." She cut the engine, got off her machine, sat down at the base of a nearby tree, and used the trunk for a backrest.

"Hey, what's goin' on? How are you adjusting to civilian life?" Jesse answered the phone.

"First week was great," Frankie chuckled. "Second one, I started to get bored. I just landed a fantastic job with a private security firm. Tommy's here with me, and Ned and Beau are coming in next week. We just need you to get our old team back together. Tommy has talked to the boss man, and he's got no problem with us working together. What do you say?"

"I'll have to turn you down. I came home to help on the

ranch, and I found out I've got a nineteen-year-old daughter that I want to get to know," Jesse said.

"Will you think about it? Starting pay is six figures with a benefit package that will blow your mind," Frankie said. "And how did you get a daughter that old without even knowing about her?"

"Long story." Dollar signs flashed in Jesse's mind.

"Bring her with you," Frankie said. "Girls like the beach."

"Beach?" Jesse removed his cowboy hat and fanned his face with it. "Where is the headquarters for this job?"

"Miami. Nice beaches. Warm weather, but we'll be sent out on missions all over the world. It'll be like old times," Frankie said. "Give yourself a few days to think it over, and I'll call back at the end of the week. Sure be nice if we were all together again. After that first week at home with the wife and kids, I missed you guys."

"How does Nora feel about moving to Miami?" Jesse asked.

"She loves the idea," Frankie said. "Got to run now. Talk to you later. Promise you'll think it over seriously?"

"Promise I'll think it over, but I'm pretty sure my answer will be the same," Jesse answered. "Give Nora my love."

"Will do, and she misses you, too," Frankie chuckled again. "She kind of liked being the hostess for all of us. See you later."

Jesse opened up the saddlebag and took out a bottle of water, carried it over to where Mia was sitting, and sat down beside her. "You ever think about living anywhere other than here in Honey Grove?"

"I did, and you see where that got me," Mia said. "I'm just now finding out that Poppa and Nana are really mine. I would never leave them. Why are you asking?"

"I just had a pretty big offer for a job, but it would mean moving to Miami, Florida," he answered.

"You can't do that!" Mia gasped.

"Why not?" Jesse downed half of his bottle of water.

"Because it would break Nana and Poppa's hearts. All they talked about for six months before you came home was if they could just hang on until you got here, everything would be just fine, and you're going to be the boss in a few weeks when Henry moves to Colorado, and..." She stopped to take a breath. "And because the ranch needs you."

"Any other reasons?" Jesse asked.

"Mama is happier than I've ever seen her, and you need to give her another chance. She would be devastated if you left her again, but she would never say a word about it because she wouldn't want to ruin your dreams." She finally turned up her water bottle and drained the rest of it.

"Is that all?" Jesse asked.

"I don't want you to go," Mia said. "I've gone almost twenty years without a father, and we're just now really getting to know each other."

Jesse didn't realize he was holding his breath until it all came out in a whoosh. He swallowed hard three times to get past the lump in his throat that formed when Mia said she didn't want him to leave. "You don't think you and your mama would like Miami? There's beaches and lots of things to do, and the money is great."

"Sure," Mia said. "We would love to go there for a vacation, but this is home, and you need to put down roots and help us make a family. Maybe you and Mama will get back together. Maybe you won't, but the three of us can be a family, whichever way it goes."

"So how would you feel if I asked Addy out on a date?" Jesse asked.

Mia whipped around and glared at him. "You better be sure you're settled down and not wanting to run off to some military thing before you ask her. If you break her heart, I'll have to get even, and I hold a grudge forever."

"What if I talk to her about this new job, and she thinks it's a great idea and wants to move away from here for a fresh start?" Jesse asked. "Maybe she'd like to go back to full-time nursing where she works a shift and then comes home without having to do fill-in ranch stuff."

Mia shook her head. "Mama is happy here on Sunflower Ranch. She gets to be a nurse to Poppa, and that's enough. Don't make her choose. That's not fair to her. You make up your own mind, and either leave us behind again or stay. But I'll tell you right now"—she pointed her finger right at him—"I'm not leaving again, and even crossing the Red River into Oklahoma is going to be like going to a foreign country to me from now on. I've learned my lesson about testing out the grass on the other side of the fence. It's not greener, and it tastes bitter."

"I'm not going anywhere," Jesse admitted.

"Well, why in the hell are we having this stupid conversation then?" Mia hopped up and got back on her four-wheeler. "I was worried that you were serious."

"I was testing you." Jesse removed his hat, resettled it on his head, and smiled up at her.

"Did your old Army buddy even call you? Or was that Poppa telling you to check on something?" Mia eyed him suspiciously.

"Air Force, not Army, and yes, it really was my friend. His name is Frankie." Jesse settled into the seat of his four-wheeler. "I turned him down, but he's going to give me until the end of the week to think about all that money, and then try to talk me into it again."

Mia did a head wiggle. "Army, Air Force, Marines, whatever. It's all men in uniforms."

"You'd better not let a veteran hear you say that," Jesse said. "And there are women, too, you know."

"Did you tell him about me?" Mia asked.

Jesse nodded. "I sure did, and he knows that my dad isn't well, and Mama needs me, so no matter what he says, I'm not going anywhere."

"Does that decision make you sad?" She had to raise her voice over the noise of the engine.

Jesse shook his head. "Not in the least, and Mia, I would never hurt your mother."

"I'm holding you to that," she declared as she sped off ahead of him.

Had Mia given him permission to date Addy? And with their past, how did they even begin to date? Would it feel strange, he wondered, or would going out with her be as natural as the kisses had been?

* * *

After supper that evening, Addy helped Sonny get out to the back porch so he could watch the alpacas. She popped up his folding chaise lounge and set a glass of sweet tea on the table beside it. Then she pulled a rocking chair over beside him and sat down.

"You ever get bored out here on the ranch?" Sonny asked.

"Nope," she answered.

"I'm glad, but I wanted to ask. Jesse is a medic, and he could monitor my meds and do what you do. I wouldn't want to hold you back if you wanted to work in a hospital or nursing home, again," Sonny said.

"Are you trying to get rid of me?" she asked.

"Not in the least. I hope you stay here even after me and Pearl are gone on to eternity. You and Mia make this place complete, but I don't want you to ever have regrets like Jesse would have had if we hadn't supported his decision to join the Air Force."

Addy patted him on the arm. "No regrets. I'm happy right here, doing what I do. I just hope Jesse and Mia can find some kind of middle ground and have a friendship if not a father and daughter relationship."

"And what about *you* and Jesse?" Sonny turned his head and looked right at her.

She couldn't keep from blushing. *God! At thirty-eight years old, I shouldn't get red cheeks at the mention of his name.*

"It's good to have my friend back in my life. I didn't realize how much I had missed him, and Sonny, I want to apologize for not telling you and Pearl about Mia. I cheated both of you out of so many memories by keeping that to myself. It wasn't fair to you," she said.

"But you brought her back to us when we needed her the most," Sonny said. "Sure, we would have loved to have been part of her life the whole time, but we're not complaining. You had your reasons, and they were good ones. If it had been out of spite or anger, it would have been tough to forgive you, but it was done out of love for our boy, so..." He shrugged. "I'd like to see you two be more than friends, Addy. Don't waste precious time when the two of you could be together. I regret that I didn't take my sweet Pearl to all the places she wanted to go when we were young enough to enjoy it."

"We've agreed to take everything slow," Addy said.

"As long as you're going forward," Sonny advised.

Pearl came outside and slumped down in the rocker on the other side of Sonny. "I thought, at this age, we would be sitting out here watching our grandkids play in the yard, not baby alpacas romping in the pasture. But I've got to admit, I'm glad that Mia wasn't pregnant. Not that I'm so old-fashioned as to be upset by a single mama, but I wouldn't want her to have to raise a kid by that wild O'Malley boy."

"Amen to that," Addy agreed. "You've got to admit, though,

that the alpacas are cute, and you don't have to worry about one of those sweet little girls running off with a worthless guy."

"Ever wonder what your mama thought when you wouldn't name the father?" Pearl asked.

"She was upset for a while, but she told me it was my decision, and she would support me in whatever I wanted to do," Addy answered.

Jesse poked his head out the kitchen door. "Want to go for a ride?"

"Sure." Addy stood up. "Did you ask Mia?"

"Yep, but she's gone to see Justine. This time I think she really is going there rather than to the drugstore, thank goodness," Jesse said.

"Not ready to be a grandpa at thirty-nine?" Sonny teased.

"Nope, and certainly not when it would upset her to have to raise Ricky's child," Jesse answered. "Y'all want anything from over at Bonham?"

"I've got an invitation to a baby shower at the church tomorrow evening. Y'all could go into Walmart and find me a few things to give the new mother. She's having a girl. I've got a fancy gift bag and tissue paper so don't buy those," Pearl said.

"Sure thing." Addy nodded as she made her way into the house. "Just let me get my purse and I'll be ready."

"I'll be waiting in the hallway," Jesse told her.

Addy took time to brush her hair and apply fresh lipstick, then picked up her purse. Jesse was sitting in one of the ladder-back chairs in the foyer when she arrived and he immediately stood up, settled his cowboy hat on his head, and took her hand in his.

"When I was in tough situations, I used to imagine your smile, and it got me through those hard times," he said. "I'm a fool for not getting in touch with you, Addy."

"If you're a fool, I'm one, too." Addy's nerve endings were fairly well humming at nothing more than his touch. She wanted to drag him off to a secluded wooded area and have wild, passionate sex with him in the front seat of his truck. Why, oh why, had she gotten so tied up in life that she hadn't stopped to consider what was really important to her?

"Thank God, we've been given a second chance," he said.

The noise of him opening the truck door for her brought her back to reality with a jerk. "Sorry, what did you say? I was thinking of something else."

"Was I involved in that?" he asked and helped her into the passenger seat.

"Yep, you were," she said.

He leaned into the truck and gave her a sweet kiss on the lips. The tingle that traveled through her sent her right back to visualizing how great it would be to satisfy the ache being near him created in her body. He grinned as he closed the door, and then he stopped to scratch Tex's ears on the way around the vehicle before sliding behind the wheel.

"And?" he asked as he started the engine.

"I want more than friendship," she said bluntly.

"So do I." He turned the truck around and started down the lane. "But it seems to get in the way, doesn't it?"

"Why do we have to have one or the other? Is it possible to have both?" she whispered. "Pearl and Sonny seem to have found a way to make it work all these years."

"Maybe we're the kind of people who need both. I need a friend to talk to when I've got decisions to make, and I need someone to look forward to sleeping with at night and waking up to in the morning. I think we can have both, Addy," he answered.

"So tonight are we friends or more?" she asked.

"Both for as long as it takes us to get to Bonham," he said. "Has Mia talked to you about the phone call I got today?"

"Yes, but..." Addy started.

"No buts," he said quickly. "What was your first reaction?"

She turned away from him and stared out the side window. "I wanted to run away to the panhandle again. If that's what you really want, I can't stand in your way—that's friendship. But the other part of me wanted to cry, because I don't want you to leave again—that's the relationship we're starting to build."

He pulled over to the side of the road and parked. Then he reached across the console and cupped Addy's chin in his hand. "Look at me, Addy," he said as he gently turned her head around so they could stare into each other's eyes. "What do you see?"

"I hope I see happiness," she said.

"Exactly, and like I told Mia, I'm not taking the job in Miami. I would love to have a reunion with my teammates sometime in the future. We were closer than brothers, but I have no desire to work with them again. I'm happy right here, running the ranch and building on what we have. Mia said something about us being a family no matter what happens between me and you. I want that, Addy, but I want a relationship, too."

Addy took his hand in hers, kissed the palm, and put it back on the steering wheel. "Then we'll have to work things out and see if we can figure out a way to have both. Are you sure you're all right with the fact I can't have more children?"

"Dad and Mama couldn't have children either, and yet they've got three sons." He wiggled his eyebrows and went back to driving.

"I never thought of that." She wasn't sure how she felt about fostering children or about adopting.

"But all of that is another conversation for later. I should get used to one daughter first," Jesse said as he snagged a parking spot close to the Walmart entry door. "Right now, we need to go buy a baby gift, and then stop by the snow cone stand, pull over at the old barn where we went to party as kids, and eat it slowly."

"Ohhhh!" Addy gasped. "I haven't had a snow cone all summer. You still like coconut?"

"Yep." He grinned. "Do you still like rainbow because you can't make up your mind for one flavor?"

"Depends on my mood," she answered.

He held her hand across the parking lot and into the store.

Addy gently touched a cute little pink gingham dress when they got back into the baby section. "The styles are coming back around to what I used to put on Mia. I like this one." She put it in the cart and moved on to pick out a package of cotton receiving blankets, a towel and washcloth gift set, and another outfit.

"I can't believe Mia was ever small enough to wear something like that," Jesse said.

"She was a really big baby, so she didn't wear this size very long," Addy said as she picked up a package of tiny socks. "I'm sorry, again, that you missed all the fun of raising her."

"Me, too." Jesse shifted his eyes over to the left and nodded.

"What?" she asked.

He grinned and came close enough to whisper, "We have an audience. Vivien and Lylah are around that end and listening to every word we say. I caught them peeking at us a couple of minutes ago." He kissed her on the cheek and took a step back. "I think Mia is a good mix of both of us, don't you?"

"Shhh..." Addy put her forefinger over his lips. "We don't want the whole world to know. They might think you ran when you found out I was pregnant, when in reality, you didn't even know about Mia until you came home a few weeks ago. Let's get some pacifiers and check out. That snow cone is calling my name."

"Did you crave them when you were expecting Mia?" His green eyes twinkled.

"Yep," she said and then air-slapped his arm. "Shhh...folks might get the wrong idea."

"I hope so," he mouthed.

Addy paid for their items and Jesse carried the bag outside. When they were inside the truck, Jesse burst out in laughter. "That was so much fun. We should have taken the cart around the corner and acted all embarrassed."

"If you lean your head over to the right, you'll be able to hear the buzz of gossip running through the phone lines right now," Addy said.

"But now, we don't have to worry how to let folks know about Mia, do we? And you did so well by saying that about me not even knowing about her. Which one will they think is pregnant? You or Mia?" He pulled a handkerchief from his pocket and wiped his eyes.

"All over a baby shower that they'll both be at tomorrow night since it's Vivien's niece who is expecting a baby next month." Addy sighed. "The joys of small-town living."

"Want to move to Miami with me? I've got until Friday to give Frankie an answer," Jesse chuckled again.

"Don't you think moving in with you is kind of quick since we haven't even had a real date yet?" she asked.

"Well, darlin'," he drawled, "we do have a daughter together so it's not like we just met yesterday."

"Don't tempt me." She couldn't think of anything she'd like better than living on Sunflower Ranch with Jesse, but not in Miami.

Does that mean what you feel for him isn't unconditional? You wouldn't move to the ends of the world just to be with him? asked the aggravating voice in her head.

"Miami, the bunkhouse, me back in my room with you." He named off places. "Or we could build a house of our own on the ranch. It's your decision if you'll move in with me."

"I want the whole dating experience before I make a decision like that," Addy said, putting him off until she had time to figure out if he was serious or just teasing.

"Then you'll have it. Addison Hall, will you go to dinner with me on Thursday evening?" he asked.

"Why Thursday?"

"Because you have a baby shower tomorrow night after the midweek church service," he reminded her, "and you'll have a lot of questions to answer at it, I'm sure. On Thursday, we can go to dinner and talk about all of that."

"Why can't we talk about it when I get home, like when I come to the bunkhouse afterwards?" she asked.

"No reason whatsoever because, darlin', we will always have stuff to talk about," he answered. "So I can look forward to you coming to see me tomorrow evening? Should I buy another six-pack of Jack Daniel's Watermelon?"

"That might be a good idea," she said, smiling, "and yes, I would love to go to dinner with you. Where are we going, so I'll know how to dress?"

"It's a surprise, and in my eyes, you would be sexy in a gunny sack, darlin'." He was actually flirting with her.

Addy's heart did one of those flip-flop things that she hadn't felt in years and years. "Is that your best pickup line after all these years?"

"Honey, I don't need a line. All I have to do is tell the truth." He pulled his truck up behind three other vehicles at the snow cone stand. "Rainbow with cherry, banana, and grape, right?"

"Nope," she told him. "Tonight, I want a coconut cream."

He whipped his head around and locked gazes with her. "I can't believe you made up your mind for only one flavor."

"I've had either blue coconut or coconut cream for twenty years. They remind me of you," she admitted.

"This is my first snow cone since I left home, and, honey, everything reminded me of you," he said. "They used to serve them in cone shapes. I wonder when they started using paper cups?"

"They haven't used those cone things in years," she said. "What I wonder is why did we waste all those years?"

"Nothing is wasted life," he answered. "Everything we've been through has brought us to this day. I like the adults we've become even better than the kids we were."

"When you put it that way, it makes sense. God or Fate or Destiny was preparing us for something better on down the road." Addy did a quick look back over the years and realized in that moment that she and Jesse might not have made a relationship work when they were young, but now they just might do so.

* * *

"The barn is gone," Jesse groaned when he drove up to the spot where the old building had been. "I thought that thing was so old, it had petrified and would be here for another hundred years."

"I was looking forward to climbing up in the loft and watching the stars while we finished these snow cones," Addy said.

Jesse opened the truck door to find there was a nice breeze blowing. "The stars are still there even if the barn has been torn down. We'll get a much better view from the bed of my truck. I've got an emergency quilt we can lay on under the backseat. Maybe we'll see a falling star, and we can make a wish on it."

Addy didn't wait on him to help her out of the vehicle but met him at the backside of the truck with a snow cone in each hand. "You always travel with a quilt?"

"Yep, but it's been washed after the baby event." He spread it out in the bed of the truck, took the snow cones from her and set them on the tailgate, then helped her up.

They sat with their backs against the cab, and just as Jesse took his last bite of snow cone, he pointed up at the sky. "There goes one. What are we going to wish for?"

"You saw it first, so you get to wish," Addy told him.

"I wish for years and years of happiness right here in Honey Grove," he said.

"You stole my thunder," she replied.

Jesse wasn't at all surprised that they would want the same thing.

Knowing her as well as you do, the voice inside his head said, sounding a lot like Frankie's, *are you going to get bored with her and wish you were back in the life with me and the boys? If she really loves you, she would be willing to come to Miami with you.*

Jesse slowly shook his head. *She's not the problem, my friend. I don't want to go back to that life, and even if I did, my family, and that includes Addy and Mia, are more important to me than the thrill that dangerous adventures would bring.*

He slid over closer to Addy and wrapped her up in his arms and breathed in the sweet coconut fragrance of her hair. "It's your hair," he blurted out.

"What's my hair?" she asked.

"You've always used shampoo that smells like coconut. The snow cones leave a taste in my mouth like the scent of your hair leaves in my nose. That's what I like about that flavor," he said.

"That may be the most romantic thing a guy has ever said to me," she said.

Jesse tipped up her chin with his fist and kissed her—long, lingering, and passionately. "I've wanted to do that all evening," he said when the kiss ended.

She drew his mouth down to hers for another kiss, and when that one ended, they were both panting. "I've wanted to do that all evening, too. Matter of fact, I wanted to kiss you like that a lot of the times when we were out here as kids." She shifted her weight until she was sitting in his lap, and her lips were on his again.

Jesse had never wanted a woman so much that his whole body ached with desire, or that his heart had pounded so hard. His hands found their way up under her shirt, and her skin was like silk to his touch. He massaged her back while she undid the buttons on his shirt, one at a time, stopping to run her hands over his chest after she unfastened each one.

"You're killin' me," he gasped.

"What do you think you're doing to me?" she whispered in his ear.

"Are we going to do this right here in the bed of my truck?" he asked.

"What's wrong with this place? The stars are above us, and there goes another shooting one." Her lips found his again.

When that round of kisses ended, he said, "I'd thought of something far more romantic than this for our first time."

"This is our second time, and there's no place more romantic than this." She smiled.

Jesse didn't argue but simply enjoyed every minute of having Addy back in his arms, of feeling her naked body next to his, of the complete satisfaction of making love to her with his whole body, heart and soul. Then he wrapped the quilt around them, sealing them inside as if they were in a cocoon and all the world had disappeared.

"I like the idea of it being just us under the stars," he whispered.

Addy's soft breathing said volumes. She had drifted off to sleep in his arms, trusting him out there in the wide-open spaces to protect her. He buried his face in her hair and closed his eyes, planning to rest them for only a few minutes.

At midnight a distant ringing woke him. Thinking it was the alarm clock beside his bed, he reached over to slap it, only to find that Addy had her phone in her hand.

"Hello," she said in a groggy voice. "We'll be home in a few minutes. We had snow cones, and we came out to our old party stomping grounds, and both of us fell asleep."

He could hear Mia's voice saying that she was worried when she came home and her mother wasn't in her bedroom.

"You're out past curfew, too, darlin' girl," Addy noted.

"I'm a grown woman," Mia raised her voice.

"So am I. We'll be home in five minutes. Don't wait up for me," Addy said. "The snow cone was delicious, by the way."

"I will wait up. I worry about you," Mia said.

"See you in a few then," Addy said and ended the call.

"Busted!" Jesse chuckled.

"I didn't lie. The snow cone was delicious, and what came after it was amazing. Now, I suppose we'd better get dressed and go home. I don't think we can both use one quilt like a sarong." She placed her palms on his chest and leaned in for a kiss.

Her touch warmed his whole body and made him want another round of passionate sex—no, that wasn't right—he wanted to make love to her again. There was a vast difference in a roll in the sheets and making love, and what he and Addy had was definitely the latter.

Chapter Twenty

Addy hummed as she got ready for the day on Wednesday morning. She and Jesse had made love out there in a pasture with the moon and stars looking down on them. She hadn't thought of anything during those hours but his arms around her and his skin touching hers, and it had been absolutely amazing. She was still humming an old country song by Wynonna Judd, "Mama He's Crazy," when she made it to the kitchen.

"You're in a good mood this morning," Pearl said.

"Yes, I am, and I hope nothing spoils it, but I've got a feeling this baby shower tonight could, so I intend to love my good mood all day." Addy got the bacon out of the fridge and a cast iron skillet from the pantry.

"I imagine the gossip will be in full force by tonight, but there will be questions, I'm sure," Pearl chuckled.

"Phone already been ringing?" Addy asked as the skillet heated up.

"First thing this morning," Sonny piped up from his place

at the table. "Rumors spread faster than the speed of light in a small town. What happened to cause all this?"

Addy told them about Lylah and Vivien eavesdropping in the Walmart store. "We said just enough that they know Jesse is Mia's father." She went on to tell Pearl that she had taken full responsibility for Jesse not knowing. "That should take the heat off him so folks don't think he's been a horrible person."

"You done good, girl." Pearl smiled.

"Yes, you did." Sonny laid his paper aside.

"I hope so, but I bet there'll be some whispers at the baby shower tonight," Addy said.

"I'm sure there will be, and I bet since y'all were buying baby clothes that those two gossipin' women think one or both of you are expecting a baby. Lylah and Vivien are going to look a little foolish when they find out that neither of my girls are pregnant," Sonny commented and went back to his newspaper.

"Good mornin'." Jesse pushed his way into the kitchen.

"You're mighty chipper, son." Sonny looked up over the top of his paper this time.

Jesse filled a mug with coffee and then carried the pot to the table to top off his dad's cup. "Yes, I am. I had a job offer from my old Air Force teammate yesterday. He offered me a six-figure salary and a big benefit package to work with him and my team in private security. I turned him down because this place right here is where my heart is, so I am happy and chipper this morning. I've figured out where I want to be for the rest of my life, and I'm at peace with the decision."

"Good for you," Sonny said.

Pearl stopped what she was doing and hugged Jesse. "I'm so glad to hear that. I would never want any of my boys to be here unless their heart was in ranching."

"Well, mine is," Jesse said.

"Yours is what?" Mia asked as she entered the room by the back door and went straight for the coffeepot.

"My heart is right here on this ranch, and I'm not leaving," he answered.

Mia poured a mugful of coffee, added sugar and cream, and took a sip. "That's good to know after that phone call you got yesterday. Did you and Mama discuss Frankie's offer over your snow cones last night? And did Mama get a coconut cream like she always does? She never changes her flavor."

"We did and she did, and I got the same kind." Jesse smiled.

"Y'all are getting old." Mia yawned. "I got up early and did the alpaca feeding and got their troughs cleaned and refilled. It's amazing how dirty that water can get in only a day."

"Ranchin' is never done," Sonny said. "It's kind of like a relationship. You've got to work at it constantly."

"You got that right," Addy said.

* * *

Just as she had thought, the minute that Addy and Pearl walked into the fellowship hall that evening after a short Wednesday night Bible study, the buzz of conversation ceased.

"Hello, everyone," Pearl said. "This party is not about Addison or Mia or even me and Sonny tonight. This is Gloria Sue's party to celebrate the birth of her new baby daughter, who will be here in about a month. So let's get the rumors settled and let it be her night. To begin with, Mia is indeed Jesse's daughter. He didn't know until he retired from the service. Addy probably deserves a crown for having the best-kept secret for the past twenty years. To end with, neither Addy nor Mia are pregnant. They were buying presents for this shower last night when Lylah and Vivien overheard them talking. Now that's settled, let's let Gloria Sue open her presents and enjoy this event."

"I don't believe you," Lylah whispered when Addy sat down right beside her.

"What's that old saying?" Addy pretended to be thinking. "Oh, I remember: Believe nothing you hear and only half of what you see."

"If Mia is having my grandchild, I will get grandparent's rights. I've already talked to a lawyer about Justine's kid and asked for a DNA test," Lylah continued to whisper.

"Be careful," Addy told her in a low voice. "You could wind up supporting that little guy for eighteen years or else visiting your son in jail if he doesn't pay support. She told you that she didn't want anything from you or your son."

"He's not Ricky's kid. I'm just proving it," Lylah said.

"If he is, you could be out thousands and thousands of dollars in child support, plus lawyer fees, so be sure this is what you want, and not revenge," Addy said and raised her voice. "Oh, look at that cute little romper. It will be perfect for the new baby girl."

"Maybe Jesse should ask for a DNA test since you were so secretive about things," Lylah hissed through clenched teeth.

"Now, you are getting into none-of-your-business territory, and honey, you don't want to go there." Addy smiled sweetly.

Lylah got up and moved to the other side of the room. Vivien followed right behind her like a little puppy dog.

The gifts had all been opened and displayed on a table, and the hostesses were serving refreshments when Addy's phone vibrated. She fished it out of the pocket of her flowing gauze skirt, expecting it to be Mia, but it was Jesse.

"Hello, I thought you might be Mia." She stepped out into the hallway, where it was quieter.

"I'm in the ambulance with Dad. He collapsed. He's awake, but he can't say a word," Jesse whispered. "Bring Mama straight to the hospital in Bonham, please, Addy."

"We're on our way. Hang in there. We'll be right behind you," Addy said. "Jesse, this is a side effect of that trial drug. Grady will know what to do. Ask for him when you get there."

"How do you know that?" Jesse asked.

"I studied every aspect of those drugs before Sonny started taking them. See you in a few minutes." She ended the call and crossed the room to where Pearl was talking to a couple of the hostesses. "We've got to go right now," she whispered in Pearl's ear.

"Is it Sonny?" Pearl asked.

"Yes, but let's just leave quietly so there's not a lot of drama," Addy said.

Pearl picked up her purse. Addy did the same and they slipped out the side door.

"What's happened?" Pearl asked, breathless and paler than Addy had ever seen her. "Is Sonny okay?"

"Jesse's on the way with him to the hospital. Sounds like he's got stroke symptoms, probably from that trial drug he's been taking." Addy worked hard to stay calm and matter-of-fact as she got behind the wheel of her car.

Pearl clasped her hands in her lap. "Will he be okay?"

"If it's just a side effect of the drug, he should be okay once it's out of his system. We'll know more as soon as Grady has had a chance to check him out." Addy hated not to have better news, but she also didn't want to make any false promises.

Addy got out of town and onto the highway and drove ten miles over the speed limit the whole way to the hospital. When she got there, she braked in front of the emergency room doors, but Pearl didn't get out of the SUV.

"Addy, I can't go in there alone. I'm strong, but when it comes to Sonny, I can't imagine life without him. If it was a stroke, and he didn't make it, I don't want to be alone. Jesse will be in there. I know that, but I'll have to suck it up and be brave for him and his brothers when they come home. I need you there to give me the strength to do that. Go on and park, and we'll go inside together." Pearl wiped tears from her cheeks with the back of her hand.

"If that's what you want." Addy swallowed hard and drove to the parking lot. She thought about calling Mia but decided against it—not until she knew more about his condition.

Pearl opened the door as soon as Addy parked the vehicle. "I'm ready now. I might not like the news, but with you by my side right there at first, I can handle it."

Addy tossed the keys in her purse and walked beside Pearl. The automatic doors slid open, and Jesse met them in the middle of the waiting room floor. He wrapped one arm around his mother and the other around Addy. "Grady's back there with him now, but he said that you can go be with him, Mama. Dad still can't talk, but he wrote your name on a piece of paper. I figured you'd be getting here about now, so I stepped out to talk to y'all."

"One at a time?" Pearl held her hands tightly together.

Addy could feel Pearl's anxiety and sense of doom. "Can I go stand outside the door?"

Jesse shook his head and nodded toward the left. "Only one at a time goes through those doors right there. Mama, he wants you."

Addy gave her a quick hug and whispered, "It's all right. Jesse and I are both right here. If he needs a shoulder, I've got two, and Sonny will understand if you aren't strong."

"Thank you." Pearl straightened her shoulders, took a deep breath, and marched through the doors leading back into the emergency room.

Jesse collapsed into a chair, propped his elbows on his knees, and put his head in his hands. "I'm so scared, Addy. He was coming from the kitchen to the living room and he just fell on the floor. By the time I got to him, his eyes were wide, and he couldn't speak. I just knew it was a stroke, but Grady says he thinks it's the side effects of his medicine. What if he's wrong?"

Addy sat down in the chair right next to him and wrapped him up in her arms. "I should have told you all the side effects so you would have been prepared for something like this when you were alone with him. This is the very first one listed."

"Thank you for being here," he muttered.

"I wouldn't be anywhere else," she said. "Have you called Cody and Lucas just in case it's not his meds causing this?" She hated to even say the words out loud, but if she were one of the other two sons, she would want to know what was going on with her parents.

"Grady said it wasn't a time to call in the family, but I did anyway. Cody was in London for a fundraising event and said he'd catch the next plane to the States. Couldn't get a hold of Lucas. He's somewhere in France training some horses for a multibillionaire, and the phone service isn't good," Jesse answered.

Grady pushed through the doors and stopped in front of Addy and Jesse. Addy dropped one arm but kept the other one around Jesse's shoulders.

"I'm so sorry about this," Grady said in a professional tone without making eye contact with Addy.

Jesse raised his head and asked, "Was it a stroke?"

Grady shook his head slowly. "I've done preliminary tests, and it doesn't appear so. We're going to do a CT scan to confirm it's not a brain issue, and then put him in a room. We want to keep him at least twenty-four hours for observation. I still think it's the trial drugs, but we'll be absolutely sure before we send him home."

"How will you know?" Jesse asked.

"We're flushing the drugs from his system right now. If that's the problem, he will start to regain his ability to speak by morning," Grady answered. "Time is going to be our biggest asset right now. It would be best if you went home and got some rest. Pearl has already said she won't leave his side. Y'all can go in and see him for five minutes. Don't worry, Jesse. We'll make her comfortable."

"Thanks, Grady," Jesse said. "We'll wait right here until he's in a room. We want to see him before we leave."

"Fair enough." Grady turned around and disappeared through the doors.

Jesse cut his eyes around to focus on Addy. "Is he shootin' me a line of bull, or is he tellin' the truth?"

"I really think he's being truthful," Addy answered. "If it had been a stroke or a brain bleed of some kind, the symptoms would have been different. You would know that from your medic background."

"Never dealt with that kind of problem," Jesse said. "Mostly I was sewing guys up, starting IVs, and getting them ready for the helicopter to fly them off to a hospital for more extensive care."

Addy removed her arm from around him and laced her fingers in his. "Well, darlin', I've dealt with lots of stroke and heart attack patients, and so has Grady. I'm going to choose to trust him, but I am sorry this trial thing didn't work. If it had, it would have hopefully stopped the MS right where it is."

"God, I'm glad you're here," Jesse whispered.

"I'm glad you are," Addy said. "And I know Pearl and Sonny are, too. Sweet Jesus!" she gasped as she grabbed her phone from her purse. "I've got to call Mia."

* * *

When Addy and Jesse got back to the ranch house that night, Mia met them at the door with a scowl on her face. "I'm on my way to the hospital. I packed a bag for Nana." Her chin quivered for a few seconds and then she broke into tears. "I'm going to go and be there with Nana. She needs me."

"They said only one person can stay with him." Jesse drew her to his side with an arm around her shoulders. "Grady is his doctor, and he thinks that, by morning, Dad will be talking again. I can drive that bag back to Mama."

Mia stiffened her back. "He can't talk! How is he communicating? Oh, Jesse, what if he never laughs or talks again?"

"He will," Jesse said. "He's a strong-willed guy. He *will* get over this."

"What caused it?" Mia asked.

"Most likely the trial drugs he was taking for his MS," Addy answered.

"Then he can't have them anymore, right?" Mia asked. "I don't care if he gets in a wheelchair. I want to be able to talk to him as long as we can."

"He's off of them already, and they are flushing them out of his system." Jesse hugged her closer.

Addy's phone rang, and a heavy silence filled the room. She'd told Pearl to call her if things got worse so they could rush back to the hospital. With trembling hands and a shaky voice, she answered the call.

"Hello, Pearl. Do we need to come right now?" she asked.

"No, darlin', and I didn't mean to scare y'all, but I had to tell you the good news. Sonny said three words to me before he drifted off to a peaceful sleep. He said, 'I love you.' Those were the most precious words I've ever heard in my whole life. Grady says that means he'll be fine, and that we can go home after twenty-four hours. Go get some sleep and call me before you head this way in the morning."

After a few more words, Addy ended the call and turned around to face Jesse and Mia. "He told Pearl that he loved her and then drifted off to sleep."

"Thank you, Jesus!" Mia said dramatically. "Does Henry know about this?"

"Yes, he does." Jesse smiled up at Addy. "I called him from the hospital. He's letting the hired hands know that there won't be any work tomorrow because we'll all be in and out of the hospital."

"In and out, my butt." Mia swiped a hand across her face. "I'll be there all day, and I don't care if I have to sleep in the hall beside his room. I'll be there all night if Nana needs me."

"All right, but call me when you get to the hospital," Addy said, "and don't give Grady too hard of a time."

"Why not? He wasn't very nice to you." Mia picked up the small tote bag and headed out the door.

Addy slumped down beside Jesse on the sofa.

Just sitting close to him brought comfort to her, but when he reached over and took her hand in his, she realized that she wanted to hear those three precious words from him. She was a patient woman, and there was no hurry, but she didn't want to waste another twenty years either.

Chapter Twenty-One

"Don't fuss over me," Sonny said, as Jesse held the door for him to get into the house. "I had a little episode. I'm over it. Tests all came back saying that I'm going to live until I'm a hundred and ten, so don't all y'all start smothering me."

"I'll smother you if I want to," Mia declared, "and there's nothing you can do about it, so there."

"Okay, then," Sonny said, "you've got permission to worry, but nobody else. Sunflower won't run itself."

Henry came out of the kitchen with a big chocolate chip cookie in his hand. "No, it won't, and you're not going to guilt me into staying on here by pretending to be sick."

"I thought it might work," Sonny teased. "Guess you're determined to leave if my near-death experience doesn't keep you here."

"Near death, my royal ass," Henry growled. "Come on out to the porch. I made coffee, and the church ladies brought a big pan of cookies and a pineapple upside-down cake for your homecoming. I got to admit these are some damn fine cookies even if Lylah O'Malley did make them. And, Sonny, you need to lay off those stupid drugs so you can come spend some time with me in the Colorado mountains."

Addy thought that Sonny was leaning on his cane a little more than usual. She hung back and let Henry and Sonny go through the kitchen and out on the back porch, where Mia and Pearl had already gone.

"What do you think, nurse?" Jesse asked.

"For every day you lay in bed, it takes five to recover, so we should expect him to tire out a little faster than usual for a few days," she answered.

"What can we expect now that he's off the meds?" Jesse slipped an arm around her waist and drew her close to his side.

"It's a crap shoot," she answered. "He might stay like he is right now for years, but eventually, he will end up in a wheelchair."

"That doesn't scare me as much as losing him." Jesse bent down and kissed her on the forehead. "I'm sorry about our date tonight."

"There's time for those things later," she told him. "Right now, Sonny and Pearl are our top priority. We have to be sure that we take good care of Pearl, too. This is a lot of stress on her."

"Just tell me what to do if I miss something," he said. "Will you come to the bunkhouse later this evening?"

"If you'll wake me up in time to get up here and have breakfast going when Pearl gets up in the morning," she answered.

"Deal," he said. He took a couple of steps toward the kitchen, then turned around and cocked his head to one side. "Do I hear someone coming up the driveway?"

"Sounds like it, but it's pretty late for company to be dropping in," Addy answered.

The sound of a car door slamming floated through the night

air. Footsteps sounded loudly on the wooden porch. Then the thud of something dropped in the foyer caused Jesse and Addy both to turn at the same time.

"Cody!" Jesse let go of Addy's hand and rushed to wrap his brother up in a fierce bear hug. "I didn't think you'd be here until tomorrow."

"How's Dad?" Cody asked. "Is he home yet?"

"Just now got here. He's out on the back porch." Jesse took a step back and held his brother at arm's length. "You look like hell."

Cody was as tall as Jesse, but maybe thirty pounds lighter, which gave him a gaunt look. His thick blond hair lay on his shirt collar, and his blue eyes looked weary and tired.

"I feel like hell, but I want to see Dad. Hello, Addy. Didn't mean to slight you." Cody managed a weak smile in her direction.

"No problem. We can catch up and compare notes when you've had some food and a good night's rest. Can I get you a sandwich and maybe a bottle of beer or some sweet tea?" she asked.

"A sandwich and a beer would be wonderful," Cody said as he made his way across the kitchen and threw open the door to the back porch. "I hear there's a party out here."

Addy gave Jesse a gentle push. "Go on out there with all of them. I'll bring out a platter of sandwiches and some chips in a few minutes."

"Sweet Jesus!" Pearl squealed.

"No, Mama, just one tired old prodigal son coming home." Cody opened his arms and Pearl rushed into them.

"Go!" Addy told Jesse.

"Let them have a little time," Jesse said. "I'll help you with the sandwiches. Besides, I need a kiss to hold me until tonight."

"You sure about that? Cody will probably go to the bunk-house, too, since all the rooms in the house are filled." Addy brought ham and cheese out of the refrigerator.

"Does that mean you're ashamed to spend the night with me if Cody is in the bunkhouse?" Jesse asked.

"Ha! I'm not one bit ashamed," Addy said. "But I don't want to make it tough on you."

Jesse put his hands on her waist and took a step forward. "Honey, I'd be happy if you gave him your room after tonight and moved into the bunkhouse with me."

"Don't tempt me." Addy rose up on her tiptoes and kissed him.

"Hey, what's going on in here?" Mia asked from right inside the door. "You two should be out there welcoming Cody, not making out in the kitchen."

"Bossy, isn't she?" Jesse chuckled and headed for the pantry. "I'll get a bag of chips."

"We're making sandwiches. You can get down a platter," Addy answered. "And I expect Jesse and I are old enough to make out wherever we want."

Mia did one of her famous head wiggles. "Whatever! But you're also old enough to get a room and not embarrass your daughter." She reached into the cabinet and brought out a plate. "You put on the mayo, and I'll slap them together and cut them diagonally. I could probably eat half a dozen. Nana and I haven't had anything but a couple of cookies from the vending machine since noon."

"We could have stopped and gotten pizza or chicken to bring home." Jesse brought two bags of chips from the pantry.

"Poppa was in a hurry to get here, and we didn't want to take the time," Mia explained as she deftly made sandwiches. "That's plenty for now, Mama. We can make more if we eat all these. I bet Poppa will have some, too. He didn't eat worth a damn in the hospital. He said the food didn't taste like what Nana makes." She turned around to find Jesse grinning at her. "And for your information, I am bossy. I get that from Mama and Nana both, so if you don't like it, you don't have to claim me as a daughter."

"He already did," Addy said.

"What does that mean?" Mia picked up the plate of sandwiches but didn't take a single step.

"It means that we deliberately let it slip when we saw Lylah eavesdropping the other night when we went to Walmart to get a gift for Gloria Sue's shower," Jesse answered. "I'll tell you all about it tomorrow while we get the bales of hay into the barn. And Pearl announced it to the whole bunch of ladies at the baby shower last night."

"I'm just now hearing about this?" Mia raised both dark eyebrows. "I'll be in your room later this evening, Mama."

"You won't find anyone there. She's sleeping over in the bunkhouse with me," Jesse said.

Mia whipped her head around so quickly that Addy figured she would have a crick in her neck the next morning.

Addy shrugged. "You told us to get a room."

* * *

"How long are you going to be able to stay?" Jesse twisted the top off a bottle of beer and handed it to Cody.

"Thanks." Cody took the beer from him. "Honestly, I have no plans to go back," Cody answered quietly.

"Really?" Jesse tried to keep his voice down, too.

"I'm too tired to talk about it tonight, but I've got an idea to run by you and the folks in the morning," Cody said.

"Fair enough," Jesse replied. "But I'll say this, I'm glad to hear it. I can use some help on this place when Henry leaves.

When school starts back in late August, we'll lose our summer hired hands, too."

"If what I've got in mind pans out, I'll have time for a little ranching. Tell the truth, I've missed it, but now that I see Dad is going to be all right, I'd sure like to find a shower and a bed. Want to help me take my things to the bunkhouse?" Cody asked.

"You can have my room," Addy told him. "I'm staying in the bunkhouse with Jesse tonight. I'll feel a lot better knowing a doctor is in the house in case Sonny needs you."

"Well, good for the both of you." Cody yawned.

Addy stood and started inside the house. "While you shower, I'll get some clean sheets on the bed."

"Thanks," Cody said. "I can't remember the last time I slept in a real bed with clean sheets. Mostly, I catch forty winks in a hammock or on an army cot."

"I'll help you," Pearl said.

Mia hopped up from her place on the top porch step. "You're worn out, Nana. I'll help Mama."

"And I'm going to my place," Henry said. "Thanks for not dying, you old coot."

"Who's calling who old?" Sonny asked. "You and I are the same age."

"Yeah, but I didn't have to spend a night in the hospital," Henry threw over his shoulder as he disappeared into the dark.

"You need to get to bed," Jesse said to his father. "Want some help?"

"I told y'all that only Mia can smother me," Sonny reminded them. "The whole lot of you have got things to do. Cody, you get a shower and some shut-eye. Mia, you help your mama. And Jesse, you better take these leftover sandwiches down to the bunkhouse," Sonny said with a broad wink. "You might get hungry later."

"Thanks, Dad." Jesse smiled. "Never know when a guy might appreciate a little food."

* * *

Addy snuggled up as close to Jesse as she could possibly get the next morning after shutting off the alarm. "I love this cuddling time."

"I love that no one is giving us hell for spending the night together." Jesse made lazy circles on her bare back with his thumb.

"We're adults," she said.

"Yep, and we've got fifteen minutes before we have to really crawl out of this bed. What do you think we should do with that time?" He had a wicked grin on his face as his hands traveled down her back.

"I can't think of much of anything when you're this close," she answered, "but I'm willing to go along with your idea."

Half an hour later, they were scrambling to get dressed for the day, then they rushed to the ranch house. They barely made it to the kitchen when Pearl and Sonny arrived with Cody right behind them. Cody Ryan was a good-looking cowboy, but there was no way he was as sexy as Jesse—not in Addy's eyes anyway.

Jesse put on a pot of coffee. "So, Cody, are you really going to stay in Honey Grove?"

"Yep, I was on my way home to surprise everyone when I got your call," Cody answered.

"Now that a full-fledged doctor is in the house, I guess I won't be needed so much," Addy said.

Jesse took five mugs from the cabinet and filled them. He set three on the table and handed off the other two to his mother and Addy, then put another pot on to brew.

"Oh, no!" Cody shook his head. "I want to do some ranching. I've missed that, but I want to be a doctor, too. Nothing says I can't be both, does it?"

"Not one bit," Sonny answered. "Does that mean you're going to be a part-time doctor?"

"Kind of, but more like an old-time doctor," Cody answered. "I want to run my business from right here. I won't see patients in a clinic or in an office, so I won't need much in the way of staff—just a nurse." He glanced over at Addy. "I would make house calls, and if the patient's condition warrants it, I'd refer them to a specialist or send them to the hospital."

"What would you need a nurse for?" Addy stirred up the batter for banana nut muffins.

"To help, for one thing, and as a witness for another. Kind of like when you go to the doctor for an exam and a nurse is always standing by."

"That sounds like a great idea," Sonny said. "I'll be your first patient."

"Thanks, Dad." Cody nodded.

"You can have Henry's place for your office when he moves to Colorado in a few weeks. Until then, you can use my office to get things set up," Sonny told him. "You'll need to keep files and supplies and such, and his little house would be perfect."

"Why don't you take the bunkhouse?" Jesse suggested. "Since I'll be the new foreman, I thought maybe I'd take Henry's place. The bunkhouse is closer to the house, so you'd be close by if Dad needs you."

Cody looked over Jesse's shoulder right at Addy. "Would you consider being my nurse?"

Addy's first thought was what would Jesse think of her accepting the offer; then her second was that this was her life and her decision.

"Nurse for what?" Mia came into the kitchen and went straight for the coffeepot. "Mama can't leave the ranch. This is our home."

Pearl explained what they had been talking about in a few words. "No one would be leaving the ranch. We'd just be adding a doctor to the list of who lives here."

Mia took a sip of coffee, then set her mug on the cabinet and started setting the table for breakfast. "Too bad you're not a vet. We could sure use one so that we wouldn't have to pay Stevie so much."

Cody chuckled. "Maybe I can help save enough on doctor bills to offset what Stevie charges. Who is this guy anyway?"

"Not guy." Addy was glad to steer the conversation away from herself. She needed time to think about Cody's offer. "Remember Stephanie O'Dell? She would have been a couple of years younger than you in high school."

"She had red hair even curlier than yours and big blue eyes," Cody finished her sentence. "Kind of tall and thin, and she cleaned up in the science division of every academic meet we went to. Kind of embarrassed me since she was a freshman, and I was a senior."

"That's Stevie O'Dell." Addy slid the muffins into the oven.

"She'll be at the rodeo events in Honey Grove tonight," Sonny said. "She volunteers her time to be the onsite vet. I can't wait to see how the little kiddos do on the mutton busting. I love that and the calf riding and the calf scramble."

Addy had begun to shake her head before Sonny finished. "Grady said that you are to have more rest for a few days. You don't need to be sitting out in the heat at a dusty old rodeo."

"Grady's not my doctor anymore," Sonny said. "Cody is my new doctor, and if he doesn't agree with me, then that's too bad. That little episode has taught me that I'm not wasting one more second sitting around and waiting for this disease to put me on my back. I'm going to live my life. Pearl and I are going to the rodeo, and as soon as Henry gets settled in Colorado, we're going to spend a few weeks with him. After that I'm taking her to Las Vegas. You boys are home. You can take care of Sunflower."

"But we'll only be gone for a week at a time," Pearl said. "I want to spend as much time as I can with my boys."

"We'll be together and having a good time, not sitting at home waiting for me to die, and when I'm home, I don't want y'all to treat me like an invalid either." Sonny opened his arms. "Come over here and give me a hug, Pearl."

When Pearl bent to hug Sonny, he pulled her onto his lap and kissed her cheek. "I'm the luckiest man alive to have had you beside me all these years."

"You've always been a hopeless romantic," Pearl said through misty eyes.

"That's why you fell in love with me when we were just sixteen years old." Sonny smiled and kissed her on the other cheek. "Promise me you'll travel with me, and let me do what I can for as long as I can."

"I promise, sweetheart," she said. "I'll go with you wherever you want to go, but if we get any more grandchildren, I want to be home to enjoy them."

Addy had been so intent on watching the beautiful display of love that she didn't even notice Jesse getting up to stand behind her. When she sighed, he slipped his hands around her waist and whispered, "That's the kind of relationship I want."

"Me, too," she agreed.

Chapter Twenty-Two

Thank God for a breeze that ruffled the leaves on the trees on Friday afternoon, Jesse thought. He worried about his dad being out in the hot sun, too, after the episode he had had, but there was no talking him out of going to the parade. Sonny agreed to sit in a canvas chair, but he declared that he had judged the little kids' bicycle part of the parade for fifty years, and he wasn't turning his job over to anyone else that year.

"Mia, darlin', go get some nachos from that vendor across the street for me and Pearl to share while we figure out which bicycle is best." Sonny handed her a twenty-dollar bill. "And we'll want a large root beer, too. Keep whatever change there is to get yourself something to eat. We won't be going back home until after the events tonight. I want to visit with the folks."

"Dad, you could use a couple of hours rest between now and the mutton busting," Cody told him.

"I can rest when I can't go anymore," Sonny said. "Now, y'all go on and stop hovering around me like buzzards waiting for me to die."

"Sonny Ryan!" Addy scolded. "I'm not a buzzard!"

"No, honey, you're a pretty little dove, but these two are so worried about me leaving this earth that they're forgetting to live. Jesse, take this woman by the hand and let the whole town know y'all are a couple, or an item, or whatever the hell y'all call it these days. If you don't, some guy like Grady will come along and steal her from you," Sonny chuckled.

Jesse quickly grabbed Addy's hand and kissed the knuckles. "Do I need to carry a pistol?" he joked.

"I reckon not," Sonny answered. "Hey, Dr. Stevie." He waved and yelled across the road.

Stevie waved back and jogged over to where Sonny and Pearl were sitting. "I heard you had to spend some time in the hospital. You should have called me. I've treated rangy old bulls like you for a long time."

"I'd say that next time I would, but Cody has come home, and he'll be takin' care of me from now on," Sonny told her.

Jesse tugged on Addy's hand, but she held her ground. "Just a minute. I'm trying to decide if I want tacos, which are that way"—she pointed to the left—"or corn dogs, which are in the other direction."

Stevie gave Cody a steely glance. "We've got a doctor here in Honey Grove, and a dozen or more within a thirty-minute drive."

"How many of them make house calls?" Cody met her stare.

"You're crazy if you think that will work in this day and time," Stevie said.

"Maybe so, but I'm going to give it my best shot," Cody said.

"And if you fail?" Stevie asked.

"I might go back to school, get my vet credentials, and give you some competition," he teased.

"In your dreams," she retorted and stormed off toward the chutes.

"There's something between them," Addy whispered to Jesse.

"Yep." Jesse grinned. "Always has been, but neither of them will wake up and see what's in front of their noses. Remind you of another couple we know?"

Addy laughed.

"I'm thinking tacos."

"Sounds good," Addy said.

Everyone they passed wanted to welcome Jesse back home again and ask about Sonny. This was the first time some of the folks had seen Jesse since his return. Several of them took notice of the fact he either was holding Addy's hand or else had an arm around her waist. When he started to introduce her to most folks, they just smiled and said they already knew her, then asked if her folks still liked living in the panhandle.

When the two of them finally made it to the taco vendor, Addy asked, "What's going on with Stevie and Cody?"

"They went to the same college, and she kind of had a crush on Cody then. He was a senior when she was a freshman." Jesse moved up to the front of the line and ordered half a dozen tacos and two bottles of root beer.

"What happened?" Addy carried the root beers over to a picnic table that was set up under an awning.

Jesse followed her with the paper boat holding the tacos. "I'm not sure. Cody never talked about it, and I only knew because Mama found out through the gossip vine. I think she kind of told him how she felt about him, and he broke her heart. Truth is, I had forgotten all about it until I saw them together, and I could be wrong about the whole thing."

"Is she married or engaged?" Addy asked.

"You'd have to ask Mama about that," Jesse answered. "But speaking of that, are you going to move in with me when I move into Henry's house?"

"Are you asking me to?" she asked. "I thought we were going to take things slow."

He handed her a taco. "Yep, I am. We can give it a trial run in the bunkhouse. That would be the slow part."

"Do you think we need a trial run?" she asked.

The hair on Jesse's neck tingled, which meant something wasn't quite right. "Are we having our first fight ever?"

"No, not the first one," she answered. "You remember when we were in the ninth grade?"

"Oh, yeah." He picked up a taco, unwrapped it, and took a bite.

"You told me I looked like a mop that had been hung on the clothesline to dry," she reminded him.

"Well, you said I looked like some kind of bird trying to take flight when I ran because I had chicken legs," he said.

She opened both bottles of root beer. "That was our first fight ever."

"What's this one about?" he asked.

"I want to know if . . ." she started.

He laid a hand on hers. "Yes, we have moved up a step or two from being just friends, and I like where we are, but you wanted to go slow. You should have the freedom to spend the night with me in the bunkhouse, but I also want you to know if you need some space, I won't get angry if you stay in the ranch house."

"Thank you," she said. "I like the place we're in, too."

"Even in this heat?" Cody sat down beside Jesse.

"You should be used to this after the places where you've been." Jesse really wanted to talk to Addy some more about their present and future, but he sure couldn't tell his brother to get lost. "Where were you before you made that trip to London?"

"Sudan, and you are right about the heat." Cody picked up one of the tacos and took a big bite.

"What made you decide to quit and come home?" Addy asked.

"Bullets," he answered. "Things were getting rougher by the year, and I'm getting older right along with them. I'm ready for a quiet life as a country doctor and rancher. I figure I should be ready to get my practice going by fall, so I'm available to help on the ranch until then. Have you given any thought to being my nurse, Addy?"

"Not much, but I've got to admit, it's tempting. Now that Jesse is home, and you're on the ranch, I won't be needed as much," Addy answered. "Especially if Sonny and Pearl are going to be traveling a little more."

"I won't think about hiring anyone else until you make up your mind. There's no rush. I want to take the summer to relearn the ranchin' business," Cody said.

Jesse picked up another taco. "It's like ridin' a dirt bike, or a four-wheeler. You just get out there, go to work, and it all comes back to you. Do you think Lucas will ever come back here for good?"

Cody shook his head. "Not unless Dad decides to buy a bunch of horses for him to train. He loves what he does, and when he comes home for a week, he gets bored." He looked across the table toward Addy. "He's the quiet, brooding one of us three brothers. Do you remember him?"

Addy nodded. "Very well. He was a year younger than me and Jesse, and he was always sweet to me."

"Three of us, and we're all different as night and day," Jesse said.

"You got that right, brother." Cody got up and headed toward the taco stand. "I'm getting a few more. Y'all want anything else?"

"How about a plate of nachos to share? We've still got thirty minutes to kill before the parade starts." Jesse reached over and gave Addy's knee a gentle squeeze. "Another root beer, darlin'?"

"I think I'll wait for a real beer at the rodeo grounds tonight," she answered.

"That's my girl." Jesse hoped that he was still saying that when he and Addy had been together as long as his mother and father.

That means a lifetime commitment, the voice in his head said.

I'm ready, he thought, *but I need to give her time to catch up with me.*

* * *

Addy thought that Sonny looked weary by the time the mutton bustin' started with the little kids aged six and under, but he whooped and hollered for every one of them. Jesse sat on one side of her, the fingers of one hand laced in hers, the other wrapped around a bottle of cold beer that they were sharing.

"One of my first memories was trying to stay on the back of a rangy old ram when I was four years old," he said with a grin. "Someday, we'll have kids we can dress up and watch ride in this event."

"Kids or grandkids?" she asked.

"Both," Jesse said. "I'm a foster kid who was adopted. We can always get a family that way."

"I could never be a foster mother." Addy didn't want to burst his bubble, but she had to be honest. "I would get too attached, and it would kill me to have to give a child back, and I can't even begin to imagine giving back a little baby."

"How about adoption?" Jesse asked. "My folks were almost our age when they took me and my brothers in and then adopted us when they could."

"That's a whole different conversation." She pointed. "That

little girl is going to outdo all the boys that have ridden up to now. You see the way she's easing down off the side of the chute. I've seen cowgirls approach a bull or a bronc the same way. Betcha she comes from rodeo folks."

"And here's Breanne Wilson, coming out of chute six," the announcer said into the microphone as he nodded to the two cowboys to open the gate. "She's six years old, and man alive, look at her ride in those pink cowgirl boots and that shiny shirt. Folks, I believe she's going to hang on for the full time. Good Lord! The bell has rung and she's still riding. Look at that ram go!" Two rodeo clowns chased after her and finally lifted her off the ram's back. She whipped off her helmet to show a full head of blond curls and took a deep bow. "And that's the way it's done, folks. Breanne has a score of eighty points, the highest of any tonight. Congratulations, young lady."

The crowd went wild and the little girl blew them kisses before she went back to her chute, where her mother and daddy waited. "Hey, all you daddies of little girls up there in the stands, I want y'all to remember this next feller's name. It's Wayne Crawford, and he's proven for the last two years that he's a real muttin' buster. In a few years, if he comes to date your daughters, you tell him to get lost, because he does not know how to let go."

Sonny's laughter could be heard all the way to where Jesse and Addy were sitting.

"Daddies don't need to worry." Mia sat down right behind them. "Girls are smart enough to see through those kinds of boys. It might take them a while, like it did me, but..." She gasped. "Good God! That's Ricky down there in the arena. He's one of the cowboys opening the chutes."

"No, it's not," Addy said. "That's Pete."

"Thank you, Jesus!" Mia whispered.

"Hey, Mia," Sonny called from two bleacher rows in front of them, "you in the mood for some cotton candy?"

"Always, Poppa." She stood and started toward the concession stand. "How about you and Nana. Y'all want some, too?"

"Yep," Sonny said, "and two root beers."

"What was Mia thanking Jesus for?" Cody sat down beside Addy.

"That one of those cowboys out there isn't Ricky O'Malley but his brother Pete," Addy answered.

"Mama told me all about the trouble last time we talked on the phone," Cody said. "Looks like I'm not the only one who dodged bullets."

"She might have gotten grazed," Addy said. "She turned pretty pale when she thought that was Ricky out there."

"She's young," Cody said. "She'll get over it."

"Did you 'get over it' with Stevie?" Jesse teased.

"That was a long time ago," Cody said. "Lots of water under the bridge since then."

Addy's thoughts went to all the water that had run under the proverbial bridge in the past twenty years since she and Jesse had said their goodbyes. She would never have thought they would be given a second chance to have a relationship again and yet there they were, thinking about babies and grandbabies.

He hasn't even told you that he loves you, the voice in her head reminded her. *This could just be the heat of the moment for both of you.*

* * *

The folks around the breakfast table on Saturday morning had grown to seven since Henry had joined them. Now Sonny sat at the head of the table with Pearl to his right and Henry beside her, Cody on the other end, and Jesse, Addy, and Mia on the other side. Addy had thought that Sonny would be totally exhausted after the previous day, but he looked more alive and happier than he had in years.

"Henry, Pearl and I spent some time talking yesterday afternoon, and we've made some decisions," Sonny told his foreman and then addressed everyone else. "Henry's going to leave us on August first, and Jesse will take over in his place. That next week, Pearl and I are going to Colorado for a long visit. When we get back, we're going to move into Henry's house. It's plenty big enough for the two of us. Cody can have the bunkhouse for his house and office, and Jesse, Addy, and Mia can live in this place."

"It's the sensible thing to do," Henry agreed. "Pearl will have less to clean. My little place was built on a concrete slab, so there's no stairs for Sonny to worry with."

"I can't imagine living in this house without y'all in it," Mia sighed.

"Change is good for folks. It keeps us on our toes so we don't get to taking life for granted," Sonny told her. "We'll only be a quarter of a mile away, and when we're home, you can have the job of driving me around the ranch every single day."

"Mama?" Cody asked from the other end of the table. "You've lived right here in this house your whole married life. Are you good with this?"

"I'm the one who outlined the whole plan," she answered. "I'm actually looking forward to it, and to doing some traveling with this handsome husband of mine. I want to thank you two boys for coming home so we can do some of the things we didn't think we'd ever get to do, but I also don't want to waste precious time I have with you."

"Addy, have you given any thought to what Cody offered you?" Sonny asked.

She hadn't been able to sleep the night before for thinking about the idea and still hadn't made up her mind until that very moment. Her grandmother had told her that she should open the door when opportunity knocked. According to her, it was easier to invite it inside and give it a glass of sweet tea than to chase it a mile down the road when you change your mind.

"Thanks for the offer, Cody. I would love to work for you," Addy said.

"That's wonderful, but you won't be working for me. You'll be working with me. We'll make a great team, and there will still be time for us to both do some ranchin'," Cody promised. "You all right with this arrangement, Jesse? You're going to be the boss."

"I'm fine with it," Jesse said. "Now, pass the biscuits, and let's get the day's work lined out. Mia and I are going to work on the barn roof. Cody, you can drive Dad around the ranch and refamiliarize yourself with the place this morning."

"We'll knock off at four so we can get to the rodeo grounds to see the kids again tonight, and then we're not working at all tomorrow," Sonny said. "I don't want to miss the bronc and bull riding, or the dance after the rodeo is over. Mia, you'll save your old poppa a dance, won't you?"

"Of course I will, but Nana gets the first one and the last one, because she's the girl you're bringing to the dance and the one you'll be taking home. That's the rules," Mia said with a grin.

"You going to give me first and last dances?" Jesse whispered for Addy's ears only.

"Yep, she sure is," Mia answered.

"Little corn has big ears," Addy said.

Pearl giggled. "We learned that lesson years ago. Now that we've got everything lined out for today and for the future, Henry, do you have anything else to say?"

"Not without blubbering like a baby," Henry answered. "I'm just glad to have had time to watch you boys grow up and to work with my best friend, Sonny, all these years. To eat lots of meals that Pearl cooked and have five years with Addy and Mia. Now, that's enough. We'll save the tears for the day I drive away from this place and head for Colorado." He finished off his last sip of coffee and pushed his chair back. "Me and the hired hands are going to be fixing fence today. Before I leave, I intend to have the fences in good enough repair to last for a long time."

"Thank you for always being here for us through the years, Henry." Pearl wiped a tear away with her napkin. "Addy and I are supposed to be in town from ten until noon today to watch over the bake sale table for the church. We're having this one for our missionary fund."

"I'm glad I'll be roofing a barn. I hate to sit behind a table at a bake sale." Mia pushed back her chair and carried her plate to the sink.

"Better get used to it, darlin'," Pearl said. "This job gets passed down. I inherited it from both my mother and mother-in-law. Addy gets it from me, and you'll get it from her."

"But she's not your daughter or daughter-in-law," Mia argued.

"She *is* in my heart, and that's as important as DNA." Pearl smiled.

"Thank you," Addy said. She truly hoped that what she and Jesse had wasn't just a flash of heat in the pan, but that someday she would be a real daughter-in-law to Pearl and Sonny.

Guess that blew the bottom out of going slow, the voice in her head giggled. *You're thinking marriage, and he has yet to say that he loves you.*

Chapter Twenty-Three

*M*ay I have this dance?" Jesse held out his hand to Addy.

She slipped her hand in his, and he led her out to the dance floor. The cover band was playing Chris Stapleton's "Millionaire." The lyrics talked about love being more precious than gold and having it made a cowboy a millionaire. Jesse wrapped his arms around Addy's waist, and she draped her arms around his neck.

Jesse sang along about the times when his pockets were empty and his cupboard was bare, he still felt like he was a millionaire.

Addy leaned back a little and smiled up at him. "Do you really believe that?"

"I do," he said. "I'm a rich man because I've got you in my arms tonight."

She leaned her cheek against his chest. "That's a romantic line."

"It's the absolute truth. I've never felt like this before, not even that night before I left for the Air Force," he assured her, and meant every word of what he'd said.

When that song ended, fiddle music started, and Jesse grinned. "Looks like the band is singing just to us tonight. Listen to the words of this one."

"I could probably crawl up on that stage and not miss a beat," she told him. "Alan Jackson is one of my favorites, and I love 'Livin' on Love.'"

Jesse took her hands in his, swung her out, and brought her back to his chest. "He's right, you know—without somebody, life ain't worth a dime."

"Yep," she agreed.

He was about to say that he was in love with her when Grady tapped him on the shoulder. "Mind if I cut in?"

"Of course not," Jesse said with a smile. But he really wanted to grab Addy's hand and run away from the dance with her. He went to the bar across the room, sat down on a stool beside his brother Cody, and ordered a beer.

"Lost your woman?" Cody chuckled.

"Just for one dance," Jesse answered.

The bartender set his beer on a paper coaster. Cody handed her a bill and pointed to his empty. "I'll get the first one for my brother."

"Thanks," Jesse said.

"So, you and Addy had a little fling before you went to the Air Force? Why didn't you ever mention it to me? I thought we pretty much shared everything," Cody said.

"One night," Jesse said. "I left the next morning and didn't know about Mia until I got home this time. Best-kept secret in the history of Honey Grove unless you've got one to share about you and Stevie."

"Nope," Cody told him.

Jesse turned up his beer and took a long drink. "She and Grady were good friends until his girlfriend got jealous of their relationship."

"Maybe he split with the nurse, and he's ready for more than friendship with Addy," Cody suggested. "Have you told her how you feel?"

"She knows," Jesse said.

"Maybe so, but until you tell her, she won't be sure. Good God!" Cody said.

Jesse followed his brother's eyes to the mirror above the bar and saw Stevie coming right toward them.

"You going to ask her to dance?" Jesse asked.

"Hell, no!" Cody whispered.

Stevie sat down on the stool next to Cody and ordered a double shot of Jameson. When it was set before her, she nodded toward Cody.

"Put that on my tab," Cody said. "I'll buy this pretty lady her first drink."

Jesse nudged him with an elbow. "So much for that 'hell, no.' I bet you five bucks that you dance the last dance with her."

"I'd forgotten how cute she is." Cody laid a bill on the bar without looking at her. "What brings you out tonight? You plannin' on doing some dancing?"

"Maybe." Stevie turned up her drink. "If a good-lookin' cowboy who thought he was too old for me at one time was to ask me, I might show him up on the dance floor."

"Y'all excuse me," Jesse said when the female vocalist in the band took the microphone and began to sing an old Shania Twain song, "From This Moment On." He slid off his stool. "I want to dance with Addy on this one. He lowered his voice and said, "You're on your own, brother, but I'll expect a full report tomorrow morning."

"You son of a bitch!" a man screamed over the top of the music, and the sound of a breaking glass followed. "Don't you come in here trying to take my woman away from me."

The singer didn't miss a note, but suddenly, Jesse felt a

spray of something warm across his face. He reached up and swiped his hand across his cheek and brought back bloody fingers. "What the hell?"

"I'll kill you," he heard so loud in his left ear that he whipped around to see who was threatening him.

"You bastard," Patrick O'Malley said as he held his hand over a cut across his cheek.

"She only goes for the handsome ones, so I'll fix your face so she don't look at you again," the first guy said as he took another swipe toward Patrick with the broken bottle.

Patrick squared off with him and held him at bay with the legs of a bar stool. "You idiot. I wasn't flirting with your woman. I asked her which way the bathrooms were."

"You're a low-down scoundrel, Patrick O'Malley. Everyone in town knows you cheat on Lylah." He knocked the bar stool out into the dance floor, causing two couples to trip and fall flat on their butts. "Well, your lies ain't goin' to work on me."

Jesse got between them and managed to wrestle the bottle from the big burly guy's hand, but in the process he got a cut on the back of his hand. Now, he and Patrick were both bleeding.

"You idiot," Cody yelled as he waded into the melee. "That's my brother you just sliced open. Someone call 911 and the police."

Suddenly, Addy was beside Jesse and shaking her finger at the guy who had been holding the bottle. "You fool. You're drunk, and you've injured two men. Charges will be filed against you as soon as the police get here."

"Come on, Dolly." He motioned for his woman. "It's time we left."

"I'm not going anywhere with you," she declared and dropped down on her knees beside Patrick. "I'm so sorry, honey. He wasn't supposed to be here. He told me he had to work tonight."

Patrick's blue eyes rolled back in his head, and he fainted right there at Jesse's feet.

"Is there a doctor in the house?" the woman squealed.

Cody dropped down on his knees. "I'm a doctor." He pulled off his shirt, tore it in half, and threw one side to Addy. "Use that to apply pressure to Jesse's hand. That's a nasty cut and it's going to need stitches," he said as he used the other part of the shirt to apply pressure to Patrick's cheek.

"Is he going to live?" the woman sobbed.

"Of course," Cody said. "He's not dying. He's passed out from too much liquor. Do you know if he's allergic to anything or how much he's had to drink?"

"You'll have to ask his wife." She stood up and melted back into the crowd.

"Wait until Lylah hears about this." Jesse tried to chuckle, but it came out more like a groan.

"As long as they're talking about her problems, they'll leave us alone," Addy whispered. "Now, be still until the ambulance gets here."

"Send Patrick with them and take me home. Cody can stitch me up there. I'm up-to-date on my tetanus shot, so I don't need one of those," Jesse said.

"I can do that." Cody looped his arm through Jesse's and led the way through the people now standing around, staring down at Patrick. "Let's just ease on out of here."

The ambulance was pulling up as they made their way to Jesse's truck. "Want me to drive?"

"I can take him home," Addy said. "You can follow us, and we'll get him stitched up when we get to the house."

"Will do," Cody said.

"You are welcome," Jesse chuckled as he got into the passenger seat.

"For what?" Cody asked.

"I got you out of whatever was going on between you and Stevie." He slammed the door before Cody could answer.

Addy started up the engine, backed out of the parking spot, and headed toward the ranch. "I can't leave you alone for one minute," she teased.

"It's your fault for letting Grady cut into our dance. You should have told him that you didn't want to dance with him." Jesse leaned his head back. "I hate stitches more than anything."

"Cody will numb you up real good, and I'll get you a shot of Sonny's best whiskey to dull the senses," she offered. "And, honey, Grady wanted to dance with me to ask me to forgive him for saying we couldn't talk anymore. He and his girlfriend broke up, and he's got a new one that isn't jealous."

Jesse sat up straight. "What did you tell him?"

"Told him that I had committed to working with Cody. He got a little hateful and asked if I couldn't decide which brother I wanted," she answered.

"I told him that it wasn't a damn bit of his business how I lived my life, and then the ruckus started. I left him on the dance floor and was coming to get you when the lady started singing, "From This Moment On.""

"I wanted to dance with you on that song," Jesse said as she turned into the lane to Sunflower Ranch. His hand had left the shock stage and had begun to throb.

"I was coming to get you for just that same reason, but we kind of got sidetracked." She parked the truck in front of the yard gate, and Cody pulled in right behind her.

"I'll get my bag, and we'll work on him in the kitchen." Cody laid a palm on the fence and jumped over it in one fluid movement.

"I'd try to do that and impress you so you would choose me, but I don't think I better with this." Jesse held up his injured hand, which was still wrapped in half of his brother's shirt.

"Oh, hush!" Addy scolded as she opened the gate for him.

Tex met them on the porch and dashed inside the house in front of Jesse. He headed straight for the kitchen as if he knew that's where they would be and curled up under the table.

"Sit down right there." Addy pointed to the chair where Sonny usually sat and headed to the sink.

"Bossy, ain't you?" Jesse said.

"When my boyfriend's hand is cut open, I am." She filled a basin with water, opened a drawer for towels, and carried everything to the table.

"I'm your boyfriend?" he asked.

Cody slapped him on the back of the head as he passed by. "Of course you are, doofus. Addy is too classy for one-night stands or flings. You are a boyfriend. Own it and be proud of it."

"I am"—Jesse nodded—"very proud of it. I just wanted to hear her say it. Some first date, huh?"

Addy unwound the bloody shirt from his hand and cleaned the gaping inch-long wound with water. "At least we won't ever be able to say our first date was boring. Cody, we might be able to pull this together with Steri-strips."

Cody sat down and took a long look at the wound. "Nope, it needs stitches, and very close together. He'll have to do more bossin' than workin' for a while until it heals up."

"Come on," Jesse groaned. "Listen to your nurse and use the strips."

"Sorry, brother." Cody shook his head. "This is right where your wrist bends, and you are also going to need a wrist guard to keep it straight until it heals. We'll be lucky if you don't have to have therapy on it, just because of the location." He pulled out a hypodermic needle and tore the packaging away from it. "This is going to sting, but then you won't feel the stitches."

"I've said that so many times that I can't even remember them all," Jesse said.

"I just bet you have, and if this was your left hand, you could even do this yourself, but your stitching wouldn't be as pretty as mine." Cody joked as he worked. "And I bet you aren't as gentle as I am. You'll only feel the stick the first time."

"Just get on with it and stop bragging." Jesse watched as the needle pierced his flesh around the cut.

Addy sat down beside him and watched as Cody carefully stitched the skin together with tiny little sutures. "You should have been a plastic surgeon."

"Thought about it, but then I figured there were folks who needed a plain old doctor more than those who needed to be pretty," Cody said as he tied off the last stitch. "I'll take these out in ten days. Until then, you get to wear a brace to keep you from bending the wrist and ruining my beautiful work. Let this teach you to stay out of other men's fights."

"Hey, now," Jesse protested. "I was just walking across the room to dance with my girlfriend. They put me in the middle of their fight."

"That's not the way I saw it," Cody argued.

"You couldn't see right because you were focused on Stevie," Jesse reminded him.

Addy patted him on his shoulder. "Come on, tough cowboy. Let's get you down to the bunkhouse and put you to bed."

"I'm not a child," Jesse said.

"I can see where Mia gets that attitude," Addy teased, "when she sets her jaw and says she's not a little girl. If you're so big and brave that you don't need me, then I'll sleep in Mia's room tonight."

"Whoa!" Jesse threw up his left palm. "Now I see where our daughter gets her sass."

"Mia does not get her sass from me," Addy protested. "She

acts just exactly like my grandmother. Let's go home to the bunk-house and get some sleep. We'll feel better come morning."

"I'll see y'all at breakfast," Cody yawned, "but, brother, if you wanted a few days to be lazy, all you had to do was ask me to do your work. You didn't have to try to amputate your hand."

"You were the serious one when you left home. What happened to make you so funny?" Jesse pushed back his chair and stood up.

"Life." Cody grinned as he left the room.

* * *

Addy slipped her hand into Jesse's on the way to the bunk-house. "Want me to sleep on the sofa tonight so that . . ."

"No," he answered before she could even finish the sentence.

"Dancing to that song tonight was important to me," Jesse said as they crossed the distance from the back porch to the bunkhouse. "I'm not as romantic as a woman like you deserves, but when it started playing, I thought it would be the perfect time to tell my girlfriend that I've fallen in love with her."

"Damn Patrick O'Malley for ruining that for your girl-friend. I know she would have loved to have heard those words while she was dancing to the song that says all those beautiful things," Addy whispered.

"I imagine that Lylah is damning him pretty good tonight without my girlfriend heaping coals upon his head. So, as my best friend, do you really think my girlfriend is ready for me to say those words to her, or should I wait?" Jesse asked as he opened the door with his left hand and stood to one side.

"Lylah should have been there with him rather than helping clean up the church cupcake vendor site," Addy said. "I would never let my husband go to a dance without me."

"Oh, really?" Jesse raised both eyebrows. "What if your husband only has eyes for his beautiful wife and would never, ever, not in a million years, cheat on her?"

"Because Patrick can't keep his hands and eyes off other women, I suppose you're going to wait for another perfect moment to say those words to your girlfriend, aren't you?" Addy sat down on the sofa and pulled off her boots. This idea of being Jesse's best friend as well as his girlfriend was fun, and she really wanted to hear him say those words to her as his girlfriend, not as his best friend—romantic time and place didn't matter. "What's the difference in saying that you love me and that you've fallen in love with someone?"

"I love you as a friend, Addy. I have always loved you. That's in the mind, but now I'm in love with you, and that goes deeper because it's in the heart and soul. To have both is..." He sat down beside her and ran a fingertip down her cheek, "a miracle. I don't think many people get that in their lives."

Sparks danced around the room as his lips found hers in a long, lingering kiss. A fancy dinner with candles and white tablecloths and roses, or dancing to an emotional song could not have been more romantic than sitting right there on the sofa beside Jesse and feeling his lips on hers.

When the kiss ended, she gazed into his eyes and said, "I'm in love with you, too, Jesse Ryan, and everything is perfect right here, right now in this bunkhouse."

Chapter Twenty-Four

*E*verything was too perfect. Jesse had said that he was in love with her. The two of them were settling down into a routine that she loved, but Addy wasn't a teenager living in a world of unicorns and rainbows. The other shoe would drop, and that terrified her. She didn't want the sweet little world she and Jesse were living in to crumble.

The temperatures were already in the high nineties that morning when she and Jesse headed into the office to finish up the week's computer work. Jesse was getting restless, but even after the stitches came out of his hand, Cody had declared he needed another week of easy exercises before he went back to heavy lifting.

"I'm sick of this office," he grumbled. "I want to be out there with Cody building the new barn."

"It's only until Monday," Addy said. "We'll be done with the office work by noon, and then we'll drive into Bonham to get sheet metal for the roof. You'll be out there in this miserable heat with him on Monday, so suck it up, cowboy," Addy said.

"Is that my best friend or my girlfriend fussing at me?" he asked.

"Both," she told him. "Weren't you ever put on desk duty in the Air Force?"

"Only once, and I bitched about it the whole time," he admitted.

Addy pulled a chair around to sit beside him at the desk. "You're doing great with this, darlin'."

"I can do it, but I don't like it. I wish Lucas would come home. He's as great at this stuff as he is with training horses," Jesse said.

"Maybe he will sometime soon." Addy had been around Jesse when he was in a foul mood, but that had been twenty years before, not recently. As they got the bookwork ready to go to the CPA to be checked for the next time quarterly taxes rolled around, she had to take the bad with the good, just like Jesse had to do with her mood swings.

They had just emailed all the material off to the CPA when Pearl poked her head in the door. "Grady is here and wants to talk to you, Addy. He's out on the front porch swing."

"What does he want?" Jesse asked.

"He didn't volunteer, and I didn't ask," Pearl answered. "I just took out two glasses of sweet tea for y'all. The temperature has hit the triple digits now."

Jesse stood up and flexed his wrist. "I guess if I was supposed to go, you would have taken three glasses of tea, right?"

Pearl nodded. "You can come on in the kitchen and help me make sandwiches for dinner. Mia and Cody are going to be in here in half an hour, and they'll be starving."

Addy kissed Jesse on the cheek before she left the room. "This won't take long, and then I'll come help get dinner on the table."

"Maybe we can stop off for some ice cream or a snow cone after we get the sheet iron." He smiled up at her.

"Sounds like a great idea to me," she agreed.

She tried to stay positive, but she felt like she was in one of those dreams where she was trying to run and her boots felt like they were filled with concrete. Something wasn't right. She could feel it all the way to the bottom of her heavy heart. Hopefully, the other shoe dropping didn't have anything to do with Sonny's health, not now, not when he and Pearl were finally going to have some freedom to travel.

"I thought when the other shoe dropped, it would be something between me and Jesse," she whispered as she went out to the porch. "Hello, Grady, what's going on?"

"Please, sit with me." He patted the place beside him on the swing. "Have some tea."

She picked up the full glass and sat down on the other end of the swing, keeping a couple of feet between them.

Don't prolong the issue. Come right out and ask him what the hell he's doing here, the voice in her head scolded.

Grady took a long drink of his tea and set the glass back on the small end table. "I need help in more ways than one, and we used to be friends, so I came to you."

Addy drank part of her tea and held the cold glass against her cheek. "Spit it out, Grady."

"I need to get away for six months," he said, "maybe a year."

"Why?" Addy asked.

He removed his glasses and cleaned them with a white handkerchief that he pulled from his pocket. "I called my new girlfriend Amelia when we were..." He stammered and blushed. "When we were..."

"When you were in bed?" Addy asked.

"Yes," Grady said. "You were right. I was just trying to replace my wife with another woman. I'm not ready to move on yet and I'm confused, so I've agreed to a stint with Doctors Without Borders. Do you think I should go?"

"That's your decision, not mine, and even if we were still good friends, I wouldn't make the decision for you."

"Addy, I've never been good at decisions. My folks decided that I should be a doctor. Amelia asked me on our first date. She's the one who proposed to me and planned the wedding. She decided that we should stay in this area when we were offered jobs in big cities. Then Aurelia decided I couldn't be friends with you, and now Crystal—I went out with her because she had a name that didn't sound like Amelia—has dumped me. Tell me what to do," Grady said.

"I'd say it's time for you to examine your life and decide what makes you happy," Addy said. "Take control and learn to stand up for what you want."

"I don't know if I can do that," he almost whined.

"Well, it's your job to do if you're ever going to be happy," she said.

"Are you happy? I hear that you're living with Jesse now." Grady's tone turned a little cold.

"Yes, I am, and I've promised Cody to help him with his new project," she said.

"Maybe you should check into Jesse's past before you make up your mind. He wasn't an angel those twenty years that he was in the military." Grady tapped a folder that was lying between them on the seat.

"What's that?" she asked.

"Just a little research that I thought you might be interested in," Grady said.

Addy felt a chill chase down her spine in spite of the heat when she saw Jesse Ryan's name on the outside. "What's in it? You had Jesse investigated? Why would you do such a thing?"

Grady's smile looked more like a sneer. "I figured out a couple of years ago that Mia belonged to him, and then when I heard he was coming home for good, I thought you might be right where you are today—in love with him all over again. So I did a little background research on him. That's what friends are for, right?"

Addy stared at the folder as if it were a rattlesnake. The other shoe had definitely dropped. "That's just wrong. You shouldn't pry into his past."

"He's got an exemplary military record, but his personal life is what you'll want to take a look at. Do you want to spend your life with a man who hopped from one woman to another? He'll grow tired of you in six months, and then you'll be asked to leave the ranch. You don't have a thing in common with him."

Grady stood up, but he didn't pick up the folder. "You can take that thing with you, and if you hadn't ended our friendship, I damn sure would today. What you did is inexcusable."

"Read that before you get too involved." Grady crossed the porch and yard, and went to his SUV.

Addy picked up the folder and went into the cool house. She sat down on the ladder-back chair right inside the door and stared at the bright red folder.

"What's that?" Jesse startled her when he peeked around the kitchen door.

"Grady isn't the friend I thought he was," she said.

"Okay, but what's in that folder?" Jesse sat down in the chair beside her.

"This is a full investigative report on your military and your personal life for the past twenty years. I'm not sure how he got all this, but here it is," Addy said.

Jesse inhaled deeply and let it out slowly. "Why in the hell would he do that?"

"He says that he knew I'd fall in love with you, and I should know what kind of man you are," Addy answered.

"I have not been a saint, Addy," Jesse admitted in a husky voice.

"I didn't think you had been," she said. "I haven't even opened this, but Grady read it and said that you hopped from woman to woman."

"I did have a few relationships, a few one-night stands, and some second and third dates. None of them lasted because I kept measuring all the women by your standard, and they all came up short," he admitted.

Addy stood up and headed for the office with him right behind her. "I'm all for leaving the past in the past, darlin'," she said as she stuck the whole folder into the shredder. "I love you, Jesse. What either of us did or didn't do the past twenty years is over and done with. We don't need to hash out all that old news, and I'm not worried about the future."

* * *

Jesse took her in his arms and held her close to his chest. "You are one amazing woman, Addison Hall."

"Thank you for that, Jesse, but just for the record, how many women are we talking about?" she asked.

"Show me yours, and I'll show you mine," he teased.

"Fair enough." She giggled as she went up on her tiptoes for a kiss. "We'll just nail that box shut with tenpenny nails."

"I agree, but I can promise you one thing," he whispered. "There won't be any children coming out of the woodwork."

"Other than Mia, you mean?" she asked.

"That's right, and I can promise you another thing. I'm right proud to be Mia's father," Jesse said. "Now, I hear folks coming in for dinner and the noise of Dad's cane tapping on the hardwood floor. Let's eat and get a visit before we head off to Bonham. I was right to measure all the other women by your standard." Jesse took her hand in his and led her across the hallway into the kitchen. "You always put other folks before yourself."

"Hey, what was Grady doing here?" Sonny asked.

"I'll tell you all about it after you say grace." Jesse was in a state of shock that Addy had shredded the file without even looking inside it. He doubted that the thing was as complete as Grady had thought because it simply didn't look thick enough to have covered all his military commendations plus the women that he had spent time with through the years. Besides, how on earth would anyone know about some of those ladies? They were scattered all over the blasted world.

Sonny bowed his head and said a short prayer, then reached for a couple of sandwiches. "I'm ready now. Did Grady have bad news about me?"

"Nope, it was bad news about me." Jesse chuckled and told them what Grady had done.

"Sweet Lord!" Mia gasped. "That's downright dirty of him, and to think I actually liked the man at one time. Why would he do that anyway?"

Addy poured chips onto her plate and then passed the bag over to Jesse. "He wanted me to be his friend and tell him how to live his life. When I refused, he gave me that file."

"That makes him even worse," Mia said.

Jesse kept quiet and let Addy tell the rest of the story. With every comment from Mia, his heart got lighter and lighter. After those first few rocky days, it was great to see his daughter standing up for him and her mother.

"If he goes through with joining Doctors Without Borders, he will probably get sent to one of the small African villages." Cody reached for the pitcher in the middle of the table, refilled his glass, and then passed it around the table. "If he's not fully committed to this, he'll be miserable. When he puts his name on that contract, they don't come get him until the time is finished."

"He deserves it," Pearl said, "but he seemed so nice when he was treating Sonny and was Addy's friend. I can believe he has trouble making decisions. He was one of those kids—one that his parents did everything for him, and he never really had any hard knocks in life. He was married to Amelia when his folks died. I guess he just never learned to take care of things on his own. Hard to believe he'd do something so shady as to have Jesse investigated."

"Yep, but then one never knows what they'll do if they want someone to do something they won't do," Addy said and then focused on Jesse. "You ready to drive to the lumber yard and get these folks some more building material?"

Jesse laid his napkin on the table and stood up. "Only if they'll promise that they will slow down a little so I can, at least, say I got to have a hand in building our new barn. I'll want to tell future generations that I helped build the barn the year I came home from the military."

Cody picked up another sandwich with one hand and the bag of chips with the other. "We promise we'll save a nail or two special just for you. Mama, it's so nice to be able to sit down to a meal in air-conditioned comfort. I'll never take home for granted again."

"Me either," Jesse agreed.

Driving to Bonham, even with a trailer hitched up behind his truck, took fifteen minutes, barely enough time to cool down the cab. Jesse turned the radio to the station that played the older, traditional country music, and the first song the DJ played was Shania Twain's "From This Moment On."

He braked and pulled the vehicle over to the side of the road, parked in the gravel, and turned up the radio as high as it would go. He hopped out of the truck, rounded the front end, and opened the door. "My name is Jesse Ryan, and I've been admirin' you for a while now. May I have this dance?"

Addy put her hand in his, slid out of the truck, and wrapped her arms around his neck. He two-stepped with her all around the truck and didn't even miss a beat when two vehicles went by and honked.

The lyrics said that life had begun from this moment, and that she belonged right beside him. Jesse breathed in the scent of her hair and hummed along with the song.

Addy leaned back slightly and sang right along with Shania, saying that from this moment she had been blessed, and that she would give her last breath for his love.

When the song ended, Jesse dropped down on one knee and took her hands in his. "I don't have a ring, and this isn't romantic, but after listening to that song, I want to say this. I love you, Addison Hall. With my heart and soul, I love you. Will you marry me?"

As luck would have it, the very next song on the radio was "Cowboy Take Me Away" by the Dixie Chicks. Addy dropped on her knees in front of him and nodded. "Yes, a thousand times, yes."

Jesse jumped up, scooped her into his arms like a new bride, and spun around in circles until they were both dizzy. Then he put her on the ground and began to dance to the music. "I'm so happy that my heart is pounding."

"I can feel it," Addy said. "This song is from me to you. Like it says, cowboy, take me away and fly me as high as you can for the rest of our lives, Jesse."

"I'll do my damnedest to make you happy," he said.

"Right back at you." She nestled her cheek against his chest. "Someday, I want to tell our grandchildren about the day you proposed, and how romantic it was."

"I'm glad it doesn't take much to please you." Jesse knew that he was the luckiest cowboy in the whole state of Texas.

"I love you so much," Addy said as she sealed their new promises with a long kiss.

Chapter Twenty-Five

Addy would have been happy to go to the courthouse, get married in ten minutes, and go home, but Pearl and Mia weren't having any part of that idea. They decided that the last day of July would be a nice day for a wedding. Henry would still be at the ranch and could attend. Pearl and Sonny had decided to drive to Colorado with Henry and help get him settled into his new home on the first day of August, so everything would work out just fine. Lucas even said that he could fly in for a couple of days to attend the wedding.

Now, the day had arrived, and Addy was so nervous about the whole affair that she really wished that she and Jesse could run away and elope. For a whole five minutes, she was alone in the Sunday school room that they used for a bride's dressing area. She sat down in a rocking chair and stared out the window at big fluffy white clouds. Twenty years ago, on the last day of July, she had taken a pregnancy test and found out that she had gotten pregnant that last night Jesse was home.

Whoever said that a girl couldn't get pregnant when she and a guy had only had sex one time had rocks for brains.

Mia came in from the hallway with Addy's bouquet in her hands. A sunflower with a bit of baby's breath around it looked lovely in her dark hair, and her deep yellow dress fit her every curve just right. "You've got fifteen minutes, Mama, and then Grandpa is coming to escort you down the aisle. Are you ready for this?"

"Are there a lot of people in the church?" Addy asked.

"Yep, but it is Saturday night, so it's like date night for everyone, and we've got quite a spread in the fellowship hall besides that truly gorgeous cake. It's also a time for everyone to get all dressed up and fancy. Speaking of which, you should see my father. He's so danged nervous that I had to keep assuring him that you would forgive him if he forgot a line of his vows. He wants this day to be perfect for you."

"Thank you, Mia, for working so hard with Pearl to make this day special. How you two got all this together in two short weeks is amazing," Addy said.

"Hey, not every girl my age can say that she got to be the maid of honor at her parents' wedding," Mia said. "Now, get your boots on, and take these sunflowers. I'm glad you decided on these instead of roses."

Pearl peeked into the room. She wore a dark green dress with a pretty floral scarf around her shoulders and an emerald necklace. "I brought you a little present. My mother-in-law gave me the same one on my wedding day, and I thought you should have them." She handed Addy a tiny satin bag tied with a drawstring at the top.

Addy opened it to find sunflower seeds. "Oh, Pearl, this is a wonderful present," she said. "I will plant them around the back porch."

Pearl dabbed at the tears in her eyes. "That's a perfect place. And honey, you can call me Mama, you know."

"I'd love to." Addy hugged her.

"Be careful," Pearl warned. "I don't want to get makeup smears on your pretty dress. Mia was right about you wearing champagne lace. It looks lovely on you."

"But I had my way about the boots." Addy pulled up her dress to show off a pair of boots with phoenix birds sewn into the fronts. "Jesse and I are rising from the ashes, so these seemed proper."

"Good God, Mama, you're supposed to wear the off-white lace boots," Mia fussed.

Pearl headed for the door. "I hear the music that tells me they're about to seat me and your mother, Addy, so I'm leaving."

Addy gave her a hug. "Thank you for the sunflower seeds ... Mama Pearl."

"I like that a lot, and the seeds are just my way of welcoming you to the family that you've already had for five years," Pearl said.

Addy's eyes twinkled as she focused on her daughter. "I can't dance in new boots, and be damned if I go on my honeymoon with blisters on my feet, and you've only got about two minutes before you have to leave this room. Before you go, thank you again, my child, for everything, but most of all for accepting Jesse."

"It's in my DNA," Mia said, smiling, "and Mama, your honeymoon is just a weekend in a cabin up on the Red River. It won't be that different than staying in the bunkhouse."

"A honeymoon isn't where you are or how long you get to stay there. It's who you are with." Addy dropped the full skirt of her lace dress. "Are you sure about this, Mia Hall?"

"I'm sure about everything. Are you, Mama?" Mia fired back at her.

Addy nodded. "Absolutely."

Denison Hall, Addy's father, knocked on the door and then entered without being asked. "I hear there's a bride in here who needs an escort down the aisle." He was a tall, thin man with gray in the temples of his black hair and clear blue eyes.

Mia stepped aside. "Here she is, Grandpa."

"You are beautiful." Denison smiled and offered her his arm. "Mia, you'd best get on out there. It's time for you to walk down the aisle."

"Whoa!" Addy handed Mia her bouquet. "You'll need this."

"She isn't ever going to stop bossing me around." Mia picked up her single sunflower with dark green ribbons streaming from the stem.

"That's a mama's job," Denison told her.

* * *

Jesse hadn't been this nervous during harrowing near escapes with wounded soldiers that he and his team had rescued. But after Mia had taken her place and he could see Addy coming down the aisle on her father's arm, everything and everyone disappeared. Suddenly, all the angst left him, and his trembling hands were as steady as a rock. As long as he had Addy before his eyes and in his life, he was fine.

Waiting for Denison to bring her all the way to him wasn't easy, but the moment he could reach out and take her hands in his, he whispered, "You are so beautiful, and I'm such a lucky cowboy."

"Who gives this woman to be married to this man?" the preacher asked.

"Her family and I do." Denison kissed her on the cheek. "Be happy. Both of you, be happy."

Addy had asked for a simple, quick ceremony, and the preacher delivered just that, but just before he told Jesse to kiss the bride, he nodded at Mia.

She stepped away from her place beside her mother and took the microphone from the preacher. "You two have already joined hands, and now I'm going to lay mine on yours. Today, Jesse Ryan, I take you as my father, and I change my name from Hall to Ryan. I promise to respect you both as my parents and try not to be so bossy."

Some folks chuckled, but several laughed out loud.

Jesse had to swallow twice to get past the grapefruit-sized lump in his throat. He had not known that Mia was going to do either of those things, but pride swelled up in his chest. "I promise to love and cherish you as a daughter, Mia, and I won't expect too much when it comes to that bossy part."

More laughter came from the congregation.

"And now that you are man and wife, and we are a family, the preacher has said that I can tell my daddy that he can kiss the bride." Mia removed her hand and stepped back into her place.

Epilogue

Addy woke up on Thanksgiving morning snuggled up to Jesse's broad back. She had one hand thrown over his chest, and the moment she stirred, he laced his fingers with hers and flipped over to face her. So much had happened in the last four months that she could hardly take it all in. Sonny and Pearl had made two trips to Colorado and were planning one to Las Vegas in a few weeks. Mia had made the decision to finish her education with online classes rather than ever going back to college. Sonny and Pearl now lived in Henry's house, but they were in and out of the ranch house every day.

"Good mornin', darlin'," Jesse said. "Happy first Thanksgiving as Mrs. Jesse Ryan."

She gave him a quick kiss on the lips. "I have so much to be thankful for, and being your wife is in the number one spot on the list. I hear noise coming from the kitchen, so I guess that means Pearl and Sonny are already here."

"I hear something coming from across the hall that sounds like Mia humming a lullaby. I guess that means she beat you into the babies' room. I can't believe that we already have a set of twins." Jesse hugged her tightly.

"Two boys to grow up on Sunflower Ranch like you and your brothers." Addy slipped out of his embrace and off the bed. She quickly dressed in a pair of jeans and a bright orange sweater. "I'm glad that teenage mother chose us. After having them for only four weeks, I can't imagine life without them. They might not have grown in my belly, but it sure hasn't taken them long to grow in my heart."

"Or mine." Jesse slung his long legs over the side of the bed and stood up. "If I'm dreamin', darlin', don't wake me up."

"If we have to change diapers, you'll realize that you're not dreaming." She tiptoed over to him and kissed him again on the lips. "I love you, Jesse."

"I love you, Addy," he said, and she believed him with her whole heart.

Jesse was still getting dressed when she crossed the hall and went into the nursery. "Happy Thanksgiving to all my children." She smiled at Mia.

"Sam is in a pissy mood this morning, and Taylor is hungry," Mia said. "And my brothers and I say Happy Turkey Day right back at you. I told them if they were good until next year, I'd make sure they got a bite of pumpkin pie, but today they'd have to make do with a bottle of formula."

Mia handed Sam over to Addy and then picked up Taylor. "I've already changed them, but I'll take this sweet boy with me to the kitchen to make the bottles."

Jesse yawned as he made his way into the room. "I can hold Taylor while you make bottles."

"Sure thing, Dad." Mia handed the baby to Jesse. "That way, Nana and Poppa won't fuss over which one gets to hold him first. I swear, these babies have put new life in Poppa, even more than all the medicine he takes."

Jesse sat down in one of the rocking chairs in the nursery. "Six months ago, I didn't have any children, and now I have three, plus a gorgeous wife."

"Seems only fair that you get double diaper and feeding duty this time around," Addy teased as she dropped a kiss on his forehead. "I figured it would take at least a year for us to get into even the foster program. It's a miracle that we got to go straight to adoption this quickly."

"Thanks to Cody and his connections." Jesse grinned. "My brothers are good for something after all. Of course, now he says that he gets to be the favorite uncle."

"Seems fair to me, but Lucas may have other ideas," Addy said. "I think they're going to have your blue eyes."

"Of course they are," Jesse said. "I'm their daddy."

Every chair around the dinner table that day was filled. Sonny said grace and his eyes got all misty as he glanced at the table full of food and at all the folks gathered for the holiday. "I'm thankful today for every one of you. It's good for an old man to live to see his grandchildren and know that what he's worked for his whole life will go on in good hands."

"I'm grateful for family, too," Pearl said. "And to finally have a daughter."

"I'm thankful that Addy and I are getting the practice up and going," Cody said.

"That I'm coming home to stay next summer." Lucas smiled. "I'm tired of these short visits when I barely get here until it's time to go again. Besides, after coming home for a couple of days in July when Dad had that episode, I've been downright homesick."

"For Addy," Jesse said when it was his turn to speak up.

Addy kissed Jesse on the cheek. "Thank you, darlin'. I'm grateful for my life with Jesse, my children, and all y'all."

"I'm thankful that I have two new brothers and not a child

of my own, and that I have a father," Mia chimed in. "Now, can we please eat? I'm starving."

"Look!" Cody pointed at the window. "It's snowing. I hope it doesn't get too slippery. After we eat, I've got to go up to a little cabin on Coffee Mill Lake and check on Tommy Jones. He called this morning and said that he had a cough that wouldn't go away. I'm not surprised. He's living in a little cabin with a wood-burning stove, so he's probably breathing in smoke."

"Need me to go with you?" Addy asked.

"I can take care of this one," Cody said. "You can stay inside with the babies."

"I won't argue," Addy told him. "Be careful, though, and call in if you need help with anything, and I'll drive up there. But I'd rather stay here all cuddled up with my husband and watch the snow fall." She leaned over and laid her head on Jesse's shoulder. "I'm glad you're a cowboy now and not a soldier."

"I'm glad I'm a husband now and a father." Jesse kissed her on the cheek.

Don't miss Cody and Stevie's story, *Texas Homecoming* coming in early 2022

Small Town Charm

**A sweet Southern story of family,
forgiveness, and true love.**

Growing up, Cricket Lawson was never one of the popular girls. And that was just fine with her. If the Belles couldn't deal with her curves or tell-it-like-it-is attitude, she didn't want to be friends with them anyway. She's perfectly content running her little bookshop and tending to her garden.

Then Bryce Walton comes to town. He's sweet, friendly, and successful, and suddenly all the ladies in Bloom, Texas, are pulling out every ounce of Southern charm they have to win him over. But they're shocked when the only one Bryce wants to spend time with is Cricket.

When one of the Belles reaches out to her for help, Cricket will have to decide whether it's one more heartache in the making or a real show of friendship at last.

Chapter One

If the punishment for being a curvy woman was being sent to live in a big city, then Cricket Lawson would have had to make peace with her maker, because she would surely die if she ever had to move from Bloom, Texas. She'd always been slightly overweight, and she'd tried to lose weight more times than she could count on her fingers and toes. Then she'd come to the realization that *diet* was a four-letter word—and those were a sin to think or even say out loud.

The thermometer on her porch said it was past ninety degrees, so when she got home from working all day in her secondhand bookstore, Cricket changed into a pair of cutoff jeans and a chambray shirt, which she tied up under her breasts, leaving her midriff bare. For the past two days Bloom, Texas, had had rain, rain, and more rain, so she kicked off her shoes at the edge of the garden and waded out in the mud in her bare feet. No one else was within a mile of the huge vegetable garden where Cricket picked tomatoes and beans that hot evening.

"Romeo," was blasting through her MP3 player, and Cricket

sang right along with Dolly Parton. When Billy Ray Cyrus began to sing his part in the song, she did a few line-dance steps. Mud flew up and stuck on the backs of her legs, but she didn't care. She lived so far out of town that no one could see her. If they could, it would sure enough give everyone in the town something to talk about.

She put her hands on her knees and did a little twerking. "That would really set their tongues a waggin'," she giggled. "Someday, my Romeo will come along, and he'll sweep me right off my feet, but the way I look right now, I hope it's not today."

It seemed like an omen when the next song on her player was "Something to Talk About." Holding a cucumber as a microphone, she sang along with Bonnie Raitt and danced around a half-bushel basket almost full of green beans. She'd just finished doing a little two-step with an imaginary partner when she caught a movement out of the corner of her eye.

Her brother Rick and sister-in-law had just taken their two kids on a vacation to the beach the day before and wouldn't be home for two weeks, so it couldn't be either of them. She whipped around too fast, slipped in the mud, and fell flat on her butt. Dirty water splashed all the way up her bare midriff and across her arms. She didn't even try to get up but just sat there and stared at the man standing at the edge of the garden.

"Hello, I'm Bryce Walton," he said. "Were you practicing for a country music video?"

"No, I'm taking a mud bath," she snapped at him. "What are you doing on my property?"

"Lettie gave me your phone number, but there was no answer when I called. She gave me the directions out here and told me you could sell me some fresh vegetables," Bryce explained.

"How do you know Lettie?" Cricket's tone softened a little.

"I bought the Bloom Pharmacy," Bryce said. "Today was

my first day to work, and I'm renting Lettie and Nadine's garage apartment until I can find something to buy. Do I need to give you a résumé to buy okra and tomatoes?"

Cricket knew that the pharmacy had sold—everyone in Bloom knew that two hours after the papers were signed. But she hadn't expected the new pharmacist to be so young—or so tall. She'd thought he'd be middle-aged, bald, and wearing bifocals perched on the end of his nose. Lettie had told her that he'd moved into the apartment, but Cricket was so busy that she hadn't even gone to the pharmacy to get her daily limeade that day. Now she wished she had.

Bryce had clear blue eyes, a full head of dark hair, and was probably about her age of thirty-one. He wasn't muscled up like a weightlifter, and maybe looked a little soft in his belly, but all in all, he was a good-looking guy.

"I'm Cricket Lawson. I'd shake hands, but I don't think you want a fistful of mud." She got to her feet and made her way out of the garden. She picked up the water hose, sprayed the mud off her body, and then asked, "How much okra and how many tomatoes do you want?"

"Pleased to meet you," Bryce said. "I'd like a basket of each if you have them. I hear that you own the Sweet Seconds Book Store right next to my pharmacy and that you usually have fresh produce in that store."

Cricket vowed that she would carry her phone in her pocket from then on, even if she had to put it in a Ziploc baggie. Lettie and Nadine were her good friends and gossip gals. No doubt, they had tried to call her several times that evening to tell her about Bryce coming out to her little farm. Bless their hearts, they were always trying to fix her up with someone, and she kept telling them that she was going to grow up and be like both of them—old maids who kept track of everything that went on in Bloom.

"I've got plenty," she answered. "There's a little more than a pound in each basket. Do you want big boy tomatoes or the small cherry tomatoes? And yes, I own the bookstore, and I sell produce as well as used books. Do you like to read?"

"Every chance I get." Bryce's smile lit up his whole face. "I'll be over to visit your store as soon as I can. And I'd like the small tomatoes, please."

"What I've got gathered is in the house. Wait right here, and I'll bring them out to you." She walked past him and glanced up at his wide shoulders. Yep, the man was at least six feet, four inches tall—maybe even a little more than that. Cricket was only three inches over five feet and she barely came to his shoulder. She predicted that there would be a lot of sick women in Bloom in the next few weeks—especially those who were single or divorced. She could just imagine them lined up waiting to get prescriptions filled, or to buy bottles of aspirin, or even to get a soft drink or limeade at the soda fountain. The bar stools in front of the counter wouldn't get cold with one woman sliding onto one the moment another left.

"I'll be right here," Bryce said.

If Lettie and Nadine liked him enough to give him her cell phone number, then Cricket thought she should invite him in, maybe even for a glass of sweet tea. But if she did that and he mentioned it in town, the gossip vine would burst into flames. She could hear the clucking from the old women's tongues, sounding like mother hens gathering in their baby peeps before a storm, as they pitied her for trying to latch on to a man like Bryce. No, ma'am! Cricket didn't need or want anyone to feel sorry for her.

Besides that, everything she'd worn to work that day was hung over the back of kitchen chairs, including her bra and underpants. She'd taken them off in a hurry and changed into what she called her work clothes—an old bra, a shirt she could tie up under her breasts, and a pair of cutoff jeans. She couldn't bring a good-looking man like Bryce into her house to a sight like that, much less to sit down at the table with him for a glass of sweet tea with mud caked in her hair.

"Some days you win," she muttered as she picked up a basket of okra and piled a few more pods on the top. "Most days you lose." She added half a dozen more tomatoes to that basket.

The phone rang as she was walking out the back door, but she ignored it. If anyone found out that she hadn't answered her phone, the news would probably make the *Bloom Weekly News* under the HEARD column on the front page. She could see the little article already:

Cricket Lawson did not answer her phone. The whole town is wondering if she is sick, and several church ladies are preparing casseroles to take to her.

Everyone in Bloom knew that Cricket liked gossip too well not to answer a call if she was within hearing distance of the ring. Why on earth she'd forgotten to tuck her phone in her hip pocket was a mystery.

"Nice garden you've got here." Bryce had walked down to the end of the plot and was on his way back toward the house. "How do you work full-time and take care of this, too?"

"My brother Rick does most of the work, but he and his family are on a two-week vacation, so I'm doing double time while he's gone." She set the okra and tomatoes on the porch. "At least, it rained a lot this week, so I didn't have to water."

Bryce made it to the porch and pulled out his wallet. "I'm surprised that you've still got a crop as hot as it's been. How much do I owe you?"

"Consider those two baskets your welcome to Bloom present," she said.

"Well, then thank you very much. I plan to make a skillet full of fried okra tonight to go with my pork chops." Bryce picked up the vegetables. "What time do you close the bookstore, so I'll know next time I want fresh produce to get on over there and buy it?"

"We're open until six Monday through Friday and from nine to noon on Saturday, but you are always welcome to come out here and get veggies," she answered.

Was he lingering? she wondered.

Of course he is, that pesky voice in her head told her. *He's just moved to town. He doesn't know anyone, and he's going home to eat alone tonight.*

"Maybe I'll see you tomorrow when you come in for a limeade." Bryce started for his vehicle that was parked next to her car in the driveway. "The ladies at the store told me you like limeades. I'm not psychic!"

"I'll be there," she called out.

He got into his SUV and stuck his hand out the window and waved.

She hurried into the house and grabbed her phone from the table. There were ten messages from Lettie and five missed calls from Nadine. She plopped down into a chair and scrolled through her contacts until she found Nadine Betterton and called her first.

Nadine answered on the first ring, but instead of saying hello, she started fussing. "Where have you been? I was about to get in the car and drive out there. You're never without your phone."

"You haven't been allowed to drive in years, and I was in such a hurry to get to the garden that I forgot to take my phone with me," Cricket told her.

"We've got the phone on speaker. You've got me, too, and I was worried about you, girl," Lettie yelled.

Cricket had repeatedly told them that they should just talk in a normal voice, but they both thought they had to raise their voices when they had it on speaker.

"Did Bryce Walton come out there for okra and tomatoes? Is he still there?" Nadine asked.

"What did you think of him?" Lettie butted in before Nadine had finished the last word.

"He seemed nice enough," Cricket answered.

"We're inviting him to Nadine's birthday party Thursday night," Lettie said. "After all, he lives in our apartment building, and, that way, he can meet some folks. Did you know that he loves books?"

"He mentioned that he likes to read," Cricket said, and then went on to tell them about falling in the mud.

"He must think you are beautiful if he asked if you were making a video for television," Nadine said.

"Or he was being sarcastic," Cricket told them.

"If he was and I find out about it, he won't be invited to my party." Nadine's voice rose even higher.

"Wouldn't Jennie Sue and Rick be happy if they came home to find you in a relationship?" Lettie sighed.

"Hey, they're only going to be gone a couple of weeks," Cricket said. "I just met the guy tonight, and he could be engaged or already in a relationship."

"Nope, he's not. I asked him if his girlfriend would be coming to see him or maybe moving to Bloom, and he said he didn't have a girlfriend," Lettie informed her.

Cricket's heart threw in an extra beat, but she scolded herself. "Bryce Walton is way out of my league, Miz Lettie. He's educated, downright handsome, and he's a pharmacist for cryin' out loud."

"Bull crap," Lettie argued.

"Well, let me tell you..." Nadine lowered her voice to her gossip tone. "Mary Lou Cramer has already let it be known that her daughter, Anna Grace, will be married to Bryce by Christmas. She even sent an ivy plant to the drugstore today as a welcoming gift from the Cramer Oil Company, and then a peace lily arrived from the Sweetwater Belles. It would be a feather in Mary Lou's cap to have a pharmacist in the family. Why, Anna Grace might even get elected to be the president of the Sweetwater Belles Club if she could snag Bryce. Sugar Denton is grooming her daughter, Laura Lee, to step into the president's place of their fancy little elite club, but she's only married to the CEO of her daddy's construction firm."

Anna Grace, like most of the daughters of the charter members of the Belles, had been a cheerleader in high school, but she had risen even further on the social ladder because she had been elected homecoming queen and still got to ride in the parade every year. She had gone on to college, joined a sorority, and then come home to work in her daddy's oil business. She was thirty-one now, and her mother, Mary Lou, made no bones about the fact that it was time for Anna Grace to settle down. What Mary Lou wanted, she got—plain and simple.

"Think a pharmacist is good enough for Anna Grace?" Cricket asked. "A couple of weeks ago, I heard her telling Jennie Sue at the café that she had been dating a dentist, but she really wanted to marry a doctor."

"Her mama seems to think that a pharmacist would be just fine. I heard through the grapevine that she was already looking at wedding venues," Lettie whispered.

"Good Lord!" Cricket gasped. "Bryce just took over the pharmacy today!"

"Yep, but when a good-lookin' bachelor comes to town, you can expect Mary Lou to try to snag him for her daughter. She would like to have grandkids before she's ninety," Lettie said.

"So would we," Nadine sighed.

"You've got Jennie Sue and Rick's two daughters," Cricket reminded them.

Even though neither Lettie nor Nadine had ever married or had children, they had been surrogate grandmothers to Cricket's two nieces. They had taken Jennie Sue under their wing when she came back to town six years ago, and Cricket couldn't remember a time when they weren't her friends.

"But we want a grandson," Lettie said. "And your biological clock is ticking, girl."

"Then you'd better adopt Anna Grace," Cricket said.

"We'll do without before we do that," Lettie declared. "She looks down her nose at me and Nadine like we're aliens."

"We ain't Sweetwater Belles." Cricket steered Lettie away from the alien subject. Aliens got the blame for everything in her life. If she lost her car keys, then the aliens stole them. If she burned a pan of biscuits, then the aliens had abducted her for a few minutes, and it was their fault. "If you ain't a Belle, then Anna Grace doesn't waste her breath speaking to you."

"That's the truth," Nadine agreed. "I'm so glad that Jennie Sue told them to go to hell after her mama and daddy died."

Cricket giggled. "I'm not sure she said it just like that, but they sure knew what she meant. I was there when the Belles all came to the house after Charlotte and Dill died in the plane crash. I'd always thought I wanted to be in that crowd, but good glory! I learned real quick that I'd rather be pickin' beans as puttin' up with those women. That reminds me. I've got a bushel of beans and a bucket of tomatoes that I need to bring in and wash, and I'm still covered with mud."

"Go on then," Nadine said. "We'll be in town tomorrow, so we'll stop by the bookstore. I've still got a chapter of *The Great Gatsby* to read before we come to the book club meeting next Monday."

"I'll bring the cookies to club that night," Lettie offered. "I know you're super busy since Jennie Sue and Rick are off on their vacation."

"Thank you," Cricket said. "That will help a lot. See y'all tomorrow."

"Bye, now," Lettie and Nadine said at the same time.

Cricket laid the phone back on the table and headed back outside. She brought in the beans and tomatoes, took care of them, and put them in small baskets to take to the bookstore with her in the morning.

"Poor Bryce," she muttered as she rinsed the mud from the beans and laid them out on paper towels to dry. "He'd better be fast if he hopes to outrun Anna Grace."

Chapter Two

*B*ryce was grateful that the two employees who had worked for the previous owner had agreed to stay on when he bought the drugstore. Ilene, a gray-haired lady who had worked there for thirty years, managed the soda fountain and helped stock shelves. Tandy, a middle-aged pharmacy technician, helped him but wasn't too proud to stock shelves, manage the register, or do whatever needed done. They had made sure the transition was an easy one when he took over the store, and on Wednesday, his second day at work, they were waiting at the back door when he arrived.

"Good morning, ladies," he said as he slid out of his SUV and headed across the small parking area to unlock the door.

"You might be singing a different tune by noon," Ilene told him.

"I thought you'd have more time, but it looks like the vultures are circling," Tandy laughed.

He turned the key in the door but didn't open it. Instead he looked up at the blue sky without a cloud anywhere in sight. "Vultures? What are y'all talking about?"

"You've been earmarked to be married by Christmas to one of the town's most elite women, Anna Grace Cramer. Her daddy owns Cramer Oil Company, and her mother is one of the Sweetwater Belles."

He opened the door and stood to the side to let them enter before him. Ilene flipped on the lights and reset the thermostat, then went to open the front door.

"What's a Sweetwater Belle?" Bryce asked and wondered why the upper crust of Bloom would want their daughter married to him when they didn't even know anything about him.

"A group of women formed a club about thirty years ago here in town. They call themselves the Sweetwater Belles, and they've got their fingers in everything, including the holiday and homecoming parades."

When two women came in right away, Lettie rolled her eyes toward Tandy and Bryce. Tandy patted him on the back. "The older one is Mary Lou. The tall, blond, younger version of her is Anna Grace. You better think fast because you are about to have to sink or swim."

Bryce finished putting on his white lab coat and glanced toward the front of the store to see two well-dressed women slide onto the bar stools in front of the soda fountain. The older one was wearing black slacks, a white silk blouse, and her diamond earrings sparkled under the fluorescent lights. If rich was a perfume, she would have reeked of it. The younger of the two was wearing a tight red skirt that showed half her thighs, and high-heeled shoes that matched her skirt. She had that competent air about her, but she didn't come across as royalty like her mother did.

"Sink or swim!" Tandy said out of the side of her mouth.

"You're joking, right?" Bryce asked.

"Not in the least." Tandy patted him on the back. "Mary Lou wanted her daughter to marry a doctor, but she's decided that a pharmacist will do since Anna Grace has passed the thirty mark."

Bryce wiped sweat from his brow. "But I only just got here yesterday. You're pranking me."

"I wish I was." Tandy removed her glasses and cleaned them on the tail of her blue scrub top. "I can never locate my glasses in the morning, and when my kids do find them, they leave smudges on the lenses. Someday I'm going to get contacts."

Bryce wasn't interested in Tandy's smudged glasses or her four kids right then. He wanted her to tell him that she was hazing him. "Prank? Yes?"

"Prank. No." Tandy twisted her brown hair up and secured it with a long clip. "Lettie Betterton called me last night and told me to warn you."

"But…how…what…" Bryce stammered.

"This is a small town," Tandy said. "Everyone knows what everyone is doing, who they're doing it with, and where they did it. We only read the paper, which comes out today by the way, to see who got caught. Anna Grace won't be subtle, and she won't take no for an answer. Mary Lou has made up her mind, and when she does, it might as well be set in stone. Nobody crosses a Belle, except Lettie, Nadine, and Cricket. Oh, and Cricket's sister-in-law, Jennie Sue," Tandy whispered. "They never come in here for coffee in the morning, so you've probably got about five minutes to think up a reason not to do whatever she wants you to do. That is, unless you like what you see."

Bryce's neck itched with heat that was fast traveling up from his collar to put a blush on his cheeks. Lord have mercy! He had been a science geek in high school and in college. He'd never been one of those guys that the girls pursued and had no idea how to handle such a thing.

He'd been in town only a couple of days, and he had been

brought up not to lie. What was he going to say if she asked him to dinner or to a party? Would not accepting her invitation ruin his business? He sure wished he had time to call his mother, or even his grandmother, and ask them for advice. Even though Bloom Drug Store was the only pharmacy in town, it wasn't all that far to Sweetwater where folks would have a choice of several places to fill their prescriptions. What if he lost all kinds of customers because he refused to fall down at Anna Grace's feet and kiss that big turquoise ring he could see sparkling on her finger? No wonder the previous owner gave him such a good deal on the drugstore—the old guy probably got sick and tired of playing small-town politics.

Tandy picked up a bottle of spray and a dust rag. "Ilene is taking her sweet time getting their coffee. She's trying to give you time to get your ducks in a row, so to speak."

"Bless her heart and thank you for the warning and for explaining to me about the Belles." Bryce let out a long breath of air and tried to think of plausible excuses. His mama and daddy had taken him to church every single Sunday from the time he was born until he went to college. Then he went home on weekends that first four years and drove them to church. He sent up a silent prayer asking God to help him out of this big mess.

Before his prayer ended, Lettie and Nadine pushed through the glass door at the front of the store and headed straight back to one of the little bistro tables with the four chairs around it.

"Mornin', Ilene," Nadine called out. "Me and Lettie will have our usual. Neither of us wanted to cook breakfast this morning."

"Two honey buns and two cups of hot chocolate coming right up," Ilene said.

Anna Grace slid off her bar stool and started toward the

back of the store, where the pharmacy was located. There was something about her pasted-on smile and the look in her eyes that let Bryce know Tandy and Ilene were not pranking him.

"Hey, Anna Grace, I heard that you and your dentist boyfriend broke up last week," Lettie said.

"Is your poor little heart just plumb broken?" Nadine asked.

"No, I broke up with him," Anna Grace answered.

"Well, honey, if you get down in the dumps, I suggest you watch a good movie. Me and Lettie like all the *Home Alone* movies when we're feeling blue. They make us laugh," Nadine said.

Anna Grace's smile faded, and she tilted her chin up a notch. "I'm sure that little movie would appeal to old folks like y'all, but I'm just fine. Like I said, I broke up with him, so my heart is just fine." She focused her attention on Bryce and pasted her smile back on. Her high heels on the tile floor sounded to him like .22-caliber bullets heading straight for his heart—or maybe for a spot between his eyes. He needed to think fast, come up with a plan, but his mind was totally blank.

"Hello, I'm Anna Grace Cramer, and I'd like to welcome you to Bloom. We're having an informal little cocktail party at our house tonight, and we would just love it if you would join us." Her smile seemed sincere, but it sure didn't reach her eyes.

"Hey, Bryce," Lettie called out, "didn't you tell Cricket that you would help her gather vegetables tonight? She's kind of swamped since Jennie Sue and Rick are out of town."

Anna Grace whipped around, and Bryce could only imagine the go-to-hell looks she was giving his two elderly landladies.

"Yes, I did." Bryce crossed his fingers behind his back like a little boy who had told a lie. "I'm sorry, Miz Anna Grace, but I have plans."

"Some other time then. Maybe I can pick you up tomorrow night, and we'll go for ice cream?" Anna Grace pressed.

"That's my birthday party night." Nadine raised her voice.

"Sorry again," Bryce said with a smile.

"Then don't make plans for Saturday night. We're going to Sweetwater to the Community Theatre. That's the opening night for the newest musical they're doing this summer. I do love musicals, don't you?" she asked.

"Not so much, and I've already asked Cricket to go fishing with me that night. Why don't you just leave your number with Ilene, and when I have some free time, I'll give you a call?" Bryce hoped that the sassy Cricket wouldn't shoot him when he told her they had plans for at least three evenings that week. Thinking about her telling him that she was taking a mud bath put a broad smile on his face.

"I'll be looking forward to your call." Anna Grace's tone was suddenly as cold as ice. When she got back to her bar stool, she whispered something to her mother, and the two of them left without even waiting for their coffee.

"You're welcome." Nadine grinned at Bryce.

"Thank you," he said, coming around from behind the counter and joining them at the table. "That woman is pretty brazen."

"Yes, she is but not as much as her mother," Lettie said, "and Mary Lou always gets what she wants."

Ilene brought coffee and warmed honey buns to the table for Lettie and Nadine. "Thank goodness y'all didn't want to cook breakfast this morning."

"And that you called us, so we were prepared," Tandy added from the checkout counter.

"But now you've caused Mary Lou to put on her war paint," Ilene said.

"What does that mean?" Bryce asked.

"She will never, ever let it be said that her daughter lost out to Cricket Lawson," Nadine giggled.

"Why not?" Bryce asked. "I liked Cricket when I went out to her farm to buy vegetables last night. She's honest and funny, and she seemed down to earth. Why would anyone not like her?"

Lettie rubbed her hands together and giggled like a little girl. "This is the most exciting thing that's happened in Bloom since Jennie Sue came home from New York and thumbed her nose at the Belles. We've got to get a bet going."

"Cricket has never run in the same circles as Anna Grace," Ilene answered. "She hasn't got a dishonest bone in her body, and she'll speak her mind even if doing so gets her put in jail."

"Speaking of Cricket, it looks like she's just now turned down the alley to park behind the bookstore," Nadine said. "Maybe you ought to run over there while there's no one needing prescriptions and tell her that you'll be picking peas with her tonight and fishing with her on Saturday."

"What if she says no and slaps me for being so presumptu-ous?" Bryce asked.

"Be sure to tell her the whole story about why you made dates with her without asking. She'll understand," Nadine told him.

"I hope so." Bryce pushed back his chair and headed out of the drugstore.

* * *

Cricket turned on the lights and unloaded her tote bag, putting her lunch in the small, dorm-sized refrigerator, and then rolled the cart with the newly bought, used books out to shelve them. She had seen Lettie and Nadine's vehicle parked in front of the drugstore, so when the bell above the door rang, she figured it was her two friends.

"Y'all have a seat. I'll make a pot of coffee, and I brought blueberry muffins," she called out without even looking up from her work.

"Sounds good, but I'm alone," said someone with a deep, Texas drawl from the end of the romance book aisle.

She looked up into Bryce Walton's smiling face. "I thought you were Lettie and Nadine," she said.

Bryce shook his head. "They're over at the drugstore having hot chocolate and honey buns, and they saved me this morning, so I shouldn't even charge them for their breakfast."

For one of the very few times in her life, Cricket was speechless for a whole minute. "Saved you?" she finally asked.

"Yes, and now I'm here to beg a couple of favors from you." His blue eyes locked with hers and held for a moment until he blinked. "I've got a bit of a problem, and it is named Anna Grace Cramer."

"You better sit down and have a muffin and some coffee." Cricket pointed to the sofa at the front of the store. "It's too early for customers to need medicine, and the doctor doesn't call in prescriptions until he closes at four, so you've got a little while before you get busy." She left the cart in the middle of the aisle and went to her desk, where her tote bag was still sitting. She poured two cups of coffee from her thermos and removed the cover from a plastic container of blueberry muffins.

"How do you know all that?" he asked as he sat down on the end of the sofa.

"I've lived in Bloom all my life. That's all just common knowledge," she answered as she set the muffins on the coffee table and went back to her desk for the coffee. "Now, tell me about the Anna Grace Cramer problem."

Bryce reached for a muffin. "It's embarrassing."

Cricket set the two mugs of coffee on the table and took a

chair across from him. "Hey, you're talking to the woman who took a mud bath in front of you yesterday." She smiled. "What could be more embarrassing than that?"

"I was born and raised in Amarillo, but outside of town on a small farm," Bryce said.

Cricket didn't want his whole life story. She was just interested in the bit about Anna Grace, but she kept quiet and picked up her coffee.

"I'm not used to small-town politics," he admitted as he reached for another muffin. "These are delicious."

"I made them this morning. Next year, I'm hoping my blueberry bushes are producing." She wanted him to get on with the story. Lettie had sent her a text that morning reminding her that Anna Grace had probably set her mind to become a pharmacist's wife. She wondered what any of that had to do with her.

"Anna Grace and her mother came into the drugstore this morning." Bryce turned a faint shade of red. "She asked me to a cocktail party tonight. To begin with, I'm not *that guy*." He put air quotes around the last two words.

Cricket wondered what kind of guy that was, but she just kept sipping her coffee. So Lettie had been right, and Anna Grace wasn't wasting any time at all.

"I lied and told her that..." he stammered, and the blush got even redder, "or maybe I didn't really lie, but just went along with what Lettie said. She told Anna Grace that I was helping you pick peas tonight, so Anna Grace asked about tomorrow night, and Nadine said that was her birthday party. Then she insisted on Saturday night, and I lied and said I was going fishing with you?" His voice rose at the end, as if he was asking a question.

"You know anything about picking peas or fishing?" Cricket asked.

"My granddad had a farm kind of like what you have, and my dad and I both love to fish," he answered.

"Then I guess you'd better be at my place about six thirty tonight. After we get done in the garden, I'll fix us some supper. And after work on Saturday, we'll dig some fishin' worms and go to the creek out behind our place. There's some pretty good-sized bass out there. If we catch some, maybe we'll fry them for supper one night soon," she told him.

"Thank you, Cricket. I thought you might slap me and tell me to never darken your door again." He grinned.

"It will take an army to save you from Anna Grace." She smiled. "I'm just one soldier, but I'll do what I can."

"Why would you do that for me?" Bryce asked.

"Because I could never forgive myself if I didn't help you..." she said, "and because Anna Grace has treated me like dirt since before we even went to school. I wouldn't want my worst enemy to get tangled up with her, and besides, I can use help in the garden. Jennie Sue and I go fishing about once a month, but she's not here, so I'd love some company."

Bryce took a couple of sips of his coffee and then stood up. "I'm available any evening you need me to help out."

"Thank you. I will remember that and just might call on you. And I'm available to use for an excuse any time that Anna Grace tries to hoodwink you into doing something you don't want to do." She followed him to the door and out onto the sidewalk. "I've got some beans, okra, and tomatoes to unload. I sell a lot of produce out of the bookstore."

"I'll be glad to help you," he said.

"I'll be glad to accept," she told him. Just wait until Mary Lou heard that he had come over to her bookstore and even unloaded produce. That would be like throwing down a red flag in front of a raging bull. Cricket couldn't have wiped the grin off her face if she'd been sucking on a lollipop made of alum and lemon juice.

Chapter Three

Cricket rushed home after work that evening, changed into a pair of cutoff jean shorts and an oversized T-shirt with a picture of Betty Boop printed on the front, and made sure the kitchen and living room were in good shape. She closed both bedroom doors, gathered up her harvest baskets, and was in the garden when Bryce arrived.

For the second time that day, she was struck speechless when he got out of his SUV. He was wearing a pair of bibbed overalls and a faded T-shirt. He sat down on the back porch, rolled the legs of his overalls up to his knees, and kicked off his flip-flops. Lord, have mercy! In Cricket's eyes he was even handsomer than he had been in his khaki slacks and white lab coat. One thing for sure—Anna Grace had her work cut out for her if she had any notion of ever turning him into a guy who liked cocktail parties.

"This is great," he said as he carried a basket to the end of the first row of peas. "I used to go home every single weekend just so I could smell fresh dirt. I got so tired of being cooped up in the library, studying every spare minute."

"Did you live in the dorm all those years?" Cricket finally found her voice.

"I had a full ride academic scholarship for the first four years," he answered. "Dorm, food, books, and tuition, but the last four years, I worked for a research lab and went to school to help out with the finances. My grandparents were willing to foot the whole bill, but I didn't feel right about letting them do that when I was able to work. Besides, I liked doing research. Not as much as I enjoy farming, though."

"You must've been really smart," Cricket said.

"I just had some good study habits and didn't want to disappoint my parents or grandparents. They had sacrificed a lot to save up the money for my schooling." He tossed pea pods into the basket.

"Are they still alive?" Cricket asked.

"Yep, and still living on the family farm. Granddad is almost eighty now, but if you took the garden away from him, he'd probably only last another week. He and Granny take produce to the farmer's market in Canyon every Saturday. That's their social outing for the week. He bought me that vehicle out there for my graduation present and gave me the down payment so I could buy the drugstore," Bryce said as he kept working. "Mama teaches school, and Daddy is a farmer."

"They must be really proud of you."

"When I finished my first four years, I got a partial scholarship to pharmacy school in Austin. That's seven hours from home, and it was a year-round program, so I only got home for holidays. I missed times like this. What about you? Where did you go to school?"

"The University of Hard Knocks," she answered. "I wasn't smart enough to get a scholarship, and I'm not so sure I would have gone if I could have. I like living on this little patch of ground, and I love my bookstore. My sister-in-law Jennie Sue bought the store, and we ran it together for a while. Then she had two kids and decided to be a stay-at-home mama."

"What does your brother do?" Bryce asked.

"He spent time in the military, got injured pretty bad, and was in the hospital for months. Then he was given a discharge and a disability. He was kind of lost for a few years until Jennie Sue came into his life. The farm was like therapy for him, or so he says. These days, he runs the farm for the most part. When he's home, he takes care of the garden, and he and Jennie Sue go to the farmer's market on Saturdays," she answered.

Bryce stood up at the end of the long row and said, "Peas are done. Want to take care of what tomatoes are ripe?"

"Sure thing." She got two smaller baskets from the back porch and handed one to him. "What does a science geek do for fun?"

"Pretty much the same stuff as a lot of guys: Go fishing, watch football, and I've never met a book I didn't like to read. I'm an eclectic reader. I'll read anything from Faulkner to the back of the Fruit Loops box." Bryce gently pulled tomatoes from the stalks and put them into his basket. "I'll be over to the bookstore to look through your mystery and western sections when I get a chance. I'm kind of on a kick lately with those two genres."

"Ever read *The Great Gatsby*?" she asked.

"Sure," he answered. "I had to read it for a lit class, but it's been a while."

"Well, we've all read that for our book club this month. We meet next Monday night. You'd be welcome to come if you want," she said.

"I'd love to. What time?" Bryce asked.

"We usually meet at six thirty. I don't even leave the store on those nights," she answered.

"I'll be there as soon as I close up the drugstore, and I'll bring a pizza for our supper," he said.

"I'll have the sweet tea ready." She was looking ahead to the evening when they reached the end of the row.

He picked up the basket of peas and tucked the smaller basket of tomatoes under his arm. "Want to get these washed before supper?"

"No, I'll do them later. You must be hungry." *So this is what it's like to have a guy friend*, she thought. *Bryce is much too good of a man for Anna Grace. I kind of even feel sorry for her for only seeing him as a pharmacist and a notch on her social belt.*

Bryce set the two baskets on the porch and sat down on the steps. "Mind if I use the garden hose to wash off my feet? I wouldn't want to track mud into your house."

Cricket turned on the faucet and handed the hose to him. "When you get done, I'll do mine, but my kitchen has seen its fair share of dirty feet over the years."

He reminded her of her brother when he stood and sprayed off his legs and then sat back down on the steps to let them air-dry. Rick did that every night before he put on his shoes and headed back out across the field to his home with Jennie Sue. She missed him living in the house with her, but she couldn't have been happier for him to have fallen in love with Jennie Sue.

"I'm making chicken and dumplings for supper. We'll have corn on the cob, and a cucumber and tomato salad to go with it. I popped a blackberry cobbler in the oven when I got home. It should be ready to take out right about now." She sat down beside him on the steps.

* * *

"Just like home," he sighed. "I never thought I'd get a meal like this when I came to Bloom. I expected to cook for myself or else eat in that little café a lot, and by the way, blackberry cobbler is my favorite dessert."

Bryce wasn't a romantic person, but he could have sworn there was chemistry between them when Cricket's arm brushed against his. That was crazy, though. As sexy as she was with all those curves and those big hazel eyes, she could have any guy in the whole county. She would never be interested in a plain old geeky guy like himself, Bryce thought.

"One thing my mama did before she died was teach me to cook, which is something I like to do," she said, "but eating alone does get lonely. Pretty often, I either eat with Jennie Sue and Rick or they come over here. The girls love to help in the garden. Aubrey is five, so she really does know how to pick beans and peas. Dina is only three, but she's learning."

"I can't remember a time when I didn't know how to work in the garden, or when I wasn't happiest there," Bryce said.

"Whatever put you in pharmacy school then?" Cricket got up and headed inside the house.

He stood up and followed her. "I thought about being a doctor, but I'm not real fond of the sight of blood. Then I figured I could work in research, which I did when I got into pharmacy school, but for some reason, pharmacy kept calling out to me. Maybe it was Fate."

She opened the back door and went on in ahead of him. "If it was Fate, then maybe you should go out with Anna Grace. After all, you were brought here for a reason."

"I don't think it's got anything to do with that woman," he said. "I'll set the table for us if you'll point me toward the cabinet where the dishes are."

She flung up a hand and it brushed against his biceps. Yep, there were definitely sparks, and Bryce didn't even believe in love at first sight. In his previous two relationships, he and the women had been friends for months, and there hadn't ever been electricity with either of them like he felt with Cricket.

"Sorry about that," she said. "I'll get the food dished up and on the table. Plates are up there. Utensils are in the first drawer to the right of the sink. Paper napkins are on the table. Glasses for tea to the right of the sink."

"Just like Mama has her kitchen set up." Bryce took down two plates and put them on the table. "Everything for efficiency."

"It's the only way to run a farm kitchen," she said as she scooped up chicken and dumplings from the slow cooker.

When everything was on the table, he asked, "Where should I sit?"

"At the head of the table. I always sit right here." She started to pull out her chair, but he beat her to it.

"Allow me," he said and then took his place when she was seated. "Do you say grace?"

"Usually silently," she answered, "but since there's two of us, maybe you could do the honors."

"Gladly." He bowed his head and said a short prayer, and then picked up the crock bowl full of dumplings and started to pass it to her.

"Help yourself first," she told him.

He took out a healthy portion and then sent them over to her. "I got a confession. I've never sat at the head of the table before. That's always been Granddad's place on one end and Dad's on the other."

"Have you got brothers and sisters?" she asked.

"Nope, there's just me, and I come from a long line of only children. My dad and mama both are only kids, and so were my granny and grandpa," he answered as he took his first bite. "These are amazing dumplings. They taste just like what my granny makes."

"That's some high praise." Cricket passed the salad and then the bowl of buttered corn to him.

"Just statin' facts, Miz Cricket," he drawled. "You reckon Anna Grace can make dumplings like these?"

"The cook at their place might be able to," she answered. "You should tell her that you really like dumplings and see if she invites you to Sunday dinner after church."

"Does she go to the same church as you do?" Bryce took a sip of tea.

"Oh, yes, she does." Cricket nodded. "She and her friends, the Belles' daughters, sit together on the back pew so they can hurry out as soon as the benediction is over. I guess she wouldn't invite you to Sunday dinner. They all gather up and go to some place in Sweetwater for dinner every Sunday. I hear they have a standing reservation."

"Does that mean she goes with her friends, and I'm safe for that day?" he asked.

Cricket shook her head. "Not really. The Belles that don't have anything else on their calendars and their spouses and kids all go, so she might rope you into going with them. Mary Lou, that's her mother, would be happy to have her daughter settled. I've heard that Anna Grace has had a long-time affair with a teacher in Sweetwater when she's not trying to find a husband that would make Mary Lou happy."

"That's crazy!" Bryce had heard of small-town rumors and gossip, but he had no idea what he was getting into when he bought the drugstore. "Why doesn't she just take that teacher to Sunday dinner."

"You might be super smart when it comes to books," Cricket said, "but you need to be educated in the ways of small towns. Anna Grace can sleep with the teacher. She can fall in love with him, and even have an affair with him the rest of her life. But she will marry someone Mary Lou approves of.

Anna Grace wouldn't dare disgrace herself in front of the club members by marrying a plain old teacher. Mary Lou would be mortified, and her father would fire her from the high-paying, window-dressing job she has at the oil company."

"Why would he do that?" Bryce asked.

"Because if Mary Lou ain't happy, ain't nobody happy, and her husband doesn't cross her when it comes to Anna Grace," Cricket answered.

"Holy sh…smoke," Bryce muttered. "What else do I need to know about?"

"That's enough of a social lesson for tonight, but if you've got doubts about anything, just call me or else ask Lettie and Nadine. They know everything about everything in Bloom, going all the way back to when they were young, and Nadine will be ninety-five tomorrow," Cricket told him. "Lettie is a couple of years younger than she is, but neither of them act that old. You do know that Lettie believes in aliens, don't you?"

If Bryce hadn't swallowed fast, he would have spewed tea all over the table. "You're kiddin', right?"

"Nope, not one bit, and if you don't want to have to find another place to live, don't ever try to convince her otherwise," Cricket said.

Bryce was so glad that he'd come out to the farm to get some produce the day before. Cricket was a fountain of information. Her cooking was fabulous. He got to play in the dirt and could look forward to going fishing. And she was so damned cute that it took his breath away.

Chapter Four

Cricket had just flipped the lights on at the shop and set down her tote bag on Thursday morning when her phone rang. She fished it out of her purse and smiled when she saw Jennie Sue's name pop up.

"Good mornin'," she answered. "How's the vacation going?"

"Absolutely wonderful," Jennie Sue replied. "We had planned to go to a waterpark and the zoo today, but Aubrey and Dina both cried. They wanted to build another sandcastle on the beach and play in the sand. Rick is getting them into their bathing suits. I've gathered up the sunblock and snacks. Now, tell me all about this new pharmacist and how you are being the damsel in shining armor who is rescuing him from a life of misery with Anna Grace."

Cricket giggled. "I don't know about all that, but he has to be saved, and I'm doing my part to help with that. He helped me pick peas and gather the tomatoes last night. Then he ate supper with me."

"Lettie thinks there might be a little attraction there," Jennie

Sue said. "She said that when she and Nadine came to the bookstore yesterday, your eyes were sparkling."

"Anna Grace bullied me in school and has continued to be hateful to me every chance she gets. Getting back at her would make anyone's eyes twinkle." Cricket unloaded her tote bag and made a pot of coffee while she talked.

"Well, don't lose the sparkle. I want to see it when I get home," Jennie Sue said. "We went to a T-shirt shop yesterday, and the girls picked out two for you."

"That will make my eyes twinkle for sure." Cricket poured herself a mug of coffee before it even quit dripping and carried it to the sofa. "I miss those two little angels so much."

"We're ready," Rick's deep voice came through the line.

"Beach, Mama, beach," Dina said.

"Did you get the snacks and the juice boxes and the towels and the buckets and shovels and..." Aubrey ran out of breath.

"They aren't acting much like angels right now," Jennie Sue laughed.

"I love hearing their voices, and they'll always have little wings and a shiny halo in their favorite aunt's eyes," Cricket said. "Give them a hug from me and go enjoy the day. The damsel in shining armor has things under control here."

"Love you, sister," Jennie Sue chuckled. "See you at the end of next week."

"Lookin' forward to it," Cricket said and ended the call.

When Jennie Sue first came back to town a few years ago, Cricket had felt the same way about her that she still did about Anna Grace. She'd thought Jennie Sue was uppity and had been glad that she'd fallen on hard times. But with time, and especially after Rick and Jennie Sue started seeing each other, Cricket had seen that she'd been wrong and that she should have never grouped Jennie Sue in with the other Belle girls.

Maybe you're wrong about Anna Grace, too. Cricket's mother's voice was clear in her head.

"Mama?" Cricket whispered.

But there was no more from her mother, and before she could figure out why she'd heard the voice so clearly, the bell above the door rang, and Anna Grace came into the store for the first time ever. Cricket blinked a dozen times, but the tall blond woman did not disappear.

"May I help you?" she finally asked.

Anna Grace was wearing a cute navy dress that day with matching high heels and had a matching bag draped over her arm. She crossed the floor with the grace of a runway model and sat down in the wingback chair across from Cricket's desk. She crossed one long, slender leg over the other and took a deep breath. "I need to talk to you."

Here it comes, Cricket thought. *She's going to tell me to leave Bryce alone or else she'll ruin my business.*

"About what?" Cricket sat down in her desk chair and got ready for the bullying.

"I want to apologize for all the times when I've been hateful and mean to you, and to ask for your help." Anna Grace kept her eyes on a spot on the wall behind Cricket's head.

"Thank you for that, but I don't believe you." Cricket reached under the desk and pinched her thigh, proving she wasn't asleep but fully awake. "I think you are here to tell me to step aside where Bryce Walton is concerned, that you intend to start up a relationship with him, and eventually marry him because he's a pharmacist."

"If my mother was sitting in this chair, you would be right. She gave me orders to do just that this morning, but..." Anna Grace actually blushed.

Cricket folded her arms over her chest. "I think you will do anything to get what you want, and then later, you and your friends will laugh at me for being so gullible. Well, I'm an adult now. I'm not a teenager who wants to be included in your circle of friends, and I'm not someone you can bully anymore."

"If I was sitting where you are, I would feel the same way," Anna Grace said. "I don't want to date Bryce. I don't want a relationship with him. I'm in love and have been for a long time with Tommy Bluestone, a biology teacher who lives in Sweetwater. Mama won't hear of it, and Daddy says if I marry him, I'll have to move out of the house and find a job elsewhere because he's not living with Mama when she's that mad. So I just let them think I'm dating other guys, but I haven't dated anyone but Tommy in more than three years."

"Are you serious?" Cricket eyed her carefully. "I heard you just recently broke up with a dentist."

"I have to invent a reason to break up with my imaginary boyfriends when Mama begins to insist that I bring them home for a weekend, or that I invite him to go out to eat with us so she can meet him." Anna Grace looked absolutely miserable when she admitted that.

Cricket shouldn't feel sorry for her after the way Anna Grace had looked down on her all those years, but she did. "That must be tough."

"You can't even imagine." Anna Grace looked like she might break into tears any minute. "I wish Jennie Sue was here so I could talk to her, but then she probably wouldn't even answer my calls after the way we all shunned her when she married your brother." She lowered her voice and looked around the store. "I was proud of her for what she did. I'd never admit it to anyone else, but I was. She stood up to her mother and all the Belles when she came back to town. I want to know how she did it, because I can't live with all this stress any longer."

Cricket still wasn't sure this wasn't just playacting. "She

had the guts to go after what she wanted, even before she met Rick. She rented an affordable apartment and cleaned houses for enough money to live on. You know all this, and yes, all her old friends did shun her for doing it. What makes you think she'll even talk to you?"

"I wouldn't blame her if she didn't," Anna Grace said. "I want to make Mama happy, but I can't make her happy and be happy myself. Tommy has asked me to marry him." She pulled a black velvet box from her purse and popped it open to show Cricket what looked like an engagement ring. "Mama would throw a Southern hissy if she even knew I had this. The diamond is barely half a carat, and I think it's gorgeous. I love it. Tommy saved up for a long time to buy it for me."

"That reminds me of your sweet sixteen ring," Cricket said.

Anna Grace held out her hand to show a ruby ring on her right hand. "This is my sweet sixteen ring, and I guess other than my engagement ring having a diamond instead of a ruby, they kind of do resemble each other. My birthday is in January. Mama didn't think a garnet was fancy enough, so she bought a ruby, which is about the same color. But how did you . . ." She frowned.

"I remember every one of y'all's rings. You came to school showing them off and bragging about them," Cricket said. "I was sixteen that same year, and we were still mourning my mother's death. Rick was in the service and couldn't even come home. I was lucky that Lettie and Nadine brought me a cake that day. So yes, I remember that and every mean thing y'all did to me. I hated school because of you."

"I'm so sorry." A tear made its way down Anna Grace's cheek and dripped off her jaw.

"Apology accepted," Cricket said. "What did you tell Tommy when he proposed, and how did he ask you to marry him?"

Cricket figured Anna Grace would stutter and stammer, but she smiled.

"We took a blanket out into a field of Texas bluebonnets to watch the sunrise. He's very inventive with our dates, and we have so much fun together. He's taught me that money isn't everything and helped me find my inner self," Anna Grace answered. "Right when the sun came up that morning, he brought out the ring and asked me to marry him, and I said yes. Now what do I do?"

"Well, since you said yes, I suppose that you should marry him," Cricket answered, but she still didn't believe all of this was real.

"I've always dreamed of having a big wedding with the fancy dress, at least eight bridesmaids, a blowout reception, and all the trimmings, but I know if I tell Mama that I'm engaged to Tommy Bluestone, I'll have to give all that up." Anna Grace sighed.

"A wedding is a day. A marriage is a lifetime," Cricket told her. "Jennie Sue and Rick didn't have a big wedding. They went to Las Vegas and got married in one of those funny little chapels out there. You have to decide whether you want a big wedding or a marriage. At least, that's the way it looks to me." Cricket didn't give a flip about a huge event, if and when she ever got married, but she did want a man to look at her the same way her brother looked at Jennie Sue. That was pure love, and it beat the hell out of a fancy dress, a string of bridesmaids, and a four-foot wedding cake.

"Tell me more about Tommy. Why are your folks so set against him? Teaching school is an honorable profession."

"That's what I told them back when we had been dating a few months," Anna Grace sighed. "But they informed me that I'd been raised in a better lifestyle than he could ever offer and reminded me that I made five times what he did in a year working at Daddy's oil company, but my job would come to an end the day I married Tommy. That's how much they're against me and him having a happy ever after."

"What's money compared to love?" Cricket asked. "You go to work. You come home, have supper together, talk about your day, and then spend the night in each other's arms. Tell me where you would live if you decided to go against your folks."

"Tommy has a small, one-bedroom apartment in Sweetwater. The whole thing is about the size of my walk-in closet. The Belles will shun me worse than they did Jennie Sue if I do this. Mama and Daddy swore three years ago that they would disown me if I marry him."

"Do his parents accept you?" Cricket asked.

"Oh, yes! He's the baby of eight kids, and they all are so sweet to me. They invite me to everything—birthdays, anniversaries, holidays—and they are just awesome. I love spending time with them," she said.

"What do his folks do, as in jobs?" Cricket asked.

"His mother was a high school math teacher. His father was a history professor at the Tech College. They're both retired now," Anna Grace answered.

They sounded like pretty influential folks to Cricket, but then in the eyes of the Belles, she could understand where the Bluestones might not make the social cut.

"How much money do you need to be happy?" Cricket asked. "You could get a job at a rival oil company. That would really piss your folks off."

"Truth is, I'm not qualified for another job," Anna Grace said. "I'm just window dressing at the company. I answer Daddy's phone calls, take coffee to him, and take care of his appointment book. I don't know anything about managing money or living on my own."

Cricket remembered sitting in the café and seeing Jennie Sue get off the bus when it stopped across the street. Cricket could hardly believe that the famous and very rich Jennie Sue, the daughter of a Belle, was coming home with just a suitcase and riding on a bus instead of driving a fancy sports car. "I guess it just depends on what you want most. Tommy or money."

"That's harsh," Anna Grace said.

"Maybe so, but it's the gospel truth, isn't it?" Cricket was almost believing her, but not quite.

"Tommy wants us to get married at the end of summer on the beach at Padre Island. He has a friend who has a cabin down there that he's willing to let us have for a whole week for our honeymoon." Anna Grace sighed again. "Daddy said that if I make Mama happy, then I can have a honeymoon on the Riviera in France."

"Again, Tommy or money? What will make you smile like you did when Tommy opened that box you've still got in your hand? What are you going to remember the most about your wedding and honeymoon on your fiftieth wedding anniversary?" Cricket asked. "Answer those questions, and you'll know what means the most to you."

Test her, the voice in Cricket's head whispered.

"Want a cup of coffee?" Cricket asked. "There's also some leftover blueberry muffins under the cake dome if you want one."

"I'd love both, but I'll get them. You don't need to wait on me," Anna Grace said.

"I didn't plan on it." Cricket took a sip of her lukewarm coffee and pushed her office chair back. "I'm going to heat my coffee up in the microwave. Those muffins might be better if you give them about ten seconds."

"I can't cook. I don't know jack about cleaning, and I'm afraid I'll be a big disappointment to Tommy." Anna Grace dabbed at another tear with a paper napkin.

Cricket put her coffee in the microwave. "Looks to me like you've got three months to learn. Do you even know how to run one of these to heat up that muffin?"

"Not really." Anna Grace grimaced. "When I want something like that done, I tell our cook and she takes care of it."

What would Jennie Sue do? Cricked asked herself.

She would help Anna Grace. The pesky voice in Cricket's head didn't help one single bit.

"All right, I hear you loud and clear," Cricket muttered as she carried her second cup of coffee and a muffin back to her desk.

"What was that?" Anna Grace's heels made a tapping sound on the tile floor as she followed Cricket back to the desk.

"I can cook. I'm an expert at cleaning and gardening. I have an extra bedroom you can use. And I'll give you a job here in the bookstore dusting shelves, waiting on customers, sweeping up dead crickets every morning, and dumping the occasional dead mouse out of a trap and into the Dumpster out back. Your current friends don't come in here very often, but if and when they do, are you willing to let them see you doing that kind of work?" Cricket said.

Anna Grace hesitated for a moment but then nodded.

Cricket went on to say, "At the end of the day you'll go home with me and help me in the garden, then learn how to cook and clean. It will be a crash course in life. That's what I can offer if you love Tommy enough to leave your fancy lifestyle."

"You'd do that for me after the way I've treated you?" Anna Grace's expression showed total shock.

"No, I'll do it for you because that's what Jennie Sue would do," Cricket said. "Leave your high heels at home. The closet in the spare bedroom at my small house isn't very big, so you will need to limit what you bring to no more than two suitcases. If you don't have anything fit to pick beans or dig up potatoes or even to clean house in, you can borrow some of my old shirts, but my cutoff jean shorts will be too big for you."

"I can't believe I'm even considering this," Anna Grace

gasped. "I don't know how much you'll charge me for all that, but I do have a little bit of savings, so I can pay you."

"Nope. I'll give you minimum wage for working here in the bookstore forty hours a week. I've been thinking about hiring some help so I can take a few hours off now and then anyway, but the rest of it is free for the help you'll be giving us in the garden and helping me clean the house. You might even pull a few more dollars in if you offer to clean Jennie Sue's house, or Lettie and Nadine's for the rest of the summer. We only work half a day on Saturday and we're closed on Sunday at the bookstore," Cricket told her. "And trust me, I can't believe I'm offering this any more than you can."

"When would I start?" Anna Grace asked.

"I'm going to a party tonight at Lettie and Nadine's. I'll leave the front door open. If you're there when I get home, then you've started. You've got twenty-four hours to make up your mind. If you're not there, then I figure this was a prank, or that dollar bills mean more to you than love. But Bryce is off-limits, no matter what you decide. Not because I'm in love with him or want to be a pharmacist's girlfriend, but because he's much too nice of a man for the likes of you if you throw Tommy over and give him back that gorgeous ring for prestige and money," Cricket said. "And another thing—jeans and T-shirts are just fine for work in this place. You can leave all your fancy suits at home, too. Who knows? You might be able to save up enough money by the end of summer for you and Tommy to drive out to Vegas and get married there."

"I just might see you out at your place later." Anna Grace smiled.

"I can honestly say that I hope not," Cricket told her, "but it's up to you. I'm not easy to live with, and I speak my mind. You won't bully me ever again, or I'll kick your skinny butt out in the yard."

"I've lived with my mother for more than thirty years," Anna Grace said. "That doesn't sound too bad at all, and I can never repay you or thank you enough for this offer. There's just one problem. Daddy says if I ever leave, I won't even have a vehicle. If he's serious, then he'll send someone to take my car or else make me give him my keys. Mama will be mortified, and Daddy doesn't like it when she's not happy."

"If you need a ride, call me." Cricket didn't figure she'd ever get that call. "You can ride to work with me, and if you want to go somewhere in the evenings, there's an old work pickup truck out at the farm. It doesn't have air-conditioning, and you'll have to put your own gas in it."

Tears began to stream down Anna Grace's face. "Not one of the Belle daughters would ever offer to do all this for me. They'd all be too afraid of my mother and their own mamas."

"Honey, Mary Lou had better be afraid of *me*. I'm determined that no one is ever going to make me feel inferior again." Cricket had actually stretched the truth, because, deep down, she felt rather plain and chubby in Anna Grace's presence.

"You haven't dealt with my mama," Anna Grace said, "but I'm not going to argue with you. Can I have your cell phone number?"

Cricket picked up a business card for the shop, wrote her number on the back, and handed it across the table. "Welcome to the world of the poor and proud."

Anna Grace pulled a tissue from a box and wiped the tears from her face. "I'm going to call Tommy and talk to him on the way back to the office. Thank you again, Cricket. I damn sure don't deserve this, but I appreciate it more than you'll ever know."

She pushed open the door just as Lettie and Nadine were about to open it. She stepped aside and allowed them to enter, then went on her way.

"Am I seeing things?" Lettie asked. "Was that Anna Grace leaving this store without a black eye or bloody nose?"

"Yep, and I still don't know if she tried to pull a prank on me, or if what she said was real, but I think I shut down the joke if it was one, and I made her feel like crap." Cricket went on to tell them what she had said and done.

"Holy hell!" Nadine sputtered. "What are you going to do if she shows up at your house tonight with her things in tow?"

"Teach her how to work and how to cook and clean," Cricket said. "Jennie Sue gave me a chance when I treated her like crap, so I'm paying it forward."

"This is like that one book we read a few months ago, or was it years ago?" Lettie drew her dark eyebrows down and tapped her chin with her bony finger. "Doesn't matter how long ago it was, but I remember that someone said that the heroine was letting the villain define her actions. You just proved that Anna Grace doesn't have any power over you anymore. I'm right proud of you, girl."

Nadine shook her head slowly from side to side. "Man alive, you've got your job cut out for you if you think you can teach that girl a blessed thing in just three months. She's probably never even pushed the button down to make toast."

"Don't I know it," Cricket agreed. "She doesn't even know how to work a microwave."

"I want pictures of her the first time you take her out in the garden and teach her how to cut okra." Lettie headed for the coffeepot. "That'd be something even more bizarre than aliens."

"Oh, no!" Nadine grabbed her chest. "If she does this, she will be at your house on Saturday when you're supposed to go fishing with Bryce. Do you think she's just initiating—no that's not the right word—" Nadine pursed her lips. "*Insinuating*— that's the word—into your life so she can get next to Bryce? Is this just a ploy to be a pharmacist's wife after all?"

"I warned her about that," Cricket said. "If it is, she's going to find herself landing out in the yard flat on her butt, and I hope it's good and muddy when it happens."

"I'll help you," Lettie said. "Just give me a call, and I'll be there in ten minutes."

"Let me drive and we'll be there in five," Nadine declared.

Cricket just hoped that she never had to make that call.

Chapter Five

$\mathcal{R}$ather than get dressed for a party, Bryce would have liked to put on his overalls and go out to the farm to spend the evening with Cricket. Time with her was refreshing to his soul. Even from the beginning, she didn't put on airs or try to cover up what she was thinking, and he liked that in a woman. But tonight, he would be going down the stairs from his apartment into the garage, and then into Lettie and Nadine's house to celebrate Nadine's ninety-fifth birthday. He'd known them for only a few days, but he already wanted to grow up and have the kind of attitude about life that they had. One that said he loved life and living, and that he was so confident in his own skin that he didn't give a rip what people thought of him.

On his way out the door, Bryce picked up his present—a box of fancy chocolates that he'd bought at a local gift store. He'd called his mother to see what he should take, and she'd suggested a bottle of wine, but his grandmother said a box of candy was a better gift since he didn't know if Nadine liked wine or, if she did, what kind.

When he had gone down the stairs and crossed the garage, he stood at the back door, not knowing whether to go in or to knock. A breeze wafted the scent of roses across the space to him. He turned to look over his shoulder, and Cricket waved at him.

"Hey, good evening." She smiled.

She was wearing a cute floral sundress printed with roses, and red sandals. Her brown hair was twisted up on top of her head and held with a bright red rose clip. Surely, he wasn't just imagining that beautiful, clean smell that got stronger as she neared.

"You sure look pretty tonight," he said.

"Thank you." Her smile grew even wider, seeming to light up the whole garage. "You clean up pretty good yourself."

"I do my best with what little I've got to work with," he chuckled. "I didn't know whether to knock or not."

"No, just go on in. Judging from all the cars and trucks parked along the road, we're not the first ones here." She brushed past him and opened the door.

He motioned for her to go on in ahead of him and then followed that enticing scent through the back door. Nadine was in the kitchen, swiping her finger across the icing on a cupcake, and she just grinned when she saw them coming into the house.

"Busted!" she giggled. "Just remember, when you get to be ninety-five, you can do whatever you damn well please."

"Nadine Betterton!" Lettie shook her forefinger at her sister as she came into the kitchen. "That's the third cupcake I'm having to set back."

"It's my birthday, and besides, I'll have those three for my midnight snack tonight." Nadine slapped her finger away. "You've made too much food anyway."

"Where do we put presents?" Cricket asked.

"We've got a table set up in the living room," Lettie answered. "I'll take them if you two young'uns will guard this woman and keep her from ruining anything else."

Bryce handed over his gift but wasn't sure how he was going to guard Nadine without hurting her feelings.

"Are we the last ones here?" Cricket looped her arm in Nadine's and pulled her toward the archway leading into the living room. "If so, it might be time to cut the cake and start eating. You sure look pretty tonight. Blue is definitely your color. I hope I look as beautiful as you when I'm eighty years old."

"Eighty nothing! I'm only thirty in my mind," Nadine laughed. "And you know very well that my birth certificate says I'm ninety-five, but thank you for the compliment."

Cricket was absolutely awesome, Bryce thought, and he couldn't wait to go fishing with her the next evening. For that matter, he already planned to spend as much time with her as he could in the coming days and weeks.

"Hey, hey," Nadine called out, "the gang is all here."

"And all ninety-five candles are on the cake. Amos, will you help me light them?" Lettie asked.

"Be honored to help, but only if you've got the fire department on standby," Amos laughed.

"Amos and his wife, who passed a few years ago, owned the bookstore before Jennie Sue bought it," Cricket whispered as everyone watched Lettie and Amos light all the candles.

Amos reminded Bryce of the late Mickey Rooney. He was short, had a smile that covered his round face, and by golly, Bryce liked the man before he even said a word because he'd worn bibbed overalls to the party.

When they'd finished, Nadine stepped up behind the table. "Okay, Lettie, now you have to help me blow them out. You could have bought a couple of those candles that are shaped like a nine and a five. You didn't have to put one for every year."

"Oh, no!" Lettie shook her head. "You're the one who's lookin' a hundred smack in the eyeball. You blow them out, and you better hurry because the ones in the middle are about to burn to the bottom. They'll ruin the icing and that's your favorite part, so don't take another second to make your wish."

"I'll remember this when you need saving from the aliens." Nadine took a deep breath, started at one end, and blew out every one of those candles.

A tall man with just a rim of gray hair around his head started the "Happy Birthday" song in a deep baritone, and everyone else joined in. Bryce paid particular attention to Cricket, who had an alto voice and carried a tune very well. Was there nothing this woman couldn't do?

When the song had ended, Amos and the tall guy helped Lettie remove all the candles, and then Nadine cut the first piece.

"I like a corner because it's got the most icing," she said with a smile. "I believe in having dessert first because life can be short. Not that I know anything about that business of it being short, but I do like chocolate cake. The rest of you feel free to enjoy all those finger foods that Lettie has worked on for a week, and please eat it all, or she'll make me have it for breakfast, dinner, and supper until it's gone."

"Tables are set up in the backyard," Lettie announced. "Thank goodness it's a decent night and not too hot."

Cricket wasn't a bit shy about loading her plate with finger foods, so Bryce did the same.

"This is some spread," Bryce said. "I was expecting cake and punch."

"Not at this house. Lettie and Nadine love to entertain," Cricket said. "And they're offended if you don't eat hearty."

"Well, I sure wouldn't want to offend anyone, especially my landladies." He liked these people. They were like the country folks he had grown up around.

The tall guy who'd led the "Happy Birthday" song fell into line behind Bryce and introduced himself. "I'm Frank Bartell, the pastor at the church that most of the folks here attend. I've been meaning to get down to the drugstore and welcome you to Bloom, but this has been a busy week. We've already had a funeral, and two members of my congregation are in the hospital in Sweetwater. But welcome, and I'd love to have you join us on Sunday."

"Thank you, sir," Bryce said and then turned to face Cricket. "Is that where you go?"

"Yep, been going there my whole life. Lettie took care of me in the nursery," Cricket answered.

"Can I drive out and pick you up for church on Sunday, and then maybe take you out to dinner?" Bryce asked.

"That sounds great. I'll be ready at ten thirty. Church starts at eleven," she said. "Come on outside and sit by me. I need to tell you about today."

"Lettie said she saw Anna Grace go into the bookstore. Is everything all right?" Bryce asked as they made their way outside, where multicolored balloons were tied to the ends of two eight-foot tables. Framed pictures of Nadine in every stage of her life were strewn down the middles. "Now, this is a party," he said as he put his plate on the table and sat down beside Cricket.

"Everything is fine, or, at least, I hope it is," Cricket answered. "I figured someone would have seen her in the bookstore and spread the gossip." She told him the short version of what had happened that day.

"That's pretty sweet of you after the way she's treated you, but I've got to admit, it sure takes a load off my shoulders. I was dreading even filling prescriptions for her and her family," he said in a low tone.

Cricket shrugged. "I treated Jennie Sue like crap, and she gave me a second chance, so I should do the same for Anna Grace. Besides"—she leaned over and whispered—"if she was just playing a mean trick, I turned it around on her and took the power away from her."

"If she's not, you have to live with her for three months," Bryce said.

"If she's not serious, she won't last a week in the garden or the kitchen, and she'll leave for sure on Saturday afternoon when I tell her it's her turn to scrub the bathroom." Cricket picked up a stuffed mushroom and popped it in her mouth. "I love food, but then that's evident from the way I look."

"I think you are gorgeous," Bryce said with all sincerity.

* * *

Cricket was glad she had food in her mouth and could use that for an excuse not to say a single word. She was even happier that she didn't have a mouthful of sweet tea, or she would have spewed it all over a picture of Nadine when the elderly lady was probably about sixteen.

"Well, at least you don't have to worry about breaking me with a big hug," she finally said, "and the way I like to cook and eat, I never will. But I've got to admit, I'm probably the clumsiest woman in the whole state."

"I'll catch you if you fall," Bryce said.

Was he flirting with her? Sweet Lord! She had never learned how to bat her eyelashes and flirt like the Belles. While they'd been learning all about fashion and how to make a man fall all over himself to get to kiss their pretty sweet sixteen rings, she had been learning how to cook and plant a garden.

"If you do, I'll probably just drag you down with me," Cricket said.

"Sounds like fun if it's in a muddy garden. We could take mud baths together, and then wash up with the garden hose," Bryce teased, and stole a small tomato off her plate.

A shiver chased down her spine when his hand brushed against her bare arm. Cricket had started to think that she would grow up to be like Nadine in more ways than just age. She would probably be an old maid who knew all the gossip in town and who took care of her two precious nieces. But that little spark she felt gave her hope that Bryce was serious and that there just might be a better future ahead for her.

Nadine sat down beside her, and Lettie claimed a chair across the table. Cricket loved both of them, but tonight, she wished they had sat at the other table with Amos, Ilene, Tandy, and the other guests.

"Bryce, has someone introduced you to our preacher?" Nadine asked.

"Yes, ma'am." Bryce nodded. "We met when we started around the food table. By the way, this is an awesome party."

"I do my best, even though living with her is like sharing a house with an old bear one day and a teenager the next." Lettie nodded at Nadine.

"Hey, if I got up in the same mood every single day, you'd get bored." Nadine winked. "Don't worry, sister, when you get to be ninety-five, I won't smother you with a pillow even if you act like a teenager. Unless I catch you making out on the sofa with some old bald, toothless man."

"I could still catch a young guy." Lettie fluffed up her dyed black hair with the palm of her hand. "I betcha I could even get one who has hair and teeth and doesn't use a walker."

"I've got ten bucks that says you can't," Nadine said.

"You're on, but you can't fuss at me for getting protection

down at the drugstore. I don't want to be catchin' one of the STFs at my age, and besides, if the aliens ever do choose me to go up in the sky with them, I wouldn't want to spread it around to them." Lettie grinned. "And it could take a while, so let's say you have to pay up on my ninety-fifth birthday."

"It's not STFs," Cricket whispered. "It's STDs."

"Close enough," Lettie said out the side of her mouth.

Bryce nearly choked on a sip of tea, but Cricket wasn't a bit shocked at what they were saying. She'd heard them place two-dollar bets on all kinds of things. "That's why they sit with us rather than with the preacher," Cricket told him.

"You got that right," Lettie said, "but we do try to be nice on Sunday. Which reminds me, you two want to have Sunday dinner with us after church?"

"We've already got plans," Bryce said. "I'm taking Cricket to church and then out to lunch."

"Is it a real date, then?" Nadine asked. "If it is, that's the best birthday present you could give this old woman."

"Old, my stars!" Cricket felt the blush before it started burning her face. "You will never be old, no matter what the numbers say."

"Thank you, darlin', but I just love it that you are going out on a date." Nadine grinned.

Thank God Bryce didn't ask why that was such a great thing, Cricket thought. Then the preacher came over, with a huge square of cake on a Happy Birthday plate, and sat down beside Nadine.

"Lettie, you outdid yourself on this cake. It's amazing," Frank said.

She put on her sweet little angel expression and cocked her head to one side. "You let me know when your birthday rolls around, and I'll make you one just like it, but one without ninety-five holes poked in it."

"I'll only need sixty-five, and my birthday is at the end of August," Frank said. "I plan on retiring in September. The committee will be looking for a new preacher at the end of this month. You ladies going to be up for interviews?"

"You bet we are," Lettie assured him.

Bryce leaned over and whispered, "I guess it's all right then if we go get cake now?"

The sensation of his warm breath on her neck sent even more of those delicious little shivers down her spine. She pushed back her chair and stood up. "We're going for cake. Can I get y'all anything while we're in there?"

"No, we're good for now," Nadine answered for both sisters.

"I'm just fine," Frank said.

Cricket could hear them talking about new preachers as she and Bryce started into the house. "They've been on the hiring committee for probably fifty years or more. What kind of scares me is that Lettie might fight to hire a widower who has hair, his teeth, and walks without a cane just so she can collect on that bet."

Bryce chuckled, but the second they were in the house, he couldn't hold the laughter in anymore, and he guffawed. "You've got to be kidding me."

"They take their bets very serious, and a ten-dollar one is big. They usually only deal in a dollar or two at the most." Cricket headed for the cake. She handed the knife to Bryce and said, "Don't be shy. I sure don't intend to be. I love Lettie's chocolate cake."

"Blackberry cobbler is my favorite dessert, and chocolate cake comes in right behind that." He cut off a big square, then handed the knife to Cricket.

When she finished putting her piece on her plate, she turned around to find him grinning down at her. "What?" she asked.

His eyes glittered when he ran a finger through the chocolate on the top of his cake and then wiped it on her lips. Before she could blink, he leaned down and kissed her. "That's the way to taste chocolate icing," he said when the kiss ended.

Her knees felt weak, and her heart thumped in her ears, but not to be outdone, she set her cake on the table, swiped a finger down the side, and smeared it on his lips. Then she rolled up on her tiptoes, wrapped her arms around his neck, and brought his lips to hers for an even longer, more passionate kiss.

When that kiss ended, she leaned into the hug for another moment, mainly because her knees still felt like they were filled with jelly. "You are so right," she said between breaths.

Bryce wrapped his arms around her and drew her even closer. "I'd rather have your kisses as chocolate cake. I'm not real good at the romance stuff, but I've wanted to kiss you ever since I saw you in the garden."

"Really?" Cricket couldn't keep the amazement out of her voice.

The back door opened and they both hurriedly picked up their cake and started back outside. "Hope y'all left me some cake," Amos said.

"There's plenty." Cricket's voice sounded a bit high and squeaky in her own ears. "But I happen to know that Lettie made cupcakes in case the cake runs out."

Amos passed on by them and headed to the dining room. "That's good to know. I might beg a couple of those cupcakes to take home for my breakfast tomorrow morning."

"I'm sure you won't have to beg," Cricket said as she hurried out the door that Bryce was holding open for her. "Me, too," she said as they crossed the yard.

"If you're going to take cupcakes home, then I might be brazen enough to ask for some, too," Bryce said.

"I wasn't talking about cupcakes," Cricket told him. "I like kissing you better than chocolate."

"That *is* romantic." Bryce beamed.

Chapter Six

$\mathcal{C}$ricket felt as if her car were floating on air all the way from the party out to the farm. The idea that Anna Grace might be at her house was completely gone from her mind, but it came flooding back when she saw the older-model pickup truck parked in front of her house.

"She really did it," Cricket muttered.

She sat in her car for a few minutes before she finally got the plastic container out of the backseat. Lettie and Nadine had sent home cupcakes and little bits of the leftovers, including the rest of the stuffed mushrooms that she liked so well.

The door flew open before she even cleared the porch steps, and a tall guy with dark hair said, "Can I help you in any way? I'm Tommy Bluestone, and I want to thank you so much for helping Anna Grace."

"I've got it all," Cricket said. "Pleased to meet you. I'm Cricket Lawson. Y'all want a cupcake or some of the party leftovers?"

Tommy sure didn't look anything like she had imagined.

He might be as tall as Anna Grace, but not if she was wearing her signature Prada shoes. He had golden skin, jet-black hair, a round face, and a tattoo of a dreamcatcher on his arm. He wore black-rimmed glasses, a faded T-shirt, and well-worn jeans.

"I'd love a snack," Tommy said. "When Anna Grace called me to say that she was really moving out, I didn't even take time to get a bite of supper. It's a wonder I didn't wind up with a speeding ticket."

"It seemed like hours instead of thirty minutes until he arrived," Anna Grace said as the two of them entered the house. "I hope it's all right if I already put my things away."

Cricket carried the container of leftovers to the kitchen and took a half-gallon jar of sweet tea from the refrigerator. "Y'all help yourselves, and Tommy, you are welcome here anytime, but be forewarned, if you arrive right after six any day of the week, I might make you help harvest vegetables from our garden."

"Not a problem. I grew up on a farm in Oklahoma, and I know all about gardening. My granddad is a member of the Chickasaw tribe, and he thinks that all children need to learn about the land and about growing food." Tommy removed the lid from the container. "Oh, man! This all looks so good. Thanks for bringing stuff home for us. Come on, darlin', let's dig in." He picked up a mushroom and fed it to Anna Grace.

"My God," she gasped. "That is amazing, and those cupcakes are homemade, aren't they?"

"Yep." Cricket nodded. "You'll judge all chocolate cake by them forever after you take the first bite. Y'all make yourselves at home. I'm going to have a shower and go to bed."

"Thanks again," Anna Grace said. "What time do I need to set my alarm for?"

"Six thirty, but I'm surprised that your folks let you keep your phone?" Cricket asked.

"I have a clock, and I'll be getting one of those pay-as-you-go phones at the Dollar Store tomorrow," Anna Grace answered. "My mother checked my purse and took away all my credit cards, my phone, and wouldn't even let me bring my hair dryer or curling iron with me. I have one month to change my mind about all this, she says, or they'll take me out of the will."

Tommy gave her a hug and kissed her on the forehead. "You'll survive. You are strong, and I love you."

"Good night." Cricket left them to encourage each other and headed down the short hallway to the bathroom, which she now had to share with Anna Grace. She turned the water on in the shower, put the toilet lid down, and sat on it. She fetched her phone out of the pocket of her dress and called Jennie Sue.

"You're never going to believe what I did today, and what happened tonight," she said.

* * *

Cricket was whipping up eggs in a bowl when Anna Grace came in the kitchen the next morning. "You can make the toast. Put two slices in the toaster oven."

"I usually just have a kale shake for breakfast." Anna Grace yawned and looked around for bread. "What's a toaster oven, and I don't see a loaf of bread."

"I make our bread. It's in the green plastic box right there by the toaster oven." She pointed toward the small appliance sitting on the cabinet. This was going to be a bigger chore than she'd thought. Hopefully, Anna Grace was a fast learner. "The bread has been sliced. All you have to do is put two slices in the tray, close the door, and turn the knob to toast."

Anna Grace followed the directions without being told a second time. Cricket kept a close eye on her while she scrambled eggs to go with the bacon she had already fried.

"Now take it out and smear butter on it. You've eaten in enough restaurants to know how to do that," Cricket said.

"I made toast!" Anna Grace beamed as she carefully spread butter on the thick slices of homemade bread. "This smells so good. How do you make it?"

"That's a lesson for another month." Cricket finished the eggs and piled them up on a plate beside six slices of crispy bacon. "Pour two mugs of coffee while I get the orange juice."

"Mother would scream at me for eating like this," Anna Grace sighed. "I've been taught my whole life that you can never be too thin or too rich."

Cricket set the plate of eggs and bacon on the table, then brought out a half-gallon container of juice. "I guess those are two lessons you'll have to unlearn. I'll say grace this morning. We'll take turns. Tomorrow it will be your turn." She sat down and bowed her head.

"Thank you, Cricket," Anna Grace said when the short prayer ended. "I've never prayed out loud before."

"Another lesson you'll learn here." Cricket served herself half the eggs and three pieces of bacon, then passed the plate over to Anna Grace. She poured herself a glass of juice, slid the jug over toward Anna Grace, and picked up a piece of the toast from a plate that was in the middle of the table.

"We never ate together except at dinners when we had guests." Anna Grace followed Cricket's lead and put the rest of the eggs and bacon on her plate.

Cricket hoped that Anna Grace learned to like this new world because, from what Tommy had said, this was the kind of upbringing he had had. If she didn't learn to be independent, all the love she had for him might not be enough.

"If we eat like this every morning, I'll need new clothes," Anna Grace said.

"You'll work it all off." Cricket opened a jar of homemade elderberry jam and put a spoonful on her toast.

"I go to the gym after work at least three times a week, but I'm sure my mother will cancel that membership. She's probably made a list of all the places she'll need to call today." Anna Grace finished off her breakfast and took a sip of her coffee. "Do you think I could make breakfast for Tommy by Sunday morning? And is it all right with you if he sleeps over on Saturday night?"

"You're an adult. You don't have to ask me whether your boyfriend can stay the night here," Cricket said. "I'll give you a crash course in something simple. We'll make French toast and ham for supper tonight, and you can write down the instructions as we go. It's fast and easy."

"I hope so." Anna Grace smiled. "I'll go get dressed. I brought jeans and a shirt like you said to wear to the bookstore this morning."

"Not before we get the dishes done and the kitchen put to rights." Cricket finished off her coffee. "And Anna Grace, if you can read directions, you can cook. During our downtime at the store, why don't you go through some cookbooks?"

"Do they have one called *Cooking for Dummies*?" Anna Grace asked.

"Maybe so," Cricket answered. "I'll wash. You can dry and put away, so you'll learn where things go."

No one ever texted or called Cricket early in the morning, so it startled her when her phone rang as she was washing dishes. She quickly dried her hands and pulled it from her hip pocket, scared that something might have happened to Lettie or Nadine. When she saw Bryce's name, a wide smile broke out, and Anna Grace raised an eyebrow.

"Hello." She carried the phone outside to the porch.

"Good morning! I dreamed about you last night, and wondered if I came out and helped with the garden right after work, if maybe we could get a couple of hours of fishing in tonight before it got dark?" he asked.

"I don't see why not," she answered. "Anna Grace and I are making French toast and ham for supper. We could make a sandwich out of ours and take it to the creek with us."

"That sounds wonderful. See you then, if not before." He lowered his voice. "So she moved in, did she? Lettie is betting Nadine that she won't last a week, and she's put ten dollars on it, so she's serious."

"Did you get in on that bet?" Cricket asked.

Bryce chuckled. "I'm in for five. I saw that woman in the store. She looks like she's all fashion and makeup. What about you?"

"The jury is still out, but I might have to throw a dollar or two into the pot," she answered. "See you after work."

"Lookin' forward to it," he said and ended the call.

Cricket returned her phone to her pocket and went back into the house to find that Anna Grace had finished the dishes, put them away, and wiped down the stove top, the cabinets, and the table. "I've seen our cook do this, so I figured that was the rest of what you meant by cleaning up."

Cricket smiled and nodded. She was going to put in five dollars on the positive side. If Anna Grace kept this up, Cricket might win the whole pot, but even if that didn't happen, she felt like she'd already won the lottery when Bryce called.

* * *

Lettie and Nadine were in the drugstore before anyone else that morning. They sat down at one of the tables and ordered cherry limeades. Ilene had just gotten their drinks set down when Amos came in and joined them. Since Bryce wasn't busy, he rounded the end of the pharmacy counter and sat down at the table with them, too.

"That was some party last night," Amos said. "Ilene, would you be a doll and bring me a cup of coffee?"

"Comin' right up," Ilene answered.

"We was glad for a good turnout." Lettie took a sip of her drink. "I think I need a bag of chips to go with this, Ilene."

Ilene picked up a small bag from the end of the counter with her free hand and brought it to the table along with Amos's coffee. "I hear we've got a pot going about Anna Grace making it for a week." She laid a five on the table. "I don't think she'll make it until Monday, so put my money on that side."

Lettie whipped an envelope out of her purse and added the bill to it, then wrote Ilene's name on the outside. "If anyone bets for *her*, they're going to win a lot."

"This is so exciting!" Nadine said. "We haven't had a good bet going like this in more than a year."

Amos handed her two dollars. "Put me down for her not making it until Sunday. She'll be back in Mary Lou's good graces by church time Sunday morning."

Lettie did the bookwork and then focused on Bryce. "Now, we want to know if you're going to ask Cricket on a real date. So far, you've just done what you had to do to run from Anna Grace, even though it's looking like you didn't need to."

"Already did," Bryce said. "We're going fishing tonight, and if she's willing, I'm going to ask her to go with me for ice cream tomorrow night."

Lettie smiled and winked at Amos.

"What's that all about? Are y'all taking bets on me and Cricket?" he asked.

"We never tell the folks that we're betting on," Nadine said. "That would be cheating."

The phone rang and Tandy motioned for him. "Doc just called to say he was faxing over a whole page of prescriptions for the nursing home patients."

Bryce pushed back his chair, but he looked over his shoulder and noticed that Lettie had an envelope out. Amos handed her another bill. Bryce was too far away to see how much he was betting, but he figured they had a pot going where he and Cricket were concerned.

The afternoon went by in a flash. There was a constant flow of customers in the store, and the bar stools and tables were full most of the time. Bryce filled a hundred prescriptions before closing and had at least twenty on his counter to start filling the next morning. At five o'clock, he closed shop and rushed home to his apartment. He got all his fishing gear together and changed into his most comfortable jeans and a comfortable old T-shirt.

He whistled all the way down the stairs leading into the garage, pushed the button to open the overhead door, and loaded his gear into his vehicle, which was parked out on the curb. The radio came on when he started the engine, and the song playing put a grin on his face. Bonnie Raitt was singing, "Something to Talk About." That was the song that Cricket had been singing at the beginning of the week when he met her for the first time. Just hearing the lyrics put a visual of her in those shorts with her midriff showing.

The song ended, but he kept humming it through five minutes of commercials. The words were still playing through his head when he turned down the lane to the farm. He got out of the SUV and headed around back to the garden, where he could hear two female voices. He could hardly believe that the woman in shorts and a faded T-shirt with her hair pulled up in a ponytail was Anna Grace. She had freckles across her nose, and dirt had collected in the sweat beads on her neck.

"Hey, I'm here," Bryce called out. "Where do you want me to begin?"

"Could you bring in the watermelons and cantaloupes?" Cricket asked. "Having this much help is great."

"Before you start, could you take a picture of me picking beans?" Anna Grace asked. "I want to send it to Tommy."

"What about your mother?" Cricket teased.

"Her, too," Anna Grace laughed. "I figure if I can make it through dusting shelves and sweeping floors at the store, then picking beans here and helping cook supper, I'm on my way."

Bryce just nodded and hoped that Cricket hadn't asked her to go fishing with them, too. He had been looking forward all day to spending time alone with Cricket.

"Tommy is driving up here tonight." Anna Grace's voice sounded excited. "He has to take classes this summer to keep up his teaching certificate, but he's got time off until Monday. Cricket says that he can stay with us, and he's even offered to help out in the garden and at the store."

"Fantastic!" Bryce could have danced a jig right there in the wet dirt. That meant Anna Grace would be busy with Tommy, and he could spend time with Cricket.

Bryce pulled his phone from his bibbed pocket and shot a picture of Anna Grace, and then turned it slightly to take half a dozen shots of Cricket picking tomatoes. He slipped the phone back into his pocket and checked the pigtail on the first watermelon vine. It was still green, so he moved on to the next one, which was brown. When he picked the melon up, it came off the vine easily.

"Looks like you're going to have a lot to take to the bookstore tomorrow," he said. "You want to put some in my vehicle? I'll bring them over when you open up tomorrow."

"That would be great," Cricket said. "And thank you. I've been selling everything I take in by noon each day, but I haven't had watermelons in two days. Folks have their name on a list for me to call when we harvest some more. Lettie and Nadine are always at the top, so you can just drop one at their house."

"Will do," he answered and went on to check the next

melon. By the time he finished, there were ten cantaloupes and half a dozen watermelons in the back of his SUV. He washed off his feet with the garden hose, sat on the back porch until they dried, and slipped on his flip-flops. The women had gone into the house earlier, and the smell of cinnamon and the sizzle of ham frying met him when he opened the back door.

"Something smells good in here," he said.

"French toast and ham," Cricket said. "I've got a small container of maple syrup in my tote bag, and there's a bowl of fresh fruit, and a chunk of leftover blackberry cobbler in the fridge that I'll tuck in for you."

Bryce's stomach growled loudly. "That sounds wonderful."

Cricket explained everything to Anna Grace as she cooked. When the ham was browned, she put it on a platter and divided it into four pieces. She dipped two slices of thick home-made bread in an egg, milk, sugar, and cinnamon mixture and browned them two at a time. When she had done eight, she made four sandwiches, put them into individual containers, and slid them down into her tote bag.

"We're ready to go," she said. "Bryce, you can get your fishing gear and the beer, and I'll carry this and my fishing stuff."

"Yes, ma'am," he said. "Are we driving to the creek?"

"We'll take the old work truck," she said. "We can get within fifty yards of one of the best fishing holes in this part of Texas."

"Will you show me where that is sometime?" Anna Grace started whipping up an egg mixture. "Tommy loves to fish. I've never been, but after today, I'm ready to try new things."

"Sure thing," Cricket told her.

"Maybe y'all could go tomorrow evening. If Cricket is willing, I thought she and I would drive down to Sweetwater and get a snow cone," Bryce said.

"I'm willing." Cricket nodded. "I'll show you where to go tomorrow morning before we go to the store, Anna Grace. Are you sure you can do this cooking tonight? I can stay until Tommy gets here if you want me to."

"Get on out of here." Anna Grace waved toward the door. "Tommy will be here in a few minutes, and I wrote down what you did step by step. I'm feeling pretty empowered right now."

"All right then." Cricket picked up her tote bag and headed out the back door.

"Where's your fishing pole?" Bryce asked.

"In the back of the truck," Cricket answered. "It's parked beside your SUV."

She was behind the wheel by the time he got his gear and beer all situated in the bed of the truck. He climbed into the passenger's seat and started to roll up the window, but she shook her head.

"The air conditioner hasn't worked in years. Neither has the heater, but it took us to the farmer's market on Saturdays before I started selling our produce out of the store, and it makes a great truck to drive back and forth to Rick and Jennie's house. Keeps the old rutted pathway from rattling my car all to pieces," she said.

"Grandpa has a truck that might even be older than this one." Bryce propped his arm on the edge of the window. "I got to admit, I never expected to get this lucky when I moved to Bloom. I knew it was a small town, but I figured, for the first year, I'd be sitting in my apartment every night either watching television or reading."

"Why's that?" Cricket drove toward a wooded area.

"Because folks in small towns tend to be a little standoffish until they get to know a newcomer," he answered.

"So is Bloom," she told him. "At least, for some folks. Us commoners are a little more sociable."

"Well, thank goodness for y'all. I feel like I fell into a gold mine," he told her.

"Me, too," Cricket said. "I was dreading the two weeks that Jennie Sue and Rick were gone, but now I've got company and lots of help."

Bryce would have liked to hear her say that she had buried her old feelings about Anna Grace and that he was her boyfriend, but that would have been expecting a miracle since they'd known each other less than a week.

* * *

Cricket parked the truck under a whole grove of pecan trees, slung open the door, and grabbed her tote bag. "This is it. We'll make camp at the edge of the water, toss in our lines, and have supper while we wait on the fish to bite."

"I'll bring all the rest of the stuff," he offered.

"Thank you. I'll get the blanket and the food," she told him. *Is this a date? Or is it just fishing?* she wondered as she spread out the blanket on the grassy edge of the creek and set out the plastic containers of food.

"This is the best date ever." Bryce dropped all the fishing gear and his tackle box, then set the small cooler with a six-pack of beer inside it on the edge of the blanket.

"Is this a date?" Cricket asked.

Bryce sat down beside her and kissed her on the cheek. "I hope it's a date and that we have lots more in the future."

Cricket turned to face him. Her heart pounded in her chest, and she wanted to forget fishing and make out with him until the stars popped out, or maybe until the sun came up the next morning. But before the electricity that she felt went on another minute, she had to know the truth. "Are you serious? I don't want to start something that will just end up breaking my heart and making me feel horrible."

"You really are straightforward, aren't you?" Bryce said as

he cupped her cheeks in his hands and looked deeply into her eyes. "I know this is fast, but you're so special, Cricket. I feel like I've known you forever, and that I'm one lucky son of a gun to have found you. Do you believe in Fate?"

Cricket felt like Bryce could see straight into her soul. "I didn't until Jennie Sue came into my brother's life. That had to be Fate, so I guess in some circumstances I do believe in it."

"Well, Fate brought me to Bloom. I was looking at two small drugstores and had decided on the other one. The deal for it fell through at the last minute when the guy's son and daughter-in-law decided to move back home and run the drugstore, and now I'm glad it did." His eyes fluttered shut.

She barely had time to moisten her lips before his mouth closed over hers. She'd been kissed a few times in her life, but mostly she had just wished the experience would be over. This time, when the kiss ended, it seemed as if her whole life had changed. The water in the stream was brighter. The sky was bluer, and she could swear that the clouds had formed into a heart just for her.

Chapter Seven

Anna Grace was already in the kitchen and had the table set for two when Cricket came out of the bedroom the next morning. She took one look at Cricket and a broad smile covered her face.

"You and Bryce had sex last night, didn't you?" she asked.

"No, but we had kissing and we're having ice cream tonight, and, I hope, more kissing," Cricket answered. "What do you want to learn to make today?"

"Quiche," Anna Grace said, "but we'll have to do that another day. From the recipe I read, it will take a while."

"Not really." Cricket pulled a readymade piecrust from the freezer and unwrapped it. "I keep these on hand for times when I'm too lazy to make the crust. Get bacon, half-and-half, cheese, and eggs from the fridge."

"Are you serious?" Anna Grace asked. "I was just teasing. Quiche is something that the Belles always serve when they have a brunch meeting, and I love it, but it has to bake, and we need to get to work."

"We can get ready for work while it cooks and take about half of it with us. Tommy can have the rest when he wakes up," Cricket said. "Put four pieces of bacon on the bottom of the crust while I beat up the eggs. Then we'll add the half-and-half, cheese, and other ingredients, and pop it in the oven."

"Is it really that easy?" Anna Grace asked. "From the way Aunt Sugar talked, I thought it took a long time. The recipe in the book I looked through yesterday looked harder than that."

"Do you know anything about cheeses?" Cricket asked.

"No, but it said to grate the cheese, and doesn't that take a long time?" Anna Grace measured the half-and-half for Cricket.

"Not if you buy it already grated," Cricket answered. "There are some shortcuts. You will have to go shopping with me one evening after work."

"That would be great," Anna Grace said, "and now, back to the kissing. How did it make you feel?"

"It was totally different from when any other guy kissed me," she said.

"That's the way I felt when Tommy kissed me good night on the second date," Anna Grace sighed. "It was like two soul mates found each other, and he says the same thing."

"But what if Bryce doesn't feel the same?" Cricket asked. "He told me that he was lucky to have found me, but what if that's not real, and when something better comes along, he breaks my heart? I've been hurt bad before, and I don't want that again."

Anna Grace put all the ingredients back where they belonged. "Just trust your heart. I did mine, and I'm happy for the first time in forever. And, Cricket, the way Bryce looks at you tells me that he's not going to break your heart. He really does like you a lot."

Cricket slid the pie in the oven and started for her bedroom. "Thank you for that. Who would have thought I'd be getting romance advice from you?"

"Who would have thought I'd be sharing a house with you and learning to cook and garden?" Anna Grace stopped her long enough to give her a side hug. "This is a whole new world, and I'm loving it."

Cricket hugged her back and then stepped away. "I don't think I'd love your world if our situations were reversed. When Jennie Sue's parents were killed in that car wreck, Rick and I came to the house with her."

"I remember that night," Anna Grace said. "You stayed out by the pool most of the evening."

"Yep, because I let the whole bunch of you intimidate me," Cricket admitted. "But that's in the past, and we're living in the present."

"And so, looking forward to the future." Anna Grace grinned.

* * *

Amos, Lettie, and Nadine were all waiting at the front door when Bryce opened the drugstore that morning. The three ordered coffee and honey buns and sat down at one of the tables together.

"Heard you went fishin' last night," Amos said. "Catch anything?"

"Nope," Bryce said. "They weren't bitin'."

"Goin' back tonight?" he asked.

"No," Bryce answered. "Tonight, Cricket and I are going to Sweetwater after work for ice cream and a drive through the country."

"So y'all are dating?" Amos asked.

"I hope so," Bryce said with a grin.

"We've got a whole raft of prescriptions coming in," Tandy yelled from the back of the store. That started a day busier than any he'd had all week. Bryce could hardly believe it when he looked at the clock, and it was ten minutes until five. Ilene was wiping down all the tables, and Tandy was counting out the bills in the cash register.

At exactly five o'clock, Ilene locked the front doors, Tandy put a bag of cash into the safe and locked it, and Bryce hung up his lab coat. "I can't tell you two how much I appreciate your efficiency. I'm so glad you stayed on to work for me. This could have been a nightmare if you hadn't."

"You ever think maybe we're putting a little more pep in our step because we don't want you to be late for your date?" Ilene teased as they all three left by the back door.

"Well, thank you for that, too."

Bryce got into his vehicle, drove around to Main Street, and parked in front of the bookstore. He turned off the engine, waited until half a dozen cars went by, and then slung open the door and slid out from behind the wheel.

Anna Grace was sitting on the sofa with a glass of sweet tea in her hands when he went into the store. She looked up and pointed toward Cricket's desk. "She's in the bathroom right now, but you can wait on her. How was your day?"

"Fast and furious," he answered. "I don't think I stopped counting pills from the time we opened until we closed, but that's good. That's what I'm in business to do. How about y'all?"

"The same until about five minutes ago. Cricket says that she sold more books today than she usually does in a month," Anna Grace answered.

"It's been crazy," Cricket said as she crossed the floor. "Are you ready to go get ice cream?"

"Don't you have to wait until six to close up shop?" he asked.

"Not when I have help. Anna Grace can turn off the lights and lock the doors," Cricket replied.

"For real?" Anna Grace asked.

Cricket tossed her the store keys. "Didn't you ever close up shop at the oil company?"

"Yes, but..."

Cricket shook her head and held up a palm. "No buts. When six o'clock gets here, lock it up and..." She dug around in her purse and laid her car keys on the coffee table. "And go home. Tommy said he would make sure anything in the garden that needed picking got picked. There's food in the pantry and fridge. You're on your own. If you're afraid to cook anything else, make sandwiches and take them to the creek for a picnic. Jennie Sue says that you can skinny-dip this time of year." She sent a broad wink toward Anna Grace. "Nobody will be home for a while to catch you!"

Bryce ushered Cricket out the front door with his hand on the small of her back, opened the vehicle door for her, and waited until she was settled before he closed it. He hurried around the back of the SUV, made sure no cars were coming, and slid into the driver's seat.

"This is a real treat, getting to leave this early," he said, "but what do you say we stop by the Bloom Café and have a burger for supper before we drive down to Sweetwater to the ice cream shop?"

"That sounds great." Cricket smiled. "But you do realize that if you take me there to eat, folks are going to talk."

"Then we'll keep the phone lines hot tonight." He grinned as he drove to the end of the block and snagged a parking place.

When they were out of the SUV, he draped an arm around her shoulders and kissed her on the cheek. Only one booth toward the back of the café was empty, so he drew her close to his side and whispered in her ear all the way from the entrance to it. The whole place was buzzing when they walked in, but even a deaf person could have heard a pin drop until the moment they both slid into the same side of the booth, and he brushed a sweet kiss across her lips.

* * *

Sparks flew around them, and even though it wasn't funny, Cricket giggled.

"I hope my kisses aren't that bad," he whispered.

"Not at all. They make my knees go weak and my heart race. I can't stop laughing at all the people's faces. What they've heard about the new pharmacist in town is true. He's spending time with Cricket Lawson when he could have had any woman in Bloom," she whispered.

"But I like Cricket," he chuckled. "She's my kind of woman."

Laura Kay, the café owner, came over to their table and asked, "What can I get y'all to drink?"

"Sweet tea for me," Cricket said, "and I'll have a double bacon cheeseburger and fries."

"I'll have the same, and with an extra order of fries," Bryce added.

"Have it right out," Laura Kay said, "and welcome to Bloom. I've been meaning to get down to the drugstore and meet you, but it's been crazy in here all week. I'm Laura Kay Franklin, and I own this café."

"It was busy at both our places today, too," Bryce said, "and thank you for the warm welcome."

"Sure thing," Laura Kay said. "Hope to see you in here often."

"Maybe not, since Cricket has been cooking for me," Bryce said.

"Well, I'm sure what you get in here wouldn't be as good as what she makes," Laura Kay said and rushed off to pour refills of tea for other customers on her way back to put their order in.

"You do know that she's telling all the folks where she's refilling tea glasses what you said, don't you?" Cricket looked up to find that he was staring at her.

"I hope so," he said. "You have the most beautiful eyes, and your smile lights up the whole room."

"Flattery will get you—" she started.

He put a finger over her lips. "That's not flattery. It's the pure facts."

She closed her hand over his finger and kissed it. "With all this to feed the rumor mill, the gossip about Anna Grace will fall by the wayside."

"I told you we'd give them something to talk about, but it's not rumors, it's the truth," Bryce said.

Laura Kay must have refilled the customers' tea glasses five times each because no one seemed to be in a hurry to leave the café. The place was buzzing with conversation when Cricket and Bryce finished their burgers and fries, and when he paid for the food, the noise got even louder.

They had barely gotten into his SUV when both their phones rang at the same time. Cricket answered hers, and Bryce stepped out of the vehicle and sat down on the bench in front of the store to talk.

"Hey, I hear that you went to supper with Bryce at the Bloom Café," Jennie Sue said. "I should leave town more often."

"Holy smoke! We just walked out of the place," Cricket laughed. "How did the news get all the way to Florida that quick?"

"You know what they say," Jennie Sue giggled right along with her. "There's three ways of fast communication: telegraph, telephone, and tell-a-woman. The latter is the fastest by far. Someone in the café called Lettie and she called me, but she thought y'all were going for ice cream tonight and burgers tomorrow night. She's not going to be happy when she finds out that someone else jumped the gun on her when it comes to gossip."

"Tongues were wagging." Cricket told her what Bryce had said about giving everyone in town something to talk about. "He did an amazing job, but he said it was all real, not just for show."

"Like I said, I should leave town more often," Jennie Sue said, "and you should keep me informed a little better. I don't like getting things secondhand either."

"Yes, ma'am," Cricket agreed. "Bryce got a call at the same time I did, and he's on his way back. Talk to you later."

"I'll expect details," Jennie Sue said.

"I know, I know," Cricket groaned.

* * *

A quarter moon hung in the dark sky with bright stars dancing all around it when Bryce walked Cricket to her door that evening at ten o'clock. They'd had ice cream, talked about anything and everything while they ate it, and then talked some more on the way home. She'd never been so comfortable with a guy in her whole life.

"I told you that the call back at the café was my father, and I've been trying to figure out a way to ask you to meet him and my mother. Is that too forward or too soon for you? Dad and Mama are coming to Bloom on Saturday and staying over until Sunday after church. Since my place is so small, they'll bring their motor home. I called Lettie right after I talked to them, and she said they could park it in the driveway and hook up to the electricity in the garage. They want to take us out to dinner so they can meet you on Saturday evening. If you're not comfortable with that, or if you think I'm rushing things…" He hesitated.

"I've got a better idea," Cricket said. "Bring them out to the farm when they get into town and have gotten things hooked up. We'll grill some pork chops and cook supper at home. We can visit more that way. Tommy and Anna Grace will be there, too, so we'll have a perfect group—three guys and three ladies."

"Like I've said before, you are amazing," he said. "Will you go to church with us on Sunday morning? They'll have to leave right afterwards. Maybe we could take another picnic to the creek after we say our goodbyes?"

"I'd love to," Cricket said, "on all of it."

Bryce caged her by putting a hand on the door on each side of her, and then he leaned down and kissed her good night. Just like all the other times, he could have sworn the earth moved under his feet.

Cricket rolled up on her toes and wrapped her arms around his neck for the second kiss. "This has been the most awesome week of my life. I'm still not sure if it's real or if I'm dreaming."

"If you're dreaming, then I am, too, and I don't want to wake up." Bryce kissed her one more time, and then whistled all the way to his SUV.

Cricket waved at him until she couldn't see his taillights any longer and then went into the house to find Anna Grace cuddled up beside Tommy on the sofa.

"You look like you're in love," Anna Grace teased.

"So do you," Cricket shot back.

"Guilty as charged, and happy to boot," Anna Grace said. "Mama called this evening just before I closed up shop and begged me to come home. She said that Daddy would give Tommy a job in the oil company, and I could have my big wedding. She'd already contacted a planner."

"And?" Cricket stopped in her tracks.

"I told her no," Anna Grace said. "Tommy likes what he does, and I've decided I don't want a big wedding. I do need three more months to learn more about being independent, though, before we have a small ceremony on the beach on Padre Island. I told her that she and Daddy could come to the wedding, but none of the Belles are invited. Not one of my friends has tried to get in touch with me since I moved out of Mama and Daddy's house."

Cricket slumped down in a rocking chair. "As strong as you've gotten in just the past few days, you should be able to bench-press an Angus bull by the end of three months."

Tommy chuckled. "That's similar to what I told her, and she cooked supper all by herself. We had chicken enchiladas."

Anna Grace blushed. "It was a simple recipe. I can read; therefore I can cook."

"Yep," Cricket said and remembered what Jennie Sue had said. "I should leave you alone more often. Hey, just a heads-up. Bryce's folks are coming over on Saturday for dinner."

"I'll do what I can to help." Anna Grace nodded.

"And I'll take the guys fishing so you ladies can talk about us," Tommy said.

"Thank you both." Cricket pushed up out of the rocking chair. "I'm glad you're staying all summer, Anna Grace."

"Will you and Bryce come to Padre with us, and will you be my bridesmaid?" Anna Grace asked. "I'm only having one, and it will be really simple. We've decided on the first weekend in August."

"I'd be honored," Cricket said, "as long as the dress isn't too frou-frou."

"I can guarantee that," Anna Grace assured her.

Cricket went to her room, and sent Bryce a text: *Will you go with me to a wedding on Padre Island the first weekend in August?*

The answer came right back: *Yes!*

She fell back on her bed and stared at the ceiling. If someone had told her a few months ago that her life would turn completely around in one short week and that Anna Grace Cramer would ask her to be her only bridesmaid, she would have thought they were drunk or insane.

"But it's real," she whispered, and picked up her phone to call Jennie Sue.

Chapter Eight

"Cricket, I'd like you to meet my parents," Bryce said. "This is my mother, Darlene, and my father, Tim."

"I'm pleased to meet both of you." Cricket shook hands with them. "And this is my friend and roommate, Anna Grace, and her fiancé, Tommy Bluestone."

"This is really sweet of you to invite us out here," Darlene said.

"Yes, it is, and I hear there's a good fishing hole right here on your property," Tim said.

"There sure is," Tommy said. "I caught several catfish yesterday. I thought us guys might grill them along with whatever we catch today. Or we can have a fish fry. Whichever way y'all like them best."

"Grilled," Darlene and Tim said at the same time.

Bryce leaned down and whispered in Cricket's ear. "Do you want us guys to stick around awhile?"

Cricket shook her head. "Anna Grace and I have already made a blackberry cobbler and a chocolate cake for dessert, and the vegetables are prepped for supper, so we thought that us girls would go fishing with y'all."

"Well, halle-damn-lujah!" Darlene grinned. "I love to fish. Let's have a contest. If the ladies catch more fish, the guys have to do cleanup after supper. If they bring in a bigger haul than we do, then we'll do cleanup."

Bryce shook his head. "That's not fair. We'll be doing the grilling, and that's half of making the meal."

Cricket raised both eyebrows. "And we've made dessert and will be making the sides."

Darlene took a step over to stand beside Anna Grace and Cricket. "I think they're afraid we'll show them up, girls."

Cricket liked this woman. She reminded her of Lettie and Nadine twenty years ago. "Losing a fishing contest would be humiliating," Cricket added, taunting the men.

"You're on," Bryce said. "And we won't lose. Let's gather up the equipment. Can we all go in the truck?"

"Sure." Cricket grinned. "You guys can have the back of the truck. Just hang on tight. I'm driving, and I could hit a few potholes."

"Want some pillows to sit on?" Anna Grace teased.

"We're tough." Tommy gave her a quick kiss on the forehead. "I'm just glad that dessert is already made. If you ladies lose the bet, you might burn it, and my sweet tooth would cry if a cobbler was ruined."

"I'll get the keys then and meet y'all at the truck." Cricket headed into the house. She went straight to the kitchen, opened the refrigerator door, and took out a plastic container. She put it, several bottles of water, and some cookies into her tote bag; grabbed the keys for the truck from the end table; and went back outside.

The guys were already sitting in the back of the truck, but none of them was brave enough to sit on the tailgate.

Anna Grace pointed to her bag. "What's that?"

"A few cookies in case we get hungry, some water if we get thirsty, and what's going to help us win this bet," Cricket answered. "And we are willing to share with the guys. We don't want them to say they lost the bet because they were so thirsty and hungry that they couldn't concentrate on their fishing powers."

Anna Grace giggled. "I can't believe I've missed out on all this fun for so many years."

"Why's that?" Darlene asked as she got into the truck and slid over to the middle of the bench seat.

"You're the smart one," Cricket said, smiling, as she settled in behind the steering wheel, "but there are no gates between here and the creek."

"What does that mean?" Anna Grace asked.

"It means that the smart farmer always sits in the middle. Then she doesn't have to get out and open and shut the gates," Darlene explained. "Now, tell me why you missed out on fishing."

"A week ago, I was employed by my father in an oil company," Anna Grace began and went on to give her a brief explanation of what had happened in the last week, "and Cricket was kind enough to forgive me and hire me, and she's teaching me to be independent. Today is the first time I've ever been fishing. I hope I don't hold y'all back any and cause you to lose the bet."

"You'll be our ace in the hole. Beginner's luck will be with *you*." Darlene patted her on the knee. "And Cricket, please be careful with the potholes. I would like grandchildren in the near future."

Cricket laughed out loud. "Yes, ma'am." She had always been skeptical of people until she really got to know them, but she really did like Darlene—just like she'd been drawn to Bryce from the first time she met him. She parked under a tree, and a vision flashed through her mind of those kisses she had shared with Bryce a couple of nights ago. A nice rosy glow filled her cheeks, and her pulse jacked up a few notches just thinking about the way his lips on hers had heated her from the inside out.

"The race is on!" Bryce called out as he and the guys unloaded and carried the fishing rods and tackle boxes to the edge of the creek.

"I have no idea how to bait a hook," Anna Grace whispered.

"I'll teach you," Darlene said. "There's nothing to it. Just think of the worm as a piece of spaghetti. Come to think of it, we could use cooked spaghetti."

Cricket opened the truck door. "That's part of my secret recipe for bait. I brought some along, and we won't be sharing that with the guys."

"Do you share your recipe?" Darlene asked as she and Anna Grace got out on the other side.

"Not with many people, but I might with you," Cricket whispered. "Men think that bait has to stink to high heaven. I'm of the opinion that any smell will bring a catfish to see what it is. Let's see how you like it before you write it down."

"Fair enough." Darlene nodded.

The guys went upstream twenty yards and sat down on the bank. Cricket took Darlene and Anna Grace downstream about ten yards. "This is a better spot. It's a little deeper and a little colder, and there's shade. Catfish like murky waters. If you follow the creek that way"—she pointed to the west—"the water clears up, and it's a perfect place to lay out and let the clear water cool you off on a hot day."

"Or go skinny-dippin'," Anna Grace giggled.

"I remember being young and doing that," Darlene said.

Cricket got a visual of Bryce with the clear creek water flowing over his body, and immediately felt her cheeks burning.

She took a deep breath and let it out slowly. "Okay, ladies," she said to get the picture out of her head, "grab a fake worm and put it on your hook."

"Are those fettuccine noodles?" Anna Grace asked. "But what's the smell?"

"A little cinnamon, some nutmeg, and ginger whipped up in a flour mixture and made into balls, then the noodles are wrapped around them so that when they get into the water, the pasta kind of comes undone and wiggles like live worms," Cricket answered.

"Beats the devil out of stink bait." Darlene grabbed one of the balls, slipped it onto her hook, and tossed her line out into the creek.

"Okay, here goes," Anna Grace said when she'd baited her hook. "I watched how y'all did it, so I'm going to give it a try. I hold this button down, and throw, and oh my gosh, I did it! I can't believe I did it!"

"Beginner's luck. It's going to be with us today," Darlene assured her.

Minutes after Anna Grace sat down on the bank, her red and white bobber went under and her line got tight. "What do I do now, Cricket? Help me!"

Cricket laid her fishing rod down and hurried over to Anna Grace. "You reel it in just a little at a time. Looks like a nice-sized one, but the bigger they are, the harder they fight. Easy now, just a turn or two, and let him think he's won."

"I can't believe I'm catching a fish," Anna Grace squealed.

"It's not caught until it's on the bank and on ice," Darlene reminded her.

"All right, now a little more," Cricket said.

"Tommy, I'm catching a fish!" she yelled.

"That's great," he hollered back. "Need some help?"

"No, we've got it," Anna Grace answered.

In another five minutes, they brought the catfish to the bank, and Anna Grace stared at it as if it were made of pure gold. "I can't believe I caught the first fish."

"Now you pick it up like this." Cricket held it up. "And put it in the cooler on the back of the truck."

Anna Grace flinched only once when she took the four-pound catfish by the gills and carried it to the cooler. Cricket was as proud of her as she figured she would be when her first child started kindergarten.

"She's doing pretty dang good for a woman who's never done anything for herself," Darlene whispered.

"Love kind of does that for you." Cricket grinned.

"Yes, it does." Darlene nodded.

Cricket noticed that the woman was staring at Bryce when she said it and wondered what was on her mind. "We should have bet on the greatest number of pounds rather than how many fish."

"We'll win either way," Darlene said with so much conviction that Cricket believed her.

By the end of the time they had to fish, both teams were tied with two fish each. Bryce had caught two, and Darlene had caught the second one on the girl's team.

"Looks like we'll be sharing the cleanup," Bryce said as they all piled back into the truck to return to the house. "But we do have enough to grill along with the pork chops you've got marinating. Let's make a deal. We'll clean the fish and fillet them if y'all will do cleanup."

"You got a deal," Anna Grace said. "I'm not quite ready for the fish-cleaning lesson just yet."

"Honey, I'll always take care of getting the fillets ready, and I'll be the master of the grill at our house if you'll always have a dessert ready." Tommy stopped and gave her a quick kiss on the lips.

"That sounds good to me," Anna Grace agreed as she

climbed into the truck behind Darlene. "That was so much fun. Can we go again soon?"

"You and Tommy should go together. Take a blanket with you and some beer. If you don't catch a single fish, you'll still have fun." Darlene winked at Cricket.

Sweet Lord! Had Bryce told her that he and Cricket had gone fishing and wound up making out on a blanket?

* * *

On Sunday morning, Bryce knocked on the door of his folks' RV. "Y'all awake in here?" he asked.

"Come on in," his mother said and stood back to let him enter. "We had breakfast burritos. There's one left. You want it?"

"You bet I do. I just grabbed a doughnut and a glass of milk." He felt cramped in the tiny trailer, even when he sat down at the small, booth-type table with his father.

"We're going to drive the RV to the church parking lot so we can leave right after services," his father told him. "I want to know how you really feel about Cricket."

"That was blunt," Bryce said.

"We like her a lot," Darlene said. "She speaks her mind, and she's so much fun to be around. We don't want to influence you, but she fits right in with our family so much better than your other girlfriends."

"I really like her a lot," Bryce confessed. "I feel like I've known her forever, like we grew up next door to each other. I was disappointed when that other opportunity for a small drugstore fell through, but I'm so glad it did because I've got Cricket in my life now."

"Good enough." Tim grinned. "Finish up that burrito and let's go to church."

When he'd finished eating, Bryce helped his dad get things

unhooked and ready to travel, got into his SUV, and rolled down the window. "Wait for us in the parking lot, and we'll all go in together," he said.

Tim waved in agreement, and Bryce hummed Blake Shelton's "Honey Bee" all the way to the farm. When he knocked on the door, Anna Grace answered and motioned for him to come on into the house. "Cricket will be out in a minute. Would you mind if Tommy and I rode with y'all this morning?"

"Not a bit. Afterwards, let's all four go down to the café and have Sunday dinner," Bryce suggested. "I hear that Laura Kay has a chicken and dressin' special on Sundays."

"I'd love that," Tommy answered for them. "I've never eaten at that café, but now that the cat is out of the bag about me and Anna Grace, we can go in there together."

"I'm ready," Cricket said, coming in right at the end of what Tommy was saying. "I broke the strap on my sandal and had to find another pair of shoes. I almost decided to put a toe ring on and go barefoot."

Bryce tucked her hand into his and gave her a kiss on the forehead. "Anytime you want to do that, let me know, and I'll do the same." He led her outside.

Anna Grace and Tommy headed on out to his SUV and got into the backseat.

Bryce stopped and said, "Hold up just a minute."

"Is something wrong?" Cricket asked.

"How do you think her old friends are going to react to her decision? This will be the first time she sees them since she moved in with you." Bryce had something else on his mind, and he knew he was stalling, but he wasn't quite sure he was ready for her answer.

"She's pretty tough," Cricket said in a low voice. "I think she'll be fine with whatever comes her way today. I heard you offer to take them to dinner with us. That was so sweet."

"I'm a sweet guy," he said with a smile, "who would be even sweeter if he could tell everyone that Cricket Lawson is his girlfriend."

Cricket looked up at him with a twinkle in her eyes. "Really?"

"Never been more serious in my whole life," he said. "I want us to be dating exclusively. I don't want to share you with anyone else."

"Yes!" she squealed. "Yes, I will be your girlfriend, and honey, after spending so much time with you this week, I don't even want to date anyone else."

He picked her up and swung her around until they were both dizzy. "I'm so happy that..." He stopped and kissed her. "There are no words, except that I think I'm falling in love with you."

"Me, too," she said and wrapped her arms around his neck and tiptoed for another kiss. "And I love this feeling."

Epilogue

Several weeks later.

"Good morning," Anna Grace called out as she came in the back door of the bookstore. "Looks like it's going to be another hot one."

Cricket looked up from her desk. "How was the honeymoon?"

"It was amazing." Anna Grace smiled. "Mama called this morning and offered to give me my old job back, and Daddy wants to buy us a house right here in Bloom as a wedding gift."

"And?" Cricket's heart fell to her shoes. She didn't want Anna Grace to leave the store. If Bryce hadn't moved in with her the previous week, she would have been super lonely at the farm. Jennie Sue and Rick didn't pop in as often now that gardening season was over.

"I told both of them no," Anna Grace said. "I like it here, and we've found an old farmhouse on an acre of ground about halfway between Sweetwater and Bloom that we will be signing a contract on this week. It's a lease-to-own thing, so that all the rent money goes toward buying it in three years. It will be a great place to raise the six kids we want to have."

Instant relief washed over Cricket. "Have you seen the *Bloom Weekly News*? I picked one up off the newsstand on the way in today." She flipped the newspaper to the society page and pointed. "Who would have thought we'd get our pictures in the paper in the same week?"

"Well, would you look at that." Anna Grace smiled and read the first few lines of the article out loud: "*Anna Grace Cramer of Bloom married Thomas Arrington Bluestone of Sweetwater in a private ceremony on the beach at Padre Island. Bluestone's brother, Harry, served as best man. Cricket Lawson served as her friend's bridesmaid…*

"I told Mama if she didn't put it in the paper exactly as I wrote it that she would never see her six grandkids." Anna Grace laughed. "Besides, by now Lettie and Nadine have already spread the news. Folks just read the paper to be sure those two haven't lost their touch."

"Ain't that the truth?" Cricket smiled and flipped the paper around so she could read: "*Cricket Lawson and Bryce Walton have announced their engagement. They plan a December wedding right here in Bloom. Bryce is the owner of the Bloom Drug Store, and Cricket is the proprietor of the Sweet Seconds Book Store in Bloom…*"

"One marriage, one engagement. Hopefully, by Christmas next year, there will be two baby announcements," Anna Grace said.

"One marriage, one engagement, and one very good friendship that started most of it." Cricket held up her coffee.

Anna Grace took a bottle of sweet tea from her purse and clinked it against Cricket's cup. "May the friendship last forever!"

"Amen." Cricket nodded.

Read more about
Cricket and her family
in *Small Town
Rumors*.

About the Author

Carolyn Brown is a *New York Times* and *USA Today* bestselling romance author and RITA finalist who has sold more than 8 million books. She presently writes both women's fiction and cowboy romance. She has written historical and contemporary romance, both stand-alone titles and series. She lives in southern Oklahoma with her husband, a former English teacher who is not allowed to read her books until they are published. They have three children and enough grandchildren to keep them young.

For a complete listing of her books (in series order) and to sign up for her newsletter, check out her website at CarolynBrown Books.com or catch her on Facebook/CarolynBrownBooks.

Looking for more Western romance?
Take the reins with these cowboys from Forever!

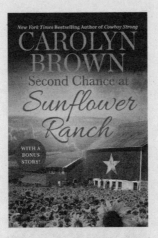

SECOND CHANCE AT SUNFLOWER RANCH
by Carolyn Brown

Jesse Ryan is shocked to return home after twenty years and find the woman he could never forget gave birth to a little girl about nine months after he left—*his* little girl. Addy Hall has her hands full as a single mom. The last thing she needs is Jesse complicating her life even further, especially since she's always had a crush on the handsome cowboy. But the more time she spends with him, the more she wonders what might happen if they finally became the family for which she'd always hoped. Includes the bonus story *Small Town Charm!*

Discover bonus content and more on read-forever.com

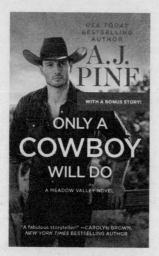

ONLY A COWBOY WILL DO
by A.J. Pine

After a lifetime of helping others, Jenna Owens is finally putting herself first, starting with her vacation at the Meadow Valley Guest Ranch to celebrate her fortieth birthday. Colt Morgan, part-owner of the ranch, is happy to help her have all the fun she deserves, especially her wish for a vacation fling. But will their two weeks of fantasy lead to a shot in the real world, or will their final destination be two broken hearts? Includes a bonus story by Melinda Curtis!

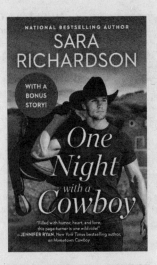

ONE NIGHT WITH A COWBOY
by Sara Richardson

Wes Harding is known as a devil-may-care bull rider—but now, with his sister's pregnancy at risk, Wes promises to put aside his wild ways and take the reins on their ranch's big charity event. Only he didn't count on his co-hostess—and little sister's best friend—being so darn distracting. One kiss with Thea Davis throws his world off-balance. But with her husband gone, Thea's focused only on raising her two rambunctious children. Can Wes convince her that he's the man on whom she can rely? Includes a bonus story by Carly Bloom!

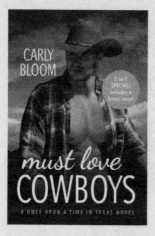

MUST LOVE COWBOYS
by Carly Bloom

Alice Martin doesn't regret putting her career as a librarian above personal relationships—but when cowboy Beau Montgomery comes to her for help, Alice decides to see what she's been missing. She agrees to help Beau improve his reading skills if he'll be her date to an upcoming wedding. But when the town's gossip mill gets going, they're forced into a fake romance to keep their deal a secret. And soon Alice is seeing Beau in a whole new way...Includes the bonus novel *Big Bad Cowboy!*

THE HEART OF A TEXAS COWBOY
(2-in-1 edition) by Katie Lane

Enjoy these two Western romances heating up the Lone Star State! Slate Calhoun's longtime flame, Hope Scroggs, is back in his life, but the feelings between them are unlike before. By the time he discovers "Hope" is her identical twin, Faith, he's head over spurs in *Going Cowboy Crazy*. Colt Lomax can't forget the night of passion he once shared with local sweetheart Hope Scroggs, a night he wouldn't mind repeating. She tries her darnedest to resist his Texas charm, but something unexpected is about to tie their fates together...and oh, baby, will it ever in *Make Mine a Bad Boy!*

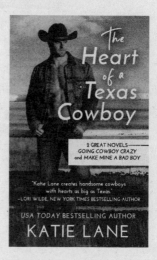